The

Other

Mother

The

Other

Mother

· *A Novel* ·

RACHEL M. HARPER

Counterpoint
Berkeley, California

The Other Mother

Library of Congress Cataloging-in-Publication Data
Names: Harper, Rachel M., 1972– author.
Title: The other mother : a novel / Rachel M. Harper.
Description: First hardcover edition. | Berkeley, California : Counterpoint, 2022.
Identifiers: LCCN 2021044906 | ISBN 9781640095045 (hardcover) | ISBN
    9781640095052 (ebook)
Subjects: LCGFT: Novels.
Classification: LCC PS3608.A7747 O84 2022 | DDC 813/.6—dc23
LC record available at https://lccn.loc.gov/2021044906

Jacket design by Robin Billardello
Book design by Laura Berry

COUNTERPOINT
2560 Ninth Street, Suite 318
Berkeley, CA 94710
www.counterpointpress.com

Printed in the United States of America

10 9 8 7 6 5 4 3 2 1

Music was the one way of keeping the past alive, his father said. There's more future in the past than there is in the future . . .

—JACKIE KAY, *TRUMPET*

Only the vanished truly leave their mark.

—PAULA McLAIN, *CIRCLING THE SUN*

BOOK I

The Son

September 2015

· 1 ·

Through the fence, between the powder black wrought iron pickets, he can see the bell tower. The clock-face is green with age, so bright it seems to glow. Its hands are folded together, signaling twelve o'clock, yet nothing happens. For a long time, he stares at it, waiting for the bell to ring. His first day on campus.

He checks his watch, then looks again at the tower—from limestone base to soaring red brick trunk—and wonders if he's made a mistake. Is there another bell tower on the green? While other first-years brush past him, heading to orientation, Jenry leaves the group and walks in the wrong direction. He abandons the sidewalk, steps directly onto the grass. His eyes scan the domed cap, searching the shadows for a hint of copper coloring—the wide waist of the bell, the curved lip—but all he sees are phantom shapes, and after a few moments he wonders if, all these years later, the bell has been removed.

When his mother went to school here, when she stood in the same spot more than twenty-five years ago, it did ring. She used the sound of the bell to mark time, to pace herself during walks around the quad, struggling to memorize the periodic table, and to make sure she was never late to class. His father was also a student here, but Jenry doesn't know much more than that; doesn't know if his father ever counted the crows as they landed on the edge of the balustrade, or why, after growing up in Providence, he chose to attend Brown University; and perhaps more importantly—if he would have wanted his only son to do the same.

What Jenry does know is that he doesn't belong here, which is how he's felt about almost every place he's been. Call it the mark of illegitimacy. But somehow this campus feels different. He's come here to find something; more specifically, to find someone, which alone gives his presence a purpose. He has come to find his father. Not the actual man, who died when Jenry was two, but some version of him—re-created out of facts and stories, resurrected like a ghost.

The word *father* doesn't mean much to him; or rather, what it means doesn't elicit an emotional response. It doesn't move him. He's never had a father, so the word exists as only an idea. An absence. Like how the stump evokes the presence of the missing arm more powerfully than the arm itself. What Jenry has is a name, and the idea of what a father should be; that is what he is looking for. He wants to know the man who should have been his father. And now, imagining him here, Jenry hopes to justify his own place in this world, to see how he measures up, to prove that he belongs.

His grandfather is the closest thing to a father Jenry's known, but Victor lives in the shadow of the other man, the one who exists in a few black-and-white photographs, images taken from a yellowed copy of *Life* magazine found under his mother's bed when he was a child, looking for answers she refused to give. Jasper Patterson is the name—the myth, the legend—but who was the man?

"Are you lost?"

The voice—female, sharp—brings Jenry back to the sun on his face and the grass under his feet, to the view of a clock tower in the distance.

"Can I help you find something?" She is smiling at him. A pretty smile.

"No, I'm okay."

The girl keeps moving, her messenger bag knocking against him as she passes by. "Don't look so panicked, classes don't start till Wednesday. You've got plenty of time."

"The clock, on the bell tower—"

"It's broken," she cuts him off. "For like the last twenty years or something." She stands with her back to the sun, her hair haloed by the light.

"Someone climbed up there to fix it and then fell off and died. Or maybe he broke it as he fell, I can't remember." She rolls her eyes and laughs again. "But it's been wrong ever since. The old president left it stopped to honor the dead."

"Oh, okay," he says, trying to feign nonchalance, "I thought it would ring. For meals or something." He's not sure why, but he feels disappointed.

"You should have come here in the sixties, when they still wore ties to class and the girls went to Pembroke."

He's heard stories of the Pembroke campus from his mother: how she'd lived there for the first two years of college, rooming with a soccer player who had to be close to the athletic fields for their two-a-day practices; how she volunteered at the Sarah Doyle Women's Center and found a new group of friends, activists who experimented with vegetarianism and smoked clove cigarettes, one of whom ended up starting the first Cuban Student Alliance during an all-night game of spades in the boiler room and now works for President Obama; how she spent her free time at the Sci-Li, collecting work-study hours to supplement her scholarship. He thinks of sharing one of these anecdotes but decides not to. He doesn't want to hear another person tell him how lucky he is to be a double legacy and how the school had no choice but to let him in. Never mind the 4.0 GPA and SAT scores that made his mother cry.

"By the way," the girl says, yellow hair gleaming in the sunlight, "orientation is that way, on the Main Green."

He follows her eyes to the row of brick buildings behind them, trying to think of something clever to say. His mind draws a blank.

"It's not just you," she adds. "All the first-years look a little shell-shocked."

Jenry feels his face turn red, though she won't recognize it. He likes how his complexion can hide feelings of embarrassment or shame, how his natural expression betrays no emotion. His mother used to call it his mask, telling him, "I could skate across that face, it's so frozen," until he eventually gave in, melting for her. "There, that's my boy," she would say, his face dissected into angles she could finally recognize.

Jenry shifts his weight, crossing his arms as he wonders how to salvage the moment, and why he cares. "Maybe you can help me with something else," he says. "If I wanted to research someone who went here a long time ago, where would I go? They must keep those records somewhere."

"Sure." She nods. "You could start at the Alumni Center, across from Res. Life. But you might be better off going straight to the Archives, if the person was really important. Those are at the John Hay."

"The library?" He remembers hearing it mentioned on the tour.

"Right there." She points behind him. "They have all the rare books and special collections. Things you couldn't imagine anyone still caring about."

He glances at the large building on the corner, its white marble gleaming in the sunlight. "Okay, thanks."

"But bring a jacket. It's always freezing in there, and they won't let you take in a bag. Just a pencil, I think. They're very strict."

"How do you know so much?"

"English major," she says. "I spent last semester TA-ing for Professor Dennison. She had me in the basement for weeks, looking for old playscripts."

"Sounds fascinating."

"It is. Assuming you care about anything that happened before the invention of the iPhone."

"What makes you think I do?" His tone is playful, bordering on flirtatious.

"Most people don't notice the tower even has a bell. And I don't think they arrived on campus worrying about alums."

He tilts his head to avert the sun from his eyes. "Oh I see," he says, lowering his voice to draw her closer, stoking the tiny embers that smolder between them, "you're saying I'm weird?"

She breaks into an easy grin. "Either that or interesting." She backs away, one small step at a time. "Don't worry," she says, her voice rising playfully, "your secret's safe with me." She walks away with a purposeful step, confident he's still watching.

Jenry's gaze follows her across the green: the cut-off shorts loose on her hips, her pale calves rounded like mangos, leather flip-flops wide enough to fit a man. An athlete, he thinks, soccer or field hockey. Tennis. An East Coast sport popularized by the bored and wealthy. He won't say it out loud, but he finds most athletic endeavors tedious. Something to bridge the time between therapy sessions and online shopping. Even if he weren't strapped to a piano all day, he doubts he'd ever pick up a racket. Still, he regrets not getting her name.

He loses her in the crowd and soon the feeling is gone. He didn't come here to date or fall in love, that isn't what drove him a thousand miles away from home. He came here to get answers—to learn about the past so he could face his future.

· 2 ·

Every part of the John Hay Library's exterior, even the staircase, is made of white marble. From across the street it had looked almost new, but as he gets closer, Jenry notices the markings of age: the steps are stained gray, with rust-colored grooves running like veins along the dulled surface, no longer shiny and flat, but worn down in the center from a century of daily use. When he opens the library's heavy wooden door, a thought arrives like a headache, sudden and sharp. *This is where I'm supposed to be.* It lingers in his head as he repeats it, questioning something he wants to be true.

He asks the receptionist where to find the University Archives, and is directed to the Special Collections Reading Room, two flights down. He takes the stairs, his footsteps echoing in the stairwell. A middle-aged librarian sits behind a desk in the foyer, just outside the entrance to the Reading Room. She removes her glasses as he approaches.

"How can I help you?"

"I'm looking for information about someone who went here—"

"Did you check our website first? To make sure they're part of the Archive?"

"I tried," Jenry admits, "but I couldn't get into any documents. Guess I did it wrong."

"Access depends on your credentials. And where the papers are stored." She rolls her chair closer to the desk, adjusting her keyboard. "Are you a student?"

Jenry nods. "Just got my ID today."

"Let's make sure you're in the system."

She motions for the card and he passes it over the desk. After swiping it, she starts typing.

"Okay, Mr. Castillo, let's start with the easy part. What was his name?"

"Jasper Patterson."

"One or two *t*'s?"

"Two."

She types quickly, the tips of her manicured fingernails clattering against the keys. "Do you know his graduation year?"

"Um . . . yeah," he pauses, trying to remember. His mother was the class of 1992, and he knows Jasper was a few years older. "Nineteen eighty-nine, I think. Or maybe '88."

"Not a problem, I'll search both."

Jenry glances at the floor, unable to look at her while he waits. He feels nervous, as if waiting for test results he's not sure he's ready to hear. The sound of her typing is erratic but also comforting, like a piece of music he was composing.

The woman coughs into the sleeve of her sweater and takes a sip of water. There's a part of Jenry—the part that doesn't want to bother anyone, the part that will work, even at his own expense, to make other people comfortable—that considers turning around and leaving the library. Who would care, if he ended his search before it's even begun? But it's more than that: he feels afraid; afraid to be so close to what he's always wanted, to getting answers that reveal not just Jasper's past, but something about Jenry himself, now, in the present.

When Jenry started high school and finally got his own computer, he would occasionally comb the internet for Jasper's name, long tired of asking his mother for details she claimed to forget or never know. He would invariably end up with the same results: the *New York Times* obit, the Wikipedia page, a few articles in dance magazines. And of course, the images of Jasper performing—in *Romeo and Juliet* or *Don Quixote*, wearing that embroidered jacket; shirtless and soaring across the stages of the Met or Lincoln Center, toes pointed and captured in flight. He'd seen those photographs dozens of times, as familiar to him as the images of famous figures in American history, men like Abraham Lincoln or Martin Luther King Jr., and equally remote. His mother tried to remind him that it was a different time: the internet didn't exist like it does now, and everything wasn't catalogued and tracked. But Jenry wanted to know—not about what Jasper did, but who he *was*. He was convinced there was more to find.

"All right," the librarian says, "I found him."

Jenry sees her squinting at the computer screen. His heart beats faster.

"Jasper Lucas Patterson, dancer and choreographer," she reads, "graduated on May 26, 1988, summa cum laude, major in Theatre Arts, minor in French." She stops to adjust her glasses. "Is that who you're looking for?"

Jenry nods. "Is there more?" he asks, his voice thick with anticipation.

"Shall I read the whole summary? Or would you prefer that I print out a copy?"

Jenry feels his eyes suddenly focus. "I'd like a copy please."

"He was quite accomplished. That must be why his name sounds familiar. I'm surprised I can't place it."

Jenry shrugs. "He died a long time ago."

"Some of our archives go back two hundred years." She removes the paper from the printer, handing it to Jenry. "The nineties are practically yesterday."

Jenry reads over the summary, impressed by the contents of the collection.

Materials include photographs, video/film recordings, bio-
graphical information, correspondence, writings, print
material, pen and ink sketches, clippings, dance awards,
pamphlets, and other documents dating from 1976–1999.

"This list of materials, is that all kept here? I mean, can I see it?"

She smiles. "That's why we have it. But let me check something first." She scans the computer screen again. "Unfortunately this collection is housed off-site. You need to make a request via email and then come back in forty-eight hours to look at the files."

"Forty-eight hours?" He thinks of the time he has already waited, practically his whole lifetime. "I don't know if I can wait that long."

The librarian gives him a strange, almost pitying look. "Patience is the heart of all research, don't you agree?"

She goes on to tell him that their library has a very prestigious collection, with first-edition copies of *Moby-Dick* and *The Scarlet Letter*, a Shakespeare folio, and slave narratives, all under one roof; that it's a historian's dream, really, one of the best rare book collections in the nation; that people come from all over New England to use their facilities; and how fortunate he is to have been given access to such privileges, just by being enrolled here. If he can only wait two more days.

She points him toward a patron computer, where he can place the request for the entire collection to be brought to the Reading Room, all forty-nine boxes. Jenry sits down in front of the monitor. He rereads the printout, his eyes scanning each line. At the very bottom he sees a line he didn't notice before, "Related Collections: Patterson Family Archive." He returns to the librarian's desk, asking what it means.

She leans forward, putting on her glasses to see it clearly. "Hmm, let me look it up." She is back at the keyboard, clicking away. "The archives are linked, but I don't see this one listed on the main database, there must be a hold or something." She leans in, peering at the monitor. "Oh, I get it. This is a new acquisition, so it's still being catalogued. Let me see who the contact librarian is."

She picks up the phone and dials a four-digit extension. Jenry leans forward, hoping to read the screen himself, but the monitor is blocked from view.

"Hi, Rosemary, it's Gayle. Who's the contact on the new Patterson Family Archive? Oh, really? Must be important." Gayle adjusts her glasses. "Yes, that makes sense." She nods, listening intently. "Oh, I see. I didn't realize that." She is silent for a long time. "What's the availability right now? I've got a gentleman here who's interested in a related archive, for Jasper Patterson." She looks again at the screen. "No, he didn't, not yet. A first-year." She clears her throat. "Okay, I'll tell him. Three boxes. Yes, I understand. Thank you, Rosemary." She hangs up the phone and turns to Jenry.

"This must be your lucky day, Mr. Castillo. The Patterson Family Archive hasn't been fully processed, but it does include papers and media relating to Jasper. As of today, three boxes have been catalogued and are available for viewing."

"Right here? Now?"

"In the Reading Room. Just fill out this slip and leave your belongings in one of the lockers by the wall." She hands him a request slip. "Rosemary can answer any other questions. She knows everything about everyone." Then she lowers her voice. "She only takes the families with, how shall I say it, historical significance. The Pattersons must be important."

Jenry fills out the request and hands it back to her. He wants to say something to convey his gratitude, but all he can muster is a simple thank you. She gives him a tight smile and a freshly sharpened pencil, referring him to the list of rules and regulations posted on the Reading Room's glass doors. He deposits his things as instructed and carries nothing but the pencil into the room.

· 3 ·

The Reading Room is completely silent. Jenry sits at a long mahogany table that takes up half the room. The other table, its identical twin, is empty. The chairs are huge, with arms curved like lions' paws and velvet seat cushions the color of blood. It is like no room Jenry has ever seen. He taps out a beat—one, two, three— as he waits, the table's smooth surface dark and cool beneath his fingertips. The room is cold, not just from the aggressive air conditioning but because it's partly underground. A row of small windows runs along the upper edge of the wall, letting in a fair amount of natural light, but none of that warmth reaches him.

Suddenly Rosemary is there, a petite, small-boned woman with a full head of straight white hair, as thin and shiny as dental floss. She pulls a small cart behind her, carrying three file boxes, each marked with a filing system he doesn't understand. A printed label on the outside of the boxes says: PATTERSON FAMILY ARCHIVE; below that, someone's written neatly with black marker: JASPER.

"You must be the first-year?"

Jenry nods, straightening up in his chair, trying to look responsible.

She shakes her head, and for a split-second he thinks she's rejecting him, but then he realizes she's referring to the boxes. "This is not," she says, picking up the first box, "the complete Patterson archive. I'm sure Gayle mentioned that."

"Yes, she did."

She places the box on the table before him. "This represents about five percent of the collection." She lifts another box onto the table. "Just so you understand the scope of what you're dealing with." After a moment she adds, "To get the whole story, you have to put in the time. Research cannot be rushed."

Jenry shifts awkwardly in his seat.

"I have to tell you," she goes on, "I spent two years cataloging the first archive, that was just Jasper. Six boxes of correspondence, a dozen more filled with books. And then there were the photographs." She tips her head back and sighs. "Hundreds of loose prints to sort. Boxes and boxes of slides. Negatives that had to be transferred into plastic sleeves one by one. Signed posters and playbills. I swear, the media alone was one whole skid." She stops then, a smile crossing her face. "But I knew someday, someone would come."

Jenry is unsure what to say. She pats him on the shoulder. "You take your time in here. I'll be right on the other side of that glass if you need anything."

Finally, he's alone. As he touches the first box, all his anxiety vanishes. The unanswered questions recede from his mind and he's left with a feeling of stillness. He removes the lid. The box holds two accordion files, each the size of a stuffed briefcase. He opens the larger one first. Inside is a circus of papers: glossy flyers from dance shows; playbills printed on colored paper; xeroxed brochures announcing a theater's new season; black-and-white postcards depicting foreign cities, their dark rivers snaking like veins through ancient bodies of brick and stone. There are papers of all kinds—handwritten, stamped, mimeographed, typed, faxed—some bearing Jasper's name, others announcing the titles of plays, ballets, and dance troupes that Jenry doesn't recognize. The names of cities and countries are more familiar, places mentioned in news stories he watched with his grandparents as a child, waiting for his mother to come home.

The smaller file contains personal correspondence: letters to and from Jasper, all in their original envelopes, some dating back to when he was just a boy. Shuffling through the pile, he finds the oldest letter, stamped June 1975. He removes it from the plastic bag, reading Jasper's name on the envelope, followed by an address in Barrington, RI. The letter was written on hotel stationery, with a return address in Paris.

Jenry opens the letter slowly, a single onionskin page, folded into three sections. When he unfolds it, a small paper ring from a cigar falls out, big enough to fit on his middle finger. The exotic name, "Quai d'Orsay," printed in black against a yellowed band, the tiny words *Habana* and *Cuba* barely visible on either side of the emblem. The letter is typed, with *Papa* signed in inky cursive, and tells stories of Jasper's father's travels through France: the famous museums he visited in Paris; the exotic foods he tasted, pigeon and snail, when he was too proud to ask for help with translation; the crowded café where he spent a whole afternoon during a surprise thunderstorm, drinking bowl after bowl of hot chocolate with fresh whipped cream.

Jenry tries to picture the little boy who received this letter, tries to imagine what he would think of his father's adventures, how it would feel to be left behind. He can't help but picture himself as the little boy, which makes him feel sad—for himself and Jasper.

Rosemary is back, carrying a double-hinged picture frame. "This didn't fit in any of the boxes. But I thought you might want to see it."

She places the oversized frame on the table before him as if it were a serving tray, and opens it like a menu. On one side are two eight-by-ten photographs of Jasper as a young man; in one, his senior picture from college, he is wearing a striped tie and V-neck sweater, his short hair parted, the curls tamed with oil. He is smiling at the camera with a mouth full of straight teeth. The other is a full-body shot of him dancing; standing on his tiptoes, one arm raised and reaching for something, fingers extended to the edge of the frame. He wears loose cut-off sweatpants and a skin-tight tank top, both grayed with sweat; his muscled thighs are taut, solid like steel. He is not looking at the camera, nor is he smiling, yet there is a sense of joy in his posture—or maybe it's freedom. Jenry, who has never liked the way a camera caught his appearance, longs for what he sees of his father in that photograph: the strength of a stilled explosion in his body, a captured moment of flight.

On the other side of the frame, floating on a cream-colored mat, is a newspaper article that contains a third picture, pixelated in a way that contorts Jasper's face, making him appear much older than he was—an age he never actually attained. This is the image that reminds Jenry of himself, the first one he's ever seen of Jasper to do so. His father's expression is shy, almost apologetic, and his arms are folded tightly across his chest, as if he were holding himself together. *Yes*, Jenry thinks, *there I am*. This is the photo that proves he comes from someone beyond his mother, from two bloodlines—two families, not just one—that together merged to make something else, to create him.

FAMED DANCER, PHILANTHROPIST DEAD AT 33. Not an article—an obituary.

"I knew he died young, but—" Jenry doesn't finish his thought.

Rosemary points to the obit. "This one is from *The Providence Journal*. You can probably pull it up online, but sometimes it's nicer to see the original, don't you think?" She looks at him with a tender expression. "There are others here, in this box." She places the third box on the chair beside him. "*The New York Times*, *The Globe*, all the major papers." She pulls out the clippings to show him. "The best one, in my opinion, is from *The Brown Daily Herald*. It was written by a student he taught, when Jasper came back to teach a workshop the year before he died. Quite moving." She rests her hand on the box.

"Can I ask, how do you know all this?"

"It's my job," she says without hesitation, "to catalogue achievement. Do something great and one day I'll know all about you as well." She winks at him before turning to leave.

Jenry pulls out the folder to shuffle through the newspapers, not sure which to read first. He sees the date at the edge of the clipping: February 12, 1999. He wonders what he was doing that day, a boy not quite two years old. Did his mother take him to the funeral? Did he cry? He scans the obit, looking for the date Jasper died. February 8, a Monday. Where was he when his father fell through the ice?

The story he reads is the one he already knows—the snowstorm, the cabin, the accident that took the shining star, drowned in the same pond where he had learned to swim as a young boy, steps from the home his parents had built to prove they had arrived, reaching the middle-class milestone of a weekend home in the country. The weather had apparently been nice that day, a blinding sunshine that melted the snow off rooftops and sidewalks, leaving the ice with a shiny wet gloss that by nightfall would freeze in a top layer as smooth as glass.

Jenry used to ask his mother for this story at bedtime; not tales of Jasper's success on stage, not the moment they met, their brief courtship, or their passionate affair—over before it started, she'd always insisted— no, Jenry wanted to know about his death. The details his mother didn't know, or wouldn't tell him. How Jasper had traveled to the cabin alone in the middle of winter, two months after closing an international tour in Eastern Europe, his legs spent from thousands of leaps no ordinary man could ever make, his lungs compromised by a lingering case of bronchitis the tour doctor failed to diagnose or adequately treat. How he started a fire in the woodstove that was still burning hours after they found the body, frozen and curiously dressed, a purple scarf around his neck but no jacket, no gloves, no cap to cover the closely-cropped hair, trimmed weekly with his own set of clippers. This was the story Jenry longed for, the one he was forced to imagine in the absence of anything concrete.

Even now it doesn't make sense. What was he doing at the cabin during a snowstorm? Why was he alone? Surely, he would have known to dress for the weather, to wear long johns and a down coat, fur-lined gloves, a wool stocking cap. Those, in fact, were the items they'd found in the cabin, hanging neatly in the hall closet. It was all a mystery to

Jenry; not just who his father was in life, but how he came to meet an early death. How it visited so unexpectedly, with him so unprepared, so unaware.

The last line of the obit surprises Jenry, the information new and somewhat confusing. "Mr. Patterson is survived by his father, Winston J. Patterson, a distinguished university professor of history, and his sister, Juliet Patterson, a jazz pianist, also of Providence."

I had an aunt, he thinks, *a grandfather?* All these years, Jenry never imagined other relatives, his mind singularly focused on his father. He rereads the paragraph, holds their names on his tongue like a flavor. These people were Jasper's family, *his* family, yet he has no idea who they are, or if he ever met them, if they are still alive. Strangest of all: there is no mention of Jenry, Jasper's only child.

"Excuse me," Jenry says, searching the empty room for a sign of the librarian. She appears from behind a glass-lined bookcase that shines his reflection back at him, so he is looking at himself when he speaks again. "Do you know anything about the family? Who set up the archive?"

"His father. He was the executor of the estate." Rosemary leans against the table. "He donated most of the materials a few months after Jasper died, if I remember correctly, with more added every few years." She chuckles. "Just when I think it's complete, another box arrives."

"So you knew him, Jasper's father?"

Rosemary smiles. "Everybody knew him back then. You couldn't be on this campus for a week and not know Winston Patterson." She looks around the room before saying more. "I worked at the reference desk when he first got tenure. He used to come in with a ten-page list of books to put on hold for his classes. Things we'd never heard of—translated texts, old newsreel on microfilm, half the books out of print, it was crazy. A shit-ton of work." She shakes her head, still smiling. "But we did it, no complaints. Not for all the professors, mind you, but for Patterson, we just couldn't say no."

He waits for her to say more.

"Even in retirement, he still keeps us—"

Jenry cuts her off. "Wait—he's alive?"

"And kicking," she says with a laugh. "With an office on campus, right across from the green. They say he's got a better view than the president."

She offers to show him on the campus map, but he declines, claiming to know the building. Rosemary nods, but he can tell she doesn't believe him. He thanks her for her help and turns back to the boxes, waiting for his heart rate to return to normal. He looks through the remainder of the files, trying to focus on everything laid out before him, but he can't concentrate on the past, not when something new—someone alive—is pulling on his mind. A few minutes pass before he gives in. He puts everything back as he found it and leaves the boxes stacked neatly on the table, as instructed. He thanks Rosemary again, promising to come back when he has more time; she promises to be there.

Ascending the library's stairs, Jenry finds himself thinking of his mother. He pictures her dark hair, so thick it takes hours to dry, and in contrast, the striking paleness of her skin. There is a contradiction in her face, which perhaps speaks to the contradiction within the woman herself. She is outgoing and reserved at the same time, close to her parents but also solitary; forthcoming, yet closed like a fist. Sure, she had told him something—most of what he knew about his father had come directly from her—but she never mentioned the details he learned today: that he has relatives living right here in Providence, a whole side of his family that isn't a part of hers.

Outside, he squints against the shock of the bright sunlight. He thinks of calling his mother right then, to confront her with the new facts he's found, but decides to wait until he knows more of the story. She is the one who taught him to be cautious, never to attack without just cause, and when fighting, particularly against a larger, stronger person, to stand on sure, solid ground before you strike.

But Jenry isn't worried about strategy or tactics right now. His goal is simple: to meet Jasper's father.

· 4 ·

The History Department is housed in an old brick building, one of the few structures from the original campus still standing. It is a dark reddish brown, a color of brick Jenry has never seen before. The front door is narrow and surprisingly heavy, and he has to twist his body sideways to fit through. In Miami they would replace a door like this, with something strong yet lightweight, made of aluminum and glass, but here they cherish antiques, hang plaques outside houses with dates so old they seem like typos. It is strange, but not uncomfortable, he reminds himself. Like learning to stretch his pinky to reach the high register, something he can adapt to.

Inside, he finds a directory on the wall in the foyer, which he scans till he sees the name: "Patterson, Winston J." followed by the words *Professor Emeritus*. His office is located on the third floor.

Jenry climbs the steep flight of stairs. His heart thumps in his chest, more from the anxiety of the unknown than the physical exertion. He waits at the top to catch his breath. The hallway connects a maze of rooms, but 307 is nowhere to be found. He knocks on neighboring 308, its door slightly ajar. No answer. He peeks inside, despite a clear sense that he's in the wrong place. The sunlight is blinding; it shines off the honeyed wood floors making them look wet, as if still drying from a fresh coat of polish. The room, an oversized closet filled with file cabinets, is empty. As he backs out, a voice startles him.

"Looking for 307, are you?"

Jenry leans into the room. "Sorry, I've searched the floor twice."

The man smiles. "Don't feel bad, people get lost all the time. Here, I'll show you." He leads Jenry down the hall and around a corner, to a small staircase near the back of the building. Jenry had assumed it was a fire escape.

"Top of the stairs on your right, just past the piano."

When Jenry thanks him, he says, "Actually, the hard part is getting inside."

Jenry stops walking to look at him. "Do I need an appointment?"

The man pauses before responding. "Dr. Patterson doesn't keep regular office hours anymore." He shrugs. "Maybe you should come back in the morning. Give yourself time to prepare."

Jenry turns around, measuring his words. "No, I'm good," he says, feigning confidence. The man nods and wishes him luck.

As he reaches the top step, the butterflies in his stomach start to bounce around and his palms begin to sweat. This is how he used to feel at piano recitals. He always got nervous right before he stepped on stage, and it didn't go away until his fingers touched the keys. He takes a deep breath, tries to calm down. Part of the problem is how easy it's all been, so easy it hardly feels real. Doubt starts to creep in, and soon his excitement fades, replaced by a feeling of doom, heavy in his footsteps. He wants to turn around, go back to his dorm, attend the orientation sessions he's missing, but he can't stop now.

He passes the piano, perched on a small landing, and knows he's in the right place. He considers stopping to play a few chords, just to relax, but puts the thought away. When he sees the room number, he walks toward the closed office door. A clipboard hangs on the wall, pen attached, along with a sign requesting that all visitors leave a note if they want an appointment. The instructions, typed on a sheet of stationery embossed with both the university's name and Dr. Patterson's name and title, instruct the visitor not to email or call, but to drop the handwritten note into the mail slot on his door and wait for his reply, with a promise that their request will be honored in an appropriate amount of time. AND PLEASE, DON'T KNOCK! another sign reads. That alone makes Jenry want to knock, but he feels compelled to follow the rules, not wanting his first interaction with this man to be an act of defiance.

He removes a slip of paper from the clipboard and fills in the easy answers first: his name, the date and time, his contact information. When he reads the last column, REASON FOR YOUR VISIT, he pauses, wondering how to condense his answer into the three lines given. First, he writes, *to inquire about your son, Jasper.* He scratches that out and writes, *to meet my grandfather,* which he also immediately erases. On a fresh sheet he writes down his contact information and puts just two words in the final box: JASPER PATTERSON, in all capitals. He quickly tears the paper from the clipboard and slides it into the mail slot before he can change his mind.

As he turns around, his eyes land squarely on the piano, which sits like an invitation in the empty hallway. It's obviously an antique, probably from the late nineteenth century, but still in great condition, with a gorgeous rosewood case and matching bench. He's seen this cabinet style in books and old movies, but never in person, and can't imagine how much it had cost to restore, or even to get up to the top floor of this building. There are three upper panels, each inlaid with floral detailing that must have been hand-painted. He runs his fingers across the flowers, expecting to feel the image raised, but the surface is perfectly smooth.

It's a Steinway, of course, which he knows before he sees the logo on the fallboard. He lifts it to reveal the keyslip, whose wood is stained perfectly to match the case, and then what he's really come to see: the row of original keys—naturals covered with ivory, sharps with ebony. He runs his fingertips along the keys, surprised by how different they feel from the plastic-covered ones he's grown up playing, designed to absorb moisture and provide a firm grip. He plays a C major, wincing at the sound of the untuned instrument. The feeling of the ivory against his fingertips is astonishing, something he can't put into words. The keys seem raw, organic, almost alive. He's about to sit when a door opens behind him.

"Did you write this?" The voice is deep and unfamiliar. Jenry turns to face it.

A man stands in the doorway, completely still, as large and imposing as the statue of a brown bear that marks the Main Green. This is Dr. Patterson. WINSTON J. PATTERSON, the placard on the door reads. This is his grandfather.

"Yes," Jenry manages to say. He feels his cheeks flush, as if he's lying.

"I didn't hear the door."

"The sign says not to knock."

Jenry watches the old man, sees the muscles in his cheek tense and then release. He is clean-shaven, his skin the color of peanut butter. His arms are loose at his sides, hands opened against his tailored slacks. His gray suit looks brand new, though Jenry can tell just from looking at him that he doesn't buy many new things, prefers instead to take care of, to revere, the originals.

"And your name is?"

"Jenry. I wrote it down." He points to the slip of paper, dangling now like a cigarette from between Dr. Patterson's fingers.

"Yes, I can see that." The old man waits. "Perhaps I'm testing you."

"Easy test," Jenry says.

A half smile splits the old man's lean face, a flash of white teeth that matches the color of his hair, thinning with age but thick enough to comb.

"Fear not," he says. "They will get harder." He opens the office door and beckons Jenry to enter. "Come in, don't let all the cold air out."

As Jenry walks inside, he feels the temperature drop, like stepping into a flower shop. The room smells of peppermint and stale smoke. Bookshelves line all four walls, a prison cell for the literate.

"How can I assist you, young man?"

Jenry shuffles his feet, carefully unsticking each toe from the hold of his slides, wishing he'd worn real shoes. "I'm here about your son."

"My son?"

"Jasper Patterson."

The old man clears his throat. "I'm aware of his name." He looks down, appears to sort papers on his desk. "Why are you inquiring?"

The answer is an obvious phrase, one Jenry has repeated in his head again and again when he's asked the same of himself, but in this moment it fails to leave his mouth. The words arrive, but he can't make sense of them, can't figure out the proper order. Should he begin with Jasper and say: *He was my father*, or with himself, saying: *I am his son*? The former sounds hard, like an insult, an indictment, something he will have to prove with DNA reports and eyewitness testimony; the latter, a confession.

He tries to think of another way to say it, somehow less jarring to the old man, that absolves both Jasper and himself of guilt—but how? There is no easy way to disclose this type of information, to tell a man you've never met before that you are his grandson.

Dr. Patterson sits down. The chair creaks like wood splitting. "Why do you want to know about my son?"

"He was . . ." Jenry stops to clear his throat. "He was my father." Now the words sound false, too light, too easily spoken.

Jenry looks at the old man, hoping his eyes will reveal something. Instead, they seem to harden, an invisible shield forming over their surface like ice. He removes a pair of wire-rimmed eyeglasses from his jacket pocket and puts them on. They magnify his eyes, which Jenry realizes are a startling shade of hazel-gray. He has never seen a Black person with gray eyes before.

"Your father," the old man repeats, and though it's clear that he wasn't asking it as a question, Jenry nods anyway. "And how do you know this?"

"My mother told me." He plays with the cargo pocket on his shorts, buttoning and unbuttoning the flap. "Her name is Marisa Castillo."

"I know your mother's name," Dr. Patterson says, standing. He paces the floor behind his desk, lecturing to a class of one. "Marisa Castillo Ruiz. Born January 20, 1970, in Miami to Victor Castillo and Inés Ruiz, both Cuban. Graduated with distinction in sociology, May 1992. Later earned a nursing degree, specializing in pediatrics. Currently works at Miami Children's Hospital, as head nurse in the NICU." He closes the blinds, cutting the sunlight from the room.

Jenry doesn't know what to say. He reaches for the chair to steady himself. The room feels hot, and he thinks for the first time in his life that he might faint.

"Please, have a seat," Dr. Patterson offers. "Would you like a drink?"

Jenry looks around the darkened room, wonders where in the sea of books and paper this man could possibly find a beverage. Dr. Patterson leans beneath his desk to retrieve a bottle of single malt whiskey from the bottom drawer. He removes two glasses and stands them side by side on a shelf he pulls from the center of the desk, as if it were designed to serve exactly this purpose. As if he had been waiting for this moment.

"I'm not twenty-one," Jenry says.

"I know."

The bottle opens with a satisfying crack. The old man seems to smile as he pours the drinks. Jenry can count the times he's drank alcohol on one hand: beer on two occasions—the homecoming dance and a Fourth of July cookout, the cans warmed in the sun and tasting like skunk; sangria at his cousin's wedding; and Champagne at his high school graduation party, his mother insisting he give a toast to the room full of strangers, her colleagues and friends at the hospital who were impressed with her son for getting into such a good college.

Dr. Patterson hands Jenry the shorter drink. He takes the glass and brings it to his lips. Inhales. The smell makes him wince. His eyes begin to water.

"I never taught your mother. When she was a student here. She must have avoided me intentionally."

"She never liked American history."

Dr. Patterson laughs, the sound deep and hollow like a drum. "What person of color ever has?" He sips from his glass. "'History begins for us with murder and enslavement, not with discovery.' Do you know who said that?"

"Malcolm X?" Jenry guesses.

Dr. Patterson shakes his head. "William Carlos Williams."

"Right," Jenry says, "didn't he write that poem about the wheelbarrow?"

"Yes. He was a doctor, too. Smart man. A poet always needs a day job. To ensure that he won't allow the need for income to force him into telling lies."

Jenry has still not tasted his drink. He holds the glass on his knee, jiggling it slightly. Dr. Patterson nods toward the glass. "You don't drink?"

"Not really."

"That's a good thing, I suppose. Based on what the science tells us. But every man must have his vice. If not booze, something worse might come along."

Jenry shifts in his seat. "About my father—"

Dr. Patterson cuts him off. "What do you know about Frederick Douglass?"

Jenry knows next to nothing about Douglass, but he figures this is another test, so he plays along. "That he was born a slave."

"What else?"

Jenry strains to remember something. "Didn't he work with Lincoln, during the Civil War? And he wrote a book, I think."

"Yes, he wrote a book. Which means he learned how to read. As a slave. Which was not an easy task." The old man leans back in his chair. "Do you know that he escaped when he was twenty years old? And that by twenty-seven he had enough money to buy his freedom?"

"Not really."

"And do you know what the cost of that freedom was? What a Black man's life was worth in 1845?" When Jenry shakes his head, Dr. Patterson offers the answer, "Seven hundred and eleven dollars and sixty-six cents."

He repeats the figure two more times, his voice growing louder with each word. Then he sits up, pointing a long, lean finger in Jenry's direction.

"Do you know what my son was worth by the end of his life? Thirty-three years old, the same age as Jesus, and worth the price of a thousand slaves. How does that happen in a hundred and fifty years? What does that say about the country you were born in, the world you were born into?"

Jenry stares at this man he doesn't know, afraid to speak.

"I . . ." He looks away, suddenly embarrassed. "I'm not sure."

Dr. Patterson cleans his glasses with the end of his tie. "Did you know that Douglass ran for vice president in 1872, alongside Victoria Woodhull, the first woman to run for president?"

When Jenry gives no response, Dr. Patterson puts his glasses back on.

"You didn't know that, did you?" He stands up and fixes his tie, tightening the knot at his neck. "What is it about your generation? It's like you all think you invented the idea of progress. Like you are the first and only radicals."

Jenry exhales. He wants to get the conversation back on track, but isn't sure where it went off the rails. Do all professors talk like this, he wonders, where every conversation is a lecture? "Um, about my father, I wanted to know—"

Dr. Patterson slams his open hand on the desk, scattering loose papers. "What about *your father*? What is it that you think you deserve to know?"

The room is silent. The only sound Jenry can hear is the soft hum of the AC unit. The old man waits for an answer, his fingertips resting on a stack of manuscript pages held together by a rubber band. His hand looks dark against the snow-white paper, darker than he really is.

Jenry clears his throat. "Well, do you have a picture?" His voice sounds stronger than it feels inside. "I'd like a photograph, something that I can keep."

"For what purpose?"

Jenry doesn't know what to say. He's surprised that he has to justify the request, as if it isn't obvious. "Just to see him. To see if—"

Dr. Patterson cuts him off. "To see if you look like him?"

Jenry feels his face flush, suddenly embarrassed to want anything from this man. Maybe it was a mistake, not just coming here, but trying to find some connection to the past. Maybe he has all the family he needs. Jenry picks up the glass and takes a sip of the whiskey. The liquor burns his throat, but he swallows it without letting on. He has always been good at covering discomfort, a trait his mother called foolish. But it was a necessary survival skill. She didn't know how the other kids teased him—for walking to school with his grandparents; for being small and dark, for not looking Cuban; for spending hours at the piano instead of playing ball in the streets; for having a strange name and no father.

Dr. Patterson walks over to the largest bookshelf in the room, which covers one entire wall of the office. He scans the books slowly, but when he doesn't find what he's looking for, he opens the door to a closet Jenry hadn't noticed. Hanging inside are several dress shirts, still in plastic from the dry cleaners, and a camel-colored overcoat. He reaches for a box on the top shelf and pulls it down effortlessly. From within he removes a boxed set of DVDs, still wrapped in the original plastic with a red bow taped to the top, so Jenry cannot read the title. Dr. Patterson hands him the set.

"This is all I have. From his performances. I didn't keep any pictures."

Jenry looks down at the box in his lap, his father's name in raised gold lettering that covers one side. He rubs the words, as if through his touch he could bring the man to life.

"Thank you," Jenry says. He wants to say more, but is afraid to wear out what little welcome he may have.

"Is there anything else?" Dr. Patterson stands by the door, indicating that their meeting is over. Jenry, though uncomfortable, is not ready to leave. He tries to think of something to say, something that will buy him a few more minutes.

"If you have other questions, you should really bring them to your mother."

"I have asked her." Jenry's voice sounds pleading, desperate. "She told me everything she knows."

Dr. Patterson shrugs. "Then perhaps you know all there is."

"Bullshit." The word fires from his mouth like spit, surprising him. "You're his father. You knew him in a way she never could."

"You are certainly correct about that," Dr. Patterson says, his voice filled with condescension. "In a way you could never understand. Come back to me when you've had your own son, perhaps then we could meet on the same plane and hope to get something out of it." He puts his hand on the doorknob and turns it with a click.

"I'm your grandson," Jenry says, placing the glass of whiskey on the desk. "Doesn't that mean anything to you?"

"What should it mean? That we share the same blood? I don't know a thing about you."

The words are harsh, slapping Jenry across the face with their bluntness. This is not what he expected, though he realizes the old man is telling the truth. They don't know each other. Maybe it's easier if it stays that way.

Jenry picks up his bag and slings it across his shoulder. The weight digs into his skin. "Thank you for your time."

He waits for Dr. Patterson to step aside, to let him make his escape, but the old man blocks the entrance. He stares at Jenry for several seconds, as if daring him to look away. Jenry holds his gaze.

"I'm surprised you haven't asked about my daughter," he says. He takes off his glasses and tucks them into his coat pocket. Up close Jenry can see the wrinkles beneath his eyes, bloodshot from too much liquor and too little sleep. He has an eyelash on his cheek that Jenry is close enough to wipe away, but he doesn't dare. He still has not touched this man, a part of his bloodline, yet as removed from him as a figure from history.

"I was getting to her," Jenry admits. "I figured I would start at the beginning."

Dr. Patterson laughs. A deep bellow that comes from inside his chest.

"You poor fool," the old man says, shaking his head. "Don't you understand? Juliet *is* the beginning."

A surge of adrenaline tells Jenry something his body understands before his brain does.

"I don't think I follow."

"I know you don't. Because your mother hasn't told you the truth." The old man clears his throat before continuing. "Yes, the truth is a foreign concept in a family, but such a thing does exist. And in this case, I think it is the seed of what you're looking for."

Dr. Patterson closes the office door with the light touch of one finger. Jenry hears the door click and suddenly he feels claustrophobic, as if all the air had been sucked out of the room. He takes a step backward and stumbles into the edge of the desk. His leg throbs from the impact.

"The truth, you see, doesn't lie with my son. It begins with my daughter." The old man looks at him with steady, piercing eyes. "She was the one who brought you into the world. Along with your mother, of course, the vessel that carried you. But my daughter steered the ship, and the two of them brought you safely to shore."

Outside, the sound of a lawnmower rips through the air. Jenry glances toward the window, but sees only the slate-tiled roof of the neighboring building. He watches a squirrel scurry along the drainpipe, a broken twig in its mouth. Suddenly it leaps, but Jenry can't see where it lands. He feels his stomach tighten, as if he were falling. Those gray unblinking eyes stare at him.

"But . . ." Jenry doesn't recognize the sound of his own voice. "I don't understand."

"Why would you?" Dr. Patterson steps forward, his shoes echoing on the hardwood floors. "My son was never a father to you. He never planned on raising you. He was only meant to be a donor. They wanted a child and he helped them create you, end of story."

Jenry wants it to be the end of the story, wants the old man to stop talking, but the words keep coming.

"The parent you're looking for, the one who changed your diapers and sang you lullabies, fed you and bathed you—the one who named you—was my daughter, Juliet. Your missing parent is not your father, but your other mother."

The blood in his ears, rushing like a waterfall until that moment, comes to a screeching stop. A clock somewhere ticks, but when he looks for it on the wall, he can't find it. All that surrounds him are books, thousands of books he will never be allowed to touch, let alone read, objects that fill this shrine where his grandfather comes to worship daily, and where, Jenry can only assume, he will never be invited again.

The old man holds a look of satisfaction—or could it be relief?—on his face. "Any questions?"

The voice, once booming, has softened. Jenry can see that he's waiting for a reply, but he's too stunned to think of anything to say.

"I can't," Jenry starts, "I mean, I don't . . ." His voice trails off, a wave of exhaustion rolling over him. His body feels drained, as if he'd been at the piano for hours, his mind empty.

Dr. Patterson reaches into his chest pocket and pulls out his checkbook. From the inside flap, he removes a ballpoint pen. Jenry shifts under the weight of his bag, readjusting the strap on his shoulder. He waves the checkbook away.

"I don't need your money." He feels his pulse pound in his neck.

The old man chuckles. "Good. I wasn't offering it."

He reaches into the checkbook register and pulls out a business card; after writing something on its back, he offers the card to Jenry, who takes it without reading it. A part of him wants to stay and fight, argue with the old man, defend his mother; another part wants to sprint out the door and run down the middle of the street, shouting. Both are fantasies he will never fulfill. He can't afford to be seen losing his shit, not here, not on his first day on campus. No matter what he feels inside, he needs to appear calm and reserved, to show respect. He needs to prove himself; prove that he's civilized; that he was raised right; that he belongs at this school.

"I should get going," Jenry says, working to keep his voice even. He sticks out his hand.

At first Dr. Patterson looks at it, like he's not sure what he's expected to do, but then he takes it, similar in size and color to his own, and they shake. Jenry is surprised by the warmth of his grandfather's hand. He feels an unexpected sense of comfort.

Dr. Patterson follows him into the hallway, where Jenry is again drawn to the piano. He stops to admire it. "Is this yours?" he asks the older man, trying to delay the inevitable goodbye, though he's not sure why.

Dr. Patterson nods after a moment's hesitation. "I guess you could say that I inherited it."

"It's beautiful," Jenry says. "But it needs to be tuned."

The old man approaches the piano, runs his large hand across the grooves of the cheek. "No one plays it anymore. That's why it's up here, out of the way." He smooths his hand over the cabinet, tracing the fluted edge. His touch is so tender, so intimate, it makes Jenry want to look away.

"Seems like a waste," Jenry says, "to ignore such a perfect instrument."

"It's just furniture now," Dr. Patterson says with a sigh. He pats the lid, as if it were the head of a child, and returns to his office.

Jenry runs his fingers along the keys one more time before closing the fallboard. The notes ring in his ears as he walks away.

· 5 ·

All Jenry can do is walk. Not think, not talk—just move his body. He walks through the Main Green, passing dozens of first-years returning from orientation, their faces glowing. He envies their joy, which seems uncomplicated and almost naive to him now. If only he could go back and make a different choice, unlearn some of the things he's heard today. Who cares what happened two decades ago to some people he shares DNA with but doesn't even know? He wants to start over and become a different person, just let it all go.

He keeps walking, and before long he's on Thayer Street, happy to be off campus. There are restaurants and bars, a flower shop and a convenience store, but nothing makes him want to stop; he needs to put distance between himself and the words swirling around in his head—*the truth*, the old man had called it—that he can't quite believe is true. He passes dog-walkers on their phones and kids on bikes with training wheels. The occasional jogger runs by, leaving him in a wake of their scent, a salty mixture of sweat and perfume.

The sun falls lower in the sky as afternoon ends, partially hidden behind a cluster of clouds. He walks along Hope Street, further than he

meant to go. Nothing looks familiar. He cuts through a high school foot-
ball field and is soon lost in a hillside neighborhood of grand old houses.
Some are the square, boxy style of Colonials, but more are Victorian,
each taller than it is wide, with long, narrow windows and pointed roofs.
One catches his eye, with a deep, rounded porch and turreted corner
room complete with curved windows that reflect the sun's bright glare.
He wonders how they even build a round room, how they bend the glass
without breaking it.

He tries to empty his head, but the words come back. Snippets of
their conversation play in his mind like sound bites. He wants to turn
them off, silence them, but knows that won't happen until he talks to
her. Only she can answer his questions. He hates admitting that, how
much he still needs from her. It was expected as a child, natural for their
lives to intertwine, but he wanted college to be a break from that "co-
dependency," as their family therapist had called it, a chance to spread
his wings.

Jenry started seeing Mr. Carlson alone, during his sophomore year
of high school, to help him work through his anger. He was resistant
at first, not wanting to talk about any of it—the distance he felt from
other kids, no matter how long he'd known them; his discomfort in his
changing body; his desire to constantly escape—into music, *Minecraft*,
masturbation, anything to keep from thinking about himself and the
hole he felt devouring his insides. All day he poured things into it, but by
nighttime he felt empty again, or worse, consumed by a vague restless-
ness that became anxiety that bloomed into rage. He didn't think anyone
could understand or help him, or that anything could take it away. Most
sessions they talked about his mother; how it wasn't easy to be the only
child of a single mother; how she put so many expectations on him; how
he relied on her heavily yet resented the fact that she was there, the only
parent he had left; how Mr. Carlson wondered if their relationship was
enmeshed; how Jenry thought she had too much power; how his mother
believed he should be more respectful, more grateful for all she'd sacrificed to get him there.

"I didn't ask to be born," Jenry said, when they finally brought her into the sessions so Mr. Carlson could help resolve the tension between them. "I didn't ask for a selfish child," she said in reply. They both knew he wasn't selfish, but she wanted to remind him that she was the parent; in the end, she was in charge. College had been his escape hatch. His light at the end of the tunnel. And now this.

He takes a sharp left onto a narrow street with a slight incline, hoping it leads back to campus. The sky is filled with clouds, and the temperature has started to cool. He doesn't want to be caught out here in the dark, a brown-skinned teenager in a wealthy neighborhood. His mother had never allowed him to walk around their block alone at night, even if he took Peso, their part-Havanese part-Husky rescue dog. It was too risky, she would say, and you're the only son I've got. It made her feel good to protect him, but it came at the cost of his independence. A price he was no longer willing to pay.

The incline turns into a full-blown hill, and halfway up his lungs are burning. He swallows big gulps of air, heaving the breath from his lungs like it was poison. His calves start to ache. Sweat pools at his temples. His footsteps become heavy, plodding, but he cannot quit. He feeds off the pain till he's sick with it. Takes the punishment. He is alone, the only person on the street when he finally makes it to the top.

He turns around to see how far he climbed and is surprised to see the city laid out beneath him. He walks further down the street, searching for an uninterrupted view, and finds himself in a quaint, empty little park tucked into the hillside. The grass looks perfect, like the manicured lawn of a golf course, with old-fashioned streetlamps and benches scattered throughout.

He walks along the brick path, heading toward the far edge, where a wrought iron fence marks the park's perimeter. Its pickets are shiny black, like the gates surrounding the university's main campus, but here they keep everyone in. He can see the dome of the capitol building in the distance, and the dark green canopy of treetops below. It's the first time he's seen the city all at once, and the view is extraordinary. This must be why it holds such a place in his mother's heart, why she gets a wistful look in her eyes whenever talking about Providence. "I grew up," she always said, when he asked her what she did during those years after college. "But why did you stay so long?" he would ask, wanting more details, and she would shake her head before offering, "To have you, of course. To become your mother."

He sits down on a wooden bench, wanting to be off his feet. A dog, scruffy and underfed, sniffs at the roots of a nearby tree, the earth around it littered with acorns. He takes a sip of water from the bottle in his bag, warm now, and wipes the sweat from his forehead with the bottom of his T-shirt. His cell phone feels heavy in his pocket. He fingers it through the dense twill of his shorts, considers pulling it out. No, not yet. It will take several minutes for his breath to settle. Then he will face her.

A giant statue of a man looms over him—Roger Williams, according to the sign—who founded the city in 1636 after being banished from the nearby colony of Massachusetts, where he supported religious freedom and advocated for separation of church and state. Those early settlers were runaways of a sort, seeking the same freedom and self-determination that Jenry wants, which seems oddly fitting. The sun is gone now, a sea of dull clouds in its wake. He stares at the downtown area, a small cluster of gray buildings he imagines he can reach out and pluck like chess pieces to rearrange the skyline to suit his own design. He could get used to this view, the feeling of power it gives him. Where else does he dare exercise his sovereignty?

Something has to change, he knows this. He is eighteen years old and more than a thousand miles away from home, yet still feels like the little boy who can't cross the street without his mother's permission. He still lives in the shadow of her desire—what she wanted, what she did—even when he tries to follow his own. No matter what he'd said to his guidance counselor or written in his essay, he chose this school, this city, as a way to assert his autonomy, knowing she never wanted him to come here. He went against her—possibly his first act of defiance—because there was another voice, some deep internal drive telling him it was where he needed to be.

And now he's ready to have his own experience, wanting to move forward, yet it's still about her: the secrets she kept, the lies she told. One conversation with an old man, in an even older office in this old city, and his mind is filled with doubts—not just about Jasper, but about himself: how he came into the world. The injustice of it all burns in the pit of his stomach. He hates that she has the power to undo him—a power she wields as though Jenry were still a part of her body. He wants to be free, this he knows for certain, but is he ready to release her?

Minutes pass. He knows he can't put it off any longer. There is no other way forward. He unlocks his phone with a swipe, and reads through the recent calls. Her name appears several times, the word *Mami* looking foreign to his eyes, as if it's missing several letters, lacking something that would make it more substantial, and absolute.

He presses her name and watches it light up, begins to count the time as it ticks away on the call screen even before she answers.

· 6 ·

What he remembers most from the phone call is the silence. The moments when she doesn't interrupt, doesn't explain, and doesn't justify. The fact that she doesn't cover her lies with more lies. She listens, lets him talk and ask questions, lets him yell; when she does speak, all she says is that she's sorry. Sorry for the lies, yes, but more so for the truth she now has to explain, and for her cowardice, of course, in leaving the first part of the task, that enormous truth telling, to a relative stranger.

He doesn't want her apologies, not now, not ever, but the worst part is that he knows he can never get what he really wants—time. He wants to go back and relive all the moments when he'd accepted the strange explanations, the half-truths and partial-truths and straight-up lies about who and what their family was. Why he was born in Providence if they were living with her parents in Miami; why there were hardly any photos of him before the age of three; why he had only one picture of his father, one from before he was even born; why his mother, raised to be a good Catholic girl, had a baby without getting married; and finally, why she never brought any boyfriends around, never introduced him to anyone special aside from a few friends at the hospital.

This is the part of the story that he's hung up on now; this is where his mind, stretching so hard to wrap itself around a new narrative, threatens to break.

"I don't understand. I mean, why didn't you just tell me?" He skirts around the word, until finally blurting out, "Are you gay?" He is not sure he's ready to hear the answer.

"It's not as simple as that." Her voice is steady, even.

"Really? It seems simple to me. You either sleep with women or with men."

It feels wrong to talk this way to his mother, but the words come out before he can stop them.

"Well . . . I've been with both."

"So what, depending on your mood?"

"It's not—" She stops herself. "It's not something you can understand."

"You're damn right I don't understand. How you could lie to me my entire life. How you built up this man, this myth, and in the end, it turns out he wasn't even my father. I mean, he was technically, but I wasn't a son to him. I was just a bastard—"

"You had two parents," she interjects, her voice calm and unwavering.

"Are you kidding me? You think she counts? I didn't even know she existed until today."

He's getting louder now, and feels the anger flush his face. He looks around the park, but no one is in earshot.

"She was there from the beginning, *mijo*. During my pregnancy, in the hospital. She took care of you. And changed more diapers than I did."

He waits for his mother to say her name, thinking maybe that will change something, will be a clue to why this happened, but it never comes.

"This doesn't make any sense." He pinches his eyes closed, and lets out the breath he's been holding. His cell phone is hot against his ear.

"Look," she says, "I was heartbroken and alone after we broke up. I didn't know what to do—"

"You went home to your parents. You were never alone."

"But it's different than being with a partner. I couldn't share everything with them." She coughs. "They didn't accept that part of my life."

"What does that mean?" Desperate and confused, he just wants her to get to the bottom line.

"I'm saying I didn't have some elaborate plan where I sat down and figured out the rest of your life step by step. When I left Providence, I didn't know where I was going. And when I got here, I didn't know I was starting a new life. I had a baby and I needed a place to live and a way to take care of you. My parents gave me that. They gave up a lot to take us in. And I had to give things up, too."

"Like the truth?" He spits it out like a swear.

She doesn't respond right away. The word *truth* echoes in Jenry's mind like a heartbeat.

"Yes, I suppose I did."

He hears regret in her voice, maybe even shame, and for a second he starts to feel sorry for her. But then he remembers the boy he was, afraid to tell the smallest white lie, terrified of disappointing her, and the fury is back.

"That is such a cop-out. To act like you had no choice, like someone made you lie to me. I am your son, Mami. Your son." He stops, his voice breaking over the word. "Unless that is part of the lie as well."

He hears her inhale, a quick, sudden gasp, and knows he's crossed the line.

"I think we need to be done talking," she says. "I think we're done."

She is trying to help him, to save him from saying something he can't take back, but he doesn't want to be saved.

"Do you know what I think?" He walks away from the bench and steps up onto the stone ledge that traces the edge of the park. He grabs one of the pickets; the iron is cool in his grip, hard as ice. The pointed end pokes into his chest like an arrow. Like it could pierce his skin with one deep breath.

"I think you did this on purpose," he says, his voice turning hoarse. "Letting me come up here so someone else could explain your mess. I think you're a coward, Mami."

"Watch yourself right now," she warns. "You don't have all the answers." She sounds cold and unfamiliar, not like the woman who raised him.

"You're right. Thanks to you, I don't." He laughs bitterly.

"I wish you would listen. Hear me when I say I didn't plan it like this." She starts talking faster, afraid he'll cut her off. "I wanted to tell you about her myself, so many times I started the conversation. Wrote letters I never finished. But you didn't want to hear it—"

"So wait, this is my fault?"

"No. It's not about fault. It's about what happened, how we got here. Just know that it wasn't what I wanted."

He squeezes the fence post, holds the picket in his hand like a weapon.

"You must have known this would come out," he says, his voice pleading now. "I don't get it. If you didn't want me to know, why did you let me come here?"

"Her father was retired. How could I know he would still be on campus? Jesus Christ, he must be close to eighty."

She inhales sharply. He imagines she's just lit a cigarette and is now holding the smoke in her lungs, waiting for the nicotine to hit.

"You let me apply, let me accept the scholarship. You let me come."

"It wasn't me who suggested it. Your abuelo talked to the recruiter. He brought you to the audition."

"You paid for the SAT prep course. You bought the sweatshirt."

She has no response to that one.

"I thought there would be more time—" The phone crackles and her words cut out. "—all happening so fast."

"You had my whole life to tell me."

"It wasn't just my decision." She exhales. "Your grandparents, they didn't want you to know."

"So what? Don't you think knowing them could have helped me?"

"We helped you. We gave you everything."

He jumps down from the ledge, turns his back on the city.

"I was the only Black kid in our neighborhood. The only one in my graduating class. Do you think that was easy for me? Always standing out? Even at home, I was the only one who was different."

"You stand out because you're special." Her tone is softer now. "You have talent that no one in our family has."

He shakes his head. "They have it." And then, just to hear it out loud, he says, "The Pattersons."

He lets the name sit in the air between them.

"I don't know what else to say," she offers weakly. "I did the best I could." He hears the familiar tap of her packing her cigarettes. "I'm sorry."

A part of him believes her, but it doesn't matter. He's not ready for a truce.

"Are you smoking?" he asks, his tone accusatory and filled with judgment. This is an old battle between them, one he's lost hundreds of times. Still, he can't let it go.

"You've caught me again, haven't you?" she says with a hollow laugh. He imagines her face, the youthful smile. "A thousand miles away and I'm still not free to do what I want."

This surprises him, to hear that freedom is something she's wanted as well. Something she doesn't have. He hears the sound of her inhaling the smoke, and then, soft like a whisper, the sound of her letting it all go.

· 7 ·

The restaurant looks closed, but when Jenry tries the handle he finds the door unlocked. He peeks inside, scanning the unlit dining room for a body. Nothing. He considers leaving, but then hears the radio coming from the back, the bright sound of flamenco guitar. He calls out to no reply, so he walks in, heading straight to the counter like he imagines a regular customer would do. It's a long butcher block–style countertop filled with homemade jams and agave syrup in small mason jars, coarse pepper and sea salt in wooden finger bowls, olive oil in repurposed wine bottles with pour spouts—not like any diner he's ever seen. He peers into the kitchen, a showcase of stainless-steel appliances, and finally sees someone moving around in back. A flash of color streaks the pass-through. Then he hears the scrape of pots against a cast iron burner and the sound of running water.

"Hello?" he calls out in the general direction of the kitchen. A voice responds quickly, like a recording. "We open at five."

The digital clock above the counter tells him that's almost an hour from now. He crosses the dining room, walking through a cluster of Formica-topped tables, each adorned with mismatched chairs, and stands beside the closed kitchen door. He speaks to the small, round window, the view obscured. "I'm looking for the manager, actually."

"Hang on," the voice answers.

The sound of more movement as Jenry waits; a refrigerator door opens and closes, the crunch of raw vegetables being chopped, the ticking of a gas burner just before it's lit. He walks in circles around the dining room, an unfamiliar feeling building in his stomach. Not nerves, but what . . . apprehension? Anticipation? He takes a deep breath, and the feeling seems to dissipate.

The kitchen door finally opens. A woman appears in the doorway, slender in build but with the presence of someone much larger. She wears loose jeans and an even looser confidence, wiping her hands on a damp towel that hangs from her belt. Her untied work boots, obviously men's and covered in streaks of paint, threaten to fall off with every step.

She stops short when she sees him. There must be ten feet between them, but there's a curious proximity to the way she stares, her head tilted to the side as if she's measuring him, trying to fit his whole body into view.

"Yes?" she asks, her voice soft and familiar.

As he wonders if this is the woman he's looking for—the one who changed all those diapers and broke his mother's heart, the one expunged from his childhood like a minor's criminal record—he tries to remember the photo of Jasper's face, the details of his nose and eyes, but nothing sticks out as being similar except their curly hair and skin color, which is the same end-of-summer brown that Jenry's face displays.

He looks around the room, as if the words he's searching for can be found in the bright light of the diner, in the scuffed hardwood floors, the newly exposed brick, or the sign for today's specials, written in blue marker on a dry erase board that leans against the wall beside the clock. He shifts his feet.

"I'm looking for Juliet."

Her eyes widen for an instant, but she doesn't say anything. He holds out the business card he's carried in his pocket for the last three days, the corners already worn from the constant probing of his fingers. "I met her father a few days ago. He gave me this."

She eyes the card but doesn't take it. "His business card?"

Jenry flips the card over. "He wrote the address on the back. Of this diner."

"Restaurant," she corrects him.

He reads the note again. "He wrote *diner.*"

She points to the neon sign in the window: JULIEN'S RESTAURANT.

"Oh," he says, feeling instantly stupid. He looks back at the sign, his eyes tracing over the letters carefully. "But isn't the name misspelled . . . ?"

"It's not named after—I mean, it's not supposed to say *Juliet,*" she says quickly, her face flushing. "It's not a mistake. I don't own it." She wipes her hands on the towel again, annoyed now, and slightly defensive.

Jenry puts up his hands, as if to apologize. "Okay, got it."

The woman—*is this really Juliet?*—takes a deep breath and leans against the counter. She tucks a loose strand of dark hair behind her ears. "So, how can I help you?" Her face is open, interested, and, Jenry wants to believe, kind.

As he thinks of what to say, she crosses her arms over her chest, revealing a tattoo on her forearm. He can't tell what it is, but it wraps around her wrist and disappears under the rolled-up cuff of her shirt—a crisp white button-down—that doesn't seem to match the rest of her outfit. The worn jeans and work boots scream dishwasher, while her top, including her diamond-studded earrings and the gold pendant she wears on a chain around her neck, says she doesn't like to get dirty. She doesn't really look like Dr. Patterson, but there's something about her voice that reminds Jenry of the old man; not the tone or quality, but the way she speaks, the certainty.

"You still haven't told me if you're Juliet," he finally says.

"And you haven't told me your name." She shifts her feet, the boots scraping the hardwood floors. "But I have a pretty good idea of who you are."

"You do?" He looks down at her with a questioning eye.

"Yes, I do." Her face softens for the first time. Relief floods his body and he thinks that maybe, just maybe, coming here was a good idea. Then he hears the sound of a door opening in back, and a few seconds later a short, well-built man with a shaved head enters the kitchen, carrying a box of fresh green vegetables on his shoulder.

"Hey, Jules," he calls out, "I got the kale again, even though you said it was bitter last time. I think you should cook—" The man stops short when he looks through the opening and sees them standing there. "Oh. Sorry, my bad."

"No worries, Santiago. Just leave it next to the sink, okay?" Juliet gestures with the towel.

"Sure thing." Santiago drops the box and disappears into the back.

"Um, if this is a bad time . . ." Jenry starts.

"No, it's fine. Just gimme a second, okay?" She leaves for the back, propping the kitchen door with a five-gallon bucket on her way out. Jenry watches them talk, Juliet gesturing with her hands while Santiago nods, balancing a double-high tray of potatoes against his thighs. He flashes a smile, saying something in Spanish. Juliet waves him off and disappears into another room. As Santiago passes by the opened door, he winks at Jenry before he slips out the back. The screen door bangs in his wake.

Juliet returns. "We've got about fifteen minutes before the rest of the staff shows up." She checks the time on her watch, oversized and dangling loosely off her wrist, like it had once belonged to her father.

Jenry doesn't answer, looking instead out the back door, where he sees Santiago in the parking lot peeling potato skins into a garbage can almost as tall as he is.

"Here," she says, pulling out a seat for him. Her watch band sparkles in the sunlight. "Let's talk." Her voice sounds bright, like this is the exact thing she wants to be doing at this moment, as if this date had been marked on her calendar for years and she's been counting the days until its arrival. She isn't smiling, but what he hears in her voice sounds like a byproduct of happiness, or closer than that, some nascent form of joy.

Jenry sits in the chair. Now that he's here, looking at her, he doesn't know what to say. On the way over—riding two city buses and walking a half mile down Broadway so he didn't have to use the Lyft account he shares with his mother—he thought he would be angry, would interrogate her like a scene from some legal drama, but being in the same room doesn't feel like he thought it would. Mostly, he feels confusion, his own and hers, and all he wants is to lay out the pieces of his puzzled life and have her help arrange them. He takes a deep breath and sticks out his hand.

"I'm Jenry," he says. "I think you know my mother. Marisa."

Juliet stares at his hand. "Yes, I know," she says softly. "I mean, I didn't know . . . you were coming. But yes, I know you." The corners of her mouth lift slightly and she blinks several times.

He's about to drop his hand when she finally takes it; they shake firmly. He notices how smooth her hands are, and strong; they feel capable of real work. He opens his mouth, but no words come out.

"Why don't you tell me what you know," she offers, sitting back in her chair, elbow bent to lean against the counter.

"I don't know anything," he says with a small laugh.

"Well, you found me. So you've got to know something." She folds one leg over the other, an attempt to look relaxed, but he can tell she's apprehensive. The heel of her boot stamps lightly against the floor, tapping a steady beat.

"Before last week, I never knew you existed. Growing up, I heard about my father, but she never mentioned you."

"What did she tell you about him?"

"Not much," Jenry says. "How they met her freshman year, how they were friends first."

Juliet nods.

"How she first saw him at a party and could barely speak, she thought he was so handsome." Jenry pauses. "That he died young, in an accident, when they were no longer together."

"It sounds like you know a lot."

"No, not according to your father. He said that you were there. When I was born. That you were with my mother." He feels his face get warm.

"Not just with her, but *with* her, you know?" Beads of sweat start to form on his forehead.

She straightens the silverware at her place setting, lining the fork and knife up with the edge of the cloth napkin. "Yes, that's right."

"And that my father wasn't my father, wasn't going *to be* my father. That he never planned to raise me." Jenry coughs into his closed fist. "But that you did."

"Yes," she says again, nodding this time, but still not looking at him.

The butterflies in his stomach are gone, replaced by a pot of water just beginning to boil. He wipes the sweat with his sleeve.

"So what happened? If your plan was to have me together, why did I grow up in Miami not knowing you existed? You or my grandfather?" He's not mad yet, but his voice has an edge to it he didn't intend.

Juliet exhales. She looks around at the room before finally making eye contact. "Maybe your mother is the better one to answer that."

"She says that she was heartbroken and alone, that you left—"

"I never left," Juliet says. "She left." Her voice is sharp, rising in pitch.

"But you broke up with her. You ended the relationship. And then she went to Miami because she had no other place to go."

Juliet uncrosses her legs. "She went to Miami because she wanted to take you away from me."

"And you let her."

She shakes her head. "I didn't let her. She left and I didn't know where she was. I didn't know how to find you." Again, she fixes the fork and knife, straightens the napkin.

"Come on, she was living with her parents. How hard were they to find?"

Jenry feels the water boiling now, his anger a presence in the room, unmoving and visible. Yet there's a part of him that wants to protect her, so he tries to keep it restrained. Refuses to acknowledge it.

"It's complicated," she says in a quiet voice. "You don't know all the facts."

"That's why I need you to explain it to me."

She glances at the wall clock, and then at the watch hanging off her wrist. "I'm sorry. I don't have enough time to help you right now."

He stands up quickly, causing his chair to scrape its protest against the floor. "Sure, I get it. Eighteen years isn't enough time."

"I can see that you're angry—"

"Don't I have the right to be?" He grabs the back of his chair, which suddenly feels flimsy, insubstantial, in his hands. "I come here to find out about my father, and instead I find his family. Find out my life is some strange lie that's been stretched through all of these people, and I'm the only one who doesn't know the truth. Like I've got a birthmark on my face that everyone can see except me."

She stands, looking him in the eyes. "I get that this is hard for you—"

"Hard? That's the best word you can come up with?" He shoves his chair into the counter and turns away. She grabs his wrist, turning him back to face her. He's surprised by the strength of her touch.

"Listen, you're not the only one who lost something, okay? And here's the shitty thing, you don't even remember me." Her voice strains as she speaks. "You don't even know what you lost. But I do. I remember." She squeezes him, her grip like a handcuff. "I remember the first sounds you made, and how you crawled with your elbows instead of your hands, and the first time you walked—which was with me, not her—and that damn *Pizza Pat* book you made me read over and over again, and how you called cats *chicken* because you couldn't say *kitten*, and how you used to wake up after a nap saying 'All done now' and how it made me laugh every single time." She stops to take a breath. "I lost you, and I've had to carry that loss every day." She lets go of him. Steps back to steady herself. When she speaks again, her voice is much softer. "And it hasn't been eighteen years, just so you know. It's been sixteen. Sixteen years, two months, and fourteen days. Since I've seen my little boy." Her voice catches in her throat. "I think I have a right to feel some anger, too."

Jenry stands frozen in place. His arms hang by his sides as if he's lost the ability to move them. He sees tears in her eyes. Just the sight of them, and the way she blinks to keep them from falling onto her face, makes his own eyes well up. He doesn't want to cry, to feel anything for her, but he can't stop himself. Crazy as it may be, he cares about her feelings. And more than that, he wants to make sense of it all. To figure it out, and somehow make it bearable.

"I don't understand," he says, his voice beginning to break, "why you let her take me away, if you really believed that I was your son."

Juliet steps back from him, stunned into a palpable silence. Jenry feels the warmth recede from the spot on his wrist where she'd been holding him. Raw and vulnerable now, he covers it with his own hand, wraps his fingers tight around the wrist like a tourniquet, waits for the bleeding to stop. He hears the sound of the clock, its little hand the only thing in the room that dares to move.

· BOOK II ·

The Mother

September 1988

· 1 ·

Marisa would admit later that she noticed Juliet's hands first: long fingers tapered like candles, her palm square and flat like a deck of cards. Her skin was a bronze that made Marisa think she was Cuban as well, and when she handed her a drink—rum and Coke in a paper cup—she asked her in Spanish if she liked the music. The bass was so loud it made the room vibrate. It was her first college party, just one week into freshman year.

The girl—she didn't know her name yet—shook her head. It was clear that she spoke Spanish, or at least understood, but didn't care to speak it back.

"Where are you from?" Marisa had to yell over the song—British punk that had snuck onto the top forty. She wondered what they were so angry about, and why American teenagers were so fascinated by that anger.

"Here," the girl answered, flashing a vicious smirk. She pointed down at the floor with one hand, nursed her drink with the other.

"You grew up here, in this house?"

They were standing in a two-hundred-year-old Georgian turned into an Ivy League version of a frat house. They both laughed at the absurdity.

"Only a few blocks away actually. Just off Hope Street." The music stopped as the record came to an end.

"Everyone in Providence seems to live off Hope," Marisa said.

The girl finished her drink in one swallow. "That should be a bumper sticker."

"I think it is. That's probably where I got the idea." Marisa laughed again, harder than she needed to. She stuck out her hand, not sure what else to do. "I'm Marisa. I'm a freshman."

The girl shook it hard, like she was used to shaking hands with men.

"Juliet." She lifted her cup to her mouth, chewed on the ice that remained.

"Are you a student?" It was a dumb question, but Marisa just wanted to keep talking to her.

Juliet shrugged. "For now." She walked to the bar—a plastic cooler wedged into a child's red wagon—for another drink. Marisa followed, two steps behind. Her drink wasn't empty, but she held out the cup for Juliet to fill, her eyes on her hands as she poured the liquor. A drop spilled onto Marisa's finger, and when Juliet brushed it away, she felt a jolt at her touch.

Marisa sipped from her drink. She hadn't wanted to come to the party, but her roommate had insisted—begged, really—claiming that she couldn't go anywhere alone. Marisa hadn't seen her since they'd walked in, her ponytail bobbing as she disappeared into the dark.

"There aren't a lot of us here," Marisa said, peering into the darkened corners of the room, where people clustered together in groups of two or three.

Juliet looked around the room. "Women?"

Marisa shook her head. "Minority students."

Juliet made herself another drink. "I guess that's why we're still the minority."

Marisa drank from her cup. The rum felt hot in her throat.

"You always talk like that?"

"Like what?" Juliet asked.

"Like you're being interviewed."

Marisa, surprised by her own candor, was about to blame the alcohol when Juliet laughed.

"Sorry," Juliet said. "I grew up answering a lot of questions."

"Why, you famous or something?"

Juliet looked down at her hands. "I could be. If I practiced more." She stared at Marisa, as if seeing her for the first time. "I've played the piano since I was young. Classical mostly"—she paused—"jazz if my father isn't listening."

Marisa lifted her eyebrows in surprise. "You must have a gift."

Juliet exhaled. "Some people thought I was pretty good."

"What did you think?"

Juliet sucked on the ice from her cup. "I hated to practice."

"Sounds like career suicide for a musician," Marisa said. "Or self-sabotage."

"It's not like that, being a musician. It's not a job." Juliet didn't look at her when she spoke.

They watched a couple in front of them dancing too slow for the music, a pop song Marisa recognized but didn't know well enough to sing along. Juliet nodded with the beat, still not looking at her, and Marisa worried she had offended her.

Then Juliet said, "You sound like a Psych major," and Marisa, relieved, smiled in response. She had never been good at small talk, especially at the few high school parties she'd been allowed to attend, where they watched MTV videos in some kid's furnished basement and ate Pop-Tarts and sipped on blueberry schnapps, wondering what the popular kids were doing. She hoped for more meaningful interactions in college; so far, she hadn't been disappointed.

"I have two years to figure it out. Plenty of time, right?"

"If you don't waste it," Juliet said. "I spent my first year Pre-Med, before I realized nothing could make my old man happy. So I switched to Music."

"You followed your heart. Doesn't sound like a waste to me."

"It is if I'm ordinary," she said, a flat tone in her voice. Then she dragged the tip of her sneaker across the floor, toe pointed like a ballerina, leaving scuff marks on the hardwood. Marisa wondered if she was also a dancer.

"Do you still hate it?"

Juliet looked at her with a confused expression. "The piano?"

"No, silly. Practicing."

She watched Juliet tilt her head, wearing a look of complete concentration as she chewed on her bottom lip. Marisa, who had never wanted to French-kiss anyone before, let alone another girl, began to imagine how Juliet's lips would feel against her mouth.

"I miss it," Juliet said, smiling to herself, "whenever I go a day without playing." Her teeth shined brightly in the dark. "But sometimes, just to test myself, I won't play for a few days. Won't even sit at the piano."

"Why separate yourself from something you love?"

"To see if I can," Juliet said simply.

A skinny guy in all black walked by, carrying a plate of snacks. Juliet reached to grab a brownie, tossing the whole square into her mouth. Marisa watched the muscles in her jaw contract as she chewed. Then she added, "I don't want to need something that much. Like a fucking addiction."

At eighteen, Marisa wasn't afraid of need, not yet. If anything, she felt intrigued by it, desperate to be held in its clutches. She would have given anything to feel that much desire for something, especially if she was good at it—if it made people notice her.

"Don't you think," Marisa said, "there are healthy addictions?"

"Maybe. But I didn't choose classical piano. My mother played. And when she died," Juliet shrugged, "my father wanted me to be like her. Call me selfish, but if I'm going to be tethered to something, I'd at least like it to be something I choose."

Marisa nodded. She realized it wasn't her business, she didn't know this girl, why would her opinion matter? But then she found herself saying, "It's never too late. To choose something else, I mean. Not till you're in the ground."

Juliet shot her a skeptical look. Marisa felt hot suddenly. She wished they had AC in these old houses, wished Juliet would move closer to the window so she could follow her there.

"Are you religious?" Juliet asked.

Marisa wasn't quite sure how to answer. "My parents are Catholic," she said.

"I'm asking about you." Juliet leaned in closer. "Do you believe in God?" Marisa could feel the warmth of her body, could smell the rum on her breath, and underneath that, her perfume, a salty musk scent with a hint of citrus.

"I think so," Marisa began. "I mean, I want to. But I'm not sure it's a good fit. I'm not . . . like my parents."

"Well, that's reassuring," Juliet said, reaching out to tuck a loose curl behind Marisa's ear. "Most Catholics don't like me. Or my kind."

Marisa watched as Juliet's lips pulled back into a smile. She saw Juliet start to laugh, but didn't hear the sound, as if all her senses had shut down except sight. She looked at her profile—strong nose, high cheekbones, wide, almond-shaped eyes—struck by the realization that she had never seen such a beautiful face, like something out of a magazine. She memorized the rest of Juliet's body: the baggy white t-shirt (V-neck, probably a man's); the jeans that hung loose off her narrow hips (Levi's, stonewashed blue); the white-tipped sneakers etching rubber marks onto floors (Converse, faded red like a dried flower).

"We all have to make our own God," Juliet said. "I don't think I could play music if I didn't believe in something outside of myself."

Marisa wanted to respond with something smart, something clever and inspiring, but all she could think of was *I like you. I like your kind,* which sounded so pathetic in her head that she didn't dare say it out loud.

Juliet drew the tip of her sneaker across the floor again, leaving a series of wide, white scuff marks. When she was done, Marisa could see that she had drawn a cross, one matched by the small gold emblem dangling from a chain around Juliet's neck.

"Another drink?" Juliet asked, and when Marisa nodded, she led her back to the bar, reaching through the crowd to grab her hand so they didn't get separated. Juliet refilled their glasses with vodka, all that was left, topping it with orange juice from a jug on the table.

The music shifted to hard rock and soon the dance floor became a mass of bodies, thrashing around and knocking into each other. It wasn't a ritual she understood, but Marisa wanted to fit in. "Wanna dance?" she yelled over the music.

Juliet shook her head. "My brother's the dancer." She smiled as she leaned into Marisa, walking her backward through the crowd one fumbling step at a time, until they were pressed against the back wall. It was dark, the music was loud, and the force of fifty people—drunk, sweaty, young—swelled around them.

"To Providence," Juliet said, raising her cup, "and Catholics."

"And to choosing something else," Marisa added, not sure what she meant by it.

Juliet winked and they toasted, bringing their plastic cups together. Before Marisa could take a drink, Juliet kissed her. It wasn't a long or deep kiss, but it was enough for Marisa to register it, to realize that it was happening—her first real kiss—and she felt relief and exhilaration, knowing she had been right about college, this college, and this girl.

Marisa fell in love that first night. The tickle in the pit of her belly turned into a grumble, an all-out gnawing that would stay with her for months, their first encounter a subtle indication of what was to come. On the way home from the party, she told her roommate, who spent the night puking margaritas into their wastebasket and didn't remember the conversation in the morning. Marisa never confided in her again. When the crush hadn't subsided a few weeks later, she confessed to her dorm's peer counselor, a Women's Studies major who didn't believe in monogamy and encouraged her to challenge her heteronormative notions of romantic love. Eventually she wrote to her best friend from high school, now at UConn on a basketball scholarship, who had only one piece of advice: Don't tell your parents. Marisa followed that advice, but she also never told Juliet, not directly. Instead, she loved Juliet severely and secretly through all four years of college, even though she dated other women, had two long-term relationships, and had shared only that one kiss on the first night they met.

In the weeks that followed, they became friends, nothing more, and Marisa tried to convince herself that friendship was not only enough, it was preferred—lovers come and go, but friends last—and she desperately wanted, more than anything, for this relationship to last. She tried to get over her feelings for Juliet, but couldn't. No one else held her interest so completely. No one captivated her as Juliet had done in those first ten minutes, huddled together in the dark, crowded living room of an old house on Brook Street on a warm September night when she was just eighteen.

Looking back, Marisa realized that was part of the problem. Her love for Juliet was old and desperate, set up from that very first moment to disappoint her. Her thirst so great, she thought she could settle for anything, convinced herself that even a sip would be better than nothing, when, in fact, a sip would not even wet her lips, let alone satisfy her.

Years later, when she did finally get that sip—a few sips really, maybe even a whole glass—it acted instead like a poison, eating away at the very thing that created it.

· 2 ·

When Marisa first arrived in Providence, when she stepped off the airplane and onto the tarmac, walking into the unassuming T. F. Green airport, she carried a hard-shelled suitcase in one hand—the only piece of luggage she owned, a high school graduation gift—and a huge bag of oranges in the other. The oranges were from her mother, to get her through the cold winter, while her father had pressed five crisp ten-dollar bills into her hand at the gate, which she later tucked into her bra in the plane's cramped bathroom. It was the first time she had flown on an airplane by herself, and she was nervous. An only child, Marisa had grown up alongside her parents, both practically teenagers when she was born. All three of them felt equally anxious about the separation, but her parents knew something she did not: she was leaving them behind.

Victor and Inés held each other at the gate in Miami, crying only after she had boarded the plane; they both knew if she saw them, she might change her mind about leaving. She was a good daughter, self-sacrificing and loyal, and she had worked so hard for the scholarship; she was going someplace special, their little girl, and they didn't want to be the thing that stopped her. Five hours, two flights, and a thousand miles later, Marisa stepped onto the earth certain of only two things: that this strange land beneath her feet was solid, and that she was alone.

For an only child raised by doting, first-generation parents, this was quite a revelation. But there was something she had felt right away about this small city, the way it empowered its inhabitants, that made her feel as if she could endure anything, become anyone, lose and gain a lifetime of identities, and still come out whole on the other side. This affinity, and the fact that she hadn't grown up in Providence—unlike Juliet, who bolted two days after getting her diploma—made Marisa's decision after graduation fairly easy: she decided to stay.

She moved to the city's Southside, where rents were cheap, and took over the attic apartment of a three-story house that hadn't been painted since the Second World War. Her housemates worked for non-profits, which meant that none of them had any money, but they had passion and a lot of time on their hands. They started a community garden in an abandoned lot around the corner, and spent their weekends picking chunks of broken glass out of the black dirt; when the harvest finally came in—peas and potatoes and summer squash as thick as their forearms—they threw block parties where children walked barefoot in the middle of the street, Janet Jackson or hip-hop blasted from car stereos, and malt liquor was the only drink you could find on ice.

She felt like the lone Cuban in her all-Black neighborhood, and she liked it that way. The Spanish that defined the soundtrack of her childhood, already muted by four years in the Ivy League, was relegated to special occasions, pulled out when she called her parents on Sundays, or when she watched the *telenovelas* her mother recorded for her on VHS tapes and mailed in care packages with guava paste and homemade *turrón de mani*, whose sweet peanut aroma oozed from the box even before she opened it. She was used to being different, but this time it didn't make her an outsider; it made her a novelty.

Her first job was teaching at a preschool started by one of her roommates, but three months later the city shut it down for a health code violation, so she ended up working at the Boys & Girls Club. She always knew she would work with children, but was surprised to find herself in education, not health care. She started out driving the after-school pick-up van and by spring was running the after-school enrichment program. Demographics had shifted, as more Dominicans and Puerto Ricans moved north from New York City, looking for better jobs and cheaper rents; she suddenly found herself, and her Spanish fluency, in demand. Her background became useful, a tool she could pull out when needed. At twenty-four, after working only two years at the non-profit agency, she was promoted to director of youth services, the youngest director in their 126 years of serving underprivileged Black and brown kids in Providence.

The rumors about Juliet being back in town started with Marisa's housemate, Jane, who had moved onto bartending at a gay club after the preschool got shut down. One night in September she came home with a story about how Juliet had stopped in for a drink on her way to a gig in Boston, how she had been touring in Europe for a year and recorded an album of jazz standards abroad, how her hair was cut short so she looked like a boy from the back, but that she was just as gorgeous as ever, the same flaky, temperamental artist they'd known back in college. Jane rolled her eyes when she said it, but Marisa knew she thought Juliet was a genius—they all did—which was why everyone let her get away with her dodgy behavior. A week later Jane brought Juliet home, after they closed down the club with shots of Patrón and Jane had insisted she was too drunk to drive.

Marisa had spent the night playing spades with friends from work, but she was home and in bed by 11:00 p.m., as she was most nights. At 2:30 a.m., while she was yelling at her mother in a dream, pretending not to understand Spanish, she was awakened by the sound of someone falling down the back staircase. By the time she put on her robe, she could hear the laughter of intoxication from the shared hallway, followed by Jane's whisper-shouted apology for waking her up.

"Sorry, it's just me," Jane's voice rang out, "go back to bed."

It was dark where she stood, and Marisa squinted at the light from below; she saw shadows along the wall, but nothing more.

"Oh, wait," Jane called after her, "look who the cat dragged in."

Marisa had to walk down the stairs to see the person leaning against Jane in a drunken embrace, the one with her tongue in Jane's ear. She wasn't surprised or even jealous to see that it was Juliet—the first thing she was aware of feeling was relief. Aside from a few postcards and a ridiculously expensive phone call from Copenhagen on her last birthday, she hadn't heard from Juliet since graduation.

"Hey, stranger," Juliet said softly, stumbling as she and Jane stepped onto the landing in tandem. She broke free to give Marisa a proper hug, squeezing hard like she always used to, and leaning in to kiss her cheek before pulling away. More than two years had gone by, but Juliet hadn't changed. She seemed, to Marisa, to be the same person she'd always been—singular, and true to herself. Not because it was cool, but because it came naturally. She didn't know how to be anyone else. Better still, she wasn't aware of the effect she had on people, which made her even more desirable.

"It's good to see you," Marisa said, and as the words came out, she realized how true they were. "It's like you dropped off the face of the earth after graduation. And now, here you are."

Juliet smiled at the two women. "Here I am." Her eyes were glassy, and she was clearly inebriated, but she looked good—happy and vibrant, relaxed, and still beautiful. She seemed to arrive at a certain peace, something Marisa envied.

Jane unlocked her door with a key she wore on a piece of yarn around her neck and walked into the dark apartment. Juliet nodded slightly in Marisa's direction, before following behind.

Marisa hardly slept that night, knowing that Juliet was just one floor below her, hooking up with Jane in a drunken tumble neither would remember in the morning. Marisa woke early, listening for any sound in the back hallway, hanging around longer than she usually did, hoping to run into her. She eventually had to leave for work—forty-five minutes late—without catching a glimpse. Later, she asked Jane for her number and Jane said Juliet didn't have one yet; she was splitting time between her brother's couch in Manhattan and a family cabin in the Berkshires. Apparently, her album hadn't sold well in the States, and funds were low.

"Well, if she stops by the club again, give her my number," Marisa offered, trying to sound nonchalant. Jane stared at her through blood-shot eyes. "Right," she said, and Marisa knew that Jane would never pass along her number, and that her secret crush wasn't going to remain a secret any longer.

Marisa had no choice but to wait, an activity that had taken up a large portion of their friendship during college: waiting to go to dinner while Juliet finished practicing one more set of scales; waiting to turn twenty-one so they could meet at Deville's for drinks; waiting in line to congratulate her after her first performance at Sayles Hall, the one at-tended by the president of the college and the head of the Music Depart-ment, the one that cemented her reputation as being brilliant, a female Thelonious Monk, the article in the *BDH* had said; waiting for her to break up with Keesha Connelly, and then Brienne Hampton, and then Lena Monardi, and then Brienne again; waiting for the spell to be bro-ken, the infatuation to dissolve. But this time something changed. This wait, after six years of knowing each other—a third of that spent living thousands of miles apart and barely communicating—turned out to be the shortest.

Just two days later, while the sun set and the first hint of fall crisped the air, Juliet dropped by the house. She was there to pick up her jacket, a black leather deal with zippers on every pocket, no doubt European, and after getting it from the back hall closet, she walked up the stairs to the attic, where Marisa's two-room apartment was built into the eaves. She knocked three times—first two loud, last one quiet, her signature knock—and Marisa opened the door knowing it was her, her heart gal-loping with anticipation. They grabbed takeout that night, and hung out a few more times that month, and soon Juliet was stopping through on her way from New York to Boston each week for her gig at Berklee College of Music, occasionally napping on the couch before she got back on the road.

It was exactly what Marisa needed: the chance to spend time with her again, to show that she had grown beyond the shy, naive girl she'd been in college, the one who always went to class and structured her days around appointments in her calendar; who called herself bisexual—not lesbian—and pinned a pink triangle onto her backpack, yet didn't feel comfortable holding hands with a girl in public; the one who went along to queer marches, but never joined any of the clubs. She was a woman now, and she had something to offer. Marisa didn't worry about what it all meant, what she wanted or what Juliet could give; she just kept inviting her back, and Juliet kept coming.

One rainy night, Marisa cooked a big pot of her abuela's picadillo, with a plate of fried *maduros* on the side. She wanted to stay in, with a nice, homecooked meal, instead of their typical pizza or Chinese takeout. Juliet arrived late, as usual—this time from getting a speeding ticket in Connecticut—and she was soaked, her jacket beaded with rain, shirt stuck to her body. Marisa brought her a towel to dry off, but it wasn't enough. While she stood by the stove, fluffing the rice with a fork, she watched Juliet unbutton her shirt, stripping to just a tank top. She tried not to notice how hard her nipples were against the thin white cotton, and how muscular her arms looked, with strong, broad shoulders. Juliet hung her damp shirt on the back of a chair, moving it close to the radiator to dry. Towel around her neck like a boxer, she stood beside Marisa, asking what smelled so good, telling her, with a huge grin, as droplets of water fell from her hair, that she was starving.

Marisa served them bowls of white rice drowned in a stew of ground beef, potatoes, and olives. She sprinkled green beans on top, like a garnish, so they wouldn't get overcooked in the sauce, just like her grandmother had taught her. It made her feel good to cook like this, made her cramped apartment feel more like a home. They sat on folding chairs at the small kitchen table, a yard sale reject Marisa had painted bright yellow, and found themselves talking about the future. Juliet was evasive, as usual, but admitted to feeling lost at times, not doubting her talent exactly, but wondering whether she had what it took to pursue such a difficult, unpredictable career.

"You've been on this track since you were a kid, why stop now?" Marisa asked, cutting into the fried plantain with the side of her fork. She held it in her mouth and savored the sweet taste.

"I don't mean stop necessarily . . ." Juliet took a bite of her food. "But I wonder if I should change it up. Maybe focus on a new sound, or put together a new band." She used a spoon to collect the sauce in the bottom of her bowl. "Damn, this is good." She took another bite. "This is like lesbian U-Haul good."

Marisa smiled at the compliment; she knew Juliet was teasing, but she liked the idea that they might be together for more than one meal at a time, liked imagining a U-Haul in their future, however improbable it seemed.

"So, change it up then," Marisa said, a new tone of confidence in her voice. "What's stopping you?" When Juliet didn't respond, Marisa asked, "Your father?"

"He's worried about me." Juliet rolled her eyes. "He keeps saying that grad school would help me get a real teaching job."

"You said you didn't want to teach anymore."

"True. But I don't want to be broke either. Or have to beg my dad for money."

"Haven't you heard? Twenty-five is the best time to be broke," Marisa joked. "It's practically mandatory."

Marisa got up to serve her another bowl, feeling Juliet's eyes on her. When this happened with men on the street, she felt objectified and dirty, but here in her kitchen, alone with Juliet, it made her feel sexy and more free.

"You trying to spoil me?" Juliet asked. Her voice was low and flirtatious. She tugged on Marisa's apron strings as she stood before her, untying the knot with one pull. Marisa felt the weight of Juliet's hand. "You trying to catch me?" Marisa asked.

Juliet dropped the string to let her go, then sat back in her chair. Marisa was playing a game, one Juliet had perfected, but this time she felt capable, ready for whatever came next. She wanted something to change, didn't want to be the girl with the unrequited crush forever. Juliet kicked up her feet, placing them on a nearby stool, and said, "I'm game if you are," which birthed a swarm of butterflies in Marisa's stomach.

After the meal, Juliet offered to make mojitos. She pulled out an un-opened bottle of Bacardi from a paper bag she'd left by the door. "Jasper would kill me if he saw this. He's always going on about Cuban rum having the best flavor."

"Don't you mean Cuban *women*?"

Juliet chuckled. "But since we can't get Havana Club in the States"— she cracked open the bottle—"this will have to do."

Despite the downpour, Juliet wrapped the towel around her shoulders and ran downstairs to grab a bunch of fresh mint from the neighbor's garden. The leaves were still wet with rainwater as she carried them inside. She chopped off the stems with a steak knife, the only sharp knife in the drawer, and packed the bottoms of their glasses—two pint-sized canning jars left behind by the previous tenant—with the pieces of mint.

Marisa enjoyed watching her work, displaying the same precision as when she was at the piano or writing new songs in her composition journal. She imagined how it would feel to do this every night; the thought made her ache with longing.

Juliet squeezed a lime into each glass, soaking the mint with juice, then added a tablespoon of sugar and a heavy pour of rum. She muddled it all together with the handle of a wooden spoon, pressing down and twisting it to mix all the flavors together. Her hands moved effortlessly, and Marisa found herself captivated, like she was watching a magic trick. Juliet wiped her hands on the towel, then topped each glass off with an inch of club soda and a handful of ice.

They took their drinks to the living room and sat on the futon, listening to the sound of the rain falling hard against the roof.

'If you weren't worried about money, what would you do right now?"

Juliet shrugged. "Play more, I guess. And write more music."

"So you should do that. Now, while you're still young."

"I'm old when it comes to musicians. Might be too late to reinvent myself."

"It's never too late," Marisa said, sitting back to watch the rain streaming down the windows. "Look at us." She was referring to their careers—how she had stumbled into the non-profit world and moved up in a short amount of time, how Juliet had followed her fans abroad, and was now lauded in several other countries—but it sounded like she was talking about their relationship, and she didn't want to take it back.

"Us?" Juliet asked, nursing her drink.

Marisa blushed; normally that alone would make her stop, but that night she kept going. "I think we can help each other," she said. "In a different way than before." Juliet didn't say anything, just stared at her with those doe eyes, so Marisa continued, making it up as she went along. "It seems like what you really need is time, to figure out what's next. I could help you get that. You could stay here whenever you needed, I'm at work half the day anyway, and that would save you money. And give you more freedom to . . . improvise."

Juliet nodded. "And what would I do for you?"

Marisa thought for a second, then she pointed across the room, where an old-fashioned stereo system sat in pieces on the floor, speakers on their sides being used as end tables, wires unattached and leading nowhere. "You could set that up for me, attach the speakers and make it all sound good. I know it looks like a mess, but it works."

"Is that it?"

Marisa gestured to the TV, also on the floor, with a VCR resting on its top. "Maybe connect it all to the VCR so when we watch movies, it feels like we're at the theater. You know, just handle the whole electronic system in here. Bring it up to your standards."

"You're serious?"

"I'm serious," Marisa said matter-of-factly. Then she added, "Anything else we can negotiate as it comes up."

Juliet wore an unfamiliar expression, and Marisa imagined she was debating the pros and cons in her mind. A few moments later, Juliet put down her empty glass. She reached over to take a sip from Marisa's glass, which was still half full. "You don't like your drink?"

"I do, it's just a little strong for me."

Juliet took another sip, this time covering Marisa's hand with her own. Marisa's whole arm trembled.

"Are you cold?" Juliet asked. "I could find a blanket."

"No, it's fine." Marisa wanted this, to have Juliet touching her, but now that it was happening, she felt afraid. No, it wasn't fear—it was caution. She pulled back from Juliet, offering her the glass. "Here, you finish it. I have work tomorrow."

Juliet eyed the remains. "If I finish it, I'll have to spend the night."

Marisa shrugged. "The couch pulls out into a bed. You know that."

Disappointment flickered across Juliet's face. "Here's what I don't know," she said, chewing on a mint leaf, her breath sweet and tangy. "Why are you being so nice to me?" She leaned in closer, her eyelashes long and dark.

"I'm not nice, I'm—" Marisa stopped herself, not sure what she was. She wanted so badly to tell her the truth, to say everything she'd held inside all these years. But she knew Juliet wasn't ready for anything real, and if they hooked up now, it would only be a few weeks before Juliet got antsy and pushed her away. Marisa wanted a real relationship with Juliet, and she was willing to wait for it.

"I'm practical," she finally said. "That's what I am." She looked at Juliet. "What are you?"

Juliet laughed, dropping her head. "I don't know. I'm still trying to figure it out."

It seemed like the most honest thing Juliet had ever said. Marisa glanced out the window, saw the rain beginning to let up.

"But I do know one thing," Juliet said. She placed her hand on Marisa's shoulder, fingers slightly curled like she was laying them on the keyboard, about to play. "I need you." Her touch was so light, Marisa could hardly feel it. "I need our friendship right now."

Marisa nodded. This was the vulnerable side of Juliet she had rarely seen. A wave of relief spread through her body. She was right to pull back—it allowed space for Juliet to move toward her.

"I've always worried that if I stayed in one place too long, if I ever settled down, it would affect my music. That I'd lose my drive." She put her arms behind her head and closed her eyes. "Me and a million other artists."

"Maybe it's not true," Marisa offered, taking the empty glasses to the sink. "Some people build their whole lives around a lie."

When she returned to the living room a few minutes later, carrying a blanket and sheets to make the couch into a bed, she expected Juliet to be in the same position, reclined with her eyes closed, but instead found her on the floor, bent over the stereo system, beginning to put it together.

· 3 ·

Marisa gave Juliet a key to the apartment, and within a month, Juliet was spending half the week there. She finished setting up the stereo system, then helped with other things: hanging the art she bought from a student show at RISD; putting bookshelves together and fixing broken locks; installing the storm windows after the first frost. Without the pressure of having to define their relationship, they relaxed into each other, soon spending most of their free time together. From the outside, they looked like a couple, but inside they were who they had always been; for Marisa, that was both the blessing and the curse of their relationship.

Despite this hands-off approach, their bond grew stronger. The connection between them, though fluid, was potent, like a body of water teeming with wildlife; it was alive, not stagnant, always evolving. Marisa could document when the physical shifts took place—their first real kiss (during a New Year's Eve party, both drunk on Champagne); when they started having sex (the night Juliet placed third in a jazz competition hosted by Wynton Marsalis); when Juliet moved into the apartment full-time and, later, into Marisa's bedroom (after a sideman appearance at

Wally's Café, sitting in for Hank Jones)—but the emotional shift was elusive, which made Marisa wonder if it had happened at all. After six months, she still wasn't sure: were they dating, or simply friends who had sex? Friends who slept in the same bed, who used each other's bank cards, and had talks about summer homes and road trips and all the islands they wanted to visit. They talked about everything—except how they felt about each other.

Marisa thought they didn't need to. The relationship was easy, comfortable, temporary; they both understood that it wouldn't last forever. Juliet couldn't be tied down for long, even without labels and promises, and Marisa eventually wanted to put down roots and start a family. They knew this about each other. So they lived in the present, not the doomed future, and for right now Marisa was happy—she had Juliet, in the flesh—and that was enough. It might not make sense to anyone else, but Marisa knew that it was somehow necessary to her survival; that getting what she wanted, even for a short time, was going to change her life. Instead of settling for less in the unspecified future, she wanted as much as she could get right now, staying exactly where she was, waiting for the next opportunity to appear.

Spring bloomed, then summer burned hot and bright. They went to Cape Cod on vacation, napped in the tall grass above Longnook Beach, then ran barefoot through the sand dunes, Juliet screaming with the seagulls while Marisa laughed so hard she couldn't catch any of it on film. They rented a stuffy room in a ramshackle bed-and-breakfast in Province-town, with no air conditioning and an antique brass bed that squeaked so violently they had to drag the mattress onto the floor, where they had sex on top of the blankets with the windows wide open, then took cold showers before heading to town. Hand in hand they strolled down Commercial Street, blending in with other gay couples who crowded the small shops, who stopped to admire watercolor paintings set up on sidewalks and smiled at babies sleeping in strollers, who gorged on fried calamari and lobster ravioli at overpriced restaurants, who watched the moon rise over the pier at the evening's end. After three days of the same, they drove home sunburnt and happy, listening to a mix tape of old jazz standards, Juliet humming the melodies the entire way.

When fall came, Marisa wrote a grant to expand one of her programs, and when she got it, her boss gave her a raise. With the extra salary, she upgraded her furniture, ditching the thrift store chic for a living room set; she started shopping for groceries on the East Side, occasionally buying organic; she traded in her ten-year-old Mazda for a new, more reliable Toyota. To her friends, it was a sign of growing up and settling down, but for Marisa it was more than that. Every step she took toward a stable, middle-class life made her feel more confident, more worthy of being with someone like Juliet. Unacknowledged during college, there was a vast difference between the worlds they came from, the neighborhoods they grew up in, the jobs their parents had. They never discussed it, but it was alive in Marisa's subconscious, feeding her desire to make a nice space for the two of them; she hoped to one day transform their agreement from cohabitation into a shared home.

Juliet acted like she didn't care about money or the privileges it could buy, but Marisa didn't have that luxury; she didn't have a father with tenure and a retirement account, or a new Volvo she could borrow whenever her Saab was in the shop; she didn't have a brother who sent her expensive jewelry from around the world. Like most people who grow up with plenty, Juliet couldn't see how much she really had. Marisa was aware of everything she worked to attain; she wasn't ashamed of where she came from, but she didn't want to go back there. She wanted to stay exactly where she was, with Juliet by her side.

As predicted, Juliet soon became antsy. She wanted to move to a bigger apartment, so she could have her own room to work in, get her piano out of storage and do more than practice for an hour a day with a keyboard balanced on her lap. A rep from a major record label had reached out, offering to record a second album with her as leader; all she needed was her own band. Marisa wanted more space, too, perhaps with an extra bedroom and a park nearby, something in a good school district. She'd had more dreams about motherhood lately, filled with baby animals she needed to save, her body tender and full as she watched her dream-self's belly expand. At first they scared her, but as they arrived with more frequency she tried to accept them, to stay open to whatever came next.

They found a three-bedroom apartment on the East Side, with tons of light and newly sanded hardwood floors, close to Marisa's job. They could split the rent, Juliet promised, since she had a few steady gigs lined up, and could always bartend on the side if necessary; she didn't want to keep taking money from her father. Marisa agreed, happy to see Juliet excited about something that strengthened their attachment. They put both their names on the lease, the biggest sign of commitment Juliet had ever made, and moved in over Thanksgiving break.

A year had passed since that conversation on the futon, and though things were stable, Marisa was still hungry for something more. She thought she knew what that was, but didn't tell Juliet until a night in mid-December when Juliet came home from her monthly dinner with her father. They'd gone to Yang Chow, one of their regular spots, and had a five-course meal that began with dumplings and ended with Juliet at home, drinking a bottle of red wine by herself as she scrubbed the stove top and listened to Chick Corea's *Again and Again* on the record player.

Marisa was used to being alone, with or without Juliet in the apartment, and they both thought it was one of the reasons why their setup worked. Juliet had her music—hours of practicing each day, with several more devoted to listening to old recordings borrowed from the library's music collection (McCoy Tyner at the Village Vanguard, Art Tatum in cutting sessions from Birdland, Bill Evans backing Billie Holiday at the Apollo), while Marisa had her own projects—the community garden, babysitting for new moms at work, knitting wool sweaters by hand for all the kids at the Boys & Girls Club, a feat that became more impressive each year as the program expanded. So that night, when Marisa heard the syncopated beats of the piano solo pounding out an angry ribbon of chords, she almost decided to avoid Juliet, who hadn't practiced for three days straight, and even skipped her usual jam session at Southland. Marisa knew something was up.

Juliet sat on the kitchen floor, her back against the oven door. The record had stopped a few seconds before, and it was strangely quiet as Marisa slipped into the room.

"Sorry," she offered, "I was coming in for a cup of tea."

Juliet held up the almost empty wine bottle. "How about a really cheap Cab instead?"

"No, thanks." Marisa stepped over her legs to turn on the tea kettle. "Let me make you some tea."

Juliet shrugged, so Marisa picked up the wine bottle and set it on one of the unused burners. "Stove looks good," Marisa said, smiling sweetly. "Can I thank your dad for this sudden urge to degrease?"

"You can thank my father for most of my cleaning binges."

A few minutes passed. Soon the water started to rumble and the kettle blew.

"There's always next month," Marisa offered. "Plus, you'll see him again for Christmas, right?"

Juliet frowned. "Tonight *was* our Christmas." She pulled a check from her pocket, slapped it onto the floor. Five hundred dollars. "Merry Christmas, baby girl."

"Wow," was all Marisa could think to say. Juliet's father gave her money often, but it was always cash, usually small bills.

"I think it's a bribe. To keep me at a distance."

"Is the same true for your brother?"

Juliet shook her head. "Jasper gives me presents to compensate for the fact that he never comes home to visit. To assuage his guilt for leaving me alone with the old man."

Marisa fixed their tea, dipping one tea bag of chamomile between two cups. "I meant, does he bribe your brother, too. To stay away."

Juliet laughed. "I think Jasper makes more money than him, or he's invested well or something. The old man jokes about retiring early and living off the interest from Jasper's 401(k)." She twisted around to grab the wine bottle from the stove top, tipping it into her mouth.

"Must make him proud, both his kids doing well."

Juliet wasn't one to brag, but she had joined a semi-famous quartet over the summer, and the live album they recorded at the Newport Jazz Festival was getting them work all over the East Coast. But for Juliet, it wasn't enough. She wanted to lead her own band.

"This isn't his idea of success." Juliet exhaled, letting the air blow through her lips. "And who can blame him? I play the piano in someone else's band. It's a job, not a career. When he was my age, he was already teaching at City College. He was about to get married and become a father." She held the wine bottle around its neck the way a trumpet player grasped their horn. "If I gave this up and quit the band, I'd have nothing."

Marisa handed her the cup of tea. "It was a different time," Marisa said. "And he was a man. That's not a fair comparison."

Juliet blew softly on the tea, cupping the wine bottle between her legs so it wouldn't spill. "Sometimes I think they won't ever take me seriously. Because I'm not a man. Even when I play better." She let her head rest against the oven door. It worried Marisa to see her so defeated.

"The record deal fell through." Juliet closed her eyes. "There's no market for a new band right now. Not with a girl in lead."

"That's total bullshit," Marisa said, her voice sharp with anger. "Your first album sold, and you were a girl back then."

"Nobody bought it outside Europe. Jazz is basically dead here, aside from the big festivals. Unless I want to play in dark, smoky clubs for the rest of my life."

"You can't let them win. Fuck that. Go back to Europe if you need to."

"Maybe I should." Juliet sipped the tea, making a face that said it was too hot to drink. "The lifestyle over there, it was fun for a while. But if I went back, I'd be doing the same thing in twenty years. You don't progress over there. You don't graduate." She drank more tea, holding the cup with two hands. "The guys I toured with, they were in their fifties and sixties, doing the same thing night after night. The same clubs, the same restaurants, the same after-parties. But they didn't have anything. Music was their whole life. They had girlfriends or wives in different cities, a kid somewhere, but nothing was really theirs. Not even the music."

Marisa leaned over to rub Juliet's thigh. "What about you? What do you want to own?" Her finger found a frayed hole in the jeans and slipped inside. Juliet's skin was as smooth and cold as tile.

"I don't know. A house maybe, or a dog?"

Marisa laughed. "Hate to break it to you, but you have to come home when you have a dog. At a predictable time. The dog counts on that."

Juliet nodded. "I could do that. If I really liked the dog." They both laughed.

Marisa sipped her tea. "But how long until you wanted a different dog?"

It was a valid concern, they both knew it, but Marisa regretted saying it out loud. The truth, like a gust of winter wind, seemed to knock Juliet over at times, as if she were no more than a cardboard cutout, while other times, she seemed impervious to any attack, as cool and impassable as stone. Juliet stood up and poured the rest of the wine down the sink, then rinsed out the bottle and placed it in the dish rack to dry, upside down, as if it were her favorite cup. Marisa had more to say, and she knew it couldn't be hidden in a cute analogy. It had to be said directly, without excuse or apology.

"I've been wanting to tell you something." Marisa spoke to Juliet's back, the only way she could bring herself to say it out loud. "I think I'm going to have a baby." It had been on her mind for months, but she was still shocked that the words had come out of her mouth. She looked down at the kitchen floor, counted the tiles between the oven and the sink.

Juliet turned around. "Like, you think you're pregnant?"

"No, of course not." Marisa finished her tea in one swallow. "I've been thinking about doing it on my own. With a sperm bank. There's one in California that will ship anywhere in the country."

"Will they tell you who the father is?"

"It's anonymous. That way you're legally protected and some guy can't show up later and claim rights to your kid." Marisa was already practicing the way she would tell the story to others, starting with her parents. "He isn't the father, anyway, he's the donor. It's just someone's DNA in a tiny plastic vial."

Juliet leaned back against the sink. "And you think the kid will understand the difference?"

Marisa shrugged. "I don't know what the kid will think. This hypothetical kid. My future child." She bent over to play with the zipper on her boot, zipping it up and down with satisfaction. "But even if he's mad at me," she went on, "at least I'll have him. He'll exist because I made him." She pulled the zipper all the way up, till the leather was tight around her calf and her leg started to hurt.

She didn't know why she'd said *him* when she'd always imagined having a girl, but now that she'd said it, it seemed like a forgone conclusion: she knew deep down she would have a son. Juliet walked over, squatted next to Marisa. She unzipped Marisa's boot and slowly took it off, holding Marisa's foot in her hand as she peeled off her sock.

"I think you'll be an excellent mother. Really. No matter how you do it." She kissed the top of her foot, and then her ankle, her shin. Marisa felt tears in her eyes and she turned to the side, blinking them away. She felt stupid for crying at a moment like this, talking about a child she didn't even know if she would have. She cleared her throat, swallowed a huge chunk of pride.

"If you were a man," she stopped to wipe her eyes on the edge of her sweater, "would you give me your sperm?"

Juliet laughed, and then seeing the look on Marisa's face, stopped herself, turning it into a cough. "You're serious."

Marisa stared at her.

"Damn," Juliet said softly. She dropped her head, which Marisa read as embarrassment. "I don't know how to answer that."

Marisa studied the smooth muscles in Juliet's neck. Her eyes traveled down Juliet's body, from the ridges of her spine to the small of her back, where her shirt had come untucked, showing the waistband of her boxer shorts. She suddenly needed to touch her, so she ran her fingers through Juliet's short hair, the curls much softer than they looked.

Marisa kissed the top of her head. "It's okay. You don't have to. But just know that I would want that. I would want you to be a part of this baby somehow."

"That's sweet," Juliet said.

"It's the truth." Marisa stood up and brought the kettle to the sink to add more water.

Juliet moved to the record player. She switched the album, and Marisa guessed Coltrane would be next, *Giant Steps* or *A Love Supreme*, something to fit the mood, but as she watched her delicately lift the needle and lay it on the vinyl's innermost groove, skipping to the last song on the side, she recognized her mistake. It had to be Dave Brubeck's *Time Out*, confirmed as soon as she heard the first shuffle of the cymbals on "Take Five." Juliet was always going against the grain. The volume was turned way down, so it was less like music and more like a vibration, something they could feel instead of listen to, like heat warming a cold room.

"Maybe Jasper would do it," Juliet said as she read the album notes. "That way, you would have some of my DNA at least."

Marisa walked up behind her, sliding her arms around Juliet's waist. "And you'd be okay with that?"

Juliet faced her, eyes clear. "He wouldn't be the father, right? It's not like you'd be raising the kid together."

"He wouldn't be more than . . . a helper. It would just be me." Marisa rested her head against Juliet's chest. "Unless you wanted to help."

"I doubt you'll need much help. With the exception of your record collection," she teased. "You need a lot of help in that department."

Marisa smiled at Juliet's playfulness but felt her own body start to shift, become heavy with possibility. They held each other loosely in the middle of the kitchen, like teenagers at a high school dance, unsure of what to do next, of what they wanted, and of how much of themselves to expose in the harsh light of the gymnasium.

"So, what would I be, to the baby?" Juliet asked.

Marisa heard the word *baby* over and over, a record skipping on this simple word, no sound, no music beyond it.

"Whatever you want to be." In her mind she thought, *parent, aunt, friend,* but she didn't speak any of those words. She didn't want Juliet to feel trapped by a list of predetermined identities; she wanted her to choose her own word, define it for herself. She knew that was the only way it would work. For Juliet to invent a new term—her own unique label—and then be given the freedom to embody it.

They weren't dancing, but there was a rhythm to their movement, a steady pulse Marisa could feel all the way into her bones. She tried to ignore the excitement growing like a root in the pit of her stomach as she wrapped her arms around Juliet. Juliet squeezed back.

"So, a dog, huh?" Marisa said, after a long spell.

The radiator hissed as the heat kicked back on. She could feel Juliet tapping her lower back with her fingertips, a habit she had when she was working on a new song, trying to hear the notes in her head.

"I want to feel connected to something that's mine," Juliet said. "Like I'm a part of the world."

To that Marisa wanted to say: *You are my world.* Instead she said, "I hear it's quite a commitment, owning a dog."

Juliet tilted her head, looked Marisa in the eye.

"Dogs are forgiving, aren't they?"

Marisa smiled up at her. "No, actually, I don't think they are."

"Oh." Juliet leaned down to kiss her. "Well, thankfully you are."

"Yes," Marisa answered. "Thankfully, I am."

· 4 ·

There was a protocol, a *set of procedures* as her doctor described, with each step laid out in order. Marisa, who liked following directions, who bought a new planner every year to track her goals, followed it dutifully, ticking them off one by one: the insurance screening paperwork, the temperature charting and pre-ovulation test kits, the contract for donor storage and medical release forms, six sessions with an alternative family planning therapist, three cycles of Clomid to predict her ovulation, followed by three precisely scheduled rounds of IUI, each insemination performed at her OB-GYN's office, and eventually, a positive pregnancy test. The whole thing took close to nine months, which other fertility-challenged friends assured them was relatively quick. Aside from mild morning sickness, her first trimester passed without incident, fortified by an unusually warm fall that kept the leaves on the trees until Thanksgiving.

The first real obstacle Marisa faced arrived in December, when she called her parents on Christmas morning to tell them she was pregnant, still unmarried, and living with a woman she loved. Juliet had just returned home from a three-night run at Smalls Jazz Club in the Village, after starting her own band anyway. They weren't famous yet, but they had regular gigs in Boston and New York, and were slowly making the festival rounds, where critics wrote that Juliet was finally living up to the promise of her early years. Juliet had been up since dawn, slow roasting a pork shoulder for their Boxing Day party, while Marisa stood at the counter and rolled out dough for gingerbread men, peeling their floppy bodies from the cutting board before arranging them neatly on the cookie sheet. Their whole apartment smelled like garlic and ginger. Marisa held the spatula in her hand, as if it might protect her, when she dialed the phone.

Songs from Nat King Cole's Christmas album, Juliet's favorite, filled the room, but Marisa knew that at her parents' home, she'd hear Frank Sinatra's "I'll Be Home for Christmas" playing in the background. She found comfort in the anticipation of something so familiar, and when she heard Sinatra's gravelly voice, she wanted to sing along with the ballad she had memorized like a Bible verse, one of the many discarded traditions from her childhood. Her father answered and they talked weather and sports first, then health—his blood pressure was a bit high, her mother was having trouble sleeping, her grandmother's hip was slowly healing from her fall off the stepladder—and finally the holidays, their plans to give candies to the neighbor kids, to pass out toys at the club, to play bridge with his high school buddies while the wives drank glasses of coquito and looked through old photo albums.

Her mother got on the phone, talking about the food she'd been cooking all week, the last-minute shopping, the lines in all the stores. Her parents were not old, but something about their lifestyle made Marisa feel like she was talking to her grandparents, people two generations removed from her life. Victor and Inés were both in their mid-forties, still working full-time, and yet they had the air of early retirement, of building their days around social engagements and doctor's appointments, a sporting event maybe, or a drive to the ocean to watch children they didn't know fly kites along the beach.

When they had exhausted all other topics, including her cousin Pilar's new cocker spaniel, a gift to help her recover from a divorce, Marisa finally got to the point of her call.

"So, Mami, I have one more thing to tell you. Maybe you should get Papi on the line, too." Marisa sipped at the virgin eggnog Juliet had brought her.

"Victor," her mother called out, trying to drown out the sound of Sinatra's "White Christmas." "He's on the porch, *cariño*, fixing the icicle lights. A bird keeps building a nest in the gutter."

"Okay, well, I just wanted to tell you that . . ." She wrapped the phone cord around her fingers. "You know how you're always talking about becoming grandparents, well . . . that's about to happen. I'm going to have a baby."

"A baby? How?" Her mother coughed, choking on her third *cafecito* of the day.

"Well, the usual way . . ."

"But with who? Who is the father?"

Marisa took a breath. "There is no father. I'm going to do it alone."

Her mother grew quiet, and Marisa wondered if the line was dead. "Why do this now? It's so hard by yourself—"

"Well, I'm not completely alone, I live with someone, remember? My friend from college."

"Your roommate? That's not the same thing—"

"I'm not saying it's the same thing, but it's what I'm doing. I've tried to tell you before, but you won't listen. I'm never getting married. This is who I am, Mami—"

"I don't like it." Her mother's voice got louder as her agitation grew. "It's not natural, the way young people do things today. It's not God's way."

"God allowed me to get pregnant. How can you say it's not his way?"

"Well, it's not right." She sucked her teeth, a nervous tic she'd developed during Marisa's childhood. "And it's not too late, to do something about it."

Marisa felt her heart drop; she couldn't fathom what her mother, a Catholic Republican who believed even rape victims should keep their babies, was telling her only daughter. "I *want* this baby. I got pregnant on purpose."

"Why?" her mother asked. "Who does that when you're not even married? *Ay, Dios mío,*" she said, her voice starting to tremble. "Victor," she called out again, more of a bellow this time, and Marisa could hear scuffling sounds, her mother walking onto the porch in her slippers no doubt, calling up to her husband on the ladder. "Victor, come, talk to your daughter. I can't, I just can't."

She heard her father's muffled voice in the background, then the sound of something dropping. Eventually the line went dead. She stared at the phone as if it were a foreign object and realized her hand was trembling. She hung up the phone and tucked her hands into her armpits to steady them.

Juliet put down the roasting pan and draped her arms loosely around Marisa's shoulders. "You okay?"

Marisa shook her head. "I knew it would be bad, but I wasn't ready for that." Tears fell from her eyes, but she wasn't even aware of feeling sad. She was beyond sadness, beyond any emotion she could identify. "Well, I don't know what I was expecting."

"They're in shock. I'm sure they'll come around." Juliet dropped her hands to Marisa's belly, just starting to bulge, and spread her long fingers across her abdomen. Marisa felt the strength of her grasp, which seemed to be holding her up and keeping her together. She covered Juliet's hands with her own, feeling her pulse beating against her palm. It felt quick and strong like the baby's heartbeat at the last prenatal appointment, a dozen horses at full gallop under her swelling skin. ,

"I guess there was a part of me that knew, which is why I waited till the second trimester to tell them. To be out of the danger zone."

Marisa knew that Juliet thought she was talking about miscarriage, and a part of her was, but she also wanted to be protected from herself, just in case any doubts began to surface. She wanted it to be too late for her to undo what she had already started.

"When they meet him," Juliet said, "it will be a whole different story."

Marisa wiped her eyes on the dish towel hanging from Juliet's belt. "Him?" Marisa teased.

Juliet smiled. "All I'm saying is I've had three dreams about the baby so far, and in each one it was a boy. Why would my subconscious lie?"

The ring of the phone startled them both.

"Let it ring," Marisa said. "I don't want to talk to anyone right now."

They waited for the phone to stop ringing, and then Juliet unplugged it from the wall. Marisa watched as Juliet checked on the pork, basting it with its own drippings, just like her mother used to do.

"They wanted a son, when my mother was pregnant with me. The nursery was painted blue, my crib sheets had baseballs and bats all over them, and they had even picked out my name—Rafael, after the archangel." She smiled to cover her sadness. "I was a disappointment from the very beginning."

"Rafael is a nice name," Juliet said. "Until it becomes Ralph."

Marisa made a face. "Ralph is so . . ."

"White?" Juliet offered.

Marisa nodded. "And way too old."

Juliet stuck out her pinky, curved like a seahorse. "Promise me it's going to be a good name. Something unique, without an obvious nickname."

"Okay," Marisa said. "I can agree to that."

She locked her pinky around Juliet's, and they shook on it.

"And you promise me something," Marisa said, as she looked at the phone, lying uselessly on the floor. It looked fake, like a prop, which Marisa thought was fitting; the whole experience felt surreal, like she was watching someone else's life unfold on a stage. "Don't make me talk to them. No matter how many times they call."

Juliet promised, and spent the rest of the pregnancy answering phone calls from the people who didn't want to acknowledge her presence in Marisa's life—let alone her involvement—until one day the phone stopped ringing.

MARISA'S WATER BROKE at one in the morning. Asleep on her side, both legs wrapped around a body pillow. She hopped up as quickly as she could at thirty-nine weeks, her belly heavy and hard like a frozen turkey, but she didn't understand what was happening. Wetness fell from between her legs; she thought it was pee until she couldn't stop it. Juliet followed her to the bathroom, mopping up the trail of amniotic fluid with an old sweatshirt.

"Is it clear? The midwife said we're okay if it's clear." Juliet turned on the hallway light to investigate.

"Clear like snot?" Marisa called from the toilet. "Because it looks like snot." She wiped again.

"Just make sure there isn't any blood."

Marisa examined the toilet paper. "No blood."

"Okay, good," Juliet said, dropping the sweatshirt into the hamper.

Marisa held out her hands, letting Juliet pull her up from the toilet. She didn't need the help, not really, but she liked that Juliet offered it. Turns out she liked being taken care of—one of the pure pleasures of pregnancy.

"Now we go back to sleep."

Juliet found Marisa a new nightgown and laid a towel over the wet spot in their bed. She rubbed Marisa's legs until she fell back asleep.

Jenry was born almost nineteen hours later, just before eight o'clock in the evening, on the last Friday in May. The final hours of labor were a blur—nurses coming in and out, the beep of the blood pressure monitors, ice chips melting on her lips—but what she remembered clearly was Juliet, combing the hair from her face, wiping her sweat with a damp washcloth, rubbing circles into her lower back. When it came time to push—the baby was coming, they could see the head, it was almost out—all she felt was the grip of the contraction as it tightened around her belly like a corset. With a terrible feeling of desperation, she waited for the pain to end, followed by panic that it wasn't ending, that it would never end, and then the jolt of relief when it finally began to subside.

She wanted to nurse right away, so as they massaged her deflated abdomen, encouraging her uterus to contract and expel the placenta—a dark, slippery mass that slithered between her legs—then brought the baby to her breast, opening her gown to place them skin to skin. Juliet watched from the end of the bed, stunned from cutting the umbilical cord; a pair of surgical scissors was still hanging from her thumb.

"I told you it was a boy," she said softly. Tears stained her cheeks.

Marisa looked down at her son, watching his reflexive suck, his eyelids fluttering in sleep; his forehead was a field of downy hairs, soft tendrils that curved in the same direction like windblown wheat. She held his miniature hand, rubbed the translucent papery skin with a map of veins under its surface, marveling at the architecture of his perfect body, this thing made from her own blood.

"Thank you," she whispered, "thank you." She was talking to everyone in the room, from the baby to the nurses to Juliet, but she was also saying the same prayer that had carried her through the pregnancy, a conversation with God begun before she was pregnant, when it became clear that she wasn't in charge of even the smallest aspect of her own life, and realized the only power she had would be found in surrender.

Twenty-four hours later, as the sun set on the first day of her son's life, a birth certificate clerk came by their room. The clerk went through all the paperwork, eyeing the two women as she tried to put the pieces of this small family together. She left the forms on the narrow table that hung like a diving board over the bed, between Marisa's dinner tray and the plastic water pitcher.

Juliet turned on the overhead light, a fluorescent strip that bathed the room in an unflattering light, and found a pen in the hospital-issued diaper bag. "Do you want me to fill these out?"

"I'll do it," Marisa said, passing her the swaddled baby.

Juliet smiled down at him. "I've bought loaves of bread bigger than you," she said with a laugh, bringing her face in close. Marisa filled out the forms as quickly and neatly as she could, leaving the space after *Father* blank, and saving the baby's name for last.

"This is it," she said, "we're about to decide his fate." She'd meant it as a joke, but suddenly the weight of what she was doing caused the butterflies in her stomach to take flight all at once.

"Don't freak yourself out," Juliet said. "They're both good names."

"Are you sure about Sebastian?" Her pen hovered over the paper.

Juliet nodded. "As a middle name, yes. It sounds important, regal."

"And Henry—it's a good name, isn't it?" Marisa began to second-guess herself, worried that she wasn't capable of making such an important decision for another human being—her child—and she wondered if she needed an additional qualification beyond motherhood to give her the right. "Better than Enrique, right?"

Juliet nodded. "It's simple without being plain. Timeless."

"Henry Sebastian Castillo," Marisa practiced. She decided this weeks ago, yet now the words sounded heavy in her mouth. "Don't you think Patterson sounds better?" She wanted the baby connected to Juliet, to her side of the family.

Juliet looked at her. "Patterson is an Irish name. Black Irish," she laughed, "and he's Cuban."

"Half Cuban," Marisa corrected her. "And Black. With a little Irish."

"He's a bit of everything, just like us." Juliet held up the baby for her to see.

Marisa wondered at his dark hair, his face slack with sleep. "Just like us," she repeated, trying to see herself in his soft features.

"But you're his mother," Juliet added. "He should have your last name."

It made sense, yet inside Marisa felt uncertain. "I just want him to have something of yours. You've been here this whole time, you've been a part of making him."

The intercom crackled overhead as someone called a doctor to the

OR. Feet shuffled by the door, but then it was quiet again, the hospital room their own sanctuary.

"My grandfather's name was John," Juliet offered, "so they used the *J* for Jasper and Juliet as a way to honor him."

"John," Marisa said. "That's a classic name. Simple, strong."

Juliet shook her head. "No, not John. Jenry. The *J* can be for me."

Marisa repeated the name slowly, like she was trying out a foreign word. "I've never heard that before."

"Neither have I. But I like it." Juliet looked at the baby. "And he seems to like it, too. He just opened his eyes."

Juliet placed him on the bed, nestled between Marisa's legs. Marisa looked down into his dark eyes, wondering if the name fit the life he was going to live, the person he was destined to become. *Yes*, she thought, *Jenry. Jenry* and *Juliet*. They even sounded good together—one a word as new as the child himself, the other a name she had repeated in her mind a thousand times. She knew there was no point in fighting it; those two words, these two people, had the power to transform her life, and all she could do was accept it as a blessing. Which she did, writing JENRY SEBASTIAN CASTILLO in clear block letters, and then signing her name below it, blowing on the ink until it dried.

· 5 ·

They passed the summer in a fugue state, but created a routine by August, just as Marisa prepared to return to work. She nursed the baby on-demand for the first twelve weeks, as the pediatrician recommended, but now had him on a schedule: eight ounces every four hours, which she pumped into small plastic sleeves to store in the freezer, building up the supply Juliet would use when she was gone.

Marisa liked to watch TV while she pumped, so Juliet would take Jenry for a walk, either in the stroller Jasper sent—a ridiculously fancy Dutch design he claimed was the rage in Amsterdam—or strapped to her chest in a sling, depending on the weather. It was humid on the final day of Marisa's maternity leave, and the gray, cloud-soaked sky held the threat of a thunderstorm, so Juliet took the stroller. She hung a light cotton blanket over the top to cover Jenry's legs—from rain or sun or the curious eyes of dog-walkers passing by—and as Marisa stood on the porch watching them leave, she marveled at how thoughtful Juliet had become with him, always thinking ahead to predict his wants or needs: which toy would serve what occasion, how many diapers he would use when they went to the park. Beyond gratitude, she wasn't sure what she felt; was it strange that this person who wasn't his mother could anticipate his needs as well as she could? It wasn't jealousy, but she did wonder how Juliet, a woman she'd always known to be selfish in the manner of all artists, suddenly possessed a level of attunement to another person that she hadn't seemed capable of before, and certainly not with Marisa. That was what really hurt: not that she gave it to Jenry, but that she never gave it to Marisa.

Jenry was bonded to both women. He fell asleep in the arms of either, smiled at both their silly faces, but when he got fussy, he wanted Juliet. He preferred the way she bounced him in the sling, thrilled at her animal noises and exaggerated song lyrics, liked how delicately she drummed his back to dislodge a stubborn burp. Marisa wanted Juliet to love her son—but she didn't know it could rival her own connection, or that it had the power to eclipse her. She hadn't counted on feeling insecure about her attachment to her child, despite believing she was a good mother.

Marisa refilled her glass of iced coffee—decaf, extra cream—and sat down in front of the TV armed with the clicker and the hospital-issue breast pump, a slate-blue contraption the size and weight of the old 16 mm film projectors she remembered from grammar school. Fifteen minutes later, feeling depleted and slightly violated, she removed the plastic suctions from each breast, rubbed lanolin on her tender nipples, and left her shirt open to let them dry. She failed to stay awake for the final round of *Celebrity Jeopardy!*, awakening thirty minutes later to the evening news, a report about the evils of toxic mold.

After a cold shower she went through the mail. She was tempted to open a card addressed to Juliet—no return address, with a postmark from New York—but thought better of it. Then she skimmed a brochure from an artist colony in New Hampshire offering applicants their own cabin in the woods, three meals a day hand-delivered by bicycle, and most importantly, time—to write, dance, sing, create. She entertained a brief fantasy of being an artist, a person who needed to escape reality in order to feel fully alive, before tossing the brochure aside and thanking God for sparing her that particular affliction. She came across an envelope from Kodak filled with prints of Jenry's first three months, from the hospital to the first real smile. She tore through them like a box of See's chocolates, devouring her favorites first, then testing out the unknown, savoring the surprises.

She chose pictures for the baby book: Jenry asleep in the pram at one hour old; leaving the hospital in his car seat; his first bath; a close-up of his hands and feet; the first time he met Winston, the old man leaning over his crib to rest his large hand against the baby's head. She secured the photographs into the book with a glue stick, then went through its crisp pages and filled out the entries with a silver paint pen, using her best handwriting. When she got to the questions under *Mommy & Daddy*, she stopped over *Father's Name*, the ink collecting at the felt-tipped point and threatening to drop onto the page. She filled in her side first, her parents' names and birthdates, where they were born, the fact that she had no siblings. She wanted to fill in the other side with Juliet's background information but didn't know all the answers, so she left them blank.

Juliet came home an hour later, with takeout from Caserta Pizzeria in the basket underneath the stroller and a bottle of wine in the drink holder. Jenry was asleep, so they left him there to finish his nap, parking the stroller under the ceiling fan in the dining room. His cheeks were red from the heat. They ate in the shade of the back porch, Juliet drinking wine from a plastic cup. Marisa mentioned the mail, but Juliet said she'd look at it later.

"I'll get it now," Marisa insisted, "I need a drink anyway."

"You sure you don't want some of this?" Juliet held up her wine. "The doctor said you could pump and dump."

Marisa bent her head over the cup and inhaled. "It almost smells worth it."

"I'll save you some," Juliet said, pouring herself more.

Marisa came back with a tall glass of iced water. She handed Juliet the mail and sat down with the baby book opened across her lap. "What year was your father born?" she asked, shaking the paint pen.

"What?" Juliet flipped through the brochure, her eyes wide. "Why?"

Marisa gestured to the baby book. "There's a page about the father's side." She helped herself to another piece of pizza.

"Oh." Juliet glanced at the baby book, then went back to reading the brochure. She left greasy fingerprints on its glossy pages.

"You should apply," Marisa said. "It looks pretty amazing." She knew it was the right thing to say, though she couldn't imagine Juliet being gone for a whole month. But her absence wasn't the real problem. Marisa feared if she went to this colony and met people from all over the world, it would increase her chances of finding someone else, of leaving Marisa and her small world behind.

"Jasper says they take emerging artists like me as well as superstars like him"—she raised her eyebrows with a smirk, a face that said she was both awed by and envious of her brother—"so he won't get off my back about it." She dropped the brochure. "But I doubt I'd get in. The people they invite are ridiculous. Aaron Copland, Leonard Bernstein, the guy who wrote *Our Town*. It's for real artists."

"You feel pretty real to me." Marisa pinched her playfully.

"Maybe." Juliet picked up the bottle of wine. "But I'm not working on an album. And I've been lazy this summer. This whole year actually." It wasn't true—she practiced every day between the baby's naps, her band had regular gigs two or three nights a week, and she was always writing new melodies—but Marisa knew better than to challenge Juliet about her music. Jasper was the only one who could do that.

"You just had a baby. It's understandable." Marisa should have said *we just had a baby*, but it was too late to correct herself. And anyway, wasn't it true?

"Sure, it's understandable." Juliet's voice was strained, dripping with sarcasm. "For people who don't want to go to MacDowell."

Marisa considered her options: she could suggest that Juliet try drinking less, or cutting back her bartending shifts, but Marisa knew she needed those nights out in order to balance the time she spent at home with them. As if freedom were the antidote to responsibility. She decided to leave it alone. She shook the paint pen again, its metal ball bouncing around the insides.

"Do you think you should do that?" Juliet stared at the opened book. "Fill in the father's side?"

"Why not?"

"It's supposed to be his side, not mine." Juliet's eyes scanned the page.

"His side is your side."

The two women stared at each other. Juliet pointed to one of the entries. "Under *Special Talents*, you wrote piano. That's not his talent. It's mine."

Marisa looked down at the page as she spoke, trying to get her voice to match what she felt. She didn't want to yell or fall apart, but she knew she needed to be firm, clear. "You can't go back and forth," she said. "It's not fair to Jenry." She purposely kept her eyes from meeting Juliet's.

"What's that supposed to mean?"

"It means he needs both of us." Marisa was surprised when the words came out of her mouth, but she knew it was the truth. Which somehow made it easier to say. "He needs two parents."

"We talked about this last year. Before you got pregnant."

"I know. And I meant what I said. But he's here now, and he's grown so attached to you." Her voice felt strained as her own need rose to the surface. "He adores you."

"And I love him. That's not what this is about."

"Then own it. You can't be in when it's convenient and out when you get uncomfortable."

Juliet looked stunned. She wiped her mouth repeatedly with a napkin. "I don't want to lie to him. About what we are."

"This isn't about you and me, these aren't wedding vows." She shook the baby book in Juliet's face. "It's about his relationship with your family, what we agreed we both wanted." She believed it herself—that she was protecting her son, not trapping Juliet—and hoped that saying it out loud would make it true. "This is about your father—Jenry is his first grandchild—and it's about you. You either think he's your kid or you don't."

Juliet took the book from her, wiping away the droplets of water that had spilled from Marisa's glass. A trail of watermarks was left behind, puckered like blistered skin. Juliet picked up the pen, shook it once, and filled in the rest of the empty lines, writing *Winston Patterson* and *Faye Brewster* in the spot for grandparents. Her handwriting was elegant, something from an earlier time, the letters long and evenly spaced like calligraphy.

There was one question that made her pause, when it asked about the father's siblings. The pen hovered over the paper for several seconds, and then, with a quick stroke, she wrote one short word: *Jay.*

· 6 ·

That winter, to celebrate Marisa's birthday, they hired a babysitter for the first time and went out on a frigid January night. Jenry was eight months old. They still had sex regularly but hadn't been on a date in months. Like many new parents, they'd lost the opportunity for spontaneity and romance. Marisa hoped tonight would be different, a chance to focus on each other and leave responsibility behind.

They ate dinner at Leo's, the restaurant where Juliet spent most evenings when she wasn't performing; in addition to tending bar, she would occasionally fill in as sous chef if the mood struck. Marisa wasn't surprised by this—Juliet had always liked to cook—and she claimed being home with the baby gave her more time to pursue it. After finishing their meal, Juliet suggested they go upstairs to Snookers, the upscale pool hall on the second floor of the old factory building. She promised to let Marisa win.

Dessert arrived, a peanut butter cheesecake Juliet made herself, followed by a string of her work buddies, heading home early since the night was slow. Juliet invited the group to join them—the nineteen-year-old hostess named Trichelle, and Max, the first shift bartender, along with several dishwashers—and soon their romantic dinner for two became a raucous impromptu mini-party, Juliet's friends singing show tunes from musicals Marisa hadn't even heard of. They never made it upstairs.

"Sorry," Juliet leaned over to whisper in her ear. "Do you want me to send them away? I figured we couldn't eat this whole cheesecake alone."

"No, it's fine," Marisa lied, "I've always wanted to get serenaded by something from *Sweeney Todd*."

Juliet laughed. Seeing that joy spread across her face was the birthday present Marisa had wanted; a feeling of pleasure filled her, darkened only by the disappointing truth: she hadn't elicited it. When Juliet was in a certain mood—introspective or inspired, mildly depressed—she seemed to crave Marisa, or at least isolated time with her, and there were many weekends where they would hole up with Indian food and ninety-nine-cent movie rentals and not talk to another human being aside from the delivery man. She would sit at the piano and play chords over and over again, asking Marisa what she thought of different progressions, not breaking to eat or drink; all she seemed to need was the music and Marisa to play it for. Other times they would listen to old records in the dark, her eyes closed as Marisa massaged the muscles in her hands, her neck and shoulders, and finally her face; when the needle stopped and the room went quiet, they would start to kiss, sometimes lasting for hours, Marisa so aroused by the end she was on the verge of climax, Juliet's swollen lips filling her mouth.

But in times like these, when she wasn't actively creating anything, Juliet lived in a different way; she drew hordes of people around her like a storyteller, talking and laughing with the group, never one-on-one, her mood light and forgiving, her eyes bright, perusing all but penetrating nothing. Surrounded by people, she created an atmosphere of joyful abandon, but to Marisa the end result often felt false, like watching a movie scene projected onto a billowing sheet, shapes suggested but never solidified.

Both sides of her persona were engaging, each certainly had its own appeal, but Marisa fell in love with the lone Juliet, and in these moments, she found it difficult to share. It was purely territorial; she felt possessive over the part of Juliet she thought she knew better than anyone, and she desperately wanted those rights to be visible to the outside world. But they weren't. Juliet worked hard to keep her friends from one world away from the other—which was why Marisa was such an anomaly, and why she hoped to be the exception.

"So, you two went to college together? That's so cool." Trichelle was cutting tiny slivers from the slice of cheesecake on her plate and eating each one off the knife. She and Marisa were alone at the table; the dishwashers were playing darts along the back wall while Juliet and Max fetched another round of drinks from the bar.

"How about you, are you going to college?" Marisa tried to sound interested. She already noticed how familiar this teenager was with Juliet, how she chose the seat beside her and leaned in every time she spoke, her hair brushing Juliet's shoulder.

"Sort of," Trichelle answered. "I'm in culinary school."

"You must be talented." Marisa forced herself to smile.

"Well, I do make a mean gumbo. Ask Juliet."

Juliet and Max returned with a pitcher of sangria and several glasses. She raised her eyebrows. "Ask me what?"

"Just say yes," Trichelle said mischievously.

"Yes," Juliet said, while shaking her head no simultaneously.

Trichelle sucked cheesecake off her finger. "Asshole."

"Don't feel bad, she's a notorious liar," Marisa said, joining in their easy banter to cover up her discomfort. She'd heard Max's name before, but Trichelle hadn't garnered a mention, an omission that now felt intentional.

"All women are liars," Max said, smiling at Juliet like they shared a secret joke. "I grew up with three sisters. It's a known fact." He sat down next to Marisa, in what had been Juliet's seat, with Trichelle on his other side. Juliet sat across from them, sideways on her chair.

"Women have to lie," Juliet said. "It's the only way we get to keep anything. Men lie to get more; women lie to keep what they have."

Max made a face, then downed his pint of lager so he could fill it with sangria. "Sounds about right," he said, beer foam filling in his thin goatee.

A cheer erupted from the back wall, as one of the dishwashers won the game. Max poured sangria into the remaining glasses, serving everyone but Marisa. He saw her confused look and turned red.

"Did you want one? Juliet said you didn't drink. My mistake." He offered her his pint glass. "You can share mine." He glanced at Juliet across the table.

"Thank you." Marisa took a sip. "Apparently another one of her lies." She had to work to keep her voice even. She forced herself to smile as Juliet lifted her wine glass in a mock toast. "Touché."

"No, let's toast for real," Trichelle said, lifting her sangria. "To Marisa, the birthday girl. May you get everything you wish for."

Sangria sloshed onto the tabletop as Trichelle clinked glasses with Juliet. Max pulled a towel from his back pocket to mop up the spill.

"Aw, aren't you Mister Ready-for-Anything."

"The perils of tending bar," Max said, tucking the towel away. "Isn't that right, Juliet?"

"The only perils I've ever faced as a bartender involved an ex-girlfriend demanding to speak with the manager. And that was after I'd already lost the job."

There was laughter all around as Marisa drank more of Max's sangria, sucking on the lemon rind when it floated into her mouth. He squeezed her shoulder playfully. "You'd never do that, would you?"

"Of course not," Marisa said. "But then again, I'm not an ex."

A chorus of *oohs* spread around the table. Trichelle's laughter eventually turned into hiccups, which only made her laugh harder. Marisa watched as Juliet passed her the pitcher. She filled her glass, then filled Juliet's.

"You've got a fiery one," Max chuckled, throwing a few bills on the table, curved from the fold of his wallet. "No wonder you're trying to keep her sober." He and Juliet shared a look; a few minutes later, he stood up, faking a yawn. "Gotta get home to the missus."

"He means his dog," Trichelle said, "the only female who'd dare sleep in his bed."

"The only one I'd *invite*, is what you meant to say." He tossed Trichelle her coat, a bright green wool the color of pea soup. "Come on, jailbait, I'm taking you home." The coat landed on her head, messing up her perfectly moussed hair. Marisa couldn't help but laugh.

"Thanks a lot," Trichelle snapped, finger-combing her hair back into place.

"Don't worry, you look great," Marisa offered. Now that they were leaving, she felt more generous. As they said their goodbyes, Marisa heard Juliet compliment Trichelle on her coat, which gave her the chance to show it off again, spinning around to model the backside. She whispered into Juliet's ear before walking out the door. Marisa's eyes glared like searchlights across the table.

As he left, Max called out to Juliet. "And, hey, congrats on that art colony thing. Don't worry about the time off, I got you covered."

Juliet nodded to him, but her eyes were locked on Marisa. Juliet gestured for the waitress to bring the check, laying her credit card down with a snap.

"When did that happen?" Marisa was clearly upset. It wasn't the only thing that bothered her about the night, but it was all she was ready to talk about.

"I just heard. I was going to tell you—"

"But you figured it was better to tell them before me?"

"It wasn't like that." Juliet shifted her eyes, not looking at anything in particular. "I happened to be here when I opened the letter. That's all."

"I didn't even know you applied."

The waitress brought the check, saying the pitcher of sangria was on the house. Juliet thanked her as she signed the receipt.

"I'm sorry. I was going to tell you. But only if I got invited."

Marisa put on her coat, tried to calm down. "When do you leave?"

"In the summer. When you're off from work. It's just for three weeks."

"Congratulations," Marisa said, trying to mean it. "You deserve it."

A few minutes later, Marisa stood by the entrance, waiting for Juliet to finish her goodbyes. Every time the door blew open, a burst of cold air startled her; when they finally left, she was braced for the shock of cold to come.

AT HOME, THEY had to wake up the babysitter, Ben, a grad student Juliet met through her father, who had fallen asleep with his face in the spine of a book about Reconstruction. He apologized for finishing the ice cream and collected his books into a duffel bag that he hung over his shoulder like the hockey player he used to be. They asked about Jenry, who apparently hadn't made a sound all night, and then Ben told them the phone rang a few times but when he answered, no one replied. Juliet looked at Marisa, her face registering what they both knew: her parents, calling to wish her a happy birthday.

While Juliet drove Ben back to campus, Marisa opened her birthday present from the ladies at work—a bag of Dunkin' Donuts coffee beans and a gift certificate for a weekend on Nantucket, a suite with a Jacuzzi tub and a couples massage included. Juliet would enjoy the coffee, and if they got a babysitter—maybe during spring break so Ben could do it—it might be just the thing they needed to get away from the monotony of diapers and spit-up and crying jags in the middle of the night. She had other cards from the kids in the after-school program, handmade on construction paper and decorated with princess stickers and swirls of glitter, which flurried out as she opened them, leaving a layer of sparkling dust on her skin.

The last card was from her father. She recognized his handwriting instantly, overly large and sloped like it was written while he was walking on the deck of a ship. The envelope was thick, perhaps stuffed with photographs or dollar bills, but when she opened it, she found the Christmas card she sent to her mother the month before, unopened. Inside her birthday card was a fifty-dollar bill and a letter, apologizing for her mother's behavior and saying that he will always love her, even when she does things he disapproves of or can't understand. He didn't ask about the baby, but he did mention the *changes in her life*, telling her that *we all make choices*, and that it's sad when growing up means growing away from our *real family*. She had tears in her eyes as she reread the letter; he couldn't comprehend her having a family outside of them, and after tonight, she wondered if he was right.

The card to her mother contained the letter she had written, still sealed with a star-shaped sticker she had taken from one of the teachers. She was surprised by how neat it looked, every word printed deliberately, as if by making the words legible, the sentiments would somehow become tolerable to her mother. She began to read the letter, but by the second line her eyes flooded with tears and she couldn't finish.

With both cards hidden in the bottom of a storage drawer, with the shower on high and the water as hot as she could stand it, Marisa tried to forget the details of her confession: how she had fallen in love with her friend years ago, when they first met in college; how she feared her parents' rejection so she lied about who she was; how she wanted to have a baby because of Juliet, not in spite of her; how the feeling of Jenry swimming around in her belly was the first time she didn't feel hollow inside; how pushing him out was the scariest pleasure she'd ever experienced; how she didn't know that a mother could fall in love with her own child, and in doing so, could begin to love herself in ways she hadn't previously imagined. The water washed over her until it ran cold. She had taken a huge risk in exposing so much to her parents; now she knew it was all for naught. The rejection seemed more complete, more finite than any response. Denial was one thing, but refusal to acknowledge her attempt to communicate felt cruel on an entirely different plane. They did not want to know her, and they did not want to know her son.

When Juliet came home, Marisa was already in bed, all visible signs of her upset concealed. A candle the size of a small cake was burning on the nightstand; the oily scent of orange peel and cedar filled the air. Marisa wore a silk nightgown, her milk-filled breasts spilling out from the lace-fringed top. As Juliet undressed, Marisa told her about the cards from her favorite kids, the weekend on Nantucket, even the fifty dollars from her father, glossing over the details of his card. She didn't say how she felt cheated by her parents, filled with a rage she didn't know she was capable of. A door closed inside her, and she knew deep down that she would never talk to them in the same way again—if she ever talked to them at all.

Before Juliet could slip into her pajama bottoms, Marisa pulled her onto the bed. Her bare legs were cold and Marisa pretzeled her own around them, lifting Juliet's tank top to let her erect nipple fall into her opened mouth. She was aggressive in her search for pleasure, seeking out parts of Juliet's body she was usually too timid to touch, and from the moan escaping her lips, she knew Juliet was enjoying the change. Her hunger to be close to Juliet, to smell and taste her, was matched only by her need to escape her sadness, to separate from it as a way to survive it.

Before they could finish, when her head was between Juliet's legs, searching for something to take, something to keep, she heard a soft cry from the baby's room. She tried to ignore it, but eventually Juliet put her hand on Marisa's shoulder.

"Do you want me to go?"

"Let's see if he works it out," Marisa said, her tongue diving back inside to search for another cave. The crying continued, eventually getting louder, more insistent.

"Damn," Marisa whispered, forcing herself to stop. She buried her face in the warm spot beneath Juliet's hip, the sheet absorbing the wetness on her mouth.

Juliet climbed out of bed. "Kid's got great timing," she said, pulling on her boxer shorts, "I was like two minutes away."

Her voice sounded light, amused, not saturated with the disappointment Marisa felt seeping into her skin. She wanted to lose herself in pleasuring Juliet, to somehow convince her that only Marisa could give her what she needed, something indispensable, as if her happiness was a treasure only Marisa could find.

Juliet came back carrying Jenry, half-asleep, his favorite blanket draped over his eyes. She propped him in the middle of the bed, between their two pillows, and tucked her arm over the blanket so he couldn't roll.

"I think this pretty much defeats sleep training." Marisa punched the side of her pillow to fluff it up.

"It's just one night." Juliet kissed his sweaty head. "He misses us."

Marisa, still feeling the throb between her legs, wasn't ready to give up on the night. "I'll bring him back to the crib when he falls into a deeper sleep." She winked at Juliet. "So we can finish what we started."

Juliet glanced at the clock. "It's late, we should just go to bed." She pulled the covers up and snuggled in close to Jenry. "How could you deny this face?"

Marisa looked at her sleeping boy. She leaned in to smell his head. "When you grow up, no woman is going to be able to resist you."

"Or man," Juliet whispered into his ear, "just like Uncle Jasper."

"Come on, he has to be straight. Otherwise they'll blame us." She laid her first finger in his opened hand and he made a fist around it.

Juliet leaned over and kissed Marisa goodnight, the taste of wine lingering long after the kiss dissolved. Marisa tried to extend it, but Juliet had already pulled away to blow out the candle.

In the dark, Marisa felt the sadness return. Something told her she had to carry this burden on her own, so she held it inside. Juliet was lying next to her, holding her half of the baby, and Marisa understood what they shared, the responsibility of him but not of each other; they shared a life—his life—but their own joys and sorrows weren't part of the arrangement.

This was the part no one understood. Her friends thought she'd struck a gold mine, some going on about how lucky she was to have another person she could trust with Jenry's welfare, an equal partner, unlike their husbands, who begrudgingly took their children for the afternoon but needed explicit directions about how to dress them, what to feed them, and which park was safe to visit. Others extolled Juliet's beauty—*She's gorgeous*, they would say whenever she left the room, and *My God, does she really play for you every day? And she can cook, too? Damn, girl, you're lucky.*

Marisa *was* lucky, she knew that, yet something was beginning to take root inside her. A dull ache started to grow and while she tried to ignore it, to leave it buried next to the hole that held her parents, she knew it was there, knew it would have to be addressed, a debridement performed before the disease threatened to take over the healthy tissue. But that wasn't tonight's business. Tonight they lay like a family in the same bed they'd shared since bringing Jenry home, and even if she wasn't holding Marisa's body, even if she didn't say I love you—Juliet was there. And as long as she was there, Marisa still had hope.

· 7 ·

That summer, during her three weeks at the artist colony, Juliet called home every night, singing bedtime songs to Jenry from a payphone in the dining hall. She sent a postcard of her cabin, which Jenry carried around like a blankie. He had just started walking, and every morning he tottered around the apartment trying to find her, despite Marisa saying she wasn't there.

Only when Juliet came back, excited about new work, did Marisa admit to her fear of Juliet not returning. She had met some well-connected people, who helped her get exposure to bigger festivals and competitions; soon she fielded offers to tour all over the States. Juliet was happy, and Marisa was happy for her, but things between them were changing. At home, Juliet didn't talk much, retreating more and more into the bedroom she used as a home studio. She often slept in there, too, claiming it was because of the hours she kept, but Marisa could tell by the way she kissed her, how their sex had become more infrequent and less passionate, that Juliet was somewhere else.

In the fall, Juliet's band signed with a new label. They recorded an album as the Juliet Patterson Quartet, a mix of covers and original songs.

Early buzz called her arrangements innovative and fresh, with a classic swing feel. The album sold well, and when it was nominated for a Grammy, Juliet was the only one surprised. It might have gone on like that, Juliet's career heating up as things with Marisa cooled, staying together as they drifted apart, and Marisa might have been happier with that—if it meant avoiding all the heartache that lay ahead.

In February, Juliet's brother, Jasper, her protector and first playmate, her best friend, drowned in a pond in Western Massachusetts. Juliet could not accept that he was gone. She had just spent the weekend with him, and she kept saying it was her fault; she knew he wasn't well, why did she leave him alone at the cabin? Marisa tried to comfort her, but Juliet wouldn't let her. At the funeral, Juliet held Jenry for the entire service, until she walked alone to the altar to play *Moonlight Sonata*, Jasper's favorite song. She canceled her tour, wouldn't return phone calls. She stopped everything, except spending time with Jenry. He became her lifeline, the only one she would hold.

By spring Juliet was working again, but still withdrawn. One day she came home from a festival in New York and said they needed to talk. Marisa knew what she was going to say, had seen it coming for months, despite telling herself that Juliet was in mourning, and just needed time to heal. Still, she did her best to fight for their relationship, reminding Juliet of all they'd built together. Juliet didn't waver; it was over. She kept denying that it had anything to do with Jasper. There were tears in her eyes when she said, "It's better for everyone this way. Trust me, just let it go." Marisa had seen her cry only twice: when Jenry was born and at Jasper's funeral. It broke her heart that there was nothing she could do.

They agreed to keep living together. It was best for Jenry to spend time with them both, and to have his home remain intact. Weeks later, they celebrated his second birthday at a beach house they rented on the Cape. Marisa spent her evenings alone on the pier, watching the tide come in. Juliet kept apologizing, but it didn't make Marisa feel better. Time passed, yet the wound wouldn't heal.

In July, Juliet had to leave again, this time for a monthlong tour headlining festivals in Norway and Sweden. After she left, Marisa kept the door to Juliet's studio closed. Every time Jenry tried the handle, she would say, "It's locked, baby," and he would shake his head and say, "Open it, Juju inside," and then fall to the floor to wait. Juliet called home often, but it wasn't the same. He cried for her at bedtime, and as Marisa held him, she let herself cry, too. She always feared their romance would come to an end, had predicted its demise much earlier in fact, yet here she was falling apart; not surprised, but still devastated.

Marisa kept replaying their last conversation, the night before she left for Europe. Juliet claimed to still love her—*like family*, she kept saying, *you and Jenry are my family*—yet she wasn't in love with her. Marisa suspected there was someone else, likely several someones, but Juliet denied that had anything to do with ending their relationship. She claimed it was for Marisa's benefit; the breakup wasn't what Juliet wanted, it was what she thought Marisa needed.

"I'm holding you back," Juliet had said, "this thing we have. It's standing in the way of you getting everything you want."

"I want this. You." Marisa stood at the door to Juliet's studio as she packed. It was midnight; in five hours the cab would take her to the airport.

Juliet shook her head. "No, you think you do, but it's just the idea of me. How I am sometimes, or how I used to be—how I *could* be if I was a different person." She sorted through her clothes, throwing what she wanted onto the bed, ignoring the rest. Marisa watched her grab a linen jacket, a present from last Christmas, and roll it into a ball before tucking it into her duffel bag. She probably didn't even remember it was from Marisa.

"That's a cop-out," Marisa said. "You are whatever you want to be, and sometimes that means you don't want to be here. To have to account to someone. To have them depend on you. It's too much of a damn burden." Her voice was getting louder, so she stepped into the room and closed the door, trying not to wake the baby.

"You're right," Juliet said, "it is a burden." She packed stacks of music

into a leather carry-on bag—CDs and mixed tape cassettes—wrapping
them in a sweatshirt for protection. "Love is a fucking burden." As she
bent over, the bottom of her tank top rolled up, exposing a wide stretch
of skin, a perfect brown. Marisa felt a pang of love for her—every inch of
her—and it fueled her rising anger, as if Juliet were showing off all that
she couldn't have.

"So just go then, be unburdened." Marisa picked up a shirt that had
fallen onto the floor and tossed it at Juliet, hitting her in the face. "Go
to your fucking festival. Write your songs and play your music and fuck
your girls. Do whatever you want. But don't expect me to be here when
you get back." The words flew out of her mouth like bats from a cave,
words she probably didn't mean, but she was too angry to take them
back. Juliet stared at her. Marisa thought she saw fear in her eyes, maybe
the first time she had ever looked afraid.

"You wouldn't do that," Juliet said. "You wouldn't dare." The shirt
Marisa threw hung from her shoulder; now she let it fall to the floor.

"What choice are you giving me? You don't want me, you don't
want us—"

"This isn't about Jenry. Stop bringing him into this."

"See, that's the problem," Marisa said, "I say 'us,' and you think of
Jenry. What I meant was you and me."

Juliet threw up her hands. "And that's a bad thing, to think about
him?"

"No, of course not. But a family starts with the couple, they're at the
center, the heart. The kids grow from that."

The room was stuffy with the door closed and Marisa felt herself
starting to sweat. She turned on the ceiling fan, causing loose papers on
the desk to flutter.

"Maybe that's how you grew up," Juliet said, "but it's not like that
for every family." She pulled out a box of Jasper's belongings, removing
a tie and vintage gold watch. Juliet put the watch on, then packed the tie
into her carry-on, along with a framed photo of Jenry sitting on her lap,
a crushed flower in his small hand.

"Would you just stop and talk to me," Marisa pleaded. "What is this about?"

Juliet stopped to look at her. "You didn't have Jenry because we were in love and wanted a family. We were two people, two individuals, who were young and lost and needed something to hold us together. But it wasn't supposed to hold us down."

Marisa sat on the edge of the bed. "My God, how poetic. No wonder they named you after Shakespeare's most tragic heroine." Her tone was insulting, but she couldn't stop herself; her love had mutated into rage.

"See? This is exactly what I mean," Juliet said, her voice softer now. "You're becoming this mean, resentful person, and it's my fault. I'm do- ing this to you, by not giving you what you need." She zipped the bag closed. "That's why it had to end. I don't want you to hate me, or worse, hate yourself."

"I don't hate you."

"But you will. And I don't want you to."

Marisa shook her head. "That's not possible."

Juliet sat down next to her, their legs touching. Marisa could smell her shampoo, a simple pear scent that somehow smelled wonderful on her, and she turned her face away, not wanting to have anything pleasur- able associated with this moment. "When Jenry's older, when he's sixteen and has his first girlfriend, when he understands something about how the world works and how our family functions"—Juliet placed her hand on Marisa's arm—"I never want him to come to me and ask why I don't love his mother the way I should."

Something in the way she said it, or maybe the way Marisa heard it for the first time, clicked in her head. She felt that door inside her close again. Marisa found herself standing up, retreating to her own room, back to the bed they used to share. Juliet called after her, asking her to come back, but she couldn't; couldn't stand to look at her face, to see those eyes.

Hours later, when the cab honked from the street, Marisa didn't get up. She heard Juliet's footsteps outside her door, followed by the gen- tle, signature knock—two hard, one soft—but didn't move. When Juliet crept into her room to leave a card on the nightstand, she pretended to be asleep, didn't even flinch when she felt the warmth of Juliet's lips on her forehead, kissing her goodbye.

Two weeks later, Marisa packed up the apartment, putting most of her things into storage. She paid the rent and utilities through August, cleaned out the fridge, and cracked the windows an inch, anticipating summer's unforgiving heat. She left Juliet's studio untouched. Her resignation was refused twice, but she stood firm against their pleas for her to stay, telling them to hold her final paycheck since she didn't yet have a forwarding address. She almost gave in when she had to say goodbye to the kids, some she'd known since they were Jenry's age. They posed for pictures and promised to keep in touch, but she never developed the film, knowing she couldn't bear to look at them. None of her other friends, the few she'd managed to keep during the four-year absence that was her relationship with Juliet, knew she was leaving.

The hardest part was deciding what to tell Jenry. He cried as he watched their furniture disappear. When the movers lifted the couch into the moving van, he planted himself on the middle cushion saying, "My couch stay," over and over again. He walked around the empty living room, asking her where the TV was, and the table, the lamp. In his bedroom, he lay on the spot where his crib used to stand and said, "Jenry go night-night." He stood in her bedroom, in the gaping hole where their queen-sized bed used to be, asking, "Where our bed? Our bed gone?" She bent down next to him, looking into the deep browns of his eyes, so similar in color to Juliet's it was as if she were the one who'd given birth to him.

"Yes," Marisa said, tucking a loose curl behind his ear. "Our bed is gone."

Jenry reached for her hand as they walked through the empty living room. The echo was deafening. She locked the front door behind them, and from the porch window, looked back into the apartment one last time. Through tear-filled eyes, she told Jenry to say goodbye to their home, and he did.

· BOOK III ·

The Other Mother

September 2015

· 1 ·

Standing in the dim light of the restaurant, Juliet recognizes her son instantly, even though she hasn't seen him in more than sixteen years. Jenry was just over two years old that final time, asleep in the crib she'd assembled a week before his birth, wearing his favorite penguin pajamas. She's thought of that day often over the years—almost daily in fact—but in this moment, now that he's in front of her, she feels as if she'd imagined that scene, and has been replaying someone else's memory all these years. Feet peeking through the slats, curls damp against his forehead. How his mouth was slightly opened, like he was about to speak. It all comes back to her in that first instant.

He is taller than she would have imagined—at least six feet—which makes him several inches taller than her brother, almost the height of her father. His hair is shaved close to the scalp so there are no curls to recognize. But his nose is the same, a button like his mother, and he still has those ridiculously deep dimples. She has longed for this moment, but now that it's here, she doesn't know what to do, how to be.

Her mind races, though her body stands still. The timing is

terrible—her staff is about to arrive for the dinner rush, and she has to prep the duck for tonight's special, mix a marinade for the pickled beets, and whip four pounds of cream cheese into a frosting for the spice cake baked this morning—but none of that matters. This moment is his.

He looks around the room, scanning every corner. "I'm looking for Juliet," he says.

The sound of her name coming from his mouth startles her. She doesn't know what to say, how to speak even. He hands her a business card, but she doesn't take it. She has forgotten how to move. The next thing she knows, they are talking, but she can't really hear their voices. She is underwater, a swimmer looking up through the choppy surface above, seeing only the dappled light, the image of the sun in double, stretching and bending like a bright bubble in the clouded sky.

They are talking about the past, what he already knows, and what he wants her to tell him, beginning with the truth. She knows there is no such thing; there is what she remembers and what she did. What they both did.

"The truth is complicated," she begins. "For years I didn't know it myself." She has a faint desire to laugh, from the absurdity of it all, and from the blissful relief of waiting years for something to happen and finally having it occur. "I was young, selfish. I thought it would always be there for me, whenever I was ready."

"'It' meaning . . . ?"

"You, your mother. The family we created."

He nods his head, jaw clenched. "The one you didn't want?"

"Is that what she told you? That I didn't want you?"

He doesn't answer, but she can see it on his face. Marisa's version of the story, coloring his body like a pigment. She wants to deny it, defend herself, but realizes it's better to wait. Let him go first. His anger is not greater than hers, but it's closer to the surface, so she allows him to dip into it, wetting his hands. She listens as he talks about his mother, how Juliet left her, and left him behind, and it's like plunging her hands into the well, soaking her body with a rage she thought she'd buried long ago.

But it doesn't look like rage—it looks like heartache. The loss of him fills her body, courses through her veins. And now, as her memories replay over and over, she can't help but feel it all—the sadness, the loss, the love she had and perhaps still has for him—flowing into her limbs, making her skin twitch, her fingers ache, till it spills from her eyes as tears.

She sees his own eyes fill as he says he doesn't understand. "Why did you let her take me away from you," he asks, voice trembling, "if you really believed I was your son?"

His words hit her like the aftershock of a bomb. She steps back, tries to keep her balance. The back door slams, and she knows it's Santiago coming inside with the peeled potatoes, knows the conversation has to end. "Look, why don't we meet some other time, maybe you can come back—"

"No," he says quickly, shaking his head like he's trying to remove the wrong idea. "I think I should leave."

From the corner of her eye she sees the kitchen door swing open, Santiago slipping inside with a tray. Jenry walks toward the front door, and the sight of him leaving makes her heart seize up in her chest. She calls after him.

"You must think it's crazy. Some wild tale we've concocted to ruin your life. But this wasn't what we planned." She walks closer, drawn like a magnet. "I never thought it would turn out like this, or I swear, I wouldn't have done it."

He stands at the door. "Done what? Left me, or agreed to have me in the first place?"

She doesn't know him, the man he's become, but she recognizes a part of him. The calm, thoughtful person who first entered the restaurant looking for her. The peaceful baby who always shared his toys.

"Leaving wasn't my choice, not completely. And now, well, maybe we could have another chance."

"To do what, relive my childhood?" He spits the words out, but there's something else she sees beneath the anger, a nervousness she didn't expect. She watches him button and re-button the pocket on his cargo shorts. It reminds her of Marisa, how she used to play with her clothing when she got anxious, the frayed edge of her jeans, the buckle on a pair of boots. Seeing the similarity between mother and son underscores their genetic bond, a connection that simultaneously thrills and devastates her. Here he is, the boy she knew—all grown up now—and to recognize Marisa in him only serves to strengthen the link to their shared past. This is the baby she loved. The young man she dreamed of but never knew—here, now, in the flesh.

"I just want some time, to get to know you. Again." Juliet feels her face flush, the result of speaking a truth so deep she's hidden it from herself all these years, something she never dared think, let alone say aloud.

"You know what I want?" Jenry shifts his feet. "I want to know who my father was, to see pictures of him, to hear his voice, his laugh. I want to see him dance. To know if he ever thought of me—"

"Of course he did. We talked about you all the time."

"No, not from you. From him."

Yes, of course. It is always *him* they want to know about—the father, not the other mother. Juliet nods. "I'm sorry I can't give you that."

The back door slams again, and now there are voices, the chatter of Juliet's staff arriving for work. She backs up, hoping to block the interruption with her body, to hold on to this moment. She is terrified she won't ever see him again.

"I'm sorry," he says, "I shouldn't have come." He bumps into the door as he stumbles to find the doorknob.

"No, I'm glad you did." She wants to say something to keep him from walking out.

"There is one more thing," he says, cautiously. "I'd like some pictures. If you have any . . ." He doesn't finish his thought, but she knows where it's going.

"Proof?" she offers. "Some evidence to place me at the scene?" She teases him, as if it might help absorb the impact of the last fifteen minutes. He shrugs, but the look on his face is anything but casual.

"Have you asked your mom? She was the one who took everything."

Juliet thinks of saying more, of explaining how she was in Europe when Marisa packed up the apartment and left without saying goodbye, but she stops herself. She remembers the horrible shock of the empty living room, the floors so clean it was like they had never held the weight of anything. Then the nursery, stripped of every sign of Jenry's young life: the rocking chair, crib, and changing table gone; even the bookcase, once filled with books from Juliet's own childhood, wiped clean. And then, the odd discovery that her bedroom had been left untouched, preserved like some relic from a previous time: bed, desk, closet filled with clothing—all just as she left it, all waiting for her return. But everything that mattered was gone.

Juliet watches her staff ready the dining room: fill vases with fresh flowers, place clean water glasses at every table, fold stacks of newly ironed cloth napkins. They are like dancers, she thinks, every step choreographed for efficiency. Wouldn't Jasper be proud?

"I don't want to ask her," Jenry finally says, his eyes finding hers. "I'm asking you."

Later that night, as Juliet tries to focus on work, she keeps hearing that line, *I'm asking you*, the way his voice was quiet, almost a whisper, while his eyes looked pleading. The contradiction is vast—he wants to know so much but is afraid of what he will find—yet she understands how that feels. And now, as she stands over a hot flame in the restaurant kitchen, sautéing onions in a balsamic vinegar reduction as she prepares to glaze a dozen Cornish hens, Juliet finds herself hungry for information about his life, his past, what brought him here—yet fearful of what his presence will mean to the rest of her life. How their history will impact the family she's built in the wake of everything she lost.

· 2 ·

Juliet gets home after midnight. The lights are off inside; Noelle is already asleep. First, she takes a hot shower—washing off the smell of food, the stink of raw meat—then dresses in a ribbed tank top and sweatpants, her typical sleepwear for early autumn, before the chill of winter sets in. The sounds of the restaurant still in her head, she walks barefoot through the dark house, stopping in the dining room to put on a CD. Tonight, it's classical. Her record collection, which lines four walls of bookshelves in the guest room, is something she only visits on special occasions, when she has the time for reverie. Her normal routine, practiced five to seven times a week, is this: the local public radio station turned on low, a club soda with lime, and an old issue of *The New Yorker,* which she reads standing up, scanning the columns of dense script until her body relaxes enough to fall asleep.

Tonight, it takes longer than usual, and instead of joining her wife—legally married for two years, together for seven—in their king-size bed, she stops outside the small corner bedroom that used to be her music room. The floors creak as she steps inside. Even in the dark she can make out the three pieces of furniture that illustrate the new purpose of the

room: dresser, rocking chair, crib. All the essentials of a modern nursery. She pulls the chain on the lamp, a miniature giraffe dangling from
its end like a Christmas ornament, and a soft yellow light fills the room.

A game of chess sits on top of the dresser, in mid-play. The heavy
brass set belonged to her brother, one of the few things she'd wanted to
keep. It was a present for Jasper's twelfth birthday, the first year their
father had to shop by himself after their mother died. The set was extravagant, handmade in Egypt, and they were sure their father paid too
much for it. The board was made from mother-of-pearl and walnut, and
the hand-carved brass pieces were shaped like pharaohs and exotic cats;
the queen was Nefertiti, the king, Tutankhamen. It was so beautiful they
were almost afraid to touch it, but at their father's urging they began to
play each day after school. Jasper had grown to love the game, and they
played together for hours, just to hold the gods in their hands.

Juliet picks up a rook, feels its weight. She never cared much for the
game, but liked that Jasper respected her as a worthy opponent, despite
the four years between them. He would tell her stories while they played,
of their mother and the old neighborhood in Harlem, when they lived
on the top floor of their grandparents' brownstone; things Juliet was too
young to remember.

She replaces the rook and looks over at the crib; finds it empty, of
course. Two sets of sheets, already washed, lay folded on the mattress
pad—one blue with yellow stars, one pink with green polka dots—
waiting until they know. A stuffed elephant rests in the corner of the
crib, its floppy head leaning forward like it just dozed off. Juliet touches
the crocheted blanket that hangs over the side of the rail, her fingertips
slipping inside the knotted flowers. She tries to imagine the baby who
will sleep here, pictures herself in the rocking chair on nights like this
one, and a calm overtakes her. And then she thinks of Jenry, how he
looked as a baby, and how he stood before her tonight, sixteen years later,
somehow grown into a man.

She notices a sound in the hallway, then soft footsteps. She looks
to the doorway, waiting for Noelle to appear. When she does, her silk

nightgown slipping off her brown shoulder, eyes squinting against the light, Juliet feels a rush of relief.

"Hey." Noelle slips into the room, wraps her arms around Juliet and squeezes tight. She kisses Juliet's neck. "You smell like fried onions."

"Sorry, I can shower again."

"No, it's fine. Reminds me of my grandfather's backyard barbecues." She sniffs Juliet's armpit. "Ah, hot links."

Juliet playfully pushes her away, but Noelle comes back, laughing as she tries to get her arms around Juliet's waist again, eventually tucking them into the waistband of her sweatpants.

"Don't make me do it," Noelle threatens, trying to cover her smile.

"You wouldn't dare."

Noelle tugs at the boxers, trying to pull them down, but as she does Juliet bends over and drops to her knees, dragging them both to the floor. They lay together on the small sheepskin rug, laughing.

"If you wanted me on my back, you just had to ask."

Noelle uses her leg to pin Juliet to the rug. "I always want you on your back." She kisses her deeply, and afterward, lays her head on Juliet's shoulder.

"Maybe we should paint the ceiling," Juliet suggests. "To match the stars on the blue sheets."

"The ceiling is fine. Too much stimulation and this baby will go crazy." Noelle lifts her head. "And how do you know we're going to use the stars? It could be a girl. We could paint polka dots on the walls."

"The nurse said the ultrasound looked like a boy."

"Ultrasounds can be wrong. We won't know for sure till she has the baby."

"You're right," Juliet says, smiling at her. "But I still think it's a boy."

Noelle reaches into the crib for the crocheted blanket and spreads it over them. Juliet pulls up her knees, tries to fit within its boundaries.

"How was work?"

"Fine. Seven extra people showed up to the rehearsal dinner. Thankfully half were vegetarians, so I didn't have to split the hens."

"Never thought I'd hear you praise vegetarians."

"A momentary lapse."

Juliet stares at the crib, feels Noelle watching her. She has always been able to read Juliet's face, to see the worry or wonder that other people miss, to see fear when others guess anger. Juliet knows she must sense something.

After a moment, Noelle kisses her cheek. Juliet feels her breath in her ear as she whispers, "I promise you, it's going to be different this time. No one's ever going to take this baby away from you."

Juliet looks at her. "The adoption isn't final for twenty-four months. She has two whole years to decide if she wants him back."

"I'm not talking about the law," Noelle says, slowing down to choose her words carefully. "I'm talking about Jenry."

Hearing his name come out of Noelle's mouth sends a shock through Juliet. Her skin burns with heat. She needs to tell Noelle the truth: she saw him tonight, he's alive and healthy and in Providence right now. That he's grown into a young man, a college student. But she can't form the words.

Noelle sits up, her voice pointed and sharp. "You and Marisa, you had this strange relationship. She had a baby, and you loved him, I get that. But he was always her son. Not yours. You didn't set out to be a mother, so it's not the same." Juliet listens without reacting; this is the story she told Noelle years ago, but hearing it now makes her stomach turn.

Noelle spreads her hands over the blanket, smoothing it out, tucking it tight around Juliet's body. "This baby we're adopting, he's going to be ours. He will belong to both of us equally. And I hope that means something to you, just knowing that we're starting out on the same footing."

"Of course, it means something," Juliet says. "It means a lot." Still, she isn't sure *what* it means.

"This is our baby, Jules. *Our* baby. You're never going to lose him."

Juliet feels a tear slip from her eye. It feels cold against her skin, falling fast across her temple till it stops in the groove behind her earlobe. She wants desperately to believe Noelle, to trust the woman she's promised her life to, but deep down she wonders if it's something else—if she's incapable of trusting herself.

· 3 ·

The following week, home alone before work, Juliet grabs a flashlight and heads to the attic. The air is surprisingly clean, thanks to the purifier Noelle runs 24/7, along with the broken windowpane Juliet never got around to fixing, which lets in a nice breeze. Juliet hasn't been up here since they bought the house three years ago, when Noelle had grand plans for renovation and banks were giving mortgages to first-time buyers in transitional neighborhoods like the West End. The attic would be transformed into Juliet's music studio—skylights, soundproofing on the walls, a deck for fresh air and inspiration—but since then other projects have taken over: the adoption; Noelle becoming a partner in her architecture firm; Juliet's ongoing sobriety. And of course, the biggest factor to consider: Juliet had stopped playing the piano.

She never planned to quit, but her need for silence became stronger than her need to play. It started as a short break, so she could focus on getting sober, but days turned into weeks and soon six months had passed without her playing; in the same length of time, she achieved her first milestone in AA: six months of sobriety. She was sober for a full year before she tried to play again. It felt good to sit on the piano bench, to feel the keys, to hear the notes inside her head played out loud, but after stopping, she felt empty inside; later, she was filled with a sense of longing so profound it threatened to consume her. All she wanted to do was drink.

Noelle won't say anything, but Juliet knows she wants her to play again. She thought she married a musician who loved to cook, not a chef who used to play the piano. And Juliet wants that, too—but not at the expense of her sobriety. Her father always said that music was the most authentic part of her, but she knew it was also where she carried the pain; the loss of her mother, brother, and Jenry like layers of scar tissue. Without alcohol, they became open wounds, her memories too much to bear. She had to put the piano away in order to survive.

In the week and a half since seeing Jenry in the restaurant, Juliet has hardly thought of anything else. She's spent hours replaying their brief conversation, hearing his questions and her feeble answers, and each time she returns to his simple request: for photographs. Initially, she planned to ignore it, not wanting to see them herself, but each day she felt more willing to comply, more compelled to give him what he asked for, regardless of its effect on her. Which is how she finds herself in the attic, standing amidst dozens of storage bins, looking for proof.

She searches the bins one at a time, setting aside old clothes and papers until she finds one labeled "old CDs," and instead comes across hundreds of photographs. They aren't in albums, nor are they organized by date or event; instead, they are randomly packed into shoeboxes, stacked in piles of different shapes and sizes. Some are black and white, some Polaroid, some color. A few belonged to her mother, or Jasper, copies he likely took from their parents, but most of them are hers—from childhood (something embarrassing from gym class), or high school (the misfortune of playing handbells in the winter concert), or college (an ex-girlfriend she hardly recognized, her first experiment with paisley). She has to search through all of this, years of past regrets, in order to find the photographs of Jenry from the short time they were a family. Or, as she now tries to convince herself, reimagining an easier truth, when she'd played house with someone else's son.

She feels excitement and dread as she starts to thumb through them, soon coming across a stack of color photographs, all more than sixteen years old, yet startlingly familiar. She shuffles through dozens of snapshots of Jenry as a baby: crying, nursing, sleeping, crawling, laughing, eating, pointing, walking, falling, yawning, sneezing, swimming, sunbathing. How can they capture so much life in just two years? The hard part is seeing her younger self, her ease with him and with herself; knowing she took so many simple moments for granted, as if they would last forever.

She takes all the Jenry photographs and wraps them in an old bandana, which she then tucks into a gift bag brought up from the recycling shelf. If Noelle asks about the bag, Juliet will say it's a surprise, a gift she's not ready to give her yet, and Noelle, being an honest person, one who loves Juliet in a way she doesn't think she deserves to be loved, will never once be tempted to look inside. Juliet knows this about her wife, and that alone makes her want to drive to Noelle's office right now and dump the contents of the bag onto her desk, among the sketches and plans and miniature models of other people's homes, and confess everything she's held inside for the last ten days. But instead, she leaves the bag on the kitchen island—as if wanting to tempt fate—while she figures out what to do next.

JULIET CAN'T SLEEP. She gets home from the restaurant, drinks her club soda with lime, listens to NPR for as long as she can stand the political banter, and climbs into bed. Her feet are cold and her legs ache from standing on the kitchen's tile floors, so she wraps them around Noelle's warmth. Still asleep, Noelle lifts her arm, taking Juliet into the smooth curve of her body. Juliet loves this about her wife, how she opens herself even in sleep; how Noelle always lets Juliet warm her feet between her calves, or tuck her cold hands under her shirt to find the heat of her belly. Noelle never pushes Juliet away, even when she's sweaty from nights at the grill, and this acceptance—one might call it unconditional love—is the first of its kind Juliet has ever felt. It was part of what made Juliet want to marry Noelle, this daily act of sacrifice and loyalty.

Thirty minutes pass. She feels restless, her mind spinning about Jenry and what to do; how to tell Noelle about his arrival. How to figure out what it all means—not just for her, but for Noelle and the new baby; for *this* family. Her back is tight from work, the chopping and stirring, kneading dough to make flatbread. She tries to stretch but it doesn't help. She needs a massage. She needs to have sex. Leaning into Noelle, she starts to kiss her neck, running her fingertips across her thin camisole top. Noelle murmurs and rolls to her side. She holds Juliet's hand between her breasts, trying to keep her from reaching her nipples, a signal she wants to stay asleep. Juliet considers ignoring this and mounting a second attempt, but decides against the work of it, letting Noelle settle back into her slumber.

Juliet glances at the time—too late to call her sponsor—and lies back down. She closes her eyes and says the Serenity Prayer, never one of her favorites. She exhales. Pictures the shape of a wine bottle, its glass thick and dark like some exotic candy. Fuck. She opens her eyes. *Come on, God, where are you?* While not explicitly sanctioned in the AA literature, those six words have become a staple in her prayer and meditation practice. She breathes in the scent of Noelle's perfume, feels the cool smooth of the cotton duvet cover against her bare legs, tries to be present, here, now. *Come on, God,* she prays. *Help me.*

She gets out of bed and goes downstairs. Decides to make tea, though she never wanted to be one of those lesbians. She promised her brother no tea and no cats when she came out to him in high school, a promise she kept until moving in with Noelle. Juliet treads softly through the living room in the dark. Eyes the empty wall: the chosen spot where she'd put a piano if she still had one. When she and Jasper were kids, they used to play a game where they would pick the perfect spot for a piano in any room they entered. Odd that she still finds herself doing it all these years later. Tonight, she wishes she still played; she longs for the familiar feel of the keys beneath her fingertips, the relief she felt as the notes pierced the air, sound encircling her head like a scent.

Standing in the kitchen as the electric kettle boils, she regrets donating her old piano to the women's shelter in Woonsocket; she had thought it would make her decision not to play easier, as if by not having one there to look at, she would somehow forget how much she loves it. But Noelle had been right; Juliet was being hasty, impulsive even, to think she could let go of that constant source of energy, the one she'd reliably fed on her entire life. Without it, she feels diminished, a flower removed from the sun. Yes, she is sober, but how can she reconcile not feeling like herself? Her sponsor says it doesn't matter what she feels; the only thing that matters is not taking the first drink.

She pours the water, holds the mug in both hands as it steeps. After a few minutes, she sips her tea, letting the steam wash over her face as she breathes in the scent of lemon, hoping it helps her sleep. She passes the nursery on her way out and wishes the baby were already here—then she would have something meaningful to do right now, some reason to be awake in the middle of the night. When Jenry was a baby she often took the midnight shift, since Marisa worked a nine-to-five and got up earlier than she did. Juliet came to love that extra time with him. She would sing old show tunes to put him to sleep or play chords on the piano while wearing him in the sling. Thinking of him, she pictures the young man who stood in the doorway of the restaurant, who can recall none of those nights, and feels her chest tighten. What does it mean to be the only one who remembers? She thinks of Marisa and wonders where she is, wonders what she allows herself to remember, and what she's forced herself to forget.

She sits on the couch and looks out the window, hoping to see the still, dark night outside; instead, she catches her own reflection in the windowpane. A somber, middle-aged face; still pretty, she thinks, steady, and unassuming; the face of someone who has seen too many sunrises. She longs for the days ahead, when she will eventually become forgetful, old enough to be released from the burden of remembering.

Hours later, after the sun has risen and Noelle has gotten up and showered, Juliet will still be on the couch—asleep now, with her feet up and her head stretched back. When Noelle leaves for work, she stops to spread a wool blanket over Juliet's long legs, kissing her wife goodbye as she heads quietly out the door.

THE RINGING STARTLES Juliet awake, loud like a fire alarm. If it were up to her, they wouldn't even have a landline anymore, but Noelle thinks it's a safety issue—just in case they lose electricity in the middle of a storm, especially with the baby coming—so Juliet gave in. But in silent protest she usually refuses to answer, letting it go to the voicemail she never checks. Today she ignores the first call, slow to get up from her warm spot on the couch. She blinks against the sun pouring into the empty room, folds the blanket Noelle used to cover her. As she ambles into the kitchen to get coffee, the phone rings again. *Fuck off,* she thinks, cursing the persistence of what is probably nothing more than a computer-generated marketing poll. When the phone rings a third time, she spills the last of the cream she's pouring into her coffee. Angry now, she snags the cordless phone off its charging base and barks into the handset, daring the caller to hang up again. Silence first, then a single word: "Juliet?"

The voice sounds distant, yet familiar. "Who's this?"

"It's Marisa."

For some reason, this comes as no surprise. Juliet hasn't heard her voice in sixteen years, and certainly wasn't expecting to hear it today—if ever again—yet as she stands in her kitchen looking into the backyard, where the maple leaves are just beginning to yellow, she thinks, *Yes, of course, this is exactly right.*

"I'm calling about Jenry," Marisa says after a long silence.

"What about Jenry?" Juliet finds herself responding reflexively, and then, a thought of worry. "Is he okay?"

"You tell me. I know you've seen him." A pause. "He said he found you."

Juliet thinks of lying or hanging up, but instead she says, "Yes, he found me." And then, "Not like I was the one who was hiding."

She hears Marisa exhale. "This isn't easy. This whole thing. But right now, I just want to find my son."

"What do you mean? Is he missing?"

"He won't return my calls or emails. His roommate says he's in class whenever I call their dorm room—even at night—and once some girl answered the phone and said he needed *space*." She stops herself to take a breath. "It's not normal. I mean, I haven't heard anything from him in almost two weeks. It's not how we operate." There's a desperation in her voice that makes Juliet feel sorry for her, but then she remembers who she's talking to and what she's done—how Marisa left her without warning or even an explanation all those years ago—and the wall comes up again.

"He's a college student. I don't think calling home is his first priority."

"Jenry's not that kind of kid. He's a good boy."

"Don't you think *man* is more accurate?" Her taste for coffee ruined, Juliet now searches the fridge for another drink.

"He's only eighteen years old. He hasn't even voted."

Juliet laughs. "Since when is voting the best way to measure manhood?"

"Jesus Christ, that's not what I'm talking about." Marisa is silent for several seconds, and Juliet wonders if she hung up. When she speaks again her voice is calm, measured like she always was, the levelheaded diplomat to Juliet's passionate insurgent. "He's upset, and we both know why. There's no mystery."

"The mystery," Juliet says, cracking open a club soda, "is where you've been for the last sixteen years." She pours it over a cup of ice, watching it foam. Seized with a sudden thirst.

"Juliet, stop. This isn't about us."

"It's not? Then who exactly is it about?" Juliet breaks up the ice with her straw, stirring until the bubbles dissipate. She cuts a sliver of lime as garnish, leaves the knife on the chopping block, the blade still wet.

"This was a mistake," Marisa says, exhaling. "I'm sorry I called."

"You're sorry about calling? *That's* your apology?"

"Oh, come on. I know what you want, and it's just not possible."

"Fuck you for thinking you know what I want. And fuck you for taking him, for disappearing without a phone call or even a note, for hiding all these years like a fugitive." Juliet is gesturing with her glass, feeling the old anger begin to swell, as if Marisa is in the room with her.

"I don't expect you to understand, to have sympathy for my position, but we both paid a high price—"

"I'm sorry," Juliet interrupts, "what price did you pay exactly?"

"Are you kidding? I was alone, with a toddler. We traveled for months before ending up back with my parents. Do you really think I wanted to do that?"

"You had a choice. You could have gone anywhere. But what choice did I have?" Juliet feels her face get hot. "I just came home to an empty apartment, the whole place wiped clean like you'd never existed."

"You had a thousand choices before that, and you had no problem making them. You didn't want me, and you didn't want my son."

"That is not true." Juliet yells now, unable to control her outrage. "It was never about Jenry. You know that." Her hands tremble, almost dropping her glass.

"We were a package deal," Marisa says. "You couldn't just cut me out and go directly to him."

"I never tried to cut you out. I tried to cut you free."

"Bullshit," Marisa counters. "You were the one who wanted to be free. And so I let you go. This is what freedom feels like, don't blame me if you don't like it."

Juliet slams down her glass, spilling club soda onto the table. "You didn't have the right to just take him. He was mine, too."

"Was he? I seem to remember you saying we were a burden."

"I never said that. He was just a child—"

"He was a gift—" Marisa's voice rises.

"He was my son." As soon as Juliet speaks the words, she knows she is finally telling the truth, saying what she's felt all this time, but was afraid to claim. Despite what she did, regardless of all the years of distance between them, she had always believed that Jenry was her son—hers and Marisa's, equally. But she had never said the words out loud.

"Oh, please," Marisa says bitterly. "If you really thought that, we wouldn't be here. You had the chance. To make him your son. Christ, I wanted to give him your last name. And what did you do?"

Juliet wipes up the spill with a towel. "This isn't about the law. It's about what's right." Her voice softens as she takes a breath, her heart still galloping in her chest. "Would you even have him now if I hadn't been in your life? If I hadn't been part of the equation? You might have had a child, somebody else's maybe, but not this one. Not *my* son. We brought him into the world—you and I, through our choices and our intentions. Take that away, and you lose him. Erase me, and you kill him, too."

"You don't have to be so dramatic." She hears Marisa inhale, as if drawing smoke from a cigarette.

"What you did, Marisa, how you took him," Juliet says, "it wasn't right. You just don't do that. Especially to someone you claimed to love." Tears well in Juliet's eyes as her voice breaks.

"I did love you." Marisa's voice is soft, almost a whisper. "You didn't love me back."

Juliet leans over the island, her face inches from the surface. She fingers a groove in the soft wood, wonders why time wears some things down, makes them softer, more malleable, yet other things like bones and brick—things that make up structures, that are designed to carry weight—become more brittle.

Marisa clears her throat. "I didn't call you to fight. I called you because . . ." After a long pause, Juliet hears her inhale, then she finally utters a simple plea, "I need your help." Her voice cracks, like a baseball shattering glass.

Only later, after they've hung up and Juliet has placed the handset back in its base, does she sit down. Marisa's voice continues to play in her mind, at once familiar and foreign, while the desperation of her request is something Juliet has never heard before, not from Marisa. A part of her wants to help, but she isn't sure she can, even if she agreed to try. Would Jenry want her involved? Does she have the right to intervene? And if she did, what would she tell Noelle?

Juliet finishes her drink in one gulp, sucking on the lime until her mouth waters. Years ago, when she was still drinking, she used to relish eating the lime wedges from her gin and tonics, chewing the bits of gin-soaked fruit at the bottom of the glass, the bitter oil from the rind numbing her tongue as much as the ice. It was part of the ritual of intoxication, a daily pleasure she looked forward to more than sleep. But now the lime sours in her mouth. She spits the wedge into the sink, a flash of resentment filling her. None of this was fair; why does giving up one thing always result in another loss? She gave up Marisa and lost Jenry; gave up drinking and lost the piano—without gin, did she have to lose the pleasure of the lime as well?

Later that day, she goes for a three-mile run through the neighborhood, down Westminster to Dexter and back on Potters, and grabs lunch at the Hudson Street Deli. Afterward, her body feels more relaxed, her limbs strong and loose. She showers and dresses for work, moving with a sense of purpose as something in her mind starts to shift, a feeling of hope released inside her. If she no longer covets the lime, she realizes, it will hold no power over her; she will be freed from any expectation, any responsibility, as if the need had never existed. She zips her jeans and bends to pull on her boots; the tension leaves her body like a wave of pleasure. Perhaps this is the spiritual awakening the Big Book talks about, the result of handing over your will. How liberating it must be to let everything go and live fully in the present, released from the potency of the past.

· 4 ·

Six months earlier, on a damp night in April, Juliet had taken a candle to celebrate five years of continuous sobriety. Five years of avoiding happy hour, after-dinner drinks, and cocktail parties; declining Champagne toasts at weddings, cold beer at baseball games, and eggnog spiced with rum. Five years without bourbon-soaked ice cubes melting on her tongue, without late-night sex fueled by alcohol's singular haze. It was simple, but not easy; all she had to do was keep repeating, *Not today.* Tomorrow I can make a different choice, but today I'm not going to drink.

After Marisa's surprise phone call, Juliet arrives at her AA meeting early; she makes the coffee, talks to newcomers, and sets up the folding chairs stored in the church's hall closet. Her instincts tell her to be in motion, to not dwell. She doesn't understand addiction, just like she doesn't understand why sitting in a room listening to other drunks talking about the families they can't keep, the jobs they don't want, the children they don't understand, somehow keeps her from taking another drink—but it does. Or at least for the last two thousand days it has.

When the meeting ends ninety minutes later, she stacks the chairs and returns them to the closet, helps the literature person put away all the books, waves goodbye to her recovery buddies in the church's unlit parking lot, and gets in her car to drive home—just like she's done every Tuesday for five and a half years. But tonight, there's something different. She starts the car and turns on the defroster, waits for the windshield to clear, but before pulling away she notices something on the passenger seat: the gift bag. For a second, she doesn't recognize it, doesn't remember that it's packed with photos for Jenry. She grabs the steering wheel with both hands, takes a deep breath.

Later, she will think back to this moment and realize she should have waited, stayed in one place, taken more time to come up with a plan. Instead, she puts the car in reverse and pulls out of her parking spot. She doesn't take the usual route home, but finds herself driving toward the river, taking Allens Avenue to Eddy and heading over the bridge to the East Side. She stays on Wickenden, seeing the new shops and old haunts, then finds herself deeper in Fox Point, on side streets she used to cut through when she walked home after Little League practice. She passes the old library and donut shop, the hair salon where she cut off all her hair in high school, the park where she stole her first kiss from Giovanni Consiglio, an Italian boy who used to bring her calzones from his family's bakery.

It's raining by the time she reaches College Hill, driving through the campus that holds so many pieces of her past. She turns onto George Street, barely recognizing the new buildings as she crosses Thayer, passing rows of fraternity housing. The grass is wet from the rain, which makes it look vulnerable, as students trample over it in groups, huddled together under an oversized umbrella, a bear decal stretched across the fabric. She sees the Quad ahead, where she lived her sophomore year when she was a peer counselor to forty freshmen in Everett House, and without thinking, pulls into a handicapped spot outside the dorm. She leaves the car on, hazards flashing, windshield streaked with rain. A couple stands in the brick archway, struggling through a tense goodbye. Juliet watches as the girl wipes her eyes with her sleeve; the boy is pleading, arms at his sides, hands open. As other students walk by, the couple turns away from each other, pretending they aren't together. The rain continues to fall.

Juliet remembers that same trick—in the same archway—but she and Natalia Brooks had a good excuse. They had to be discreet; not necessarily because they were two women—this was the liberal Ivy after all—but because Juliet was a counselor and Natalia had a boyfriend and a scholarship she didn't want to jeopardize. They dated for three months without anyone knowing, after a social night brought the whole dorm together to make caramel apples and talk about the university's new policy on sexual harassment. Juliet later found out that Natalia didn't eat caramels, but that night she participated anyway, dipping apples on popsicle sticks into bowls of hot caramel, heated in the dorm's ancient microwave ovens. Natalia got burned halfway through, when an especially heavy apple fell from its stick, smearing hot caramel onto her hand. She kept saying she was okay, but when she left to get ice, Juliet followed her out. They had stopped here, just under the archway, and Juliet demanded to see the burn. Natalia reluctantly surrendered her hand, which Juliet held to the light. The skin covering the knuckle of her middle finger was gone completely, the raw flesh left behind white with shock.

"Jesus Christ," Juliet said, "how did that happen?"

"I peeled off the caramel. The skin came, too."

Juliet grabbed her other hand. "Come on, I'll take you to Health Services."

"It's fine." Natalia pulled away, wincing. "I just need some ice."

"You need ointment and a bandage."

Natalia hesitated. "I have a paper due tomorrow. On *Madame Bovary.*"

"English or Comp. Lit.?"

"Comp. Lit." Natalia exhaled, blowing on her finger. "Professor Bergman."

"Lucky for you, I took it last year." Juliet smiled, reaching for her hand again. "Come on, I'll help you."

An hour later they were in Juliet's room, Natalia's finger bandaged as thick as a hot dog bun. She couldn't type, so she dictated to Juliet, who hunted and pecked her way through five double-spaced pages of critical analysis.

"I thought you said you could type."

"No," Juliet corrected, "what I said was I have good hands."

"Ah. Well, I guess it's all wasted on the piano," Natalia's voice was light and flirtatious. She sat with her legs tucked beneath her, nibbling on the same apple rescued earlier, one of the few not covered with caramel.

"Nothing at the piano is wasted."

"I didn't mean it like that. What I meant was, the piano gets all of you." Juliet could feel Natalia looking at her. She knew this pattern well, straight girls with unconscious crushes who flirted without intent. Flattering, but to be avoided.

"Do you have anything to drink?" Natalia asked, tying her hair into a knot with an unsharpened pencil.

"I'm sure there's leftover soda in the lounge."

"I meant something with alcohol."

Juliet looked at her. "Aren't you only eighteen?"

Natalia shrugged, tossing the apple core away. "Aren't you twenty?"

They finished the rest of the paper while sipping peppermint schnapps from glass votives Juliet kept on her bookshelf, their tealights abandoned like checkers behind the row of books. The buzz of alcohol made the novel's passages suddenly funny, and Natalia began to translate them back into French as she read aloud, a skill she'd picked up during a semester she spent abroad in high school. As a musician, Juliet was used to moments like this—using the piano as another language she could speak, to woo or entice or apologize—but it was strange to be on the receiving end, to have someone else performing for her enjoyment.

"I've watched you play," Natalia said, using her syllabus to mark her place as she closed the book. "At the music library."

Juliet looked up. "The practice rooms?"

Natalia nodded.

"Those are supposed to be private."

"It was." Natalia smiled. "You and I were the only ones there."

Juliet laughed. "If I didn't know better, I'd think you were stalking me."

"You don't know better," Natalia said, sipping her drink. She looked at Juliet through the edge of her glass. Juliet could see the flick of her pink tongue. "You know, I've never been drunk before."

"You're not drunk now," Juliet said. "You haven't even had a whole drink."

"I want to be." Natalia took another sip. "I want you to show me how."

Juliet didn't look at her; didn't see her pretty face, the long dark hair in its loose bun, her eyes sparkling like granite. She didn't think about the agreement she'd signed to not fraternize with the freshmen; didn't smell the novelty of Natalia's perfume, a mixture of citrus and sandalwood that covered her comforter like dew; didn't back away as Natalia moved closer, reaching for Juliet with her good hand, the bandaged one held behind her back like something she was ashamed of. Juliet's skin prickled with heat. Her pulse throbbed. Natalia closed her eyes, waited for Juliet to kiss her.

"You have a boyfriend," Juliet said softly.

"You have a girlfriend," Natalia whispered in reply.

Natalia's minty breath made Juliet's eyes water. She closed them as Natalia's mouth pressed against hers. They kissed lightly at first, but soon their mouths opened wider, as their tongues searched in anticipation. Juliet felt an explosion of want throughout her body, but she focused it all into her mouth; the stiff probing of her tongue, the cool moisture of Natalia's lips as she sucked them. The taste of peppermint, the heat of the alcohol, the pleasure that began to numb her body—it all mixed together like a potion, and Juliet began to fall under the spell of this type of seduction: the intoxication of something new and illicit. She wasn't drunk, but she was blurred by the alcohol, her senses somehow sharpened and dulled, a dangerous combination that would define her sexual encounters for the better part of the next decade. And if she wasn't careful, could dictate the rest of her life.

———

THE RAIN IS falling harder now, so Juliet turns on her windshield wipers. The sound comforts her, like the metronome always used to, marking the top of her piano like an emblem marks the hood of a car. When she looks back to the archway, the arguing couple is gone. She drives on, passing other well-known landmarks: the Quiet Green, the bell tower, Manning Chapel. Juliet never visited the chapel when she was a student, and had been inside only twice in her life. Those two visits, separated by more than twenty years, were both for memorial services; first her mother's, when Juliet was seven and wore wool tights under a black velvet dress, and then her brother's, when she was twenty-eight and defiant enough to wear a men's suit, with a lavender silk shirt that belonged to Jasper. Both died in winter: her brother in early February, the sky bright and cold, with a silent wind whipping up snow that had fallen just before, the grass dusted a brilliant white; her mother in December, four days after Juliet performed in a holiday recital, the last time her mother would ever hear her play.

Juliet slows down, peering through the gates to see the chapel's familiar outline, the limestone a startling white against the overcast sky. She sees the side entrance propped open, a sliver of light silhouetting the small door, and suddenly feels drawn to go inside. She watches a man enter, and after him, an old woman in an overcoat, followed by two younger women, arms linked in a breezy platonic intimacy. Juliet checks the time on her phone, wonders what could be happening in a chapel at eight thirty at night. Years ago she would have imagined something illicit, but today she can only think of some type of Anonymous meeting, folks gathering in church basements to find spiritual solutions the church's altar does not provide.

She parks under an oak tree; soon she's walking across the green, as if an invisible force were compelling her to go back, to face her past. It feels good to stretch her legs, to feel the ground under her feet. This campus has always felt like a second home, and like home, it holds complicated feelings. Her boots turn a darker shade of brown from the wet grass, but she doesn't notice; doesn't question what brought her here tonight;

doesn't ask herself why she's avoiding the task at hand—the delivery of the photographs—when she could just as easily drive directly to Jenry's dorm and drop them off, instead of letting her subconscious follow this tour of procrastination down memory lane.

After her mother died, her father removed most of the photographs from their home. Not all at once, lest she and Jasper object, but slowly the pictures began to shift; their wedding photo, which used to be in the living room, sitting on the mantle in its polished silver frame, ended up in the library, and then on the top shelf of an armoire in Winston's bedroom, a place Juliet rarely visited. The leather photo albums from the early years of their marriage, before Juliet was born, migrated to a higher shelf in the bookcase, subtly out of the way, while the new ones filled with their motherless exploits—ski vacations to Waterville Valley, a road trip to Mount Rushmore, summers at dance and music camp in the Berkshires—were all placed within reach.

Juliet remembers climbing onto the back of a chair in order to reach those older albums, and how she would sit in the windowsill for hours, flipping through row after row of her much younger parents, in awe of her mother and surprised by the images of her father. His hair was so dark it looked fake, and his wide smile, something she rarely saw, made her sad—to know he was capable of such joy but no longer able to access it. Looking at her mother was like looking at a stranger; Juliet felt as if she were stealing through snapshots of a movie star. She'd marveled at her beauty, her fashionable dresses, many of them sewn by hand, and her perfectly coiffed hair. She wore high heels in every shot, her legs slim and strong, the same color as her camel-haired coat, always buttoned at the waist and belted, as if even then she was bracing for a storm. As a child, Juliet craved these images from their shared past, but seeing them made her longing for her parents more acute. She could picture the intact family they had lost. The photographs certainly didn't assuage her loneliness; if anything, they created a deeper longing, sparked a hunger she eventually realized would never be sated.

She doesn't want that for Jenry, but who is she to protect him from the past? Who protected her? Perhaps her brother tried, and in his own way, her father—but was it enough? Could it ever be enough?

She has almost reached the chapel when, in the distance, she sees a figure with an umbrella approaching, one who seems to be walking directly at her. It's too dark to make out any features, but his body is recognizable, along with his steady gait. She can't look away as she waits for confirmation. When he crosses under a streetlamp, the light illuminates his face: yes, she is looking at her father. Juliet wasn't expecting to see him here, not at this hour. He's lost more weight since she last saw him, his overcoat hanging loose like a dropped sail. So this is why she felt pulled here, this is the invisible force that called her back.

She stands on the edge of the path, waits for him to notice her.

"Juliet," he calls out, continuing to walk with the same measured step.

"Hi, Pop."

He nods toward the street behind her. "I thought that might be your car. So I walked back this way, just to see." He holds out his hand, gesturing, but not reaching for her. "What brings you out in the rain?"

"I was going to a meeting," she says, nodding toward the chapel. A small lie, but easier than explaining the truth, something she's not sure she owes him.

They don't hug; instead, he places a gloved hand on her shoulder. She feels the weight of it through the fabric of her raincoat, heavy and familiar. She hasn't thought much about her father's role in all this, but seeing him now reminds her: he was the one who sent Jenry to the restaurant to find her—all without a word of warning to Juliet.

Her father nods. "I've heard they host all sorts of groups." He clears his throat, a thick phlegmy sound, and she wonders if he's catching a cold. "I never figured you'd end up in God's house, but age can take its toll on all of us, can't it?"

She has always been sensitive—*super sensitive*, Jasper used to tease— and even now she can't help but take his words of observation as insults. Growing up, a comment about anything from her study habits to her shoes could feel like a personal attack; his words, like his gaze, could cut to her core. Age and maturity didn't help; to the outside world she was confident, impenetrable, almost aloof, but with her father she was insecure, halting, defensive—still a little girl desperate for approval. Now, convinced she won't get it, she finds herself with only one choice: to go on the offensive, to use his own tactics against him.

"Pretty late for office hours," she says, looking at her watch.

"I was meeting with an old student. He's looking for a position, tenure track, wants to know if I'll write him a letter of support."

He starts walking, and she falls in step beside him. "Will you?"

He smiles. "I'm still thinking about it. But the scotch was good and the conversation made up for the ambiance."

"Faculty Club?" she asks, knowing his disdain for the false glamour of the old club, with its bright lights and fake flowers, its menu of finger sandwiches and raw oysters that always left him wanting more.

He nods. "Exactly."

She notes a hint of recognition in his voice, which makes her soften. "Do you need a ride?" She points to her car as they near the sidewalk.

"No, no, my car's in the lot, an easy walk." He gestures toward the library, but she knows what he means; he's been parking around the corner, at the Horace Mann lot, since she was a child. Always the same spot, always a Volvo.

The first one was white, a four-door they got before Juliet was born, the only one she remembers her mother driving; then the metallic blue 245 DL they bought in England to save money; then the gray 760 Sedan, which looked too close to a Buick for the old man's liking; followed by the silver 960 Estate, the first with a CD player. He ushered in the twenty-first century with a V40, but only kept it for a few years because he didn't like the compact body; and finally the current one, a shadow blue XC90 he'd already put a hundred thousand miles on, promising he'll drive it into the grave. He was loyal, her father, as long as you didn't let him down.

"I'm just stopping by the office for a few things," he says, bringing her back to their awkward conversation, "and then I'm off."

"Okay, then." She gives him a pinched smile, turning to walk away.

"I sent you an email last week," he calls out after her. "About the new Jacob Lawrence exhibit at MoMA."

"I got it." She nods awkwardly. "Thanks."

They stare at each other until he speaks again. "Why don't we go up to my office for a drink?" When she doesn't respond he adds, "I'm sure I've got some tea." He'd been confused by her decision to quit drinking, saying he was skeptical of nondrinkers, just like she had always been of people who didn't eat meat. Their intolerance for health fanatics was one of many traits they shared, but unfortunately it didn't make it any easier for them to get along.

"I should go."

"I've changed some of the photographs around. You might like it."

"I'm sure it's very nice."

He peers down Prospect, pointing at the distant building with his umbrella. "When you were a child, I had that corner room, remember, by the staircase?"

"I remember."

"But after the Chair, the Pulitzer, they started to woo me." He smiles at the memory, a story she's heard several times. "Gregorian was afraid I'd go to Yale, so one day he took me to lunch and asked what it would take for me to stay. No, not just to stay—to be happy. I told him, 'An office as big as yours.' He pulled some strings and gave me the old conference room upstairs, practically my own floor."

"And did it work? Are you happy?" She already knows the answer, but likes to remind him that she's not fooled by his persona or his success.

He winks, ignoring her tone. "Happiness was his goal, not mine."

His body blocks the light from the streetlamp. She remembers looking up at him as a child, how he seemed so massive, like a mountain, the only person she knew who could block out the sun.

"You should come by," he says, eyes pleading. "It'll only take a few minutes." He raises his eyebrows, grinning at her, and she realizes he's not going to give in, that there's a reason he wants her to join him, maybe something important. She's about to agree when another thought breaks in: maybe this lapse is a sign of his age, his memory finally failing.

"I've been to your office, Pop," she reminds him, "dozens of times. Don't you remember?"

"Have you recently?" He looks down at her, his expression one of genuine questioning. "I can't recall many visits, not since you were a student. It's been a long time since you stopped by with any regularity."

She looks at him, blinking rain from her eyes. Is he serious? "I used to bring Jenry by all the time, after you moved the piano. After Jasper died."

"Okay, yes, of course." He smiles, looks relieved. "I remember how he used to bang those keys like he was trying to break them off." He angles the umbrella, rainwater falling between them like a miniature waterfall.

Juliet shakes her head, unable to take any more. "How can you stand there smiling?" Her tone is harsh, accusatory. "When you knew he was here, yet you said nothing to me—"

"He showed up at my door," Winston protests. "What could I do?"

"—and you just sent him to me, without warning."

"What warning did I get?" Winston raises his voice, startling her with an unexpected intensity. He drops the umbrella, its metal tip pointing at her like a spear. "About any of this? You didn't consult with me when you decided to live with that woman, let alone attempt to raise her child."

Juliet sucks her teeth, swallowing the sparks of anger beginning to gather in the pit of her stomach. "We did it together, okay? Both of us. He was my child, too."

Winston shakes out his umbrella, water popping from the surface like grease escaping a frying pan. "If you say so."

"Really? That's how you show your support, with a shrug and that smug look on your face? As if you're enjoying this?"

He steps toward her, and her first reaction is to step back. She isn't afraid of her father, but she often feels a sense of unease around him, one that borders on distrust. He stops short, his feet shuffling on the sidewalk. She glances down. He's wearing wingtips, not his usual galoshes, which shine in the streetlight as if they were just polished.

"I find no pleasure in your despair, sweetheart. I've lost a son, two sons in fact, and I wouldn't wish that sorrow on anyone, let alone my own flesh and blood." His voice catches in his throat. "But unlike me, you get another chance." He holds the umbrella like a cane, tapping the damp ground in emphasis. "Here, right now. You can try again."

"Try again?" Juliet would laugh if she weren't so annoyed. "As if I can make up for missing his whole childhood."

"No," Winston says. "Don't focus on the past. You can only go forward."

Juliet shakes her head. "He doesn't want that."

"He's eighteen, he doesn't know what he wants."

"He wants to know Jasper."

"And he can, through you. You can give him that." Winston's face opens up, his eyes wide and bright. "Isn't that what you want? What your brother would want?"

Juliet turns away. She can't think about Jasper right now, not before figuring out what she wants.

"Wasn't it amazing," Winston says, lowering his voice, "to see him all grown up? To see how he looks like us, like you and Jasper, like your mother?" He goes on, "And he's got that Patterson spark, as if he's ready to take on the world."

Juliet feels herself relax, lulled by the soothing timbre of his voice. These are things she, too, had thought, even when Jenry was a little boy, and she can hardly believe her father is giving them voice. She always claimed not to need his approval, but had secretly longed for this moment: for him to welcome her son.

"I know what you're thinking," Winston says, stepping closer, "but don't let pride get—"

"Pride? Is that what you think this is?" The edge in her voice is back. "I'm in shock, okay? I don't know how to feel."

"Our feelings are irrelevant. The boy needs us. He didn't ask for this."

She pictures Jenry standing in the restaurant, remembers what he did ask for. *I'm asking you.* The wind blows her coat open, exposing her neck to the damp air.

"But I know this much," she says with certainty. "I don't want to lose him again."

Her father looks down at her. "Then don't run away this time."

She shakes her head, feels her wet hair slap against her cheeks. "Why can't you understand? She left—not me. I didn't have a choice." Juliet walks to her car, turning back to him from the driver's door. "Was I supposed to spend my whole life following the trail of a ghost?"

He opens the umbrella to its full size, the dark nylon hanging like a canopy over his head, his face in shadow. "But he wasn't a ghost," he says, his voice softer now, almost comforting. "He was a living, breathing human being. He was alive, and where were you?" He pulls on a pair of thin leather gloves, eyes locked on hers the entire time. "You had a choice, Juliet, and you chose yourself, your career. I supported that, encouraged your talent and big dreams. But what's your excuse now?" He pauses to let the question sink in. "You have to make a different choice. Trust me when I tell you: *we cannot escape history.*"

She recognizes the line, taken from Lincoln's address to Congress a month before signing the Emancipation Proclamation, something he quoted so often during her childhood she knew the rest by heart. *We hold the power and bear the responsibility.* He's made his point, but she keeps it to herself. Gives him no clear sign of victory.

Juliet gets in her car as Winston walks away. She starts the engine and turns the defrost on high. The air is cool against her face, as it works to slowly defog the windows, drying her eyes before any tears can form. *We must think anew, and act anew.*

She glances into the rearview mirror, sees the blurred image of her father retreating into the darkness, like a ship pulling away from shore. Something inside her wants him to come back, to turn around, to look at her, but he doesn't. He walks on, head held high and gait steady, and soon his whole body is swallowed by the black sea of night.

· 5 ·

Juliet has the name of his dorm—
Hegeman Hall—and a room number—401—and when she shows up
carrying the gift bag, the proof he'd asked for, she feels no different than
the coeds she passes on the way in, giddy and nervous on her way to
visit a boy she hardly knows. Marisa texted her his phone number, too,
but Juliet couldn't bring herself to call. After the run-in with her father,
feeling emboldened and a little reckless, she decides to stop by unannounced. If he's home, she will show him the photographs; if not, she
will take it as a sign that it's best to leave the past where it belongs—
stored in boxes tucked away in the attic, hidden from even her memory.

Her feet echo on the floor as she enters the building, noting that the
tiles look exactly the same as the last time she'd walked this hallway,
when she was stumbling out before sunrise, hungover and hoping to get
to her freshman dorm before her roommate noticed she was gone. She
finds number 401, the corner room, and checks for light under the door.
Someone appears to be home. She knocks, and a young woman with long
blond hair answers, holding out a twenty-dollar bill.

"The ad said thirty minutes or less, so my second pizza is free."

"Excuse me?"

She looks from Juliet's face to the small bag in her hand. "You don't seem like the delivery guy."

"Nope, sorry."

She leans into the hallway. "Damn, I bet he got lost again."

"I'm looking for Jenry." Juliet peeks into the room. "Does he live here?"

"He does. Right over there, in fact." She points to the well-made bed in the corner. "But he's not here right now."

"Are you . . . his roommate?" Juliet feels about a thousand years old.

"No, no way." Then she adds, "Well, not yet." She has a confidence that reminds Juliet of her younger self. "But don't tell him I said that."

"Got it." Juliet starts to turn away. "I'll come back—"

"Hang on, he's in a study group." She points down the brightly lit hallway. "Right across from the bathroom, if you want to stop in."

"Actually, do you mind," Juliet says, stepping into the room, "if I just leave this here?" She places the bag next to a stack of library books, the top one a survey of African literature.

"Seriously, he won't mind the interruption. He'll thank you, I swear." She tucks a long strand of hair behind her ear so she can look Juliet in the eyes.

"Just make sure he gets the bag. Please." Juliet smiles briefly.

"Are you his sister or something?"

Juliet laughs awkwardly. "No, I'm definitely *not* his sister."

The young woman pulls out her cell phone. "Well, you do look like him." The flash momentarily blinds Juliet as she snaps a picture.

"What the hell was that?" Juliet's surprise makes her sound angry.

"I just texted him your picture. To get him out of the room."

"You can't just take a person's picture without asking." Juliet knows she's overreacting, but she doesn't like this generation's impulsivity, or entitlement.

"Oh. Well." The girl looks genuinely regretful. "Here, I'll erase it."

They hear a door in the hallway close, then the sound of flip-flops slapping the tiles. A few seconds later, Jenry walks into the room.

"See?" The young woman turns to her. "Told you it would work."

If he's surprised, Jenry doesn't show it. "I see you've met Lexi," he says coolly.

"Actually, not officially." Juliet offers Lexi her hand. "I'm Juliet."

"Nice to meet you," Lexi says. "Sorry about the picture." Juliet shrugs.

Jenry turns to Lexi. "Pizza here yet?"

"Nope. I think the guy got lost. We should order Thai next time."

"I heard they're giving out donuts at the Rock, if you return an overdue library book." Jenry eyes the books on his desk. "Maybe you can get us a few?"

"Very funny," Lexi says, but then Juliet sees Jenry lift his eyes and Lexi catches the hint. "Sure, I'll be back in a few." She grabs a jacket from a hook behind the door and disappears.

Juliet is about to say something, offer an explanation, when he holds up his phone, showing her the photo Lexi took. "I've seen mug shots better than this."

"You kids and those damn smartphones, like you all want to be paparazzi."

"I'm a real technophobe actually." Jenry tosses it onto his bed. "No Instagram, no Facebook. I only got this because my mom was freaked out about me being so far away," he says. "Texting's okay, but it's so . . ."

"Impersonal?" Juliet offers, which is her opinion as well.

"Exactly," he says.

Juliet laughs. "You must be real popular with your classmates."

Jenry shrugs. "I'm a Black Cuban who plays classical piano. I never fit in." After a beat, he pulls out the desk chair. "Do you want to sit down?"

"No, I'm fine. I just came by to give you these." She picks up the gift bag, pulling out the tissue paper she had stuffed on the top. "The proof you asked for." She unwraps the bandana, hands him the stack of photographs. He holds them carefully.

"I didn't mean it like that," he says, his tone regretful. "I just wanted to see . . . something."

"It's okay," she says. "Go ahead."

He thumbs through the prints nervously, not really focusing on any of the images. "Are these for me, or do you need them back?"

That hadn't occurred to her, him wanting to keep them. "Um, no. Yeah, you can keep them." She jams the bandana back into the gift bag. "Sure, that's fine."

"You can have them back." He holds them out. "I'm not trying to keep—"

"No, they're yours." She forces herself to smile. "I want you to have them."

"Maybe I can take pictures of them," he teases, "with my phone?"

"A picture of a picture," she says. "How very twenty-first century."

He reviews the pile as Juliet, desperate to look at anything else, glances out the window. She sees the spires of the church next door, its stone tiled roof appearing close enough to touch, and beyond that a hillside of red maple trees, their brilliant show of autumn leaves now black against the night sky.

"I didn't know I was so chubby," he says, holding a picture up to the light. "And almost blond."

"For the first few months we called you *Rubio*. Didn't anyone tell you that?"

"Crazy," he says, moving on to the next picture without answering. "Oh my God, look at my mom, she was so young. And her hair was so long."

He is quiet for a long time, flipping through the photographs with a sense of calm Juliet can't help but envy. Uncomfortable in the small room, part of her wants to leave, but another, stronger part wants this: to watch him rediscover their past, secretly hoping it will jog some buried memories and magically erase all the distance between them.

He singles out a picture of them in the backyard: baby Jenry wearing a cowboy hat and riding on her back like a pony. Her hair is loose, covering her face, yet she looks happy. "This is you?"

She nods. "You had a thing for horses."

He looks surprised. "No way. They're too unpredictable."

She shrugs. "Well, things change." Her voice dips, and she can feel herself getting emotional, so she forces a smile, dismisses the sadness. "Keep going," she urges, "you haven't seen the best ones."

"Wait, is this my birthday party?" He shows her a photo of him sitting in front of a plate of cupcakes.

"Actually, that was *my* birthday. You insisted on tasting the frosting from each one. Chocolate with cream cheese frosting. It was your favorite back then."

He looks up. "It's still my favorite," he says, eyes wide like she just performed a magic trick.

"Your birthday's in there, too." She points to the stack, drawing him back to the pictures. "The one where you're sitting on my lap licking the candle."

"Oh yeah, here it is." He stops to stare at the picture, dimples lighting up his face. "Damn, I was a greedy little guy."

"All kids are greedy," she says. "It's a survival instinct."

He nods, then continues to flip through the stack while she walks around the room, pretending to look around with great interest as she notices for the first time the strangely bare walls. During her college days, her dorm walls were covered—posters of Georgia O'Keeffe orchids and the Flatiron Building in Manhattan, portraits of Malcolm X and Gandhi, batik sheets and kente cloths hanging from the ceiling, Edward Hopper postcards of bleak New England towns taped in the windowpanes. Only three things hang on Jenry's side of the room: a poster of Thelonious Monk above the desk, a Yankees pennant beside the window, and a full-sized Cuban flag over his bed. His nightstand holds a travel-sized alarm clock and a used copy of *Things Fall Apart*; his single bed has only one pillow. A lack of enthusiasm seems to dominate this dorm room, which speaks to either his minimalist decorating sensibility or his current mood—Juliet finds both options somewhat distressing.

"Where's this?" Jenry considers a picture of the three of them at a local pond—Marisa holds his right hand while she takes the other, each one helping him stand in the shallow water. He looks about a year old.

"That's Lincoln Woods," she answers. "We took you all the time, since it's closer than the beach." He seems interested, so she continues, "I used to go there as a kid, with my brother. He taught me how to swim at that beach."

"Is this . . ."—Jenry's eyes narrow—". . . where he died?"

"No, no. That was in the Berkshires, near a cabin my parents owned."

He nods, then motions to the photographs. "Do you have any pictures of them in here?" His eyes are wide, as if it has just occurred to him that she could connect him to more relatives, perhaps even his entire family tree. She inhales, wonders how much to share, how much to conceal.

"My mother died when I was a child," she says. "And my father . . . well, you met him. He used to take a lot of photographs when we were kids. But all that changed once she died. He still owns the cabin, but he's never gone back, not since Jasper." She plays with the handles on the gift bag. "He hasn't quite recovered. From any of it."

Jenry looks at her, his eyes warm and open. Juliet can't be sure, but the anger he had during their talk at the restaurant seems to be dissolving, as if he's starting to feel something for them, perhaps even see them as his family. "Sorry, I know I ask a lot of questions," Jenry says.

"No, it's fine. You're entitled to them." Juliet smiles, letting him know she means it, but even as she says the words, she starts to feel a slight panic, realizing she's digging herself into a hole; every response seems to pose another question, and some of them she may not want to answer. She steps toward the door, suddenly feeling restless. "I should get going."

"Oh. Okay." He plays nervously with the stack of photographs, straightens them like a deck of cards. "I just . . . have a lot of questions. And, you know, it's cool being able to ask you . . . about the pictures. And whatever." He chews on the side of his lip.

"Yeah, I get that it's a lot. We don't have to do it all tonight."

He's looking at the pictures again, slower this time, his finger tracing the sharp edges of each print. "It's so weird," he finally says, still not looking at her. "I was this little boy."

Yes, Juliet wants to say, *and weirder still to think I love that little boy, that I love you,* but instead she reaches for the doorknob, forcing herself to stay in the present, to see him as he is now—not how she remembers him.

"Time is a very strange thing," she says, making her voice sound light and breezy as she turns the knob, a solid brass orb that feels good in her hand, and oddly familiar, as if it were the same doorknob to her childhood bedroom. She props the door open with her boot before turning around in the doorway, looking back into the room with an eager gaze.

"I can't believe I'm back in this dorm, more than twenty-five years later, and it looks exactly the same." She touches the wall, running her fingers across the painted brick. "I swear, this paint is exactly the same color they used back then. They must call it 'dormitory beige.'" He laughs and it makes her smile.

"But I bet you didn't have Wi-Fi."

She holds up her hands. "You got me there." She's teasing, but the gesture alone seems like a confession, and she quickly drops her arms to her sides. She can feel an imperceptible shift in the air as his energy changes. His mouth closes into a tightly drawn line.

"You know what's funny," he says. "When I left the restaurant that day I thought, *I never want to see her again.* I seriously thought that. I'm not just saying it to be mean."

"That's okay, I hear you. And if it's what you want—"

"No, it's not okay," he interrupts. "And it's not what I want." He shakes his head again, raising his voice. "Christ, don't you get it? I want to be mad at you. I want to be angry." The look of fury on his face causes Juliet to take a step away from him. "But I also want to spend time with you." His voice cracks and Juliet looks away, unable to tolerate his vulnerability, or her own. "And I want to ask you questions. I think I deserve that. I have the right to know what happened."

He looks at her like he's waiting for an answer, so she nods. "Of course you do." Her voice is weak and hollow, betraying how she feels on the inside. She has made so many mistakes, broken things she can never fix. Her face turns red with shame. How can she ever make up for all that?

"What does all this mean?" he cries, waving the stack of prints at her. "So what that we shared the first two years of my life—does that really make you my *parent*?" The veins in his neck bulge as his voice strains. "Do you become my mother just because you were there?"

Juliet has been waiting for this, has asked herself all the same questions. "I don't know," she says, "what any of it means." But inside she says what she does know, what she truly feels: *I became your mother when I lost you.*

Frustrated, he tosses the photos onto his desk, where they scatter to cover the surface. "What am I supposed to do with this? With you?" His folds his arms to hide their trembling. "I don't even know who you are."

The sting of his words pricks her awake, like a finger nudging her from a restless sleep. She shouldn't have come to do his mother's bidding. This isn't her place. She shakes her head. "I'm sorry. I thought I was helping, but maybe . . . maybe it's too late." She glances through the opened door, the hallway offering escape. His voice stops her, just as she's about to take it.

"So that's it? You just leave? Again?"

The sound of his voice, soft yet pleading, makes her throat tighten. She looks down at the floor, notices how small her feet look, even encased in a pair of men's motorcycle boots. This truth betrays her: whenever she tries to look strong, inside she is often weak, close to breaking. She exhales before lifting her head. "What do you want from me?" she asks, her voice even and calm.

"I don't know," he shouts. "Am I supposed to? You show up here and you bring these pictures and I feel something, I do, but then it makes me feel disloyal to my mother, like if I let you in, it somehow lessens who she is."

"I don't lessen her. How could I?"

"Exactly," he says, as if trying to convince himself. "I know you don't. She's my mother. And you . . . you're . . ." He stares at his hands, stretching the long fingers, before closing them into fists. "You're like my . . . aunt, I guess—"

"First sister, now aunt?" Juliet stifles a laugh. "Fantastic." When it's clear he doesn't follow, she says, "Before. Lexi asked if I was your sister."

He shrugs. "I'll explain it to her later."

"Is she your girlfriend?"

"Just a friend." He gestures to the library books. "We have a class together."

"African Lit is a tough course. Is Anani still teaching it?"

He nods, then asks, "So you went here, too?"

"A Patterson tradition." Then, slightly irritated, she adds, "Yes, we got tuition remission, and yes, we were qualified. In case you were going to ask."

"I wasn't."

She crosses her arms, suddenly defensive. "I'm not your aunt."

Jenry's face holds a calm, logical expression. "You're my father's sister. That makes you my aunt. It's not a huge leap."

Juliet feels her stomach tense. Maybe it's better this way. Maybe this is a truth he can swallow, something they can all live with. She forces herself to ask, "Is that what you want?" and holds her breath as she waits for his answer.

He turns away, facing the darkened window. "I don't want any of this." He sits on the edge of the bed, staring at his hands. "Not now. Not like this."

"Okay, well." Juliet doesn't know what else to say. She tried again and failed. Now she wants to get so far away it will seem like she was never here. There are many ways to leave, but only one that promises to wipe her memory clean. Later, when telling Noelle the story, she will trace it all—the slip, the relapse, the argument with her father—back to this moment.

As she reaches the door, she hears his voice, the whisper of an apology.

"I'm sorry. I'm not trying to be an asshole. You seem like a nice person."

"Don't—" She holds up her hand. "It's fine." She can already see the stairwell, can feel the shock of cold when she reaches the outside. She is already gone.

"I'm not saying you have to leave."

"It's better this way," she says, "so we don't have to keep doing this." She wraps her scarf around her neck, grateful to have something to hide behind. "The last thing you need is to have your life turned upside down. You're in college—you should be drinking too much and studying for hours. Sleeping with girls you don't know well enough and writing them songs they don't deserve."

His eyes suddenly flash, lighting his face from across the room. "Wait—how do you know I write songs?" He peers intently at her, as if her answer will determine if she passes or fails.

"You have a music scholarship." She shrugs. "I put two and two together."

"But I never told you about the scholarship." He stands now, walks toward her with purpose. His body—long and lean, more like a dancer than a pianist—soon blocks the lamp, the only source of light in the room, and she can no longer make out his expression.

She inhales, considers lying. "Your mother told me," she says.

"You talked to my mother?" He is beside her now, looking into her eyes.

"She's worried about you. You're the center of her world, Jenry. And now you're a thousand miles away and won't return her calls."

"I don't have anything to say. Not right now." He looks like a little boy. A wounded boy. "She lied to me. For years."

"You should call anyway. Or text, email, something. Don't just disappear."

"You're going to lecture me about disappearing?" His eyes look at her mockingly.

She raises a finger, warning him. "You only know half the story."

"So you're calling my mother a liar?"

"I'm just saying . . . we each have our own perspective." She's not sure she believes that, but it sounds reasonable, and for his sake, she hopes he buys it. Better for him to think she's rational and fair, instead of the long-suffering grudge holder she knows herself to be. Marisa knew that side of her, and it never seemed to do their relationship any good.

"Not that anyone cares, but from my perspective, you've both lied for years." He states this like a fact, not an accusation, yet it still riles her.

"Oh, come on, it's not that simple. To label us liars and think you understand what we did? It was a different time, it wasn't easy for anyone. There were no lesbian mom groups, no gay marriage. People didn't understand, maybe they still don't." This brings a different angle to the argument, and she wonders if he can hear it in her voice.

"Well, isn't this a surprise?" Jenry says, collecting the pictures from his desk. "To hear you defend her." He turns away before he can see the look of shock on her face. Defend Marisa, is that what she's doing? She knows she can't leave on that line.

"I'm not defending her, okay? I'm just trying to understand what she was feeling. To think about what I would want, if I was your—" She stops herself. "If it were me."

"You can say it," he says, looking at her without blinking. "If you were my . . ." He waits for her to finish the sentence.

"If I were your mother," she says, as tears well in her eyes. His face softens as if he wants to smile.

"And what about if you were me, what would you want then?"

His voice is tender like a child's, and she can see how he's opening up to her, how he's letting her see him. If she wants this, if Juliet wants to really know him, all she has to do is stay in the conversation and answer his questions. All she has to do is look at him, and be willing to be seen in return.

Juliet exhales slowly. "I don't know how to answer that." She is telling the truth, but she knows it won't be enough. He isn't testing her anymore, he's looking for advice; like most young people, he needs a path to follow. He sits down, showing that he will wait for her, give her however long she needs.

She looks around the room, sees his roommate's messy bed, his Jay-Z poster, the psychology book that looks like it's never been opened, a glass pipe that doubles as a paperweight; she sees Jenry's bookshelf—dozens of books on music theory and a few slim volumes that look like poetry, a Leonard Bernstein biography he borrowed from the library—and then her eyes come to rest on the boy himself, sitting back on his narrow bed, his legs extended like a spider, arms long and muscled, a rich brown against the pale duvet cover, while his fingers keep tapping—always in motion, never at rest. She decides to answer truthfully, to expose herself, instead of giving him the inauthentic gift of advice.

"If I were you," she starts slowly, dragging the words out to buy more time, "I would probably want . . . to be left alone. To read my books and listen to my music, maybe get high with my roommate. And if that didn't work, I'd probably want to quit—not just music, everything."

As soon as it's out of her mouth she wants to take it back, wants to say something encouraging and uplifting, parent-like. Something a therapist would sanction. But then he's nodding his head and she realizes that telling him the truth was important—not because of what she said, but because it will give him the right to do the same. It will give them a place to connect.

"I've thought of that," he admits. He plays with his bracelet, tightening the leather around his wrist like a cuff. His fingers always seem to be moving. Juliet recalls a time when the same could be said about her. "I already dropped my theory class," he continues, "and I stopped playing with the orchestra. It's crazy how simple it was, to just walk away." His dark eyes stare straight at the wall.

The news hits Juliet like a punch. "Don't quit," she hears herself saying, the exact thing people said to her. She knows how trite and hypocritical it sounds, but she means it. She doesn't want him to give it up, to make the same mistakes she did. She wants what all parents want: for her child to be stronger than her.

"Don't. Quit."

Jenry shrugs. "I can't focus. I read the same paragraph over and over and I still can't remember it. And when I try to write, the notes just blur together." He is still staring at the wall, unwilling to look her in the eye. "I can't hear anything clearly. Not like I used to. It's like I'm always underwater."

Juliet remembers that exact feeling, and the spiral that followed; first Jasper's death, and then losing Jenry—that's when she really started to drink heavily, all day long, and even though she kept playing, it wasn't the same.

"It's easy to quit," she says, moving closer to him. "And almost impossible to start again." She sits down. "Don't do it. Believe me, it's not worth it."

He looks up at her, his eyes so dark she can't see the pupils. "But you just said that's what you would do."

"No, I said that's what I'd *want* to do. Eventually, it's what I did. But it wasn't the same. I was a total mess, a train wreck." She stops, not sure if she's making it better or worse. "Listen, I get that this is a fucked-up situation. One you didn't create. But you still have a lot going for you." She's leaning over him now, gesturing with her hands, and as she does it she tries not to think of her father; tries to forget how he used to lecture them as children, as if the dinner table were no different than the classroom; tries to ignore how similar she is to him, how much he passed on in nature and nurture. "And this thing you have, this ability to turn ideas into sound, to make music, it's bigger than everything else in your life—even this moment. It's not a part of your life, it *is* your life. It's who you are. You can't walk away from it and think you won't be leaving yourself behind."

She has no idea where these words come from, isn't even aware that it's something she believes; it's possible, in fact, that she doesn't believe it, but she still understands it's the right thing to say, knows it might have made a difference if someone had said it to her, and if she had believed them.

"Maybe I want to leave myself behind." Jenry looks down, his eyes examining the buttons on the duvet cover, his fingertips running along the seam.

"Of course you do," she says, her voice filled with compassion. "We all do. But you can't. I promise you, you can't." She watches as he slips his fingers into the opening, covering his hand at the wrist. He squeezes the fabric tight, cutting off circulation.

"When I was a kid," he says, "I used to wonder what would happen if I lost my hand in a freak accident. If I would still try to play." He has a crooked smile when he says this, but his voice is heavy, sinister almost. The tone scares her.

"And yet here you are, perfectly healthy and threatening to quit." She pulls his hand out from the covers. "See?" The blood returns as she bends his fingers and pinches the flesh on his palm. "You're completely intact." Satisfied, she returns his hand to the bed, arranging it by his side like a doll. He stares at the limb as if it belongs to someone else, as if he doesn't have the power to control it.

"All those years—the practicing, the recitals—I was playing for him, because I thought he'd given me this gift. I thought it would bring me closer to him or something dumb like that, but it turns out he didn't even play. And now," he says, shaking his head, "now it's too late for me to become something else."

Juliet exhales. Of course that's ridiculous, but she remembers being his age and thinking the path was already set, that she had committed to a certain way of life. She, too, believed it was too late to reinvent herself. And then Marisa reminded her it was possible, and after getting drunk on rum and Cokes, Juliet started to believe her.

"Jenry. You're eighteen years old. It's not too late."

"Bullshit," he yells out, his voice rising in pitch as he grabs the cover, balling it into his fist. "It's all too late. You're too late and it's too late for my father and it's too late for me." Tears fill his eyes; they shine like they're made of glass.

Juliet, not sure what else to do, places her hand on his knee; her movements are slow, measured, as if approaching a bird she doesn't want to fly away. It's clear to her that she's being tested—not just by him, but by the situation. She's spent the last sixteen years longing to see him, to get to know him—to mother him—and now that she has the opportunity, will she take it?

"When a person has a gift," she says, "it's never too late." She squeezes his knee in emphasis.

"Gift?" he says with disdain. "If anything, it's an affliction. A disease I inherited and now can't get rid of."

Juliet wants to laugh, remembers saying the same thing to Marisa, but she knows he's serious. He drops the cover, wrinkled from being in his grasp, his empty hand now twitching by his side. Without thinking, she covers his hand with her own. Such a simple act: to hold a child's hand. But in this moment, it feels both revolutionary, in the fact that she initiated it, and healing, in the realization that he allows it.

"You have this thing because she wanted you to have it. Your mother. She wanted you to always have a place to go to without leaving the room."

"No," Jenry says, his voice even now, devoid of the anguish he'd expressed just a few moments before. "She didn't want me to escape. She wanted me to be like you." He speaks with certainty, as if arriving at an obvious conclusion, saying what they all know to be fact. "It makes perfect sense. I play the piano because you played the piano. Not my father, you."

Yes, Juliet wants to shout, *because you were not Jasper's son, you were mine, you have always been mine*. Instead, she says nothing, afraid her voice will betray her if she speaks. She squeezes his hand, hoping to convey something beyond words.

"She couldn't tell me the truth," he says, "but she did try to give me some part of you."

Juliet hadn't thought of this, and now that she hears it, she knows he's right. Marisa loved her, and even as she punished Juliet with her disappearance, she didn't want to punish her son. She didn't want him to lose everything Juliet had given him, so she kept one thing: the music. And through that gift, Marisa could believe that Juliet was somehow still present in his life.

"But your father told me you quit," he says, pulling his hand away, "and no one knows why."

It was too hard, she thinks, *and I was weak, and I didn't know how to hold on to anything after I lost you.* But in place of that confession all she can think to say is "It was complicated."

"Everything's complicated," he shoots back at her. "Does that make it okay to quit?" After a long silence, he tries again. "Can you at least tell me when?"

She sits back in the chair. "A long time ago."

"After we left?"

"Yes. But not right after. I played for many years." She looks out the window over his head. "Until I just . . . stopped."

"Why did you stop?"

"It was too hard."

"Why?"

"I was a drunk."

"Why?" he says again, his voice loud and unrelenting.

She glances toward the desk, sees the scattered array of photographs. She searches for a glimpse of her face, trying to remember the person she was.

"I was afraid."

"Afraid of what?"

She exhales, not sure how much to say. "I was afraid of a lot of things. To be mediocre. To be great. To face the responsibility it brings." She swallows hard. "But mostly, I was afraid to feel. To let myself touch that sadness, to actually feel those losses. My mother. My brother. You. The alcohol, believe it or not, helped me survive. Until it almost killed me." She drops her head, exhausted from telling the truth. She is looking at the floor, so she doesn't see Jenry move, just feels his hand against her back, trying to comfort her. The feeling brings tears to her eyes.

"I have an idea," Jenry says, "to make us both feel better." He gets up from the bed. "I want to hear you play." Without waiting for an answer, he grabs a set of keys from the desk.

Her first instinct is to laugh, stunned by the absurdity of a request that at one time was routine. Instead, she shakes her head. "I don't play anymore."

It sounds like a lie to say it so bluntly, but she knows it's the truth. It's been more than five years since she sat at a piano bench, longer since she heard any notes in her head. That final year, of playing without the music she'd always heard—that continual sound, as reliable as a heartbeat yet suddenly gone, like waking up deaf—was the most painful of her life, and why she'd remained in an almost perpetual state of intoxication, her drinking so extreme she felt certain that one day she wouldn't wake up at all. She'd often wondered, in the days since, if that had been her plan, if suicide was yet another thing she had failed to accomplish.

"Why should that stop you?" he says, more a statement than a question. He grabs a fleece sweatshirt and pulls it on. "I've got spare keys to the practice rooms. They aren't performance grade, but the sound's good enough."

"Jenry." She hasn't moved. "It's late. I should have been home hours ago."

"What do you have to lose?" He stands over her, his face more animated than she's ever seen it. He looks as if all his future happiness depends upon her answer, as if giving him this one thing will make up for all she hasn't done.

"I was a different person back then. With a different life." She finally stands, pushing the chair back under the desk. "I wasn't even that good."

"Don't be so modest. I've read the reviews. I want to know if you're as good as they said you were."

"If this is a contest, you win." She feels strangely defensive, refusing to prove herself to him. "I didn't stop because I wanted to stop. I quit because the music stopped coming."

"How do you know it won't start again?"

"It's not that easy."

"How will you know if you won't try?" he asks, giving her a crooked smile, showing off his dimples. Damn. Has anyone ever been able to refuse him?

Underneath the smile, she sees something else: that his need is much bigger than he lets on. Seeing her play will show him what he deserves to see—who she really is—and this, she knows, she cannot deny him. She realizes this is the moment she's been waiting for, though she's dreaded and denied it for years. She has to be willing to face her fear, to show herself to him, battle scars and all. Yes, he may reject her, but it will be the real her he is rejecting, not the facsimile she's created. With sobriety, she has learned that humility is always better than grandiosity; the simple truth always better than the outrageous lie. Perhaps she has lost her gift at the piano, but that alone is not tragic; the real tragedy would be for her to stay in the shadows, afraid to find out.

He opens the door. "Don't you want to know if I'm any good?" He holds up the keys, hoping to entice her. "Come on, you know you're curious." She smiles at him, appreciating the change in tactic.

"Who am I to say if you've got chops?" The question is her final attempt at refusal, but her voice softens, a subtle resignation that he seems to recognize.

What is a mother who won't sacrifice for her child? This is what motherhood is all about, she will come to understand later, doing what's best for your child regardless of the pain it causes you. Marisa understood that all those years ago, when Juliet was only focused on her art, foolishly thinking that the rest would wait for her: family, love, partnership. Today, Juliet has learned to put those things first; that is what has kept her sober, kept her married and faithful, committed to Noelle and their future family.

When Jenry was still in diapers, Juliet used to sit with him at the piano, her large hands covering his as they played chords together. She never imagined how they would grow to be larger than her own, with a broader span, a wider grasp; she never imagined him growing taller or stronger than her—yet here he is. As she steps into the hallway, she notices their shadows on the floor: separate at first, but merging as she joins him, his shadow enveloping hers as they come together, as she lets it eclipse her own.

· 6 ·

When Juliet wakes up the following morning, she wants a drink. Not water, not club soda, not iced tea. She wants a real drink, ninety proof or above, and the desire alone is enough to scare her. It's not even the taste, really, it's the feeling she wants—the sweet hot tingling of escape. The old-timers warned her years ago that this day would come, when the idea would arrive and her brain would have no real defense against it. But knowing it and experiencing it are two different things, and the reality of what she's facing threatens to keep her in bed all day. She buries her head under the comforter, breathes in the fresh laundry smell, feels the smooth, cool sheets with the side of her face, like a cat rubbing its whiskers against a table leg. *Stay in the moment*, she tells herself. *Stay right here. Feel the warmth of the bed. Don't be afraid.*

This works for a while, but as soon as she sits up, the desire is back— clawing at her throat as her head spins with things she hasn't considered in years: an icy pint sweating on a cardboard coaster; the smell of boiled peanuts in snack bowls on the counter; the steady spin of a bar stool, its leather seat smoothed from years of rubbing against worn jeans; the harmless flirtation with a bartender; the crunch of shells beneath her boots as she stumbles to the bathroom. *No, wait*—she shakes her head and forces herself to stand—*don't go back there.* But she can't stop it. Next she imagines the taste: the nutty hops mixed with pumpkin, black cherry, or burnt chocolate; she remembers sipping the half-inch head of a pint poured too fast, then licking off the foam mustache. No, no, no—she can't do this. She walks to the bathroom, the phrase *when you romanticize, you fantasize* stuck on repeat in her head, something she must've heard at a recent meeting, a God shot she proceeds to ignore.

She turns on the tap and remembers breaking the seal on a liter of gin, that satisfying snap. As she washes her hands, she hears the delicious, fizzy opening crack of the first can in a six-pack; pictures the remainders dangling from her pinky in their plastic necklaces; remembers their weight dragging her hand to the ground. She splashes her face with cold water. When she looks in the mirror, she sees the smooth shoulder of a wine bottle, its green glass darkened from a nice tangy red, Spanish or Argentinian maybe, something foreign—instead of her own reflection.

Fuck. She's in trouble. She knows this without a doubt, but she doesn't want to panic. Panic raises her cortisol, which makes her feel afraid, which makes her want to drink. She needs to stay calm. And busy; busy will keep her from spending all day in her head, a place she should never wander alone. But here she is. Alone in the house with hours of unscheduled time ahead of her. She dries her face with a towel. Closes her eyes. Breathes. She wonders if she should reach out to her sponsor or Noelle, but a feeling of shame starts to grow across her chest as she imagines sending the text. The thought of having to admit to these feelings, having to own and label them, is too much vulnerability for her current state. If she can just get control of it first; no need to worry them unnecessarily.

She wipes up the water around the sink, then hangs the towel on its hook by the door. It falls to the floor, but she doesn't pick it up. Doesn't turn the light off when she leaves the bathroom. Doesn't make her bed. She gets dressed—track pants and old sneakers, an oversized men's hoodie—and decides on a plan.

First step: keep it to herself. This makes her feel a tiny bit better, just knowing she doesn't have to tell anyone. Not a secret exactly, but not really anyone else's business. Her sponsor has her own problems, a busy family, an important job. And Noelle would get upset that Juliet hadn't told her about Jenry's return earlier. Telling her the truth now would just create more problems. This is where Juliet turns a corner, where things have just gotten worse, but foolishly she doesn't realize it yet. She thinks she's still in control.

Second step: distraction. She starts with a list of chores, things she's neglected all fall like changing the burnt-out light bulbs in the garage, replacing the batteries in all the smoke detectors, and swapping out the screens for the storm windows. She takes a few trips to the Salvation Army to drop off bags of old clothes and boxes of books she's stored for decades, thinking they might be useful. As if she has time to reread *Giovanni's Room* or *Their Eyes Were Watching God* when she can't even get through an issue of *The New Yorker* in the same week it comes out. Thankfully, these mindless tasks take up several hours, and suddenly it's time to leave for the restaurant.

Things don't get easier at work. She can barely concentrate at the grill and overcooks the lamb chops; her Munroe Dairy order arrives late; the apples for her tarts are bitter and the cherries too sweet; the soufflé doesn't rise properly. On edge and irritable, she barks at her sous chef all night, and in her agitated state ends up slicing into her palm as she quarters boiled beets for the special; the beet juice is so dark and her hands already so stained, she doesn't notice her blood on the cutting board for at least ten minutes. It is only when she dries them on her hand towel and sees the streaks of blood soaked into the thick white cotton that she realizes she's been cut.

"Fuck." She washes her hands with cold water, then pours rubbing alcohol over the cut. She tries to ignore the pain. The edge is smooth and she's relieved it won't need stitches. Taping her hand, she takes a break in the pantry, eyeing the wooden crates that house dozens of bottles of wine.

"Hey, Lonny," she calls out to the dishwasher, still eyeing the crates.

"Yeah, boss?"

"You got a cigarette?"

He walks over to her. "But you don't smoke no more."

She looks at him. He shrugs, reaching into the deep pockets of his checkered khakis. He pulls out a bruised pack of menthols and hands it to her. She takes two cigarettes and smokes them back-to-back without pleasure; after, she chews mint leaves to freshen her mouth, and goes back to work. The cut still throbs, but at least the bleeding has stopped. She makes it through the rest of the shift without incident, and asks Lonny to stick around while she closes up, to keep her company, and keep her out of the pantry. Miraculously, when she gets home an hour later, she's still sober.

By the second day she starts to use the tools: she makes phone calls to other people, just to ask how they're doing; reads AA literature over breakfast; increases her prayer and meditation from zero to four minutes a day; and doubles her weekly meetings. She hates all these things and is certain they won't help take away the craving, but other people—people who look sane and happy and keep stressful jobs and stay in long-term relationships—swear by them, and they have handled life without booze for decades. To help get through the wasteland of hours between breakfast and dinner, she starts hitting the noon meetings in places she doesn't normally go, like Saint Martin's Church and Butler Hospital, so no one will recognize her. She doesn't want to be seen or questioned, doesn't want to talk about how she's feeling, to think about him or say his name. Doesn't want to remember that night in his dorm room, or worse, those magical, sweet hours in the practice room—not because they were painful, but because they had to end.

A week goes by and slowly it gets easier. Juliet thinks she's gotten through the hardest part. She feels okay, stable, better. She thinks she did the right thing by not telling her sponsor or Noelle. She saved them a lot of anguish. Besides, maybe it wasn't that bad. Maybe she had only imagined how hard it was and how much she wanted a drink. So she drops the extra meetings and stops making phone calls, stops the meditation;

a few days after that, she notices she only prays when she's at a meeting. Two weeks pass since the morning she woke up wanting to drink, and without realizing it, she is back where she started.

ON THE LAST day of October, a chilly Halloween afternoon, Juliet is on her way to her Saturday AA meeting when she misses the turn onto Smith Street. Instead of circling around the block, she keeps going, decides to take the winding, hypnotic curves of Admiral until she finds herself in Elmhurst, passing Providence College and on her way to the densely wooded hills of Smithfield. She pretends to be driving aimlessly, to not realize that she's going to Haxton's, a small neighborhood liquor store that her father used to frequent during her childhood, tucked into a plaza right off 146 in North Providence, far enough from home that no one should recognize her.

Thirty minutes later she's in line, whistling to keep any thought from her mind. She buys a cheap bottle of Merlot—thinking it doesn't really count if it's not her favorite, and might make it easier to stop— and smiles at the pregnant lady behind the counter who never looks up from her phone. Juliet pays cash, using the emergency twenty-dollar bill she keeps hidden in her wallet, behind a photo booth picture of her and Noelle taken at a friend's wedding when they had first started dating, Juliet sneaking a kiss just as the timer went off, Noelle's eyes wide with surprise. Noelle later claimed that as the moment she knew Juliet was the one.

With the wine bottle wrapped in a slim paper bag and sitting upright on the passenger seat, Juliet drives back to Providence. Her palms are sweating, her body already running on the familiar burn of adrenaline. This must be how criminals feel, the drive of anticipation so strong it becomes its own high, a form of intoxication powerful enough to wipe out all traces of doubt.

An hour later she's back in Providence, driving down North Main Street as if she's just come from her meeting and is happily headed to work. But she's not happy, and she's not heading to work. In truth, she doesn't know how she feels, or where she's going; she's caught in a wave of momentum, her body on autopilot—unthinking, unfeeling. She calls Julien, the owner of the restaurant, and calmly tells him she can't work tonight, it's a family emergency; she's never called in sick before, so he lets it go, wishes her good luck. She thanks him and drops her phone after hanging up—now her whole night is free.

Stuck at a red light, she sees the grass at the edge of the road, frosted from a cold snap, notices how many of the trees have lost their leaves, with only their gray limbs remaining—but doesn't feel the brisk air encasing her car, not realizing she forgot to turn on the heat. In the distance, the city looks like a black-and-white photograph, everything cast in shadows. This thought brings her a strange comfort, as if she fits better in a world without color.

She turns onto a side street to avoid the traffic, only to get slowed down by groups of costumed children carrying plastic pumpkins with black handles, their mothers scurrying behind with gloves and hats. Juliet wonders how it could be Halloween. Time seems to elapse at an odd rate lately; her shifts at the restaurant are drawn out like she's moving in slow motion, but the rest of her life runs in warp speed—day to night, weekday to weekend, an afternoon passing in the time it takes to finish a glass of water. The same thing used to happen when she played the piano; an entire day would slip away in what felt like minutes, the way the sun setting along the ocean seems to sink beneath the horizon in mere seconds, falling off the edge of the world in the blink of an eye.

The piano. Even as a word in her head, it has power. She tries to block it from her mind, but can't. Before she can control it, her mind is flipping through dozens of stored images of pianos she's played. Instead of settling on the black Steinway she used for years as an adult, or the antique upright from her childhood, she imagines the beat-up piano in the practice room, sees Jenry playing scales in the dim light as she watched from across the room, his eyes peeking over the top of the piano to look at her, like a child peeking over a book to make sure the parent is still there. The room was cramped, the air stale and cool since the heat was turned off overnight. To appease him, she agreed to sit down, slipping into the chair beside him on the bench. He started with a classical piece to warm up his fingers, but five minutes in he switched tempo, pounding a jazz line that made her hands ache. She had to tuck them into her armpits to keep from touching the keys.

"Fine," he said, "if you're not going to join in, I'm just going to keep playing." He ignored the sheet music and played from memory.

"Good. You need the practice." She smiled playfully.

"Wow, folks got insults," he said, addressing an invisible audience.

"Not true. I like listening to you play," she said, and she meant it.

Soon his pencil came out and he was writing notations on the sheet music. He played the same run over and over again, slightly altering the tempo each time. Looking for something. Juliet unknowingly tapped her foot.

"There, that one," she said, when she heard what he was searching for.

"You think?" He played it again and she nodded.

"But then elongate the note, when you get to the D-flat." She leaned forward to play the run herself, instead of explaining with words. "You see?" Her fingers moved effortlessly across the keys.

He didn't answer, but he played it her way, mimicking the chord patterns until he did it flawlessly.

"Yes, that's right," she said, nodding her head in time with the music.

He moved forward in the piece, and when he got to another hitch the same thing happened. "Don't mess up just because I'm here," she said, urging him on. "You have to play to your own ear, not the audience."

"I can't hear it that well. This—" He played a few stilted chords. "Sounds like this—" He played a few more. "But I can't get the progression right. I know how far apart they are," he tried again, frustrated, "but I just don't *feel* it."

"Concentrate on how they're supposed to sound. Not how you're playing them. Try to hear the pure notes." She played a few chords, stretching her right arm to reach a higher octave. "Listen to each frag-ment. Pay attention to the half tones between them, don't jump the whole tone." She played the pattern again. "Now pull it out and play it over in your mind. Without touching the keys. Just imagine how it should sound." She sat back, her hands folded on her lap. "Can you hear it?" They sat quietly for almost a full minute.

"Yes," he said. "Yes, I think I do." He had a faraway look in his eyes, as if he had stumbled upon a memory, instead of discovering some-thing new.

The overhead light flickered, causing the room to take on an eerie feel. Juliet glanced at the ceiling, afraid they were being watched.

"Don't worry, it happens all the time," Jenry said, standing to tighten the bulb with the cuff of his sweatshirt.

Juliet tilted the music desk, altering the angle so she could better see the sheet music. The paper was worn thin, with dozens of pencil mark-ings filling both margins. His notes looked like hieroglyphics, a text she could hardly decipher.

"You wrote this?" she asked, a hint of pride in her voice.

He shrugged. "Over the summer. It was the last thing I did."

"Not bad," she said, scanning the notes on the grand staff, a dense mix of notes and chord charts, with a complicated series of rhythmic notations above the staff. "But it's a duet. You haven't figured out the balance, but there's way too much for one set of hands."

He placed his fingers lightly on the keys. "I like to challenge myself," he said.

She tried not to laugh. "Okay then. I challenge you to write this as a duet."

"I said challenge *myself*," he repeated, playing an ominous chord for emphasis. "Not be challenged."

She laughed again and stood from her chair. "Here, you take the higher registers." She sat beside him on the piano bench, her knees rest-ing just under the keyslip, feet flat on the ground. "And don't stop, no matter what I do."

They played that way for almost an hour, and she felt a dozen different emotions while sitting that close to him—from fear and dread to a strange sense of shame; from mind-numbing joy and relief to a feeling of peace she couldn't explain. Thinking about it now, two weeks later, as she drives through the darkening East Side streets—from Rochambeau to Camp to Doyle, no destination in sight, just the understanding that she can't go home, can't possibly face Noelle—she wonders what she's running from. Nothing bad happened that night, they didn't even argue, but she knows something shifted in the practice room; she hasn't been on steady ground since. All the feelings she's bottled for years have slowly come uncorked and she feels the force of a flood rushing through her body, threatening to drown her, to wash away anything of substance she values—beginning with her sobriety.

She turns the car onto Hope Street, speeding up to merge with the traffic, and instinctually grabs the steering wheel with both hands. Numbed from the cold, they ache with pain. Instead of relaxing them, she squeezes again, wincing as she watches her knuckles turn pale. Why hadn't she given Marisa what she wanted? Why didn't she just sign the papers when she asked?

Juliet's chest burns with regret as she thinks of it. She takes a deep breath and closes her eyes, then whips them open as she hears the scream of a truck blaring its horn. She swerves back into her lane. *Fuck.* She shouldn't be driving like this, not in her current state of mind and not with a wine bottle riding shotgun. She needs to pull over, find somewhere safe to stop. Needs to pull herself together. But then she remembers where she is and squashes the thought, continues driving. Too many people know her on this side of town.

She drives past her old high school, surprised by how close it all seems, how most of her childhood was lived between a few square miles. She rolls through a stop sign on Thayer, then watches as a mother in a chicken costume yells at her for not giving pedestrians the right of way. Her child, dressed like a farmer, sticks out their tongue, so Juliet does it back. The mom yells and gives Juliet the finger. Juliet revs her engine in reply, just to startle them, but when she sees it makes the child cry, she wishes she could take it back. Instead, she turns up the music and drives on, relieved to see coeds with backpacks and earbuds up ahead, not a costume in sight. As she climbs the hill, she can see the green domed top of the bell tower in the distance. She drives toward campus, suddenly realizing where she needs to go. How to figure out what a couple hours messing around on the practice piano couldn't tell her: Can she still play?

She reaches across the seat, peeling down the bag to reveal the wine bottle. Her heart pounds, her cold hands sweat. She is thick in the craving now, the desire to drink like a fire that rages inside her. Having Jenry back has fanned that fire, rekindling all the pain she drank to escape: the agony of losing him and her brother within the same six months; the anguish of regret over past mistakes, cursing the selfish person she was back then—who chose her career over the little boy who loved her, who neglected Marisa and pushed her to leave, who made her bed and was then forced to lie in it.

The bottle jostles in the seat when she goes too fast over a speed bump, and Juliet's hand reflexively reaches out to secure it. She squeezes the bottle's thin neck, the glass cool beneath her fingers. She was right about the risk of playing again—it made her want to drink—but it was also worth it, despite the chain reaction set off inside her. It felt natural to sit with Jenry on a piano bench, just like when he was young; she refuses to deny it. She's found the excuse she's been looking for, that addicts are always looking for, to drop the burden of sobriety and allow her demons to take over. She decides to stop fighting—the piano and the alcohol— and instantly feels better.

At the top of the hill, beside the famed Van Wickle Gates, she slows down and turns onto Prospect, squinting in the glare of the setting sun. Her phone vibrates in her pocket but she ignores it. Minutes later, she arrives at the History Department—not the Music Department, where there are several pianos in the practice rooms, nor the foyer in the President's House, which holds a nineteenth-century grand piano made by

Ignace Pleyel and supposedly played by Chopin—no, she needs a piano she knows intimately. One she can trust.

She parks in the faculty lot and pulls out a permit from her glove box, one her father gave her years before, when he still encouraged her to visit. It's long expired, but she hides the date under the windshield shade. She grabs the bottle and tucks it under her arm, sets the car alarm with a click. It's before seven, so the building is still open; she walks right in and heads up the stairs, pulling her hat down so the secretaries she's known since childhood don't recognize her. A copier runs in the distance and she hears voices at the mailboxes, others in the kitchen. She darts up the second flight and down the back hallway, stopping only when she makes it to the third-floor landing, where the piano sits like an old dog waiting for her to come home.

It looks as pretty as ever, and she can't stop herself from smiling. She runs her hands along the rosewood case, admiring the gleam of the polished wood, and lifts the fallboard to reveal the perfect line of keys, all eighty-eight shining back at her. Footsteps ring out from the floor below and she pulls her hands away, holding her breath until the sound recedes. She stares for a long time at the piano. Then she pulls the bench into the shadows and waits for everyone to leave.

Thirty minutes later, the building is dark and silent. The security lights in the stairwell cast a blue hue in the hallway, making the piano keys glow like a string of lights. Juliet sits at the bench with the bottle between her thighs, opens the screw-top with a satisfying snap. She sniffs the neck, notes the fruity aroma, a spicy floral scent, and then, without any hesitation, tips the wine into her mouth. She swallows before she can register the taste; feels the bloom of alcohol on her lips, the sweet rush of heat flying out an open window. She drinks again.

She told Jenry she hadn't played in years—which was true—but also that she didn't want to play—which was not. Not a day passed where she hadn't felt that desire, hadn't imagined what it would feel like to sit down at the bench, lay her fingers on the keys, feel the notes vibrate through her bones. But until that night with him, she had buried the urge, convincing herself it didn't exist. Then, sitting next to him in that small, dark practice room, it seemed there was nothing left to fight; why deprive her soul of the thrill of sound any longer? But it was also about him. Her chance to feed his hunger, as well as her own. How often did one get the opportunity to kill two birds with one old stone?

In truth, she didn't want to kill anything—except the voice that told her to drink. Now, as she pours wine down her throat, she feels like she is succeeding, committing a temporary murder of that darkness lurking within. She feels the guilt and sadness, the regret, lift from her body like a kite, the thin string slipping from her hand to float away. A feeling of peace spreads inside her. She lays her fingers on the keys and plays the first note—the sound clean and true, despite the piano needing to be tuned. The next thing she knows it's almost midnight and the bottle is empty and her hands ache from the blissful act of making music. Thick, pungent notes hang in the air like smoke, encircling her.

She replays that night with Jenry, remembering the stories she told him, the questions he asked, the answers she tried to give. But then she remembers what she did not say—the one thing she leaves out of the story every time she tells it—and what she still can't bring herself to accept: that she had the chance to adopt him, to legalize their relationship and prevent Marisa from doing exactly what she went on to do, and Juliet had refused.

He was not even a year old when Marisa came home late from work, having stopped off to meet with a lawyer. She walked in with the forms, a list of official documents they would need to submit, and the price of the entire transaction laid out in a bulleted list: attorney fees, the cost of the home visit, the court filing fees. It looked so easy typed up on the lawyer's stationery, a simple list of tasks to be completed, but Juliet wondered if it was too easy. All she had to do to become Marisa's equal, permanently held responsible for this child as a co-parent, was create a legal document, essentially binding them together forever. Shouldn't there be something else?

Marisa said she wanted this—to protect him, to give him a sense of well-being, of belonging to them both—but Juliet felt it as a form of entrapment. Marisa knew Juliet would never commit to her—would not marry her, even if they could—so she was using her son to tie them together. She was smiling as Juliet scanned the papers, as if she had finally figured out how to beat the house at its own game.

"I don't want you to feel pressured," Marisa kept saying—and Juliet took time to think about it, a line of questions running in her head during the days spent with him: How could she deny this child she had grown to adore? Didn't she love him like any parent loves a child? Wouldn't she do anything for him? Yes, she answered each time, kissing his curly head, smiling into his deep brown eyes in apology for her initial hesitation; she was confident in her devotion, certain she was capable of any sacrifice. She could go without if he needed something—work two jobs to pay for diapers, clothes, the best schools—but that had never been in doubt. It was her relationship with Marisa that kept her from signing the papers. Juliet knew that a commitment to Jenry meant a commitment to his mother that she feared she couldn't keep.

Juliet spent months debating with herself. She genuinely loved Marisa, felt a real kinship with her, even before the baby. Marisa had an easy way about her; she knew how to ask Juliet questions to get her to talk, yet other times gave her the space she needed to be alone. She was supportive of Juliet's career, and had been there during the dark times, too, while others seemed to see Juliet only under the lights. She felt she owed Marisa something for that loyalty. Yet, Juliet wasn't in love with her. In the end, it came down to a question her brother had asked her the last time they spoke, the day before he died: Could she stay in a relationship without passion, feasting forever on unripe fruit? The answer was no, she'd always known she would eventually want someone else, even if she hoped to get a few more years, at least until Jenry was in school. She wasn't prepared for what happened next, the horror of Jasper's death, the depths of her depression; soon enough the fruit, long forgotten, was rotten on the branch. They broke up less than six months later. Marisa never mentioned the adoption again.

Sudden sounds from below—the front door slamming, footsteps in the stairwell—bring Juliet back to the present. She snatches the empty bottle off the piano in a rush of fear. She feels the alcohol in her legs as she tries to walk, willing her body to stay upright. Her head begins to throb, and she wonders if intoxication had always felt this unpleasant. She wants to run or hide, but knows she's in no shape to do either. She sees a door up ahead—the fire escape—and slips into the shadows beside it. A posted sign says ALARM WILL SOUND if she opens it, so she doesn't move. Tries to stand completely still. Instead, her body sways like a tree in a storm. She imagines her roots being pulled from the earth, all that damp soil. She squats down, her pulse rushing in her ears, and clutches the empty bottle in her fist as she waits.

The footsteps are closer now, on the second-floor landing. She thinks she hears a faint whistle, most likely a grad student or the cleaning crew. Maybe campus police. She doesn't want to get caught. Not here, in her father's office, not in the middle of the night, and, most certainly, not drunk. The door to his room stares at her from across the long hallway. She has tried not to think of him, only of the piano and her need to play it, but now she wonders if her father isn't the real reason she's come to his office, a place that seems to hold more of his essential self than his own body. That one room, more than their home or the cabin, was where she really came to know her father, and to understand that he was a separate person, with goals, dreams, and abilities that existed outside of their family.

For the first few years after her mother died she came here after school, wading through students in line for office hours, and quietly knocked on his door; "Come in," he would call out each time, and she would open the door to see him in mid-conversation, hands flying, eyes focused and searing, until he saw her, and then—unable to help himself—he always broke into a smile. She could tell from how the students reacted that they had never seen this side of her father before, had never witnessed Dr. Patterson display such tenderness, such joy, and it immediately changed the energy in the room, this proof of his vulnerability.

He would hand her a shiny green apple taken from the cafeteria during lunch and between bites she would listen to him lecture his students on the paradox of history in America: how our caste system is older than the country itself, established in 1619 when the first Africans were sold in Virginia; how manifest destiny was a veil for expanding slavery in the western states; how John Brown's raid on Harpers Ferry was the dress rehearsal for the Civil War. His voice was steady and familiar, strong in the way it needed to be, and it was during these moments that Juliet began to understand that he had something other men didn't have, a brilliance she hoped to one day harness in herself. She felt special being his daughter, certain in the belief he would always be there when she knocked, that he would always let her in.

Now, all that's changed; she doesn't exactly want to see him, but she has to admit to a desire to be in his space. She's not sure she carries the key anymore, and if she does, she wonders if it would even work. Surely the university upgrades their locks periodically. She spins through her thick ring of keys in the dark, using the light from her cell phone to examine each one. House, garage, back door, work, storage unit, Noelle's office, her sponsor's house, the cabin in the Berkshires, three unidentified keys probably belonging to girls she used to date, Jasper's apartment key, which she refuses to get rid of, and there at the end, an oddly shaped brass key with DO NOT DUPLICATE in small letters across the top. She recognizes it even before she sees the university insignia, knows in her gut it's going to work.

The lock opens effortlessly, and she steps into the cold room. She closes the door and locks it behind her, from habit more than anything else. Instead of using the overhead light, she walks in the dark through the maze of boxes, around a small desk piled with books and a chair covered in newspapers, until she finds the floor lamp. She pulls the chain, and the room is awash in a golden light. She smiles at the space seemingly unchanged in more than two decades—aside from the upgraded computers, a pretty set of matching iMacs as thin as picture frames. One might question the fancy technology, considering he still types postcards on his IBM Selectric, preferring them to email, but then she thinks of his penchant for fairness, wanting to be extended the same courtesies as the younger faculty, who bring guest lecturers into the classroom via Skype sessions and Google Chats.

She scans the bookshelves, sees *The Negro Caravan* in its usual place beside the collected works of W. E. B. Du Bois, and then, holding up the row, a leather-bound copy of the unabridged *Life and Times of Frederick Douglass,* a gift she gave him for his seventieth birthday. On the wall behind his desk she sees his favorite Jacob Lawrence print, Panel no. 3 from *The Migration Series,* and then his numerous diplomas, framed and hung beside other honors and awards; on another wall, a painting of jazz musicians, next to a photograph of Duke Ellington at the piano, wearing a white bowtie; beside it, a smaller one of Juliet as a child, swinging at the playground in a winter coat as long as a cape, the hem dragging in the mud. Near the closet door, right above his seat, are two more old photographs: one from Jasper's high school graduation, his hair oiled with Du-Sharme; and then a snapshot of their mother ice-skating at Rockefeller Center on the eve of their wedding, her young face lit with joy.

Juliet sits behind her father's desk, spinning a full revolution in his seat. The old wooden roller squeaks to a stop. Her eyes blur, her head keeps spinning. If things are truly the same, she will find a bottle of single malt in the bottom right drawer, and two glass tumblers waiting in the drawer above. The drawer has a lock, but he's never used it. She rolls back in the chair, reaching down to grab the metal handle, not yet sure if she wants the liquor to be there or not. This is always how it begins: the slip, the fall, the crash. She says a quick prayer—*God help me*—and opens the drawer. A brand-new bottle of Macallan 12. She slams the drawer shut and sits up, afraid. Not of the dark room or of getting caught, but of freedom and escape and betrayal. She is afraid of herself.

She imagines opening the bottle and pouring it into the potted fern by the closet. She imagines drinking it, how it would taste and feel in her mouth. She imagines driving home and confessing to Noelle—about the wine, Jenry, everything. She imagines calling her sponsor. She imagines calling her brother, hearing the sweet sound of his voice, lost forever. She imagines calling her father and yelling into his answering machine, or yelling at Marisa, telling her everything she didn't have the courage to say during their last phone call, things she wrote in her fourth step inventory and had to read aloud to her sponsor, before burning the letter in the trash can as soon as she was done.

But worse than the fear is the desire. She feels it pulse in her finger-tips. She takes a deep breath, exhales. Waits for something to happen. Her hands burn as the longing builds inside her. She grabs the bottle of scotch, heavy in her hand, and plants it in the middle of the desk. Stares at it. Her head is buzzing, and then—silence. She looks for glasses but can't find any. She searches through all the drawers. Nothing. The final drawer she checks is locked. She pulls at it repeatedly, but it won't budge. She tries with two hands, and when that doesn't work, she stands and kicks at the lock. The drawer dents but doesn't open. She kicks it again. *Jesus Christ.* The lock seems to taunt her with its simplicity, its round head shining like a bull's-eye, a tiny clock without hands. Finally, she picks up the chair, slamming one leg into the face of the drawer; the han-dle eventually breaks off, but her efforts do nothing to loosen the lock. It won't be broken.

She sits down, breathing hard from the effort. The center drawer has slid open during the ruckus, and the insides now peek out at her: unsharpened pencils, paperclips in assorted colors, a handful of foreign coins. She opens it wider. There, in between a stack of new envelopes and notepads bearing his initials, WJP, embossed on the top, sits a small, white box. She opens the lid. Inside, resting on a thin square of cotton, is a tiny gold key.

It opens the drawer.

To her surprise, and great disappointment, there are no glasses in-side. Instead, the drawer holds a single cardboard box, large enough to carry a pair of men's boots. She lifts the lid. Even if she hadn't been drinking, she would still not be able to understand what she finds inside. The sheer quantity of information is considerable, what she imagines a

CIA file would look like. *How could this be?* Juliet tries to fight the panic now permeating her body.

There are dozens of photographs of Jenry, and letters from as far back as 1999 neatly folded in their original envelopes, the tops sliced open with a knife; thirteen years of report cards, mostly As and a C in Chemistry; artwork from preschool—an orange handprint against blue construction paper—all the way through high school—a self-portrait sketched in charcoal, the image looking quite similar to the boy it's supposed to represent—her boy—as he looked when he walked into her restaurant just over a month ago. *No, this can't be right.* Her hands begin to shake. How could her father have this much information about Jenry, things only a parent would have access to? Why wouldn't he tell her if he did? She feels the world closing in on her.

She is going to be sick. Her face is on fire as her mouth starts to water. She leans over and throws up into the garbage can. Three more times and her insides are empty. She spits into the can, then wipes her mouth on her sleeve. She wants to get as far away as possible, but cannot will herself to move. Later she will carry the can to the bathroom and throw out the liner, replace it with one from the supply closet, and put the garbage can back in its place as if it had never happened—but she can't do any of that yet. For now, all she can do is sit. Think. Wait.

She looks at her phone—12:14 a.m. In six hours her father will walk through the door, as he's done nearly every day for the last four decades; but this time, instead of finding the room empty, he will find his daughter, sitting in his chair, waiting for him to arrive.

· 7 ·

It's after ten when Juliet gets home the following morning, not having slept at all. Brutus, their gorgeous and ever-elusive ginger cat, meets her at the door and escorts her into the kitchen, walking in between her legs until Juliet cracks a raw egg into his food bowl. Noelle has left a note on the island—which she doesn't read—and some oatmeal, which she eats straight out of the pan with a wooden spoon. She takes four Advil with tap water before hopping into the shower. The hot water burns her skin.

She has the vague sense that she's in trouble with her wife, though she'd sent her a text sometime around 1:00 a.m, telling her she got caught up in a card game after work and was going to crash with Lonny or Santiago. Noelle was used to her late-night schedule, to sleeping alone one or two nights a week, so when she got the text in the morning, no doubt on her way to spin class, she texted a casual reply—*okay, hon. Have fun*. But Juliet can tell she's annoyed, based on the brevity of her text, and that she texted at all. Noelle prefers phone calls, always saying texts are impersonal and distant; she wants to hear your voice, have a conversation. Juliet, on the other hand, likes the declarative nature of texting, how she can say exactly what she means without worrying about the other person's agenda. She likes it precisely because it *isn't* a conversation.

Finished with her shower, Juliet draws the blinds and lies on the bed in her towel, her wet hair turning cold on the pillow. She closes her eyes, sees her father from just a few hours before, throwing his gloves on the table, his nostrils flared in anger; she remembers the stale scent of his office, like cigars and dried flowers, and can still taste the wine on her tongue, even after brushing her teeth three times since getting home; she hears the snap of his key in the lock, the click of the door closing behind him, but can't remember anything that was spoken until the very end of the argument.

"Consider yourself free," she'd said to him as she walked out the door, but now she realizes she'd been talking to herself. She is the one who is now free from her father—but at what cost?

When she opens her eyes, convinced only a few minutes have passed, Noelle is standing over her. Juliet can tell by the light that it's afternoon. The clock on her nightstand says 2:30.

"We need to talk." Noelle sits down. Juliet can smell her lotion, a rich cocoa butter, which Noelle repeatedly rubs into her cuticles.

Juliet blinks. "Okay." She knows she should say more, but she doesn't know how to begin. Her head still hurts. She wonders if she's still drunk, or already hungover.

Noelle leans forward, and Juliet sits up, expecting a kiss. Instead, Noelle buries her face in Juliet's hair. Juliet can hear her inhale. When Noelle pulls away, she has tears in her eyes.

"Are you having an affair?"

"What? No." Juliet feels herself blink. "Why are you asking me that?"

"You're acting weird. You come home late, later than usual, and you don't always pick up when I call." Noelle wipes the corner of her eyes with her sleeve, leaving a tiny mark of mascara on the cuff.

"I'm working. I can't always answer."

"I know, it's not just that." Noelle shakes her head. "Something's off with you. Last time you lied and snuck around like this you were drinking. So now . . . I just don't know what your problem is."

From how she looks at her, Juliet can tell that Noelle doesn't suspect it has anything to do with drinking, which makes what she's about to do even harder.

"I'm not cheating on you. I swear." She inhales. "I swear on Jasper's grave."

"Okay." Noelle puts her hand on Juliet's knee. "I believe you."

"But you're right," she adds quickly, before losing her nerve, "about the drinking." Juliet forces herself to keep eye contact, but all she wants to do is bury her head in the pillow. "I slipped last night. I had a drink." She considers lying again, to lessen the blow, but decides to come clean completely. "I drank a bottle of wine, actually."

Noelle's eyes go wide. "Jesus Christ."

"It was pretty bad." She runs her fingers through her hair, damp and thin, knows she looks like a wreck. Wonders how Noelle can love her.

"Have you called your sponsor?" Just like Noelle, forever the problem solver.

Juliet nods. "We met this morning. We're having coffee tonight after the meeting. She wants me to do a thirty-thirty." Juliet looks down, plays with her watch.

"Thirty meetings in thirty days? You haven't done that in years."

"Yeah. Well. When you fuck up you have to start over." She can say the words, but that doesn't mean she fully understands what happened. That she threw away the work of five years in one night. With one bottle. Day number one all over again.

"This must be hard for you." Noelle looks sincere. "The starting over."

Juliet shrugs. "I'm lucky. I could be out there, still drinking." Noelle's face registers a look of surprise laced with fear. "I know, believe me"—Juliet touches her arm—"I don't want to think about that either." She takes a deep breath. "But it's going to be okay. I know what to do."

Noelle tries to smile. "Good." She looks at her hands, still rubbing them, though the lotion has already sunk in.

"I'm so sorry." Juliet reaches for her hand.

Noelle doesn't say anything, just nods, a movement Juliet barely registers.

"I don't know what else to say." Juliet's voice rises. "I fucked up, I know that for sure." There is plenty more to say, about Jenry and her father, but Juliet feels exhausted by the first part of her confession and can't imagine revealing anything else.

"These things happen," Noelle offers. "You're human."

Juliet shakes her head. "I'm an alcoholic. I can't afford to let things like this happen."

Noelle rubs her face like she's trying to wake up. "It's just . . . I wasn't expecting this. Maybe I'm in shock or something." Noelle looks at her, eyes glassy like she's trying not to cry. "But it's a relief, I guess. That it's not worse."

Juliet nods. They stare at each other in silence, then Juliet goes into the bathroom. She washes her face with cold water, rinsing out her mouth. She spits into the sink, then looks into the mirror. Counts a few gray hairs, notes the coffee stains on her teeth, the tiny wrinkles under her eyes. She is too old to be pulling all-nighters. How will she ever survive a newborn?

When she walks back into the room, Noelle is lying down on the bed, still in her jacket. "I told them I was grabbing lunch, but maybe I should call out sick for the rest of the day. I didn't sleep well."

"You're an expectant mother," Juliet says. "Who better to call in sick?"

Noelle makes a face. "It's not like I'm pregnant."

"So? You're a month away from having a baby. You're nesting."

"I'm freaking out, is what I'm doing."

Juliet sits next to her, her hand automatically going to Noelle's belly, where she dives under her shirt and into her warm skin. "You're going to be an amazing mom."

Noelle twists a lock of Juliet's hair around her finger. "You think?" She releases the curl, sending it spiraling back to the others.

"I know." Juliet plants kisses along the notches of her ribs. Then she lays her head down, listening to Noelle's stomach gurgle. She knows she has more to confess, but she doesn't want this moment to end. It's too early in the day for seduction, especially since her wife prefers to make love in the dark, but Juliet wonders about other forms of distraction, imagining new ways to keep running from the truth.

"What else happened?" Noelle says. She is staring at the ceiling, her bent arm resting on her forehead. "Just tell me."

Juliet marvels at how Noelle always does that, sensing when she's holding back. She sits up, her back to Noelle.

"I just told my father he couldn't be a part of our baby's life. I ended our relationship."

"What?" The bed shifts as Noelle rolls onto her side. "Why?"

"It's a long and complicated story." Juliet exhales.

"Hang on," Noelle says, pulling out her phone. She types a quick text. "There," she says. "Now I've got all day." She tosses her phone onto the bed between them, like a gambler feeding the pot. "Ante up," she says, motioning for Juliet to join her. Juliet puts her phone on vibrate before laying it in the center of the bed.

Then, with the window cracked and the November wind carrying the smell of winter—of wood stoves and hot tea, of warm, wet wool—into their bedroom, she proceeds to tell Noelle everything, starting on that day in September when Jenry first walked into the restaurant and ending with the discovery, just last night, of her father's betrayal. Noelle doesn't interrupt once. Juliet is exhausted when she finishes, sucking on a lozenge she finds on the nightstand to soothe her throat. Noelle tucks her hair behind her ear, working the loose strands into a tiny ball she knots between her fingertips. A truck passes by, rattling the old windows. Somewhere, a bird whistles.

Noelle shifts her weight on the bed. "I'm not sure what you expect me to say."

Juliet continues to play with her watch, clicking the latch open and closed. "I don't have an expectation. I just want you to say something."

"We're not starting a family with you lying to me." Noelle crosses her arms over her chest; a posture of protection, Juliet realizes, not defense.

"What the hell is that supposed to mean? Our kid is due in a month."

"Exactly."

"So you're going to sabotage the adoption because you're angry?"

"Angry?" Noelle raises her voice, causing the veins in her neck to swell. "I wish it was only anger I was feeling. This is fear, sweetheart. I'm fucking terrified that you're going to get caught up in this other life, your past life, and completely disengage from what's going on in this house. *Your* house, with *your* family."

"You mean I have to choose? I can't have both?"

"Both? Are you really comparing this boy you haven't seen in sixteen years to the baby we're about to adopt? The one you're going to be legally responsible for?" She leans forward, eyes unblinking.

"I'm not comparing," Juliet says. "What I'm saying is that I have to pursue this. There's a reason he came back into my life and I need to find out what that is." She reaches for her hand, but Noelle pulls away, leaving Juliet holding the edge of her sleeve. "I have to do this. But it doesn't change how I feel about the baby and you and our family. I swear to you it doesn't." She lets go of Noelle's arm, which falls heavily into her lap. "But I can't just walk away. I know you don't understand, but I can't make the same mistake twice."

The look on Noelle's face has changed from anger to confusion. "What mistake? You looked for her. You tried to find them for months, and she didn't want to be found. She intentionally cut you out of his life—where's your mistake?"

"I could have handled things better. When we were together." Juliet speaks slowly, her voice even. "I was a total mess." She wants to say more, but stops herself, embarrassed by who she was back then, and afraid of what it would say about her now.

"Okay, fine." Noelle throws up her hands. "You were selfish and immature, and you cheated on her, I know all that. You were a shitty girlfriend. But you were also twenty-seven years old for god's sake. What the hell did you know about taking care of yourself, let alone anyone else? Shit, we're in our forties now and I'm still worried we won't get it right. But you are not the same person you were then, and you are certainly not in the same relationship."

"You're right," Juliet says, "I'm not the same." And to prove it to herself, she reveals more about her past with Marisa, admitting she was already drinking too much when Jenry was a baby; that she was reckless with Marisa's feelings, and incapable of being honest with anyone, including herself; and perhaps the biggest confession of all, that she refused to adopt Jenry when Marisa asked her to, and has been living with the guilt of that rejection for the last sixteen years. "If I had just agreed to adopt him, I wouldn't be here right now. She wouldn't have been able to take him away."

"You don't know that, not for sure." Noelle's voice is calm, reassuring. "Think of your lifestyle back then, touring all over the world. It wouldn't have been easy to show up for him every day, not like when he was a baby."

"But I could have tried," Juliet says. "She didn't even let me try."

Noelle chooses her words carefully. "I don't want to be insensitive, because I know how much it hurt you. But maybe she didn't leave to punish you. Maybe she was just trying to protect her son."

"From me?" Juliet shakes her head. "She knew how much I loved him."

Noelle squeezes Juliet's knee. "From someone who might have failed him."

Juliet looks at her, not wanting it to be true, but realizing Noelle is probably right. Her gift of perception is another reason Juliet married her.

"You can be mad at me for saying it, but I'm not that different from her. You aren't going to get a million chances." Noelle starts to cry. "You lost Jenry once and now he's back, but if you lose me—if you lose our baby—we're not coming back." Tears run down Noelle's face, and she doesn't wipe them away.

"Don't say that—" Juliet reaches for her, but Noelle bats her hand away.

"Don't," Noelle says, her voice shaking. She points a finger at Juliet's face, inches from her eyes. She looks menacing, but her tone softens. "Don't you dare risk losing me." Her voice drops to barely a whisper. "Don't you dare." She runs her sleeve across her face, finally wiping the tears.

Juliet hears Noelle's words echo in her ears, but it's somehow a comfort, not a threat—a challenge for Juliet to be held to a higher standard, one she's desperate to reach. Before she can stop herself, Juliet is crying, the tears falling like hot wax down the soft side of a candle.

"That's better," Noelle says, "I don't like to cry alone." They both laugh, and Noelle reaches for Juliet's hand. "Try to remember, this isn't some solitary journey you're on, where you get more points if you do it without assistance. This life thing, it's a group sport." She rubs the tears from Juliet's face. "You don't have to go through it alone." She kisses Juliet on each cheek, and then on her lips.

"But I feel like it's my responsibility. I created this mess—shouldn't I fix it?"

"Fix the parts you broke. But the rest of it, we carry together." She caresses Juliet's face, something a parent would do to a child, and it feels so intimate, so loving, it makes Juliet want to pull away. But she forces herself to stay, and to take what her wife has offered. "That's what marriage is. Don't you know that by now?" Noelle runs her hands down Juliet's arms until she makes it all the way to her fingertips, which she intertwines with her own. "I sacrificed a lot to be here with you. To buy this house. To adopt this baby. I risked a lot. Because I believe in us. Don't forget that we both have something to lose."

Juliet squeezes her hands. "Nobody's losing anything, okay? I promise you. But you have to trust me."

Noelle looks her dead in the eyes. "Then be trustworthy."

It seems easy when Noelle says it like that, and infinitely possible. Since the beginning of their relationship, something about her has made all the things that Juliet ever wanted in life seem possible. Juliet leans forward to kiss her long and hard on the mouth. "I love you very much," she says, holding Noelle's face in her hands.

"I love you, too."

Noelle closes her eyes, a sign of resignation or simple exhaustion. Juliet kisses her eyelids, tasting the salt of her tears, then brings her face to rest next to Noelle's, their foreheads touching. They stay like this for some time.

"So, when are you going to see him again?" Noelle asks. Her eyes are still closed and Juliet watches as her eyelids flutter, like someone in deep sleep.

"I told him to stay out of my life. Forever. I was so angry."

Noelle sits back. "Not your father. Jenry."

It's strange, to hear Noelle say his name. As if they were speaking a shared secret language. But it also feels nice. "I don't know," Juliet says.

Noelle reaches for her phone to check the time. "Well you're going to have to deal with it. No matter what happens between the two of you, he's Jasper's son. He's always going to be a part of our family."

Noelle is trying to be generous, but Juliet isn't sure what that even means. In her mind, he can be her son or nothing at all.

"Why don't you start by being his aunt," Noelle says, "his father's sister. Don't worry about being his other mother."

It sounds so simple when Noelle says it, and a part of Juliet wants to agree, to make it easier for everyone. But she knows something Noelle does not, a secret she's carried for years and swore never to reveal; one she is still holding, even after her father's betrayal.

Being his aunt might be the perfect solution—if only it were true.

· BOOK IV ·

The Father

February 1999

· 1 ·

The pain was so great, Jasper could barely move. He didn't know why. Why he should suffer this way. What sins he was being punished for.

He tried to sit up. The muscles in his stomach ached. His head pounded. He rubbed his temples, hard enough to generate a new sensation of pain. That provided a short relief. He imagined crushing his skull like a fruit, the inside dripping sticky sweet onto his fingers, his brain a mass of seeds unwilling to die or germinate. Even though the pain had not subsided, the image brought him comfort.

He was dying, this he knew. Had been for a long time. There was no surprise there, no new wound. But this was not what he signed on for. For his body to feel this heavy, this burdened by its weight, yet to be so fragile he feared if he stood too quickly, he'd leave half his limbs behind. The hard part, the real betrayal, was the truth of his occupation, the fact that his body was his work for so many years. His house and his home. He didn't know how to deal with no longer living there. With the idea of eviction. He was a dancer, which meant his body was his life. It knew to stand up straight, to sit, to stretch, to walk on bare feet, to touch things. To touch everything.

He ran his hands over his legs: red-boned, muscled, and hairless, thanks to the mixed blood—Cherokee, Irish, African—that continued to pump through his weakened body. They looked strong, but he wondered if they could still hold him. He stretched one, then the other, flexing muscles that had carried him around the world, as he contemplated whether or not he could make it to the bathroom without stopping to rest. He scratched his gaunt face, shocked by his smooth cheeks, even though he hadn't shaved in days. He leaned forward to check his reflection in the mirror beside his bed. *There you are*, he said to himself. *You are still here.*

He looked tired and skinny, sallow even, but not old. At thirty-three he still got carded at the clubs he visited between shows, where he met lawyers, accountants, or chiropractors named Hank, Robert, or Steve, who thought it was cute that he made his money dancing—as if he was a go-go dancer, parading half-naked across a stage, instead of an esteemed ballet dancer, refined and disciplined even in street clothes and sitting on a vinyl bar stool, too humble to explain that his position might not be as lucrative as Wall Street, but was far more prestigious. He didn't say much more than *Please* and *Thank you* and *You're kidding* on those nights, and usually expected to come home alone.

He tried to smile at himself in the mirror, but ended up coughing instead, which made him choke on the phlegm in the back of his throat. He hid his face in the blanket and coughed so hard he vomited into his mouth, then reached for a water glass from the night before. The taste was bad, he imagined, but he couldn't know for certain; he'd lost the ability to taste anything other than the flat metallic wetness of his tongue. Nothing was sweet or tart. Nothing spicy. The hot throbbing of his favorite ethnic foods had become something close to a vibration now, like the dull ache he used to feel when he knew sex was coming, but before the act was consummated. Eating, once his greatest pleasure next to dancing, was now a chore. He labored through bites of cold egg whites and congealed oatmeal, banana mashed in yogurt to hide its texture. He stopped drinking hard alcohol completely, and now drank only juice and clear liquids, like a woman in labor.

To say that his life was regimented was a grave understatement. Before getting sick, his days followed a set routine; like a performance, each step memorized. He walked four miles, without fail, and ate the same breakfast (a cup of oatmeal, two soft-boiled eggs, half a grapefruit, a pot of green tea) within an hour of the sun rising. He weighed himself daily, and his weight never fluctuated more than three pounds; he wore the same size twenty-eight jeans since freshman year of high school. He was always clean-shaven, preferring to shave at night, and often fell asleep with a hot towel draped over his face. He never owned a vehicle, not even a bicycle, and didn't have a driver's license. He read every day—at least one page from a book before going to sleep, regardless of the time, his state of sobriety, or if there was a person lying next to him—and awakened to *The New York Times*, no matter the country. He asked to be called by his full name, Jasper, which he loved mostly because it had no nickname. He allowed only his mother and sister to have pet names for him, and they were the rare exception. No lover had ever called him anything but his given name, not even "sweetheart."

He always wore a touch of color, usually purple, even when the rest of his outfit was entirely black. He gave up dairy and artificial sweeteners and friends that smoked. He sacrificed the possibility of a stable, long-term romantic relationship, along with a family, despite having occasional yearnings for both. All this, because he was a dancer. It was everything he knew about himself and yet it seemed to be nothing at all. How did one build a life around a ninety-minute performance? Around grueling rehearsals and nonstop tour dates and benefit performances where Baryshnikov was the only modern dancer guests could name? Around calluses and ingrown toenails and pulled hamstrings and sweaty dance belts and three liters of water a day and massages and steam rooms and hand jobs from strangers in bathroom stalls that barely fit one man. Despite being one of the lucky ones—a principal dancer, internationally recognized—he often wondered how all of that became his life.

He swallowed four Advil without water, his daily vitamins for the past decade, and waited before trying to stand. His head was pounding, a steady drumbeat in the baseline of his skull that was so familiar it almost become a comfort. His headache, like his heartbeat, was the metronome of his life. He looked at the scabs on his hairless arm. They were small, penny-sized, dark like drops of molasses left to dry in the sun. Sometimes he scratched them off just to see the skin beneath. He didn't bleed any more, not real blood. Too much work. His cells barely had the energy to survive.

He struggled to put on his bathrobe, knowing he should cover the sores before Darius arrived. Darius didn't want to see any signs of what was coming next, for Jasper or himself. Unlike Jasper, Darius was a good patient: he was taking his meds and sleeping ten hours a day and not fucking anymore, and he even sent his mother a birthday card—what more could the gods ask for? He'd done his penance, he told Jasper during their last visit to a nightclub several weeks ago. He had this thing beat, he was sure of it.

No one wondered the same about Jasper—he had always been graced with good fortune. Blessed with all that a young man needed to thrive in the late twentieth century: good genes, good timing, and good luck. He'd built a life on getting everything he wanted. But he didn't want this: to be sick, to be dying at thirty-three. To die was okay, *to be dead*, but the act of dying? No, that was not something he could tolerate.

Unable to stand, he picked up a book from his night table. An anthology of Black, gay poetry. He flipped to a poem about someone dying. Another brother gone too soon. The new cocktail slowed things down but wasn't a cure; someone was always dying. The poet was haunted by his own impending death, afraid of the moment when he wouldn't hear his heartbeat anymore, would know the end was near. Jasper feared the uncertainty of not knowing, the fact that he couldn't control the timing. He was surprisingly unsentimental about dying; the failure of his body was the greater disappointment. As it slowly shut down, he felt himself pulling away, abandoning his organs one by one. He felt nothing for his heart now. His lungs, even his mind. He was detached from all of it.

Replacing the book on the nightstand, he knocked over a framed photograph of his nephew. He righted it quickly, as if it were the boy himself. The picture was several months old, taken when Jenry was just over a year. He was sitting on his sister's lap, wearing a cowboy hat the color of straw. His cheeks were cut with dimples as he smiled, showing off his new front teeth. Juliet was smiling, too, but not at the camera. All of her attention—which their father noted in high school had the precision of a nuclear missile—was focused on her son. She didn't seem to know the picture was being taken.

Jasper couldn't help but see his sister in the boy: her unapologetic need to laugh, her bright eyes, the untamed curls, but he knew it wasn't possible. Jenry was her son, but not related by blood. That was a simple truth. One that devastated Juliet, though she refused to admit it. And what was worse: it was his fault, or rather, the fault of the disease slowly deconstructing his body. Juliet and Marisa asked him to be the father, or more accurately, to be *the donor*, but he declined. Said it was his touring schedule and the drugs he did after college, the depression that ran on their side of the family; who would want to burden a child with that legacy, on top of having two mothers?

But Juliet knew the truth—really, it was him. His blood was bad, he told her, after his third refusal. He was diseased, marked, ruined. He was positive. "Just like the old man warned," he said, brushing off the hug Juliet tried to give him, her face threatening to break. "It's fine, I'm still healthy. Healthier than most." He was convincing, and his little sister chose to believe him. It was no longer a death sentence; they would still have plenty of time.

Jasper didn't have to ask her not to tell anyone, especially their father. They were used to keeping secrets from Winston, and agreed it would only make him worry. Well aware of his limitations, as a man and a father, they imagined it would likely carry over into his role as grandfather. He could tolerate their shortcomings only because they were his children; they were family. Jenry needed to be the same, needed to carry the Patterson blood, if Winston was going to accept him. The story they told Winston couldn't change: Jasper had to be the biological father.

"Tell him I said yes," Jasper insisted as they said goodbye. "Don't ever tell him the truth." Juliet promised, and they never talked about it again. Jasper still didn't know the identity of the actual donor; he never thought to ask. Jenry had two parents, didn't he? And Jasper had his own role: to be the uncle; to send money and love him from a distance; and to let Winston believe the baby was his son. That was how Jenry became Winston's grandson—not because Winston believed Juliet was his mother, but because he *knew* Jasper was his father. It was a small price to pay to see his sister happy, and a valuable gift to give to the boy, who not only had his mother and Juliet, but could claim a father and grandfather as well. Positive male role models, as the psychologists said, something every fatherless child was looking for.

He knew it wouldn't be difficult to lie to his father—not about Jenry or his own HIV status. He had hidden a part of himself for so long, it seemed natural to do so. Lying was easy; it was the truth that challenged him. There was a burden that came along with telling it, a vulnerability he could not accept or hardly fathom. He feared not the other person's shock, nor the rejection, nor even the pity—which he imagined would be great—it was the silence. The non-reaction was worse, he had decided. He had all the silence he could ever want right now, in his two-thousand-square-foot loft on Mott Street, in his phone that no longer rang, in his empty date book. What did he need with his father's silence as well, when they already had so much distance between them? Why put up another wall?

The intercom by the front door buzzed, but he ignored it. He never had visitors before noon. Probably Chinese food delivery for one of his neighbors, or a bike messenger ringing all the units until they got into the building, a converted factory once used as a textile mill. Jasper's loft was on the top floor, but there was no penthouse treatment; he had to answer his own door. The buzzer rang again, and he looked at the clock above his bed. It was later than he thought. Darius must be early.

Jasper took a deep breath and stood up too quickly. His head spun. He used the wall for support, its exposed brick rough against his hands. When he pulled away, he lost his balance, grabbing on to the first thing he saw: a marble sculpture of a woman with her hand buried in her chest, searching for her own heart. The sculpture was smaller than he was, and it wobbled slightly under his weight, before settling. It felt as smooth and cold as ice. Jasper rested his cheek on her head as he hugged her, as if embracing a friend he hadn't seen in years. The buzzer went off again.

"I'm coming," Jasper said to the empty room. He didn't even try to raise his voice.

Some people, like his father, thought the loft was too industrial and cavernous, but Jasper loved how it was essentially one huge room, with thirteen-foot ceilings and massive white-paned windows that drowned the space in light. But today the blinds were down, the room cast in shadows. He shuffled across the concrete floor, polished to a high shine like a roller rink. When he first moved in, back in the summer of 1989, he threw an impromptu Fourth of July party and hosted the entire event in roller skates. The thought of that night still brought a smile to his face. He'd been single, of course, and invited several exes to the party, along with a few guys he was interested in. By the end of the night he had made out with four of them, given one a blow job, and set up dates with two others, including a friend of one of his exes. His audacity was occasionally surprising, even to him.

He stopped in the kitchen to catch his breath, leaning against one of the many timber columns that ran along the length of the unit, each one marking a distinct living space. Then the lock turned and the front door opened, and his sister walked into the room. She floated like an angel, an answer to a prayer he didn't remember saying.

"Juliet?" He said her name with a touch of confusion.

"I was afraid I'd missed you, so I let myself in."

"I forgot I gave you a key."

She held up a brass key on an NY State keychain. "Since the late eighties. You want it back?" She held it out to him, a wry smile on her pretty face.

"No, of course not." He looked at her. "How sweet of you to still have it."

She flicked the row of light switches, flooding the space with fluorescent light. Jasper blinked as his eyes adjusted. He preferred the lamps in the living room, or even candlelight, but didn't bother to tell her. She crossed the room to check the thermostat. "Is the heater broken? It's freezing in here."

"I hadn't noticed. I've been in bed."

She turned the dial and a few seconds later the furnace kicked on. Her boots clicked against the floor as she walked back to him.

"You don't look good. Are you sick?" He made a face at the question, rolling his eyes. "You know what I mean," she said. "Not pneumonia?"

"Just a cold." He sat on a bar stool at the island. "Something we all picked up in Romania. I just can't seem to shake it." He shivered, more from the lie than his fever. He didn't want to worry her.

She felt his face. "You're burning up. Have you taken anything?"

"Yes, Mom. I just did. Give it a second to kick in." He gestured toward the kitchen. "Can I get you something?"

"No. I don't really have time to eat. I'm here on business."

"Business? I didn't realize we had any."

"Not you and I, silly. With my manager. A bunch of offers have come in since the Grammy nomination, but I'm not sure which direction to go in." Juliet filled the kettle with cold water and put it on the stove to boil. "We can extend the tour, but I'd be gone all spring and summer. Or stay home and record another album, then hit the festivals next year." She found two mugs and a basket of mixed teas. She shuffled through the tea bags, searching for something acceptable.

"What do you want to do?" he asked, trying to make his eyes seem bright.

Juliet stared at him with a half smile on her face. But he knew she was annoyed. "Don't you read my letters?"

"Of course, I do. When I get them." He picked up a stack of unopened mail. "Sometimes it takes a while."

"I sent it three weeks ago. I told you I'd be here for the weekend and we could spend some time together, hashing out the pros and cons. When I didn't hear from you, I thought that meant it was okay."

Jasper laughed, which sent a jolt of pain through his ribcage. He coughed to cover the discomfort. "Interesting logic."

"You know what I mean. I usually only hear from you when there's a problem. I thought everything was fine."

He pretended to sort the mail. "Yes, well, it is fine. Everything is fine."

She looked around, cataloguing all the things he had neglected. "I can tell." Her voice was flat, sarcastic, but not mean. She walked through the apartment, neatening stacks of magazines and folding blankets he'd left on the furniture. At the far edge of the living room, she pulled up the blinds, exposing the wide bank of windows. "You need sunlight, and fresh air." She turned the latch, but couldn't open the window.

"It's broken," he said, "but a few of the panes are cracked, so plenty of air gets in."

He rested his head against a flower vase filled with old lilies. He breathed in the smell of the dying flowers, marveled at the rotten stench.

"Jasper. When's the last time you ate?" She walked back toward the kitchen.

"Not sure. Probably Thursday."

"It's Saturday afternoon, sweetheart."

He glanced out the window. "Is it?"

When he turned back, he saw that she'd already peeled and sliced a banana, and was now looking through the cupboards. "Where's the oatmeal?"

"Bottom left, next to the sink. But none for me, thanks."

"You need to eat something hot."

"I'll eat later, I need to shower. I'm expecting someone." What he needed was a break, from performing for his sister. He closed his eyes, bracing for the pain that would come once he stood.

"A date?"

"No. Nothing like that. Just a friend who's going through a hard time."

He stood up slowly, gripping the island with both hands. Juliet had her back to him, so he allowed the pain to register on his face.

"Since when do you have 'just friends'?"

He measured his breath before speaking. "What do you mean, dear? All I have are friends. I don't settle down like you people."

"My people?" She chose a teabag and an empty mug. "You mean lesbians?"

"Whatever terms you prefer this week. Who am I to throw around labels?"

He walked toward the bathroom but stopped halfway there to rest. He sat on the wide arm of an old leather couch and tried to look like he was lounging. The kettle whistled. Juliet poured the boiling water into each mug, filling them to the top. She handed Jasper his cup of hot water, and then a bag of loose green tea.

"Thank you." He dropped a handful of tea leaves into his cup. The aroma always comforted him: sharp, earthy, fresh. He felt his stomach growl for the first time in days. Maybe she was right, maybe he did need to eat something.

When the oatmeal bubbled on the stove, Juliet turned it off. She fixed him a bowl and placed it on the coffee table beside him to cool. The way she moved through a kitchen reminded him of their mother, how effortless she made it seem, a perfect choreographed routine, and how she was more comfortable using food than words to show love. He watched Juliet push up the sleeves of her wool sweater, then pull her hair back with a clip, a few loose curls around her face. She looked just like Faye then, from a series of photographs his father kept that he thought the children didn't know about. Throughout their childhood the album was hidden in the top drawer of his dresser, a dark red leather the color of wine. He thought of saying something to Juliet about the resemblance but wondered what would be the point. Was anything between them unburdened by the weight of the past?

They sipped their tea. Juliet walked around the dining room, inspecting things as if it were an open house. Nothing had changed in years, but she looked with eagerness, as if she hoped to find something she'd never seen before. He followed her eyes as she took in the artwork on the wall. She stared at one of the watercolors, trying to make out the signature. Jasper leaned into the couch cushion, its leather warm from his body.

"Do you remember our mother?" he asked, his tone as casual as if he'd asked her to turn on the light.

"What kind of a question is that? Of course I do."

Jasper shook his head. "I mean really remember. Conversations you had. The way she smelled. Her laugh."

Juliet blew on her tea. "She smelled like the outside, lilacs and sweet grass, and I remember that her hands were always warm." She moved closer to him. "Mama had a world in her pocketbook, candies and maps and nylon stockings, a pair of leather gloves I used to try on but never fit. And she always carried a bag of roasted nuts, just in case."

He nodded. "Cashews. Lightly salted."

She stood behind him now, and he closed his eyes.

"What else?" he asked her.

"She was always in the kitchen. Always cooking."

He felt her hands hovering over his shoulders, and then the heat of her touch. "If I didn't know better, I'd think you were copying her." He laughed weakly. "That you were our mother's ghost. Come back to heal me."

She fixed the collar on his bathrobe, smoothed over the wrinkles with her hands; they felt as solid as an iron and almost as hot. When she removed her hand, the skin left behind felt tight, as if it were seared.

"I still can't eat cashews," she confessed.

Jasper looked out the window. He could see the buildings of Lower

Manhattan, and the sky covered with a sheet of bright white clouds, an endless expanse before him. Where did it end, he wondered. What lay beyond it?

He covered her hands and squeezed lightly. The way she hovered over him reminded him of being a boy, of holding hands with his mother as they walked through the crowded streets of his childhood. He held on to her as if it were his job, and when they arrived at their destination, he was still holding on; she was always the first to let go. He did the same when she died, too afraid to let go of her hand. During her funeral, he stood beside the casket still holding on, until the reverend said his final prayer and the pallbearers closed the lid before they put her into the ground. That was how he held on to his sister right now, their fingers entwined. Despite his weakened state, his grip was still strong, as if channeling that eleven-year-old boy who refused to say goodbye.

He wanted to tell her they were running out of time, that like their mother, he wouldn't be around to see Jenry grow up. But the words never came. He closed his eyes and thought of how lucky he was; she was his witness all these years—co-conspirator in childhood, confidante in adolescence—and for that, he owed her. If not the full truth, then some approximation.

He heard her exhale as she squeezed his hands, her fingers hard like knots of wood. He couldn't remember ever loving anyone more than he loved his baby sister right then. Tears fell, and he did not wipe them away. A feeling of peace permeated his body. And with it, a deep fatigue.

Moments later, he fell asleep, still holding her hand.

· 2 ·

Jasper awoke to the smell of bleach. The sound of a mournful whistle. He opened his eyes. The room was empty. He blinked. He lifted his head from the arm of the couch. A note from Juliet sat on the coffee table. He blinked a second time. When he heard the whistle again, he realized that Darius was there, and that he had not died in his sleep. These facts were a comfort, and a feeling of relief flooded his chest.

He cleared his throat, tried to speak but thought better of it, drank a sip of his tea instead. The tea was cold and refreshing, and he finished it in one long gulp.

The note she left him, written on the back of an invitation to the opening of a new gallery in the West Village—one he feared he would not be alive to attend—was too long, so he didn't bother to read it. But he could make out "Juliet," printed in block letters at the bottom like a street sign, a heart before her name.

He waited for Darius to discover him awake, instead of calling out; it didn't take long. Darius exited the bathroom with a bucket in one hand and a wet sponge in the other. He was overdressed for the job, as he was for most events, today wearing Armani—dark jeans, a white linen shirt so thin it showed his nipples—and cowboy boots that smacked the concrete floors like a slap. He passed the corner that held Jasper's bed and stopped at the statue of the woman, running the sponge over her pale body before drying it with a dish towel. It looked to Jasper like a father bathing his child.

On his way to the kitchen, Darius glanced over, finding Jasper awake. He smiled and waved, water droplets running down his arm.

"Hey, sleeping beauty."

Jasper smiled back. "Black beauty to you."

"Of course," Darius said, "the lighter they are, the Blacker they want to be."

"I don't have to *want* to be Black, I *am* Black." Jasper leaned back against the couch. "The difference between the two is vast."

Darius walked into the kitchen. "Just like being gay," he said.

"Or sick," Jasper added. "It doesn't matter what you want, you are what you are."

Darius wrung out the sponge and placed the bucket underneath the sink. Though Jasper stared at him, Darius wouldn't make eye contact. He cleaned the kitchen instead, while Jasper watched from his perch on the couch. When Darius was finished, he washed his hands with a bar of soap as square and black as charcoal. Jasper noticed how odd the gray lather looked as it foamed over Darius's skin, like it was washing off his color; he thought of a joke but decided not to say it. Race was a taboo subject among Black gay men, especially the brown-skinned ones, who would rather talk about money or marriage—or even their fathers—before talking about the color of their skin. Jasper learned that lesson the hard way, stunting several relationships in the dating phase with too much discussion of discrimination and their status as a double minority.

"Let me ask you a question," Darius said, his voice booming across the quiet room. "When was the last time you talked to your father?"

Jasper made a face.

"I'm serious." Darius rested his hands on the sides of the sink. "You think you've got all this time, but you don't. You need to think about somebody else—"

"Why? It's my life."

"And it's always been that way. The shows, the tours, the choreographers—you, you, you. You've always gotten what you wanted."

"You're jealous."

"You're depressed."

"You're a mean son of a bitch." Jasper had a smile on his face.

"And you're a fool. Sitting here all alone in your cold-ass apartment. As if it's noble to die alone. You have a family. A sister, a father, hell, even a son—"

"I don't have a son any more than you have a husband."

"You have people who care about you—"

"And if I don't care about myself, what then?"

"You self-pitying bastard! Don't you get it? This is the time to lean on other people. To give them the chance to help you. To *see* you."

Jasper leaned back to look at the ceiling, the wooden beams as thick as railroad ties. Tears formed in his eyes, but he didn't let them fall.

"Listen, I know how scary that is," Darius said, his voice softer now. "Believe me. You think I wanted to tell my momma and all her church lady friends? You think I wanted them praying for my soul?" Darius dried his hands on the dish towel, then hung it neatly over the faucet. His bald head shined in the spotlight. "I did it because it was the right thing to do. And because, misguided as she is, she loves me. I might be a faggot, but I'm her only son."

After a long pause, Jasper sat up. "Did you tell your father?"

Darius looked surprised. "Come on, you know I haven't seen that SOB since he got remarried and moved back to Georgia."

"And I don't see you running down there to tell him all about your life."

"You think it's the same? Your father and mine?" His voice got louder. "Your father raised you. He supported you. My father took me to a few basketball games when he had a new girlfriend he was trying to impress. He bought me hot dogs and sent me to the corner store to buy him cigarettes. He was only around when he needed something. But when I needed him, he was never there."

"Okay, you're right." Jasper lifted his hands in surrender. "I shouldn't have compared them." He moved to the edge of the couch. "But just because my father was there doesn't mean he said the right things. Or said anything at all." Jasper felt his throat tighten as he let himself remember. "I was ten when she got sick, and after she died, he became this other person. He never wanted to talk about her. Never asked me if I was okay, or why I spent hours in my room playing chess. When I was older, he never asked about it when I snuck out of the house and went down to the river to hook up with older men, never asked why I came home smelling of liquor and another man's cologne. But you're right, he was there. I knew who my father was. But he didn't want to know me."

After a few moments, Darius said, "This isn't you, Jasper. To hide like this."

Jasper exhaled. "I'm not hiding. I just don't want to be on display."

"You're a fucking liar. You've lived your life on display."

Jasper looked over to see Darius smiling. But it was an angry smile, one that covered a fury so deep it was essentially void of emotion. It simply existed, without explanation or apology. Jasper recognized it of course; it was the same bitter fruit he survived on. Two Black men. Two gay men. Two positive men. Two fatherless men. Two sick men. Two invisible men. Two young men. Two dead men. They both ate from the same tree, both carried the seeds of the same anger—not toward each other directly, but toward the situation, the world, and their place in it—and though they tried to contain it, to bury it underground and ignore it, it was determined to grow, driven like all seeds to find the sun. In moments like this, when it finally broke through the surface, something was always threatened; the foundation their friendship was built upon was inevitably punctured, the sidewalk left riddled with chunks of broken concrete. They would both carry on as if nothing had happened—step over the debris, try not to trip—but they never questioned it, never expected it to disappear. Never expected it to change. And so it didn't.

Jasper stood. He instantly felt light-headed, but he tried to ignore it. He was used to moving through pain. Darius looked at him, his face hard. The distance between them was no more than twenty feet, interrupted by the island and one of the thick wooden columns that stood in the room like a telephone pole, yet they couldn't connect. Jasper didn't want to be reached. When he stumbled, Darius moved toward him, coming to his rescue instinctually, but Jasper threw up his hand.

"Don't. I'm fine."

Jasper took another step forward. From there he reached out to straighten one of a dozen frames that adorned his white walls, this one the poster from *Don Quixote* at Lincoln Center. He heard the score playing softly in his head, and remembered the opening night's show, when he made history dancing with a sprained ankle to a packed house with both Juliet and his father in the audience. *The first Black leading man*, his father said to him backstage, mopping the sweat that poured from Jasper's forehead with a handkerchief as soft as silk. A surprise embrace had brought tears to Jasper's eyes, which he'd struggled to contain.

"That part of my life is over," Jasper said softly, his voice without pity.

Darius picked up the towel and wrapped it around his hand like a boxer taping his fists before a fight. "You're not dead yet," Darius said.

Jasper took a breath, still fighting the urge to cry, and lost his balance. His fingers skimmed the wall as he caught himself, knocking down the poster. It fell with a crash, the glass breaking over the image of his body extended in flight, cutting his legs in half. Then the room was still, reminding Jasper of the silence that followed just after a thunderous applause.

As Darius got the broom to clean up his mess, Jasper stood in the pool of broken glass. Soon he got tired, and had to lean against the wooden column, swaying a little to one side, as if dancing.

· 3 ·

The sun had just set by the time Juliet returned to the apartment. Jasper was back on the couch, bundled in wool; Darius had gone home. She brought carryout from her favorite Chinese restaurant around the block, one their parents had discovered on their second date, after seeing Abbey Lincoln and Ivan Dixon in the 1964 film *Nothing but a Man*. Juliet returned to the restaurant whenever she was in the city, as if it held some familial significance, but Jasper never went there on his own. He was not as nostalgic as his sister, and though he autographed a black-and-white headshot for the owner's daughter—one that still hung on the restaurant's back wall—he only liked to perform for a paying audience.

He picked at his cold rice noodles while Juliet ate everything she could reach with her chopsticks: Mongolian beef, pork dumplings, fried tofu with spicy bok choy. She always had an insatiable appetite. He wondered if the same would be true about Jenry, if his nephew would inherit that tendency just by watching her, despite the lack of a biological connection. He remembered how he'd started to mimic their mother's habits and style at a young age, before he learned it was wrong for a little boy to copy his mother instead of his father. Was it genetics that connected them so fiercely, or proximity, or just blind luck? And who was to blame for both children ending up gay?

Juliet was gesturing wildly when he returned his attention to the room, catching the tail end of her debriefing. She talked about the assholes at her meeting, told him that she could only tolerate the city when it was covered in snow, and said that motherhood was not like she expected, difficult in all the wrong ways. She didn't move from one topic to another; she carried on all three conversations at once. His sister multitasked as a way of living all the lives she had imagined for herself simultaneously. On a good day, Jasper struggled to keep up; today he didn't even try.

"It's too hard," she said, fixing their drinks. "To be somebody's everything."

"That's why I'll never have children." His voice was raspy like an old man's.

Juliet shook her head. "I'm not talking about children. I'm talking about grown-ups. About relationships." She used the bottle opener on her key chain to open a bottle of Red Stripe, taken from the six-pack she'd bought the last time she visited. She'd found it in the fridge, alongside a two-hundred-dollar bottle of Champagne she'd given him to celebrate the opening night of *Swan Lake*, his last Manhattan premiere, just before Jenry was born.

"Oh, well." Jasper dropped his fork. "I'll never have one of those either."

She laughed, as if it was a joke. "You know that's not the answer. To quit."

"I know you wouldn't understand, Miss High IQ," he teased, "Miss Perfect Score on Her SATs, but not everyone skips a grade and graduates from high school at seventeen." He folded his hands over his stomach. "For the rest of us mere mortals, quitting is a legitimate option."

"Oh, if Pop could hear you now."

Jasper stifled a cough. "What would he say? It's not like he never quit anything."

"Oh yeah? What did he quit?"

Jasper was quiet for a long time. "Me," he finally said. "He quit me."

Juliet placed a cup of hot tea on the coffee table, on top of a mosaic tile coaster he'd bought in Morocco, back when he used to take vacations. Jasper wished he could take back his words, or rather, that he could make them untrue, but they both knew better. He wasn't sure when it happened, but the fact of it was crystal clear. Winston Patterson would proclaim that he had a son, had two successful, accomplished children, but they didn't interact in any way that was typical or desirable; he no longer visited Jasper or talked on the phone with any frequency, and they had stopped sending each other birthday cards or Christmas presents. He was a father in name only, and Jasper was a son only in memory.

"It's life that's disappointed him, not you." Juliet jabbed a shrimp with one of her chopsticks. "You have to realize that by now."

"We've all done our fair share of disappointing him."

"Why, because we're not married with a house in the suburbs and a tenure-track job and a Volvo?" Juliet gestured with her chopstick. "So what? We're not the children he wanted. There's nothing we can do about it now."

Jasper sipped his tea. "But you do have a Volvo. The old man told me he gave you his old 960 when he got a new one."

"The maintenance was too high. I traded it in for a Ford Explorer."

Jasper laughed, causing his sides to ache. "Well, at least you gave him a grandchild."

She spit out the shrimp in her mouth. "Come on, he doesn't think of Jenry as my son. He thinks my friend had a baby and I went along for the ride. He might put up the pictures, but that doesn't make him a grandfather. Let's face it, if he didn't think you were the donor, he probably wouldn't even do that."

"Do I sense hostility in your voice, my dear?"

She glared at him.

Jasper went on. "But more importantly, is he right? Are you just along for the ride?"

She shook her head. "You've got a lot of nerve, Jay."

He let the steam from his tea coat his face. For the first time in days, he felt warm. "Don't be so sensitive. You know I'd never judge you."

"That's like me asking you if you became a dancer to date cute boys."

"But I *did* become a dancer to date cute boys." He winked at her. "Or maybe just to sleep with them."

"Jesus Christ, don't you ever get enough?" She was back at the couch, standing over him like a giant.

"Yes." Jasper pushed the food away from him. "I've had enough of this."

Juliet peered into his bowl. "You barely ate anything."

"I'm sorry. I'm just not hungry."

Juliet felt his forehead for a fever. When she spoke, her voice was even, practiced.

"I think you should go to the doctor, Jay. I've never seen you like this."

"I've already been. They told me it's just the flu. My T-cells are fine, I promise." He had told this lie so often over the last few months, a part of him believed it was the truth. "I just need sleep. You know what it's like coming back from a tour. It takes time to adjust."

"Can't they give you something? For the pain at least."

"I'm fine, Jay," he told her again.

She smiled when he called her Jay, an interchangeable nickname they'd both used since childhood. Their mother used to call them Blue Jay and Brown Jay, but neither one remembers who was who; in the interest of fairness, they've both simply become "Jay."

"Christ, you're just like Mom." Juliet sipped her beer. "Coughing blood into her hands and saying she's okay."

He opened his eyes. "I didn't think you remembered that."

"How could I forget? All her handkerchiefs were stained with blood. I remember Pop soaking them in bleach after she died because he didn't want to throw them away."

"God, he's a cheap bastard," Jasper said under his breath.

Juliet shook her head. "He wasn't being cheap, Jasper. He was griev-
ing. He didn't know how to let anything go."

Jasper waved her away. "You still defend him, just like when we were
kids. Excusing the many shortcomings of the great Winston Patterson—"

"I'm not defending him. I'm explaining him."

"Why? Does it make you feel better about your relationship?"

"It'd be pretty hard to feel any worse," Juliet said, "unless he was
dead." She snapped her mouth closed, as if that could somehow erase
the admission from her lips. Then she stood to clear the dishes from the
coffee table and put the leftovers in the fridge.

Jasper spoke to break the silence. "How often do you see him?"

"About once a month. I bring Jenry over to visit and we end up sort-
ing all his newspapers. He still has *Jet* magazines from the 1970s. Won't
throw a damn thing away."

"Just like the cabin, I guess."

She laughed. "Exactly. He still says it's the only thing he really owns."
She boxed up the garbage to take to the chute in the hallway, tying the
handles into a bow.

"I bet he still has the same sheets on their bed. Still uses that old
coffee pot from their first apartment."

Juliet opened another beer. "She was his first love."

"And it ended more than twenty years ago."

"So?" She walked back to the living room, standing over him again.

"So, she's been dead longer than he knew her."

"That's just time," Juliet said. "Love can't be quantified."

Jasper looked up at the ceiling. "He won't mourn us like that."

She flipped the bottle cap into the air like a coin. "How do you know?
Die and we'll find out." She had a playful grin, but it was lost on Jasper.

He looked out the window to the darkening sky.

"Okay," he said.

· 4 ·

Jasper woke on a bed of ice. Chills flushed his body. He was dreaming about his mother, how she used to dance with him standing on her feet in the cabin's sunlit kitchen. She was the one who convinced him he could fly.

He heard the click of old pipes as the heat kicked on. The damp air burned his throat. In the dark, he reached for the glass on his nightstand, the water cold like a stream. He looked at the clock: half past three. So many hours left before dawn. He closed his eyes and returned to the dream, picking it up like a book he still had to finish.

On that night, the one he was dream-remembering, his mother had chosen the soundtrack from *Porgy and Bess* as his instruction, and in the middle of Cab Calloway singing "It Ain't Necessarily So," his mother dipped him low, his hair just grazing the kitchen floor, and there, watching them through the screen door, stood his father. In the shadows he looked darker than he really was, and his expression—one of disgust and outrage—looked so perplexing upside down that Jasper wondered if his eyes had somehow inverted it, and really his father was delighted to see his wife and son dancing to one of his favorite albums. He blinked hard, blood rushing to his head, and when he opened his eyes again his father was gone.

Yes, he thought now. That's when he left me. In that cabin, on that darkened porch.

And so it was there that he had to go to say goodbye.

· 5 ·

In the morning he felt rested in a way that had eluded him for months. Juliet was groggy before her morning espresso, not fully awake when she agreed to drive him to the cabin on her way back to Providence. It wasn't too far out of her way and the Berkshires were so beautiful in the snow, he told her. Plus, she hadn't been there in years. Not since college, she admitted, when she took girls from Mount Holyoke up there for the weekend, trying to convince them that sleeping with her did not make them gay—or mean that she was in love with them.

The drive took three hours. Jasper slept most of the way, lulled by the radio and the rhythm of the car thumping along the expressway. He had always been able to sleep in transit: airport lounges, bus stops, train stations, his head propped against a cloudy window he knew he'd never touch again—each had offered him as many restful nights as his own bed. Maybe more. His head fell back as they rounded a tight curve exiting the freeway, mouth tilted to the sky; Juliet rubbed his cheek with the backside of her hand, touching him like she touched her sleeping son, so soft it might be imagined.

The line between city and country was unmarked; like falling in love, it was impossible to know exactly when it'd been crossed. A few miles off the Mass Pike and the only certainty was that the cars weaving through the newly paved roads were outnumbered by cows three to one. They passed through the town of Lenox, tourist signs scattered along the road: Tanglewood, the Norman Rockwell Museum, the home of Edna St. Vincent Millay. All places they'd visited in their childhood, dragged on hot summer days by nannies from Germany or Sweden while their father stayed behind, working on a book about the impact of slave revolts on the abolitionist movement, in the hay loft he'd converted into an office soon after their mother died.

Juliet laced her long fingers through Jasper's, so similar they could be from the same hand. The third finger on his left hand was ringless like her own. Still sleeping, he pulled her fingers into a fist with his, their knuckles knotted together like braids of bread. They rode like that for the remainder of the trip.

When they arrived, Juliet pulled into the unmarked driveway slowly, careful not to jostle him. She was, like all new mothers, deliberate with her movements, extracting her fingers from his loosened grip so slowly she appeared to be motionless. There was old snow along the driveway's edge, piled into crusty banks, but the center of the gravel road was clear and hard, easily passable. Though almost a half mile away, the cabin could be seen through the leafless trees, one of the few benefits of winter. It stood small and dark against the surrounding white field.

The sound of the engine cutting off was what woke him. He sat up, his head beginning to pound as soon as he opened his eyes. He blinked against the bright white snow.

"It's so beautiful here," he said. "So clean. Not like what I remember."

"You were probably thinking of summertime."

He nodded. "All that color was distracting. I like the snow better."

"Nowhere to hide," Juliet said, getting out of the car.

She carried his bags in, leaving Jasper to carry his down jacket and a lukewarm cup of tea she picked up at a gas station by the Turnpike. He stopped to sip the tea twice during the short walk from the parked car to the front porch, an excuse to catch his breath. When he got inside the cabin, he sat down on the first thing he saw: a wooden trunk as long and wide as a casket.

Juliet built a fire before he could register the cold. She carried two bundles of firewood in one arm, kindling and newspaper in another, all scored from the stash on the back porch, filled by a neighbor who maintained the grounds for them.

"I love how butch you are," Jasper told her with a smile.

"Someone in this family had to be." She made a torch out of a rolled-up magazine and lit it with matches found in the junk drawer. In five minutes, there was enough heat coming from the wood stove for him to remove his winter coat. She brought him a crocheted blanket, probably something their mother made, and tucked him in on the couch, his shoes facing the fireplace.

"Tell me if it gets too hot."

"Mmm," he said. "You'll know when you start to smell the rubber."

She laughed and he watched her walk into the kitchen, unpacking groceries from an A&P bag. He wondered when she stopped for food, what she would force him to eat.

"Hope you're in the mood for chili," she yelled out, reading his mind.

"Would it matter if I said I wasn't?"

"Nope."

"Then chili it is."

An hour later they were sharing the couch, eating bowls of chili with plastic spoons and spilling crumbs of cornbread onto the braided rug they used to beat with croquet mallets in the summertime to keep it clean.

"I had an affair," Juliet said without any preamble. "Am having an affair. Present tense."

She took a bite of cornbread, filling her mouth as if to stop herself from spilling more of the truth. He continued to stir his chili, not yet having taken a bite. "Does Marisa know?"

"No. I don't think so. Not yet." She poured red wine into two glasses, offering him one. When he shook his head, she drank from that one, leaving the other untouched.

He kept stirring. "Are you going to tell her?"

"I haven't decided. Part of me thinks I'll just break it off and never say anything about it."

He blew repeatedly on his first bite before taking it. "Good. It probably won't help anyway. Her knowing. It's just something she'll hold over you for the rest of the relationship."

"No, I meant break it off with Marisa."

He swallowed hard. "Oh. I see."

They listened to the wood snap and hiss as it burned.

"Do you love this other girl?"

She took a swallow of her wine. "No, I'm not in love. It's lust, something I haven't felt for Marisa in a long time. Maybe I never did."

He was back to stirring, the spoon held softly between his fingers. "Sex is a huge part of a relationship," he said bluntly. "Don't let straight people convince you it's not. That's the problem with long-term relationships—after a year the frequency falls by half, and if you have children, forget about it. I don't understand how any of them can live."

Juliet shifted in her seat. "The sex is good, don't get me wrong. But it's more than that. It's freedom, too. Not having the next twenty years mapped out." She tucked her feet beneath her, sitting like a child. He marveled at her graceful movements, the ease with which she folded her frame. "Marisa is great, she's fun, and she's a great mom—"

"But she's your friend. Not your lover."

"She's my wonderful, amazing friend. I love her. She's my family." Juliet looked down, into her own lap. "But I'm not in love with her."

He set down his bowl, reaching for his sister's hand. "Here's what I know about you. You're an artist, Juliet. And artists—I mean *all* artists, I don't care if you paint, dance, or sing—feed off passion. Without that, you're going to starve." He wasn't saying anything new; they'd talked about this a thousand times since high school, but something told him she needed to hear it. "Remember last summer, when you got back from MacDowell? You were so excited. I thought you were having an affair back then." He watched her drop her head, blushing. "Are you kidding, and you didn't tell your big brother? That is not right."

"I'm sorry, there was a lot going on. The band, the new album."

"Exactly." He pointed at her. "That's what I mean—passion."

"I know. That's not the problem."

"So what is?"

"I just don't know how to find the balance." She picked up the second glass of wine and held it loosely in her hand, like she was trying to measure its weight. "When I'm home, it's great. We play with Jenry and laugh, and it feels great." She took a sip of wine. "And then I go off to a gig and I love that, too. I feel alive, like I'm making something real, something that didn't exist before. I don't think I can ever give that up."

She had given him an opening, and now Jasper had to take it.

"That would be a mistake. A tragedy even." When she didn't respond, he kept going. "You have a gift, just like Mom. You shouldn't waste it at home changing diapers."

She looked up. "That's not fair. I love being home with him."

"I know you do, and it's beautiful. But he has another mother. There is no other Juliet Patterson showing up in your place at the piano."

She picked up his bowl, stirring in the skin that formed on top of his chili. "You're not impressing me with your appetite." She spooned a bite into his mouth. "Nobody starves on my watch."

"Always mothering, aren't you?" He pushed away her hand as she tried again. She was smiling, but he knew it wasn't for him. She was thinking about Jenry, the one she'd made all these sacrifices for. "There isn't anything wrong with wanting more. Needing more. It doesn't make you a bad person."

"I know that," she said, but he wasn't sure he believed her.

"Let's get real for a minute." His tone was serious. "If you do leave, what happens to the baby?"

"I didn't say anything about leaving. Even if we break up, I'm not going anywhere. I mean, I usually sleep in my own bed anyway. It wouldn't be that different." She paused, thinking. "Or it wouldn't have to be."

"Clearly you've thought about this."

She nodded. "I just don't want a big mess. Divorce is so hard on kids. How can people who claim to love their children put them through that? Having two bedrooms, two backpacks—it's like being two different people."

"And if she doesn't go along with your plan? This is his mother, after all, she might think it's a package deal. You leave her, you leave him."

Juliet shook her head. "I would never leave him." She poured more wine into her glass, and then into the second one.

"I'm just saying. She has to agree, doesn't she? She's holding all the cards."

"Maybe you can't understand this. But I love him, Jay. Like he was my own son." When she looked at him, her eyes filled with tears.

"Of course you do," Jasper said, reaching out to squeeze her arm. "He is your son. And we all know how you feel about him. But according to the law, a child only has one mother, you know? I'm just worried about her using that against you. Like maybe you won't get to have your cake and eat it, too."

"Oh please, men have been doing this for centuries. Shit, probably since the beginning of time." She took another drink.

Jasper sat back on the couch and recrossed his legs, letting the heat from the fireplace warm him. He felt like he was being held by the warmth, and that feeling of acceptance, of wholeness, gave him the courage to speak again.

"Most people think you can't be an artist and have a family—or maybe you can if you're not a great artist, but who wants to bother with that? I'm not trying to be a buzzkill, Sis, but I hope you don't lose too much of yourself in this. I think it's great, you wanting a family and everything, but who's your role model here, Pop?" Juliet snorted. "Exactly.

And he had a steady gig, and he was a man, and straight—I mean no one does it all."

"What about Mom?" Juliet offered weakly. "She was so talented. And she was a good mother."

Jasper nodded. "But Mom is dead," he said, his voice even, almost apologetic. "She didn't get the chances you got. To have a real career."

They sat together for several more minutes, neither one talking. Juliet filled the silence by picking up his bowl and feeding him another bite of chili. His stomach was beginning to protest, but he took it anyway; he wanted to give her something, however small, that would allow her to feel necessary, and in control.

"What if I adopted him?" Juliet exhaled. "She asked me a while ago, but I keep putting her off. I don't know . . . maybe it would be better for all of us, if I made it legal."

"That's a big step," Jasper said. He always thought Juliet liked the fluid nature of her role, to be legally tied to nothing. It was the way she'd always been, never wanting to promise a future to anyone, a trait they shared.

"Bigger than what I'm doing now? I'm with him almost every day."

"I don't mean with him. I mean, away from your career."

"Why can't I have both? Most of my gigs are at night anyway. I told my manager I could tour in the summer, and on weekends. We'll make it work."

"Okay, fine. So then why change it now? Did she threaten you?"

Juliet shook her head. "She would never do that." She put down Jasper's bowl and he lay his head back to rest. "When she was pregnant, we talked about all of this. She said she wanted me in his life forever, even if I don't adopt him. Nothing will change that. She made me a promise and I believe her."

Juliet fixed the blanket, wrapped it tight around his legs. With only his arms exposed, he reached for both of her hands and held them. He fixed her with his gaze, his eyes dark and somber.

"And what about you, what promise did you make?"

Juliet rolled her head back and closed her eyes. She looked so young and innocent, and he wanted nothing more than to let her off the hook and not prod further, but he couldn't do it. They had always been close, but there was also a space between them; it was, after all, the way they were raised. To be together, but in their own rooms—the way Winston Patterson preferred it. Intimacy with boundaries, where even tenderness had a limit, perhaps even a lock on its door. But that night, Jasper felt called to do more, to let his sister fully inside; whatever he had, whatever he was made of, he wanted to share it with her. He wanted to feel seen, and he would risk anything to attain it.

"Forget that," Jasper said. "Forget the promises you made her. I want you to make me a promise."

Juliet looked at him.

"Whatever happens to me, and whatever you do with Marisa, make sure you stay focused on your career. No matter what. And try to have a relationship with Pop—a real one, better than mine. So you don't have any regrets."

"What do you mean, whatever happens to you?"

"We're all going to die, Jay. Sooner or later."

"What aren't you telling me?" Juliet sat up. It was hard for him to see her worry. "Did the doctors say something?"

He shook his head, tried to keep her calm.

"This is about you, not me. Your relationship with your father. And if you can't do it for yourself, think of Jenry. He didn't ask to be born into this mess. No offense, but this isn't the cleanest stable in the barn, if you know what I mean." Jasper laughed at his choice of metaphors, imagined his father mucking a stall, wearing work boots and overalls, being the type of man to get dirty. "Pop needs someone to love. Maybe this will give him another chance, to give Jenry what he couldn't give us. He already thinks he's my son, so just keep—"

"Lying to him?"

"He needs to think there's a blood connection. That's how he forms bonds. Hell, it might be the only type of bond he *can* form."

"That's pretty shitty, if you ask me."

"Yep, but he's the only father we've got."

Later, while Juliet washed the dishes, Jasper went to lie down in the bedroom. The sheets smelled like all the summers of his childhood rolled into one, and he only had to close his eyes to go back to that distant time, when they were a family and he felt whole and complete, when he knew their entire lives still lay ahead.

· 6 ·

After a nap they played Scrabble, the only game they kept in the cabin that their father would participate in. A battle of words—now that's a fight Winston Patterson wanted to win. Juliet got up after winning with *justify*, to check on the lasagna she made for dinner, and to wrap the leftover cornbread into single-sized servings Jasper could pluck from the freezer and microwave once she'd gone. He wanted to tell her to stop, to save her energy, save the food, but he knew that cooking was her way of saying *I love you*, since she didn't often use the words.

"Do me a favor, will you?" he called from the couch. "When you're done making all this food I'll never eat, come in here and entertain me."

He heard her laughing through the thin walls. A few minutes later, she was standing above him, wiping her hands on a dish towel. She eyed the Scrabble board.

"You ready for round two?"

"How about playing me a song? It's been a while since I've heard you live."

She glanced across the room to the piano, tucked against the wall in the dining room. "It's been years since we tuned that thing. It'll sound atrocious."

"Come on, I won't be able to tell." He gave her a pathetic look. "Please."

"Let me do these dishes first."

He snatched the towel from her hands, tucking it into her belt so it hung down her front like a sash. "You're done working for the night. Now play."

Her smirk spread into a grin as she walked into the corner and lifted the fallboard to expose the perfect line of ancient keys. The piano, an antique Steinway with a rosewood case, was a wedding gift from their mother's parents, with explicit instructions for all their yet-unborn children to learn to play. Faye, never one to buck authority, started their lessons before kindergarten, but it was Juliet who showed real promise, studying all through grammar school, even in the summers, which was how the piano came to live in the cabin. She had a gift, the musicians from Tanglewood used to say, the ones their father paid each summer to give her weekly lessons, a different one each year so she wouldn't copy one particular style, but would instead have a worldly sound that would make her not just a pianist, but a star.

She sat down, cracking her knuckles dramatically, and played a few bars. "Oh God, that's awful." She made a face. "Maybe this thing has never been tuned."

"It's fine. Keep going."

She started again, playing for longer this time. Her fingers were slow at first, hesitant, but after a few stuttering mistakes she seemed to cast off whatever rust had built between her joints until they begin to fly over the keys, stretching, pounding the notes like she was drawing water from bones. After a while Jasper closed his eyes. This was the balm he'd wanted, the medicine he'd been waiting for. To be in this cabin and hear his sister play made him feel once again like the healthy, energetic child who never stopped moving, the boy that walls couldn't tame.

"Don't tell me I'm putting you to sleep," Juliet called out. "That's every pianist's nightmare."

"Just the opposite," he said, eyes closed. "I am traveling through time."

"I'm testing you," she said as she continued to play. "Name that song."

He listened, thoughtful, swaying to the beat. "Since you're in a sentimental mood, I have to go with Bud Powell." He opened his eyes to see her smiling.

"Song?"

He sat up. ""Round Midnight'?"

"Guess again."

"'In Walked Bud.'"

"Nope. One more try and then I'll put you out of your misery."

"I'm all out of ideas." He poured himself a tiny glass of wine. "Tell me, or you don't get any more wine."

"I have to slow down anyway, or I won't be able to drive home." She looked over at him. "Doesn't alcohol interfere with your medication?"

He shrugged. "Wine hardly counts. It's like sophisticated juice."

She laughed. "I like that. Maybe Jenry and I can have juice dates from now on. He'll have grape or orange—the crude class—and I'll have Cabernet or Chianti, the *sophisticated juice*."

"You could do an ad campaign. Make t-shirts, the whole deal."

"And I could write a catchy jingle." She changed her playing now, turned the song into something worthy of a thirty-second spot during daytime television. "And you could dance in the commercial."

"I only perform for live audiences," he joked. "It's in my contract."

She ran her fingers quickly down the keyboard and came to an abrupt stop on the final key, holding the note until the sound dissipated. Neither one of them moved.

"Well, there goes our fifteen minutes of fame," she said.

"Don't worry, baby sister, I've already had mine." He raised his glass. "But you, yours has just begun."

She raised hers as well and they toasted the air.

"So, what was the song?" he asked.

Juliet finished her wine, then went back to what she was playing before, the chords so familiar Jasper felt an ache in his chest, like smelling a lover's perfume.

"'Anthropology.'" Juliet continued to play.

Yes, he should have known. His mother's favorite. Juliet's hands were really in motion now, fluttering across the keys like a bird possessed. "She told me she played it while I was in the womb, hoping to brainwash me."

"Apparently it worked."

Jasper stared at the bookshelf by the window, filled with more records than books. He remembered helping his mother organize them, first by album title, and later, when the collection grew, by artist. She said their history was on that shelf, and if he wanted to know whose shoulders he was standing on, he didn't have to look beyond those three feet.

"You know why he got her all those albums?" Jasper asked, and then went on to answer his own question. "Because it was the only time she'd stand still."

Juliet nodded. "Maybe she needed to escape. From him. Or us."

Jasper had never been a parent; he didn't have to straddle two worlds. But his sister did, and his parents had; given the circumstances, they had done okay. Now, he wanted to remember the best of his parents, those moments of tenderness he saw between them, the love they were able to give to each other that they wouldn't share with anyone else.

"She used to ask him to be her radio," Jasper said, pouring more wine, "and he would pull up a chair next to the record player and play song after song that she requested. Especially during those last few months, when she hardly got out of bed. Even during the night, he never let the music end."

Juliet stopped playing. She looked at him from across the room. "Who knew he was capable of that?"

Jasper ran his finger along the lip of his wine glass, releasing a soft moan. "She knew. That's why she married him."

Juliet stood to look through the albums. "That's not the man we knew."

Jasper watched her flip through the album covers, remembered how she used to pull them off the shelf in tall stacks and carry them to the couch for story time, years before she could read. "Read it, Jay, read it," she used to beg, until he took the cover from her and made up a story on the spot, while she pointed to each photograph saying, "This one?" until she'd memorized every musician's name and most of their record titles.

"Pop changed a lot after she died," Jasper told her. "It's cliché to say, but it's true. He actually used to do things with me, like take me to the park and for ice cream cones. Before you were born and when you were a baby. Before Mom got sick." He refilled his wine glass, the most he'd drank in years, liking the heat in his belly and how it made every sound in the room amplify. "There was this Italian bakery on Federal Hill and he used to buy cannoli from the old lady who owned it every Friday. I didn't even like them, what kid wants cheese in his pastry, but I'd eat one anyway, so I could hear the story of how he picked that one just for me, with the most chocolate chips on the ends, and then he'd count them just to prove it. Our old man, counting chocolate chips—can you believe it?"

Her eyes narrowed. "No, I can't." She pulled out a McCoy Tyner album, reading the songs on the back. "You make him sound like Mr. Rogers."

"Well, no, he was never a white man in a cardigan"—Jasper laughed—"but he was a lot more . . . I don't know, *open* than he is now. He could talk without making everything a lecture. He could spend time with us, like we were a normal family."

"As opposed to now, when we're . . ." She looked up, her eyes asking him to give her the answer.

He shrugged, too tired to play the dutiful older brother. "I don't know what we are." He drank more wine. "Maybe it's just life. Growing up, getting older. People grow apart, they lose touch. It's nobody's fault."

She put the album cover back, and pulled out another. "I think it's the parents' responsibility to keep the family together. They started it, and if they want it to survive, they need to take care of it. Make sure all the kids come home for Christmas, buy the damn plane tickets if they have to, but get everyone in the same room. When Jenry's older, I'm gonna smack him if he doesn't come home for all the holidays. Martin Luther King Day, Presidents' Day, Easter."

"Cinco de Mayo?" Jasper suggested.

"Yes, whatever. We'll celebrate them all."

Jasper got off the couch, struggling to stand from the combination of wine and a still-breaking fever. He shuffled toward her.

"Well, Sister, today is not a holiday. But it is a special day, because you and I are here together, and I want you to know that I promise, from here on out, to spend every single holiday with you for the rest of my life. Deal?"

She looked at him, not certain if he was joking, so he stuck out his hand and she shook it. Then, before she could let go, he pulled her into a hug, holding her as close and as hard as he could. Still sitting, she returned the hug, burying her face in his sweater. He leaned over to kiss the top of her head, breathing in the familiar pear scent of her shampoo. He couldn't remember the last time he enjoyed a fragrance so completely.

"I think you should call him," she whispered into his chest. "Right now, from here, while we're together."

"What if he answers?"

"Then we say hi, we're at the cabin, and we were just talking about you, what a great father you used to be, until you got heartbroken and became kind of shitty." Juliet paused. "Or maybe *piss-poor* is a better adjective?"

After a second, they both started cracking up.

"Well, this is going to be fun."

Jasper got the rotary phone from the side table and brought it to the piano bench, stretching the cord straight so it would reach, like a combed-out curl. He sat down next to his sister, who started to play another song, this one something she wrote herself. He dialed his father's home phone number, the first one Jasper ever memorized, and waited for it to ring. Juliet pressed her leg against his, letting him know she was there, that she was beside him; that was all the strength he needed to keep going. He listened to the phone ring again and again, wondering if the next one would be the moment his father finally picked up, and if he would ever reach him.

· 7 ·

Jasper woke in the cabin alone. Juliet hadn't wanted to leave him, but he assured her that he was all right, that her real life—the baby, the piano—needed her more. She promised to return in a few days to drive him back home. The fire she built had lasted all night long, and the living room was warm, which made it easier to open his eyes. The sun was shining onto the floors, creeping up the couch to the edge of his blanket, reaching for him, and when he looked through the window at the bright blue sky, he imagined that it was warm outside, too, summertime warm, and it made him want to breathe the fresh country air and walk one last time over the snow-covered land that surrounded his parents' cabin. The first place he called home.

He got up gingerly, slowed by yesterday's wine, and peed first, then took a handful of pills with the coldest water he'd ever tasted, a cold that burned like strep throat—first his medications, pills of all shapes and colors, like swallowing confetti; then pain relievers, vitamins, fish oil supplements, and finally some ginger capsules to settle his stomach. The eggs that Juliet boiled for his breakfast stayed in the fridge. Maybe later he would find room in his belly, distended from all the cold water, but for now he brushed his teeth and got dressed, choosing a wool cable-knit turtleneck from L.L.Bean and herringbone trousers that used to belong to his father, the bottom half of the first suit his mother ever sewed by hand. They were ill-fitting when he'd inherited them—long in the leg, wide in the waist—so he'd had them tailored to his shape; when he first wore them, he felt as if a miraculous convergence had occurred, not that the pants had shrunk, but that he had grown to fit them; his father's frame could only be filled by expansion.

He added several more logs to the fire, stoking the embers like Juliet had shown him, urging them to accept the new wood in a fiery embrace, to become a living thing, bent on destruction. On the way out the door he grabbed his scarf, a purple cashmere-wool blend from a Danish lover who'd broken his heart by refusing to move to New York. *If he could see me now,* Jasper thought, catching his reflection in the hallway mirror—a pale ghost-like boy of a man, a dancer who could no longer dance—*he would see just how right he had been to leave me.* But then again, hadn't Jasper been the one to get on the plane?

Once outside, he noticed that he forgot his coat. The heat from the cabin, from the wine and the chili and the conversation, seemed to be with him still, his insides ignited. Oh well, the sun was shining as bright as a sun can shine midwinter, and if he moved this body and actually raised his heart rate, he trusted he'd be able to keep his temperature up for a short stroll. Just down the gravel road and back, the same walk they did each night during his childhood.

He walked along the driveway at first, crunching the snow-packed gravel until he got to the creek. The fresh air felt good in his lungs, so he kept going. As he cut across the unplowed field, he regretted not looking for boots in the closet. His loafers were frozen solid eight minutes into the walk. When he was about to go back, to quit this nature business and give in to the city blood coursing through his veins, he spotted the pond, its surface frozen smooth and black, a tinted windshield.

He tested the edge before stepping onto the ice, slipped a bit but then caught himself before hitting the ground. On his second attempt, he glided like a ship set sail. To move his body so effortlessly, to float through the air, was a feeling he thought he'd lost for good. Something awoke in him, a joy he could not deny. A few yards from the shore he found a smooth patch of ice, the snow blown off by a vigorous wind, or industrious kids building a hockey rink. He tapped the black ice with a stick and heard a deep echo in reply. He looked for cracks but there were none to be seen; the only marks that blemished the ice were the frozen bubbles trapped under the pond's surface, like swimmers coming up for air.

He stepped onto the ice and stopped. He stepped again, twisting the ball of his foot over the smooth surface. *Like a dance floor*, he thought. *A stage.* Before he knew it, he had spun three times. Then a pas de chat and a pirouette. He laughed loudly, a sound that echoed like a war cry.

It was only now—already on the ice, already moving—that he had the conscious thought to dance. His muscles burned, his bones ached, it didn't matter. He could still force them to move. The music in his head was nothing he'd ever danced to before, a mix of piano tunes and voices, memories from a childhood spent at recitals and lectures, poetry readings he didn't understand. He carried it all in his head, in his flesh, and the movement his body made was the release, a pressure valve opened. Now he was nothing more than an instrument, a conduit, which he imagined was what he'd always been. No thought, only movement. He jumped, twirled, spun, leapt, and twisted. At first, he felt nothing, then soon everything, ingesting the cold, the sun, the blue sky. He felt the rawness in his throat as he sucked the frigid air, felt the pounding of his feet against the ice—the hardest surface he'd ever danced upon—felt the vibrations of the music in his head, how it splintered and cracked like wood.

When the numbness set in, he became aware of thought. He thought of his sister in her SUV, driving the three hours back to Providence, to her home with a makeshift not-quite-legal family, and he thought of his nephew, a boy with two mothers who would surely grow up with twice the opportunity to be adored—something all children need, but especially sensitive brown boys like him—and Jasper envied them their futures, the ones he wouldn't be around to see. He thought of his lovers, and pictured them as a street parade, saw the colorful cast—mostly men, but a few women thrown in for variety—and his friends, often cut from the same fabric, friends becoming lovers becoming friends, and he felt gratitude and relief that they'd shared so much space with him—physical space, but also the space of time. He wondered if time was a form of love, a way of doling out affection in reasonable pieces, in parts small enough that you weren't aware of their size, and of what was slowly disappearing from your own form as you gave them away.

He thought of his mother, who didn't give him enough time or space, but who gave him something else entirely: a sense of pride, in who he was, but also in who he could become—beyond the labels she knew society would press upon him. The characters he became on stage were different sides of his self, but he only had that sense of multitudes from her suggestion, her acceptance. When he remembered his mother, he encountered a loss so great he couldn't see the end of it, which was the same feeling he had about his father: there but not there. Would that ever be enough, for love to be suggested without being embodied? Maybe presence itself was the embodiment of love, and since his father had been there, had raised him the best he knew how, Jasper had received all the love the old man could give. Maybe Juliet, spending all those days with Jenry, was giving him the same—and if she could love him both ways, with her acceptance and her presence, Jasper was certain that Jenry would come out better than them all.

Jasper danced. He pounded the ice harder and harder, moved with a rhythmic grace as miraculous as flight. He was flying now, a bird in a field of white, the purple scarf the only color, the only sign of life on this blank winter canvas: a heartbeat in the center of a snow-white world.

He never felt the crack of the ice as it shattered beneath his weight, never felt himself fall. This was the grace of flight—that soaring and sinking often felt the same to the ignorant bird, who knew only the fluency of movement. He didn't fall as much as he vanished, the ice opening like a door to let him in, then quickly closing in his wake, the broken chunks floating like buoys until they were licked by the icy water and glued back into place. The only remaining sign of his dance, the one thing he left behind, was the purple scarf, trapped under the sheet of ice, visible only to the birds passing overhead, flying together in perfect formation as they left in a mass exodus—a silent, singular, permanent migration.

· BOOK V ·

The Grandfather

September 2015

· 1 ·

Winston Patterson is a man who never closes his eyes. Even in sleep, they stay partly open, scanning the dark, empty room like a security camera. This habit used to bother his wife, who swore it was because he didn't trust her, didn't trust anyone really, and she worried it would take years off of his life.

Faye was foolish to worry about that—his life—when it was she who got sick in the early years of their marriage, a cherry-sized lump in her breast after Juliet was born, and then six years later, the recurrence, this time in the lymph nodes. It was quick the second time, ferocious like an untamed beast, and he was grateful that she didn't have to suffer for long, that she would only have a few months of the bone-aching discomfort, the pills she swore she'd choke on, the night sweats that soaked both sides of the bed, knowing full well that her sickness would transfer to him upon her death—not the cancer itself, but what it leaves in its wake, the annihilation of hope—and he would carry the loss of her like a branding for the rest of his life. Which so far, he has.

They were living in Barrington when she died, a small town outside of Providence, and he'd just gotten tenure—the first African American in the History Department—but after a year of living without her, in the first house they'd bought together, the one she'd painted while still pregnant with Juliet, the one she'd chosen after they'd finally saved enough money to buy a house with two stories and a small yard for her garden, he put the house on the market and moved with his children into the city proper, to an old Greek Revival on the East Side. It was twice the size—something Faye would have thought extravagant based solely on the number of fireplaces (six), not to mention the fact that the children got two bedrooms each, on the second and third floors—but Winston chose it because it was on the same street as the university president's home, and he was just a five-minute walk from campus.

When he gave his children a tour of their new home, they followed the curved banister along the open staircase to the third floor, where he came upon an ancient leaded skylight he hadn't noticed before. From it, he could see the city's modest skyline, including the blocky geometry of Rhode Island Hospital, which he found strangely comforting. Winston would spend the rest of his teaching life within the square mile the university occupied, even when he got better offers from other schools in more interesting cities. He knew he didn't have it in him to relocate again, that without his wife he lacked the imagination and drive to reinvent himself as anything other than what he was destined to become: an old, widowed professor in a grand house he could never fill.

There was occasional talk on campus about him dating, grad students mostly, and the famous undergraduates—one the daughter of a Motown legend, the other a movie star, who by twenty-two was so desperate to prove her teenaged success wasn't a fluke that she passed up a Merchant Ivory production to study history at an Ivy League college, in a state with only one international airport—but the rumors weren't true. His heart burned to ash in that crematorium, alongside his once-vibrant wife, her skin sallow and paper-thin the last time he'd seen her, bones brittle like a fortune cookie, threatening to turn to dust in his hands as he carried her from the hospital bed to the rain-speckled window, showing her one last look at the world—their world, their city—though her eyes were already closed and her rattled breath shook her chest cavity like a passing train. His passion, when he remembers to look for it, is now stored in the pages of books—photo albums from their first years of marriage, the sonnets of Shakespeare he memorized for their third date, wanting to impress her with something aside from Civil War facts— which he keeps on the shelves of his home library, a room he walks through daily, but rarely takes the time to enjoy. She was his wife for more than a decade, and Winston was raised to believe that a good man, a God-fearing Christian, was only supposed to have one; when she died, he was prepared to spend the rest of his life alone.

And he has done so, except for the children. If asked how many children he has, his first thought is always three, yet by the time he speaks he has amended the answer: *one living, two dead.* When Jasper was alive, he would say *two*, not mentioning the boy who came in between, the one he held only once and never took home. They named him before Faye went into labor, *Jaymes Houston* after her favorite uncle, and though everything about him was a surprise—from his conception while Jasper was still breastfeeding to his shockingly early birth—they considered him a blessing. The pregnancy was normal in every way except its duration; at thirty-three weeks, and for reasons the doctors could never explain, Faye's water broke, and her uterus began to contract, ushering their second son into the world on a wet night in April when Jasper was just two years old. There was no way to stop it, so the doctors prepared an incubator and warmed flannel blankets, ordered medicine to help his immature lungs—but it didn't matter. The baby could not breathe on his own. In every other way he was perfect: ten fingers and toes; a strong heartbeat, which Winston felt against his fingertips when he touched him for the first time, his hands scrubbed raw with disinfectant soap; the fine features of his mother, including her light brown eyes; and a cap of silky dark hair the nurses longed to comb.

The following day, at just twenty-three-hours old, after a night in the NICU where the attending doctor had spent his shift manually inflating the ventilator to keep the baby's lungs from collapsing, they turned the machine off and took him out of the incubator to lie in his mother's arms for the first and last time. Winston could not look at the boy; instead, he focused on his wife, her eyes bloodshot from pushing, her skin blanched with heartache. He held her hand and watched the tears pour from her swollen eyes. She didn't wipe her face clean and neither did he. He was afraid to touch her. The baby lay perfectly still, like he was dead already, but they both knew he wasn't, not yet. She didn't rock him, but there was a sway to her embrace, her mother's instinct wanting to comfort him, soothe him even though he showed no signs of distress. He seemed to be sleeping, dreaming even, as his eyeballs twitched under the delicate skin of his eyelids, a smooth and shiny silk.

The nurse cleared the room, telling them to take their time. *There is not enough time*, Winston thought, *to say goodbye to a life not yet begun.* Words left him as he tried to think of a prayer to recite on behalf of his little boy, a song to sing for the angels come early to take him home. Later, standing at the gravesite beside the small coffin, he had the Bible to turn to, and he recited three psalms to the small group, his voice clear and strong, but here in the hospital room he had no such armor; the assault of grief wiped his mind clean. Winston closed his eyes, blinking back tears, and made the sign of the cross. Faye lay motionless in the hospital bed, the baby tucked beside her. He was swaddled in a thin white blanket, arms at his sides; they both looked like dolls. Faye leaned over to kiss him, first his eyelids, then his closed mouth, lips pressed together as if they were still forming, the edges not yet unfurled like petals of a flower waiting to bloom. Winston barely recognized his wife, her face a mask of sorrow.

"Please," Faye said, her voice just above a whisper. She looked toward the window. Winston knew what she wanted. He glanced down at the hospital bed; the sheets were thin and bone white, stiff with the smell of bleach. A dark stain spread from between her legs.

"You're bleeding," Winston said.

Faye shook her head, as if it didn't matter. "Help me," she said.

He took the baby from her as she struggled to get up from the bed.

The three of them walked together to the window and looked out at the darkening night. City lights blinked on in the distance, like stars filling up the sky. Faye took the baby into her arms, leaving Winston with a strange emptiness; the feeling of his son's body, its specific warmth, had already left him, evaporating into memory, and he marveled at the boy's weightlessness, a bird removed from his hands. He forced himself to memorize the features of his son's still-forming face, every line and curve, counting each of the long, black eyelashes, and tracing the pattern of damp, brown curls with his finger.

Winston felt something slipping away, some knowledge or instinct he was certain he would need to withstand these next moments, something invaluable to their survival, yet he could do nothing to keep it. He wanted to stop everything—all the clocks ticking off time they no longer had, the beep and whir of machines tracking progress, the echo of footsteps on the polished linoleum of the hallway—all the sounds of life moving on around him; he wanted to freeze everything exactly as it was, destroy it if he had to—just so they had something recognizable to hold on to. Yet all he could do was stand there and wait. The room was cold and goose bumps erupted over his skin. Outside, the flashing lights of an ambulance. He listened for the sound of the siren but heard nothing.

Faye made a noise, a horrible choking gasp, then fell against him, her body a dead weight that almost knocked him over. He caught her roughly, his unconscious wife and the now-dead baby she clutched fiercely in her arms, and lowered them awkwardly to the ground. Winston imagined what he would say to young Jasper, what he could say to anyone, as he reached for the nurse's call button and waited on the cold, hard floor to be found.

When they did finally go home, after releasing the baby's body to the funeral home, after the doctor signed his death certificate, Winston was relieved to find he didn't have to say anything to Jasper about what happened. Faye seemed to want to handle it herself, as she scooped him from the couch where he'd been reading with the babysitter and carried him off to his room. Winston never asked what she told him, and she never offered, and things soon fell into a routine. There was always music playing, filling the empty rooms with sound. Faye never left Jasper's side, a relief to Winston, since he was now afraid to take care of his son, to pick him up even, as if his sadness would seep into the boy and infect him as well. He made him toast every morning and kneeled down to tie Jasper's shoes, zip up a raincoat, or straighten a hat, but he couldn't bring himself to hold his son.

Years later, when Jasper was studying dance in college and brought a slip of a boy home for Thanksgiving, with rich brown skin and a wide, easy smile, Winston wondered if it was his fault his son was gay, that he'd somehow encouraged it—by stepping aside to let his wife tend to Jasper's every need while Winston stood back, surveying his family like a chaperone at a school dance, watching the strained intimacy of others. He knew there was no science to support that theory, but it was hard not to feel responsible; blaming himself was better than accepting the alternative: that he had no control.

He was more comfortable with Juliet, a stout baby with a full head of hair and a permanent grin, who sang to herself in her crib and soon demanded the attention of everyone in the room, especially the father she resembled, her birth the answer to a prayer he'd begun during Jaymes's memorial. It made no sense really, that he would be more comfortable with a girl, but he assumed something had softened in him during the years in between; just the fact that she was healthy and alive gave him the hope he needed to carry her in the crook of his arm while making breakfast, to burp and bathe her, to let her fall asleep against his shoulder as he read the newspaper accounts of anti-war protests, the shootings at Kent State, and wondered about the world they now inhabited.

They were close in those early years, Faye calling her a daddy's girl as she watched Juliet migrate to her father, bringing him her perfect scores on spelling tests, sitting on his lap to watch a boxing match, learning how to trim the tip of his cigar without slicing into her finger. In her final months, Faye was comforted by this fact; she could not control that her daughter would be a motherless child, but at least Juliet had a connection to her father. By the time Winston became a single parent, he was closer to his daughter than he would ever be with his son, a fact he once tried to deny but had slowly come to accept.

The break, if one could narrow it down to one event, came in her twenties, back from a few years in Europe promoting a jazz album she'd recorded in Copenhagen, half the songs written by Juliet herself. She didn't tell her father she was moving back to the States, let alone back to Providence, where she chose to live with a woman she knew from college, a woman she called her friend but would soon be raising a child with, instead of living at home with him. It seemed like a deliberate attack, first to sneak around, but later to mislead him by refusing to disclose the details of their arrangement, claiming that she wanted to protect him from her own ambivalence. Who lies to their father, their own flesh and blood, and calls it protection? He didn't know how to trust her again.

Faye had done something similar, hiding the details of her illness until the very end, wanting to spare him the gruesome details until it was too late to fight. All she needed in those final weeks was for him to hold her, to feed and bathe her—love her, but not save her. He was angry, which helped postpone the devastation, anger being a much more motivating emotion than pure grief. He felt powerful when he was angry, and active; he used the fury to fuel him on those days when all he wanted to do was stand in the shower and cry. This was a gift, one of the last she had given him, knowing it was a tool he could wield; anger gave him an enemy, something to blame along with the cancer. Now, when he thought about his relationship with Juliet, the estrangement they shared for so many years, he wondered if it stemmed from the same trick. Was his anger really just an attempt to survive grief?

WINSTON TRIES NOT to think about that now, as he drives through the pre-dawn streets of College Hill, readying himself for the half-mile swim he faces six days a week in the university's Olympic-sized pool, the same one where his children had taken swim lessons on cold Saturday mornings, the chlorine rising off their bodies like steam. He'd thought he was leaving the past behind when they'd left the house in Barrington, but everything felt haunted to him, a man whose work was wedded to the past. Perhaps he was the ghost, not Faye, not Jaymes—not even Jasper. And if that were true, there was nowhere else to go. He might as well stay put—travel the same roads, climb the same steps, swim the same laps— all to prove that he is still alive, that his heart didn't shrivel up like a mushroom and die in those hospital rooms. Yet not a day goes by that he doesn't wonder if that would have been the better outcome, considering what has happened to his family. Considering what he's done.

He opens the pool with his own key—a perk of forty-five years of service and his newly acquired emeritus status—and undresses by the glow of the security lights. He isn't a vain man, but the sight of his seventy-seven-year-old body in a Speedo isn't the highlight of his day. Still, he never averts his eyes as he walks by the mirror on the locker room door. He knows he can't escape the truth of his body, when he's spent so many years covering up other truths. Deception is a dog he knows intimately. *Lie to me*, his wife used to say, *but never lie to yourself.* A promise he's kept for many years, choosing instead to keep others in the dark. He has learned how to justify deceit; to withhold information from a loved one for their own benefit, as Faye and Juliet had done; to lie through omission and call it protection. But perhaps it won't be necessary anymore, now that the new semester has begun; soon everything will change.

He loves the shock of the cold water as he jumps in, the brilliant ache of his skin as he pulls his body to the surface, the water like a lawn of needles he has to cross. His crawl is effortless as he moves by instinct down the lane, his pulse setting the rhythm he swims by. When he was younger, he could swim the full twenty-five-yard length in one breath, but now he takes three or four before slapping the tiled wall at the other end, counting laps to himself—*one, two, three*—until twenty minutes later when he hits eighteen and pulls himself out of the deep end without using the ladder.

His mind is always clear, almost empty, in the pool, but by the time he stands under the shower thought has returned, flooding him again. Plans for the day, opening remarks for a lecture he needs to write, the abstract for a dissertation he doesn't want to read. And then, after all that, his mind will often travel to the past. He can't set foot on this campus without remembering some aspect of his family, since he raised his children a few blocks away, and both went to college here. He often wonders if that had been his intention all along: to merge his personal life with his work life in such a way that the two became inseparable, and he wouldn't have to face the fact that neither was strong enough to stand on its own legs. It was one of the reasons he encouraged his children to attend, not only for the university's prestige, but for the proximity. He wanted his worlds fully integrated; his job as his life, his family as his job. It has been that way for four and a half decades—why change things now?

On his way out from the locker room, he passes the lifeguards arriving for their 6:00 a.m. shift.

"Donut, Dr. Patterson?" the shorter one asks, offering him the Dunkin' Donuts box. He declines, resisting the temptation, but takes the coffee they always bring for him—cream, no sugar—and the newspaper folded in half and tucked into a blue plastic bag. He leaves three dollars on the counter and nods to the young men, who wear knee-length warm-up jackets with BROWN UNIVERSITY printed across the back in white block letters.

The sky is just turning blue, and the air is crisp—surprisingly cool for mid-September. In a few hours it will be hot, so when he arrives at his office, he turns on the air conditioning, the soft hum almost comforting as he sits down at his desk. Hours pass without him stopping to look at the clock. He eats an apple from his bag and a bran muffin wrapped in cellophane that he pulls from his drawer, no doubt left there by a grad student worried about his eating habits. He writes letters, makes phone calls, ignores emails he doesn't think are necessary. Soon the sun falls behind the library, darkening his office, and he knows that it is almost time to go home.

Then he feels something odd, a shift in the atmosphere, and he glances around the empty room. He notices a slip of paper on the floor, something that must have fallen through the mail slot. He didn't hear a knock, but wouldn't have answered if he had. Without official office hours, he doesn't feel obliged to open any closed door. Still, he bends down to pick up the folded paper. The first thing he sees is his son's name, which makes his heart stop. JASPER PATTERSON, written in all capitals, as an answer to the form's question: REASON FOR YOUR VISIT.

Winston knows immediately who wrote it, before he finds Jenry's name at the top of the slip, before he recognizes the handwriting. He's had months to prepare for this moment, and now that it's here his pulse quickens with anticipation. Time for his opening move.

He unlocks the door without hesitation, well aware of the consequences of what he has set into motion, what he will find on the other side. There, in the flesh, his grandson awaits—just as he had intended.

· 2 ·

They talk for almost an hour that first time, with Jenry leaving only after Winston has given him two gifts: a boxed set of Jasper's DVDs and the truth about Juliet's role in his creation—a truth that Jenry is clearly not prepared to accept. Winston feels compassion for the boy, since he, too, had struggled to understand his daughter's role in the beginning, but his perspective has slowly evolved. The more they argue, the more he understands—not about her past behavior, but how important it is that they stay connected. He wants his family back together more than he needs to understand how they came apart.

Winston sits alone afterward, assaulted by memories, and recalls a conversation with his daughter right after Marisa disappeared with the baby, when Juliet's shock at losing Jenry was as profound as Jenry's realization of her existence.

It was August, still summer vacation, but Winston was in his office anyway, where he could be found most days, trying to keep his balance in the same wooden chair he sat in now. He remembers picking up the phone on the first ring.

"She's gone," Juliet said, her voice a desperate whisper.

"What do you mean?" Winston shifted in his chair, which creaked under his weight. "Who's gone?" He was surprised she was calling; beyond their monthly dinners, they didn't have much contact. Unless it was about the boy.

"Marisa," Juliet said, "she moved out. She took everything and left. She took the baby." She was panting now, almost out of breath.

"Where are you?" He sat up, looked out the office window to gauge the time. The sky was pink with light. Sunset, meaning nearly eight o'clock.

"I'm at home. I just got back from the airport."

At first it didn't register, but then he remembered—she had been on tour, playing jazz festivals in Norway and Sweden.

"Weren't you expected back at the end of the month?" He glanced at the calendar on his wall, to confirm that it was Monday the sixteenth of August, 1999. Just into his sixties, yet time already had a habit of getting away from him.

"Does it really matter, Pop? I'm here now and she's gone." He heard her exhale. When she spoke again her voice was restrained. "I came back early. I could tell something was wrong."

"And there was no note, no letter?"

"Nothing."

He stood up, turning around at his desk, looking for something to do. "Did you call her at work?"

"She gave notice. They're still holding her last check. She didn't give them a forwarding address. You know what that means, don't you?" He had no clue. "She left the state."

"That doesn't mean much, dear. It's a pretty small state."

"Don't be cute—"

"I only meant . . . maybe she hasn't gone far. The state line is five miles from here. We cross it to go to the cinema." He was suddenly nervous, as if everything he said would soon be proven false. Maybe she had gone far.

"I need your help. I want to look for her."

"And how do you propose we do that?"

"She used to talk about going to New York. She had family there."

"I thought she was from Miami?"

"She is, but she would never go back there. She's not close to her parents. They cut her off after she had the baby." Juliet took a breath. "But she always talked about a cousin who worked for the mayor. In the Bronx or Brooklyn, I'm not sure where."

"So you want to call the mayor?"

"Well, no . . . I don't know. I have to do something. To get out of this empty apartment."

"Why don't you come home? You can stay with me for a while." He hadn't planned for this to come out of his mouth, but now that he'd offered, he realized how much he wanted her to accept.

"I have a home."

"I know. Just until you find her."

He could hear Juliet's ragged breath through the phone line.

"I don't know where to start," she said. "I mean, I don't even know her cousin's name. She must have told me, but I can't remember." He could tell she was crying. His brave little girl, tearless at her own mother's funeral, and now this.

"Stay there," he said, his desire to protect her breaking out like a rash over his body. "I'm coming to get you."

"No, it's fine."

"I'll be there in ten minutes."

She was sitting on the porch, surrounded by boxes, when he arrived. It was dark by then, but the air was still hot, a sticky humidity that told him a heat wave was coming. She packed the trunk of his car, saying she'd come back later to pick up the rest of her things. They went to Caserta's on Federal Hill, where he ordered traditional-style pizza strips with pepperoni and black olives, her favorite when she was a child. While they ate, she made plans on the back of a paper menu, a list of people to call, then schools, hospitals, the police. She drove to

New York the following day, fighting summer traffic to talk to college friends who confirmed they had seen her a few weeks before, when she was passing through on her way west. Marisa told them it was a road trip; she had no final destination. They kept telling Juliet about the baby—how he was so big now, so cute, and a perfect angel in the car. She had called him her little traveler. *How did she look*, Juliet would ask, *how did she seem?* The same, they would say, normal, fine.

Juliet was gone for weeks. After New York she went to Philly, then D.C. and Baltimore, and eventually Chicago. She visited a string of friends and acquaintances, half of whom had seen Marisa and Jenry as they passed through town, no one sure of where they were going. She was able to get her parents' address in Miami, with a home phone number and the name of a sporting goods store where her father supposedly worked. The home number was disconnected, but when she called the store she spoke to a man who said her father hadn't worked there in years and he had no contact information for any of them. She wrote a letter and mailed it to the parents' home address, but it came back unopened. Juliet was home by October, the trail run cold. She didn't want to give up, but what choice did she have? Can a person who wants to hide ever be found?

Winston helped her as much as he could, and in the helping began to understand just how much they meant to his daughter. She talked mostly about the boy, but she also missed her friend; her face opened up and her voice raised a full octave when she told stories about them. Winston tried to understand, but he had no experience with this type of relationship. He heard the word *partner* tossed around at cocktail parties, from both heterosexual and homosexual pairings, and it sounded odd to him, as if their relationship was determined by the clause in a contract, the language dictated by lawyers. Juliet never used that word, she didn't use any label at all, which only confused him. When she spoke of Marisa directly, which was unusual, she only spoke of the action—we went to college together, we lived together, we raised him together—but never the intention behind it. Perhaps she didn't know. Or was embarrassed to tell him the truth.

He offered to clear out her old bedroom, but she wanted more privacy, taking the two rooms on the third floor, where she and Jasper once had adjoining playrooms—hers filled with wooden trains, Legos, a toy piano; his with a weight bench, a boombox, and posters from *Flashdance* and *The Wiz*. She packed it all up and Winston helped her drag the boxes down to the basement. Returning with a hammer and nails, she reimagined the space as a bedroom, hanging pictures on the sloped walls and turning the futon into a bed, which she pushed into the middle of the room, just under the skylight. Winston stared at her photos—Jenry in a cowboy hat, sitting on Juliet's lap; Marisa opening presents in front of the Christmas tree; the three of them by the side of a lake, on the floor playing blocks, under an umbrella—and he wondered how different they were from the photographs of him and Faye and Jasper from those early years. What was it that made them a family, that made him a father, aside from blood? Did he have a right to think his family was more valid than hers? And if so, what gave him that right—a piece of paper, a wedding ring, a strand of DNA?

Winston was a Democrat, but not exactly liberal, and his belief system was challenged during those months, when subtle shifts began to take place under the surface. He had always thought of the boy as his grandson, since they told him Jasper was the biological father, but he never conceived of the bond Juliet carried, certainly never thinking of her as a *real* mother. But now, in her sorrow, the depth of her loss as clear as a stone sitting at the bottom of a swimming pool, he imagined her to be not unlike himself in those weeks after Jaymes died, mourning the death of something he was just beginning to believe in. What a terrible thing, he thought, to have a loss as sudden as death without the death itself. Theft not by the hands of fate, but by the hands of someone you trusted, someone who claimed to love you. These thoughts plagued him at night, as the weeks turned to months and his once boisterous daughter turned inward, slowly giving up everything else—except the piano. It was how she'd been after Jasper's death, too, but now, with both losses so close together, he was worried she might never recover.

Then one day in winter, when Marisa and Jenry had been gone for six months without a clue as to where they were, a letter arrived for Winston, the return address in Miami. He read it on the way to his car, stopping to brush the falling snow off the white-capped hood. His breath clouded the air. The letter was from Marisa, asking him to pass along word to Juliet that they were okay, to tell her how incredibly sorry she was, and to give Juliet a recent photograph of Jenry on her birthday. She said Juliet could write to her at this address if she wanted to reconnect. Winston stared at the picture until it was stiff with cold, feeling shock more than anything else.

It was the one-year anniversary of Jasper's death, and Winston was on his way to Swan Point Cemetery to put flowers on the grave. Juliet was supposed to meet him there. On the drive he imagined how he would tell Juliet about the letter, what he would say to make sense of things, but by the time he reached the gravesite he had put the picture back into the envelope, which he tucked into his inside pocket, resting against his heart.

Juliet was waiting beside her brother's grave with a bouquet of irises. She wiped the dark stone with a gloved hand, revealing Jasper's birth and death dates, chiseled neatly into the granite. Next to it, with a matching headstone, was her mother's grave. Between the two, a small, flat grass marker lay in the ground for Jaymes. Winston leaned the yellow roses against Faye's headstone. There was a built-in metal vase welded to the edge of Jasper's headstone, where Juliet eventually placed the irises. They stood together for almost thirty minutes. Juliet stopped in front of each grave, kissed her fingertips, then placed her hand on the stones. After, she told Winston she had to leave.

"Let's get some lunch first, we should talk." He looked at her blood-shot eyes and wondered if she'd been drinking. He'd noticed how quickly he needed to restock his liquor cabinet since she'd moved back home, but he thought it was a phase, a part of the healing process. Now, he was beginning to think that it might be more than that.

"Okay," Juliet said, lifting the collar of her coat to block the wind.

They walked together to the parking lot, both cars covered with a dusting of snow.

"I'll drive," Winston said, unlocking the car. "I can drop you back at your car later." She waited in the front seat while he scraped the windshield clean. He was aware of her gaze as he brushed the passenger side, eventually revealing her sad face through the glass. He couldn't tell if she was crying. The wind blew snow-laced air into his opened coat, chilling the parts of his neck his scarf didn't cover. He pulled up his collar, readjusting the folds of the heavy wool. Something nicked his finger—the edge of an envelope—and then he remembered the letter from Marisa. He had to tell Juliet.

He climbed into the car, folding his long legs into the driver's seat. The heat blew against his cold face, making him blink. He felt his sadness like a wave of exhaustion that threatened to level him.

"Mandarin Garden?" he asked without turning to look at her. She agreed as he pulled onto the snow-filled streets outside the cemetery, following the dark, wet lines from the cars that had gone before.

She didn't want to leave the car, so they got takeout and drove to the pond in Roger Williams Park, where he used to take her as a child to watch the beavers build their dams. Engine running, they ate cartons of spicy bean curd with minced pork and fried dumplings, watching as other cars—mostly families with small children—filled up the snow-covered lot. He still hadn't told her about the letter. He kept waiting for the right moment to present itself, but it never did.

Later, at the end of the night, he kissed her cheek and watched her climb the stairs to the third floor, none the wiser. Every day that week he intended to tell her, but by the weekend she was headed to D.C. to perform with her old band, and he didn't want to distract her. Next it was her birthday he didn't want to ruin, and then it was spring and she seemed to be pulling herself out of something; he feared that any news from Marisa would set her back again. Soon she was touring with her band and traveling to New York most weekends, and eventually she moved into her own place. He was surprised by how much he missed her presence in the house, even though there had been days at a time when he wouldn't see her; somehow, it had been enough. Just hearing her footsteps in the back staircase or seeing her SUV in the driveway filled him with a sense of peace. He hid his grief over Jasper from her, wanted to seem strong, to be what she needed, but he, too, had lost something precious. Not only his son, but the promise of more time, the potential to make things right between them.

Now, there was only Juliet. And his grandson. He regretted not spending more time with the baby, though the early years were not his favorite. He liked children when they were young adults, when they had something interesting to say. When he met Juliet for lunch after the semester ended, he was glad to see how much better she seemed, excited about engaging with the world again, and with her music. He was relieved to see her so focused on her career, instead of wallowing in self-pity and doubt, threatening to quit. It would be a shame to see her waste such a gift, and to sever the connection to her mother, which kept Faye alive for both of them. Juliet was doing well, he told himself, she was back on track, and she rarely mentioned their names anymore—how would it help to tell her now? There was no clear answer.

He hadn't conceived of withholding the letter forever—that thought had yet to occur to him—so he waited for a sign that the time was right to tell her.

That June, Winston found himself attending a conference in Key West, with a layover in Miami. When his flight got delayed and then canceled, and the airline gave him a voucher for a room at the Holiday Inn, he realized the sign had finally come. Not to tell Juliet about the letter, but to have some of his own questions answered. This boy was his grandson, the last link he would ever have to Jasper, and he needed to know that he was doing fine, that he would be okay without them. Armed with a city map and the letter, he rented a car and drove to the return address listed on the envelope, a sporting goods store in Hialeah. The store had just closed for the evening, but a man stood on a ladder inside the window display hanging up a sign for a Father's Day sale. He was short and stocky, with strong arms tanned from the sun. His black hair was combed straight back and stiff with pomade. He wore a thin gold chain on his right wrist, the links straining as he moved, threatening to break.

Winston stepped out of the air-conditioned car, shocked by the humidity. It was after nine o'clock, but the air was thick with heat. There was an occasional breeze, but it only made him feel hotter. He loosened his tie and unfastened the top button of his shirt before knocking on the window to get the man's attention. The man pointed to the CLOSED sign.

"I'm looking for a woman," Winston said through the glass, "Marisa Castillo. Does she work here?"

The man slowly unrolled the sign in his hands. "And who are you?" he asked, carefully taping the curled edges of the sign to the inside of the glass. His voice was muffled, but Winston understood him. He held up the letter.

"My name is Winston Patterson. She wrote me this letter, several months ago, and she put this store as the return address."

The man peered out from behind the glass. Then he got down from the ladder and disappeared into the store. Seconds later the front door opened, accompanied by the hollow ding of a bell announcing his presence. He stood in the doorway, and Winston watched the breeze ruffle his shirt.

"Marisa is my daughter," the man said. "Victor Castillo is my name." He held out his hand, which Winston grasped in a firm handshake. He was more than a foot shorter than Winston, but he spoke with a calm confidence, as if they were looking eye to eye. "This is a big surprise, to see you here in Miami."

"Yes, well, this has all been a surprise, hasn't it?"

Victor stared at him, wiping his hands on a rag he took from his pocket. A bottle of window cleaner hung from the belt loop on his khaki pants. Winston recognized the sharp smell of the cleaner, along with an unfamiliar scent, most likely Victor's aftershave, which reminded him of pencil shavings.

"What do you want with my daughter?"

"I don't want anything from your daughter. I'm here about my grandson."

"Your grandson?" Victor's eye appeared to twitch.

Winston cleared his throat. "*Our* grandson."

Victor sprayed the window cleaner onto his rag and began to clean the windowpane on the front door. With his back to Winston, he spoke. "You just missed his birthday. He's three years old. And big already, you know, tall. You think he gets that from you?"

"I don't know what he gets from me," Winston said matter-of-factly. Then, as an afterthought, he added, "His father was average height."

"My father was over six feet, and look at me. Sometimes you never know." Victor stood on a milk crate to reach the top of the window. "He's happy here, you know. They are both doing well. My wife, she watches him while Marisa is at work. I've never seen her so happy."

"That's quite some turnaround, considering she refused to see him until last year."

Victor kept cleaning the window. "We don't travel on airplanes, my wife and me. We're simple people."

"Is that why you sent the Christmas cards back? Two years in a row?"

"You think you know us because you heard some stories?" Victor stared at his reflection in the glass. "You don't know what it was like."

"I think I have a pretty good idea," Winston said. He took a step closer.

"I spent months trying to talk to my wife, reason with her. It was impossible. She was like talking to a piece of paper. Nothing. No anger even, just nothing. And then . . ." Victor held the rag between his hands, ringing it out.

"And then what?"

Victor shrugged. "And then she met him."

Winston nodded. "Which was when, exactly?"

He raised his hands in surrender. "You have to ask Marisa about all that."

"I would love to talk to her. If only she hadn't run a thousand miles away—"

"Only a child runs away—"

"—just to hide from my daughter."

Victor's mouth tightened. "She left for a lot of reasons. Personal things. It wasn't easy." He wiped the sweat from his forehead with the palm of his hand.

Winston leaned forward to look at Victor, who was still standing on the crate, in the eye. "All I know is that she packed up and left town without any warning, took the kid and transplanted their whole life without saying a word to my daughter. Juliet loved that boy, she helped raise him, and for what—the few dozen pictures they left behind?"

Victor turned to face him. "Marisa is his mother. And your son was his father. That's biology. We can't fight that. But the connection you have is through your son. Your son, not your daughter." Victor gestured with the spray bottle, his finger on the trigger. "If he was alive, I'm sure we would have another conversation. But now, like this, what is there to say? My daughter is raising her son. And we want to help her. But my wife . . . she could never accept a child with two mothers. So that situation," he said, shrugging, "it needs to stay in the past. Marisa understands that. You can't fault her for accepting our help."

"I don't fault her. But you didn't give her much of a choice, did you?"

"She made her choice, to have a baby with no husband, all by herself—"

"Juliet was there." Winston felt the need to defend his daughter. "She wasn't alone."

"You know what I mean. You had a family once."

Winston noticed that he used the past tense, *had a family*, as if it were all over, his role of being a father, a husband, all in the past. But he didn't want that to be true.

"I still have a family," Winston said.

"Of course, I don't mean to offend." Victor raised his hands in apology.

Winston saw a look of resignation on the younger man's face, as if he had given up a lot to be standing there, but would give up even more if he had to, would keep giving until he had nothing left. He understood that instinct, but also the need for self-preservation. It was the only way he had survived this long.

"We all make sacrifices for family," Winston said. "It comes with the territory."

Victor nodded, and his body seemed to relax. "Marisa and my wife, they had to reach an agreement. So we could all stay together. If you understand that, there's nothing to argue about."

Winston pulled at the knot in his tie, loosening it further. "Is that what this is? An argument?" The wind kicked up, causing the tie to momentarily obscure his vision.

"Maybe in college they call it debate." Victor wiped the sweat from his forehead with the rag. He refused to look away.

Winston slowly undid his tie, rolling it into a tight ball, which he tucked into his pocket. Then he rested his hand on the window, smudging the glass. "You're not as I'd imagined," he said with a stilted laugh. "Not at all."

Victor took his time getting down from the milk crate. "But you, Mr. Patterson, are exactly as I imagined." He sprayed the mark Winston's hand had made on the window, wiping the glass until it squeaked.

"Doctor, not mister," Winston corrected.

Victor looked at him. "Exactly," he said.

When he was done cleaning, Victor invited Winston inside. Winston wanted to decline, but the temptation of air conditioning was enough to get him in the door. They talked for another hour, drinking warm beer in the storeroom, until a deal was struck and Victor went into the safe to retrieve a sturdy cardboard file box covered by a loose lid. They shook hands again before Winston left.

The street was empty as Winston carried the file box to his rental car. He could feel a rare excitement building in his stomach, as if he were carrying an unmarked explosive, a bomb that could detonate without warning. He couldn't know then, but he would come to understand he was exactly right about the danger of what he now possessed, the unknown power held in that innocent-looking box, the one he would bring home on the plane and store in his office for nearly two decades, keeping its existence a secret from his daughter for all those years.

Now, sitting in that same office, officially retired and yet feeling as if he will never be ready to leave, he wonders about the consequences of what he's done, and if his plan will even work. Is it possible to make up for all that lost time? He has done his part, by sending the boy to Juliet, but what he can't control is what she does from there, how she handles coming face to face with the child she lost.

Winston gets up from his desk. The room feels different now that Jenry has been here and gone; he can still smell a trace of his cologne, can hear the distinct timbre of his voice. How extraordinary to be with him in person, after years of knowing only what was held in the box—not a flesh-and-blood child but an idea, a mere glimpse of the young man he has become. The one who stood here minutes ago, unafraid to face him.

Along with relief, Winston is left with a feeling of doubt, so much of the future still unknown. For him, the stakes have never been higher than in this moment. He could lose them both—all his living family in the world—if he doesn't play his next move right.

But for now, all he can do is wait.

· 3 ·

September falls into October, Winston's favorite month. Nights cool as autumn settles in, the hillside flush with orange and gold-leaf trees, the sugar maples on campus aflame with crimson red. He chooses to walk whenever he can, often parking at the Athletic Center in the morning and not returning to his car until dark. He wants to wring the hours out of each day, to use his body while he still commands it.

Tonight his dinner plans are on campus, and though the forecast predicts rain showers and the temperature hasn't left the forties all day, he strolls unhurried through the Main Green, umbrella tucked under his arm like an unread newspaper. It's after eight o'clock when he finally leaves the Faculty Club, stuffed with slices of pink prime rib and whiskey sours. At first glance, the rain is only a threat in the cloud-filled sky, but as he walks across the desolate campus it begins to come down in full-sized drops and he eventually has to open his umbrella. The sidewalks are covered with fallen leaves, which tear like wet sheets of paper as he steps on them with his dress shoes, leaving an iron-shaped footprint in his wake; the depression that remains is subtle and surprisingly free of tread marks. He moves like a ship through water—soundless, graceful—leaving hardly any sign of his presence, almost like he wasn't there at all.

He smells smoke in the damp October air, which makes him long for a cigar, though he gave them up when he turned seventy-five. A man his age doesn't require many vices, and he has eliminated all but one—alcohol—figuring it gives the most reward for the smallest risk. He might be proven wrong about that, when his doctor finally convinces him to test his liver function, but he's made it through most of his seventies without any major ailment. He is as strong as an ox, they tell him at his annual checkups, news he celebrates with a ninety-five-dollar bottle of single malt scotch and a sliver of pecan pie.

Normally, he would turn at the bell tower and cut through the Quiet Green to get to his office, but the path looks muddy already, so he stays on the sidewalk till he comes to the end of the street. Few other pedestrians are out, and cars are a rare occurrence at this time of night, but in the rain he finds himself the lone foot soldier. A campus patrol car turns the corner, slowing as it passes. He tilts the umbrella to show his face, lifts his hand in a slight wave. The driver nods and keeps going. Winston has been teaching here since before that man was born, went to a better high school and college, has more degrees and a larger retirement account, has tenure and an endowed chair, has a half-million-dollar life insurance policy—and yet he knows the proper protocol, knows who has the power and who has to acquiesce. Like so many things beyond his control, the color of his skin has dictated much of his life, opening some doors while permanently closing others.

When he was younger, and thus, more threatening, it was a chronic problem; he often found himself smiling to diffuse awkward situations, staying seated so as to not dominate other faculty during their meetings, refusing to be labeled the angry Black man—even when he understood they often wanted him to play exactly that role. He avoided the sit-ins and walkouts, the marching that defined many in his generation; he stayed in the East when others went to the South, chose the sidewalk over the fast track, always walking under the lights so he didn't startle anyone passing by, giving them a wide berth. One benefit to aging is entering the race-less class of the elderly, where an old Black man is just an old man—someone to be helped, not harassed. Oh, to be a twenty-first-century African American; it isn't quite freedom, but the chains are looser, he has to admit, perhaps a subtle sign of progress.

He spots a car that looks familiar—with the same silvery green paint as Juliet's—and peers in the window as he walks by. The inside is spotless, leaving no clue to the owner's identity, so he checks the outside for something he recognizes. In the back window, there's a bumper sticker that says TRUST WOMEN, and he knows immediately that this is, in fact, his daughter's car. He looks around, sees no sign of her, and checks the time on his watch. He wonders what she's doing out so late—but really why she's on campus at all. Has she come to see Jenry? Have they been in touch? He sets off to look for her, circling back through the green until he sees a figure coming toward him, bundled against the rain. She walks quickly and holds no umbrella. Even with the scarf covering half her face, he knows his daughter by the way she moves, how she looks down as she walks, and by the length of her stride.

"Juliet," he calls out from the middle of the path.

She looks up but acts like she doesn't recognize him. He holds out his hand, wanting to hug her, yet she stops short of full contact, allowing him instead to rest his hand on her shoulder. She blinks as she looks up at him, her dark hair falling in loose curls as she shakes it free from her scarf. A few wet strands brush across his skin, streaking his hand with rainwater.

"What brings you out in the rain?" he asks, his voice light, non-accusatory. He tries to recall the last time he'd seen her—was it July? August? And here it was several weeks into the fall semester, yet neither had made any effort to connect. He wonders what makes it so difficult; he wants to see her, wants to know that she's doing well, but their lives are so different now. Well, no, they've always been different, but now she hardly seems interested in him at all. She has her partner, her work, her home—where does he fit in?

They make small talk about the weather, a meeting she attended, his dinner with a former student—on the surface, a normal conversation between father and daughter—and yet they both know there isn't anything normal about their relationship. They live three miles apart yet see each other on rare occasions; the last time was over the summer when they ran into each other at the Daily Bread on Wickenden. He remembers trying to stage the events, by driving home the long way to pass her restaurant or going to the arthouse movie theater on Thayer Street he knows she likes, the independent bookstore in Wayland Square, yet his efforts never seem to yield the desired results. But now, here he is standing next to her, by complete accident, and he can't help but feel a sense of happiness spread through his chest. He doesn't know how to show it, but he feels it as certainly as the drops of rain wetting his face.

"Do you need a ride?" she finally asks, pointing behind her to the car.

"No, no," he says. "My car's in the lot, an easy walk. I'll stop by the office first and then head home."

She nods and turns to leave. He feels an urge to shout out to her, to grab her and not let her go. They need to talk about Jenry, but he can't be the one to bring it up.

"I sent you an email last week. About the new Jacob Lawrence exhibit at MoMA."

She gives him a small smile. "I got it. Thanks."

He can't think of anything else to say, so he suggests they have a drink in his office. She stares at him like he's a fool, so he quickly adds, "I've got tea, too," remembering that she gave up alcohol several years ago. It's still difficult to imagine, a child of his not drinking, but he keeps his questions to himself, just as he has with her decision to quit the piano, and her choice, at fifteen, to tell him she was a lesbian, well before she had kissed a girl.

"I should go," she says, taking a step away from him.

"I've changed some things around. You might like it." He tries to think of something to make her stay, but he has nothing to offer her, nothing she wants.

"I'm sure it's very nice." She looks away, her eyes drawn together like she is trying to see something very far in the distance. He follows her gaze but sees nothing but a dark haze, as the shape of well-known buildings—Slater Hall, the library, Manning Chapel—dissolve into the foggy edges of night.

When she looks back, her eyes lock with his. "I've seen the changes," she says. "Don't you remember, when I used to bring Jenry by." Yes, that seems right, he thinks, but he can't recall how long ago that was. "After you moved the piano," she adds, seeming to read his mind. "After Jasper died."

Jasper. It still hurts to hear his name. But Winston does remember those visits years ago, when Jenry was a baby. When he played at the piano like it was a sandbox, digging for music in the keys, running his fingers like toy trucks over the smooth edges of the closed lid. Was it really that long ago, when they first moved the piano to the third-floor foyer? It couldn't have been fifteen years since she visited him in that office, not when he still thinks of her college years—a decade before that— like it was yesterday. He can picture Juliet at twenty without effort: her long hair always pulled back in a ponytail; the torn jeans and t-shirts she considered a wardrobe; the worn Converse sneakers she never took off, faded to the color of an old country barn. He remembers her sneaking into his office during finals with a key he'd given her for emergencies and how she'd print free copies on his LaserWriter for all her friends, leaving earlier drafts in his trash basket as evidence, as if she wanted him to know she'd been there.

How is it that he continues to compress time, and why? What feels like a few years ago might be decades, whereas yesterday feels as remote as a memory from his childhood. This is the tragedy of age, he thinks, his mind like an uncatalogued library with memories wedged wherever they fit on the shelves, instead of placed in a logical order. The assumption—or better yet, the ease—of chronology has become a myth he's sure a young person invented.

"Yes, of course," he says to her now, pulling on a pair of leather gloves. "When he would bang those keys like he was trying to break them off."

He imitates the movement, causing the umbrella to tip forward, pouring rainwater onto the sidewalk between them.

She shakes her head, tight lines forming around the edges of her mouth. "How can you stand there smiling? When you sent him to me, without saying anything—"

"What could I say?" he cuts her off. So that's it, she's seen him. Jenry found her and now she's angry with him. "He showed up at my door, unannounced. What would you have me do, throw him out?" His tone is harsh, but what he actually feels is relief—that she is finally confronting him, daring to attach words to her upset. He wonders if she will put it all together, if this is the moment he will be forced to come clean.

"You could have told me," she says, her voice thick with indignation, "given me a warning."

"What warning did I get?" He barks back at her, leaning forward to match her aggressive stance; they face each other like boxers late in the round, too tired to lift their gloves. If he were a younger man, and his opponent anyone but his daughter, he would cherish this moment, the power one feels right before the fight, the joy of anger as it rushes to the surface. He pictures how they would look from above, circling around each other like two pit bulls straining against invisible leashes. But then he remembers who she is, what she means to him, and all that he's kept from her, and the picture dissolves.

He is back on the street corner, wearing an overcoat and wool scarf, holding an umbrella as he looks down at his daughter through rain-soaked glasses. The umbrella's handle, wet with rain, slips from his grasp; Juliet flinches as it falls toward her. He snatches it before it can touch her, marveling at his reflexes, but there is something else: the look on her face. Why, he wonders, would his only daughter look like she's afraid of him? As if he could ever lay a hand on her. What right does she have to fear him?

The question itself—living only in his mind—fills him with outrage. After all he's done to try to fix things, by bringing the boy back to her, and trying to set things right between them, by encouraging him to find her. Winston had done what he could; he needed her to see that he had no other choice, that everything he did was for her and the boy, to help all of them find each other again. But instead of saying any of this, he starts at the very beginning, berating her with questions before he can stop himself.

"Did you ever think to consult me on any of this? When you decided to live with that woman? When you attempted to raise her child?"

This isn't a fair fight, the one he is about to wage, but knowing that isn't enough to stop him. Their exchange has opened an old wound, one that can be traced to long before Jenry was born, and on the surface, has nothing to do with his existence at all.

"Is that what I owe you, consultation?" Juliet's eyebrows narrow in confusion. "What business is it of yours who I live with?"

"For all I knew you were still in Copenhagen. You told me nothing about your life, then or now—"

"I told you I was coming home."

"In a postcard. Which I only received after you were here."

"To tell you the truth, I didn't think you would care."

Well, you were wrong, Winston wants to yell at her, *you were all wrong.* He feels his heart beating hard in his chest, like when he forces himself to swim the final lap on a single breath, and he has to remind himself to breathe. The air is cold in his lungs, and when he exhales, a cloud of white hovers between them like smoke. "Of course I cared," he finally says.

"Like you cared about Jasper?"

"Your brother and I had our own relationship. It doesn't concern you."

"That's not what he thought." Juliet zips up her jacket, raising the collar to protect her ears, pink with cold. "We talked about you all the time, whenever he brought it up. He needed you and you weren't there for him."

"Don't talk about my son—"

"Why not? You refuse to—"

"I won't be bullied by a child." Winston shakes his head, raising his eyes to look above her.

"Just like you refused to see what was right in front of you. He was sick, Pop. He was already dying."

"It was an accident, goddamnit."

"We don't know that for sure."

Winston takes a step back, leaning slightly against the umbrella to steady himself. He wants to lean against it fully, to use it as a cane like the old man he is, but he's too proud. He can't afford to show her any weakness.

"We both read the police report," he says with a measured voice. "He fell through the ice. Don't invent things after the fact."

"Why would I do that? What purpose would it serve?"

"I can't begin to imagine why you do any of the things you do," he says calmly, unable to hide the hostility he now feels. He is used to arguing about the boy, but Jasper—his son, his firstborn—that is a different story entirely. One he is not ready to discuss on a street corner where any passerby could hear. Family is a private matter, he has always believed, and if she respected him like she says she does, if she understood what he's been through, she wouldn't treat him this way.

"You don't understand how it feels," Winston says, "to lose a child."

"That's where you're wrong, Pop. I do understand. You just don't want to admit it."

He looks at her curiously, as time seems to stand still, and wonders about the truth of her words. How could her loss be the same when the boy was still alive? He can't imagine it's possible for her grief to be as expansive as his. Her eyes look unfamiliar, distant and glassy, and before he can figure out why, they are spilling tears down her face. He can't remember the last time he saw his daughter cry. It makes his heart ache—he literally feels a twinge in his chest—and he has to look away.

He doesn't want to deny her feelings, her love, that isn't it—what he can't accept is the idea that she has suffered a loss similar to his own. When Jaymes and Jasper were taken from him, it almost destroyed him. He doesn't want to imagine that agony for his only daughter, his only living child. That is the first obstacle. The second is what he has done, the truth he has kept from her all these years. If what she's saying is real, his crime is even greater than he thought; he's kept a mother from her child. Even if they reconcile, will she ever be able to forgive him for that?

"Why," he begins, finally looking back to her. The unfinished question hangs in the air between them, as Juliet stands in the rain like a wet dog beholden to the whims of her master, hair limp on her face. Winston sees in her the simple beauty of her mother, how Faye might have looked at forty-five had she lived that long. The image silences him.

"Why can't you understand? I didn't have a choice," Juliet says. "Marisa left and she didn't want to be found." She walks to the far side of the car, as if trying to get away from him. "Was I supposed to spend my whole life trailing a ghost?"

Winston raises the umbrella to cover his face, the streetlights now blinding him. He feels exposed. It reminds him of the confessional, a place he hasn't visited since he was a schoolboy, when he still believed in the unseen. That's it, he begins to understand, that's what she needs from him right now—some form of absolution. Yet who is he to grant it?

"But he wasn't a ghost," he says, his voice softer now, almost comforting. "He was a living, breathing human being. He was alive. And where were you? You had a choice, Juliet, and you chose yourself. Your career. And I supported that—until you quit."

Juliet's face registers a look of shocked pain. "How dare you," she whispers, her voice shallow as she struggles to keep her composure. The sight of his grown daughter this distraught, fighting tears he has caused, is too much for him to bear. All he can do now is get this to end, get her to leave, even if that means launching another attack.

"Me?" He raises his voice again. "How dare *you*?" He points the umbrella at her for emphasis. "For the life of me, I don't understand how you could give up on everything you love—not just the boy and your family, but the piano as well . . ." He shakes his head. "You had a gift, goddamnit, *a gift*, something your mother gave you, something that kept her alive in your body, a part of her you could share with the world. How could you walk away from that like it was nothing?"

"*Nothing?*" Juliet wears a look of astonishment. "It was everything," she says. "It was too much . . . I had to save myself."

"And for what? To fry eggs in some diner like a short-order cook? Is that what I raised you to do, serve rich white people breakfast like my father did?"

"There's nothing wrong with that. It put you through college, didn't it?"

"And I put you through college. I gave you the best schools, the best teachers, and this is how you repay me?" He opens his arms to her, his overcoat flapping in the wind.

"I lost a child," she says, "after losing my brother, and my mother before that. I don't have anything else to give you." She turns away from him, walking to her car.

"Trust me when I tell you," he says, his powerful voice now trembling, "*we cannot escape history.*" It was his favorite quote from Lincoln's address to Congress during the Civil War, one she had memorized and would recite for him whenever he fed her the opening line, but tonight, when she doesn't respond, he wonders if she has forgotten. "Maybe you don't want to hear this, but you have to make a different choice."

He wants to say more, but what words does he have to comfort her now, to comfort anyone? He has said too much already, things he will soon regret, but there is no fixing it now. His mother used to always say, *I can recover from any death but my own,* but he thinks now that it's the other way around: your own death is the easy one; what befalls the people you love most in the world, that is the most difficult thing to survive.

The wind picks up again, blowing rain into his eyes. It feels cool against his skin, and he doesn't wipe it away. He watches Juliet get into the car, the word *regret* echoing in his mind like a refrain. How naive to think it possible to live a life without regrets.

———

WINSTON FINDS HIS office surprisingly warm, the radiator hissing in the corner. It smells like cigars, though he hasn't lit one in years, which is a small comfort to him—remembering the things he used to do, the man he used to be. He hangs his wet overcoat on the hook behind his door and leaves the umbrella in the hallway to dry. With a small key he kept hidden in a jewelry box, he unlocks the largest drawer in his desk, removing the file box Victor had given him fifteen years before, and places it in the middle of his desk. It is overflowing now, filled with notes and photographs Victor has sent him over the years, holding up his end of the agreement. Winston looks through them now, as he has periodically, feeling once again the same mixture of pride and shame.

He remembers the first time he opened the box, sitting in that rental car in Miami as he waited for the air conditioning to dry the sweat on his face. First, he'd flipped quickly through the loose stacks of photographs, overwhelmed by how many there were of Juliet holding the boy—laughing with him, tickling him, kissing him—so that anyone looking at the pictures would easily guess that he was her son. Then he thumbed through the baby book, where the father's side of the family tree was filled in by Juliet herself, her handwriting a neat calligrapher's script; and at the bottom, listed under the section heading *Siblings*, he was surprised to find her brother's childhood nickname of *Jay*.

Winston saw all those things and took them for what they were: proof. Of Juliet's role in Jenry's life, of her integral part, but that was precisely what he struggled to accept. If she was what she said she was, then why had she lost her son, why was he living more than a thousand miles away while Winston was left to watch his grandson grow up from a distance, through photographs and report cards and stories told in letters, instead of in person? There was no simple answer to that question, which was part of the reason he'd put them away without showing her, without telling her about the visit in Miami at all, and why he's kept the secret for the last fifteen years.

When he came home after the conference in Florida, Juliet told him she was going on tour with a new jazz quartet; they were leaving for London in less than a week. She looked genuinely happy, like she was finally moving on with her life. How could he shatter that peace with a box of old photographs, remnants of another far-away life—one she wasn't allowed to share in any longer—when she had no legal rights to the boy and was at the mercy of Marisa and Victor and Inés, and God knows how many other members of his extended Cuban family; what point would that serve? He was protecting her, he'd told himself, saving her from what would only end in more heartache, and he felt certain that one day she would understand what he had done, how they had both sacrificed their relationship with the boy for his own good, so he wouldn't be confused about who his mother was, and would have the support of a close family nearby.

But his certainty had waned over the years, as he wondered if he had acted too hastily, agreeing to stay in the shadows while leaving Juliet completely in the dark. Wasn't it possible that when Jenry got older, they could fit more easily into his life? He was Jasper's son, after all, the only link to Jasper they had left. Didn't they deserve to know him? And the boy, now growing into a young man, didn't he have the right to know them? Winston began to imagine a different future, one where Jenry would attend Brown University just like his own children, to continue their family legacy for another generation; where he'd convince Victor to support this new plan, in exchange for Winston agreeing to cover the cost; where Jenry would live in a dorm on campus, just a short walk away from his office; where he'd postpone his retirement so he could easily be found.

So, unlike Juliet, Winston wasn't surprised that day in September when Jenry showed up on his doorstep; he'd spent the last two years planning for exactly that—conferring with Victor and his piano teachers, asking the college recruiter which festivals would enhance his portfolio, building up his college fund—doing everything in his power to ensure that his grandson returned to Providence. Returned to Juliet, and to him.

And if Winston did that, if he brought him back into the fold, perhaps he could forget about this box, forget about all the lies he told to protect it. Maybe they could all start over.

The office phone rings, bringing Winston back to the present, and his first thought is that it's Juliet, having changed her mind about the drink. He answers with a liveliness he doesn't usually express on the telephone. "Hello? Juliet?"

"It's Victor," says the voice on the other end. "How are you, my friend?"

Winston can't claim to be surprised, since random phone calls have become the norm in their unusual relationship, sometimes going months without any correspondence at all, other times talking every week. When Jenry's appendix burst after falling off a horse on his thirteenth birthday, he needed emergency surgery and, at Winston's request, Victor called with updates every couple of hours.

"Hello, Victor," Winston replies in a subdued voice. "How have you been?"

They make small talk for several minutes, until Victor finally reveals the purpose for his call, his concern over the fact that Jenry isn't returning Marisa's phone calls. He's threatened to quit the piano, putting his scholarship on the line.

"All musicians threaten to quit. It's their one power over the instrument." As they talk, Winston studies the contents of the box. He finds a picture of Jenry after a school recital, standing shyly at the piano, his eyes focusing on something beyond the edge of the frame. On the back, it says: *Jenry, 8 years old*, in handwriting he doesn't recognize.

"He sounds different," Victor says. "I don't know how to explain it." He takes a deep breath. "He's so angry. I never heard that in his voice before."

"The anger will dissipate. Eventually." Winston picks up another picture, this one taken on his last birthday; he sits in front of a cake shaped like the number eighteen. It's from the last letter Victor sent him, just a few months ago.

"He doesn't have *eventually*. He has now, these next four years, and then what? If he messes this up, he doesn't get to do it over."

Winston stares at the boy's face and recognizes himself in the photograph, the unbridled joy that comes from having your whole life in front of you, believing the hard parts are behind you, the struggles of youth discarded like an old coat in exchange for the warm, windless place called the future.

"I'll talk to him," Winston says, not quite realizing those words were about to come out of his mouth.

"You?" Victor questions. "Is that a good idea?"

"He's come to me once already—"

"Which led to all this, if I'm not mistaken—"

"Our talk didn't lead to anything but the truth," Winston says, cutting him off. "Something we agreed would be revealed as soon as he turned eighteen anyway. So by my calculation, we're already several months behind."

"It made more sense to wait, to do it in person."

"To you, maybe. But you weren't the one who had to decimate his fantasy, were you?" Winston looks up, as if he expects Victor to be standing there. His eyes are drawn to the spot where Jenry stood that first day; he remembers the stunned look on the boy's face as he heard the truth about his father, and then, about Juliet.

"We're all responsible," Victor says. "Even he knows that."

"Does he?" Winston puts the picture down, repacking the box while he cradles the phone against his shoulder. "So he knows the role you played? How you forced his mother to lie in order to make your wife more comfortable?"

"Marisa had a choice." Victor's voice has gotten hard, defensive. "She made her own decision."

"Let's give the boy the same opportunity, to decide his own fate."

"He's been given nothing but opportunities—to go to college, to do things no person in my family would ever imagine to do. Nothing but choices."

"Yes," Winston says. "He's been given a lot. We all have, don't you think?"

Victor is quiet now. Winston can hear his breath in the mouthpiece.

"Yes, of course," Victor says, which Winston takes as not only an agreement, but an admission. The deal they'd struck had benefitted both men: Victor received financial help to support Jenry's musical ambitions, including the lessons and travel that accompanied such a lofty pursuit; while Winston gained access to that life, through photos and mementos that, as a historian, he valued almost as much as the events themselves. Real life, he has come to understand, is sprawling and messy, but what he's collected of Jenry throughout the years can be held in a simple container, one he can take out and sift through whenever he wants, to feel like he is a part of it all; to convince himself that he hasn't missed the most important moments; to see that his son lives on through his grandson's life. There was a sacrifice, of course, yet he chose to focus only on the gift. But that came at a cost, and Juliet had been the one to pay. This is the part he still has to reconcile.

After hanging up the phone, Winston signs on to his computer and sends his grandson an email, perhaps the first time he's truly appreciated the benefit of modern technology. He gathers the items spread across his desk—except for one, which he places on the side table—and sets them neatly inside the file box, puts the lid back on, and returns it to its hiding place. Then he closes the drawer and locks it.

· 4 ·

Thursday morning, Jenry arrives at exactly 8:00 a.m., as instructed, and walks in through the door Winston left open. Much of his affect has changed since the last visit; gone is the halting step, the averted gaze, the nervous fingers that were always in motion. Amazing what six weeks of college can achieve.

"Have a seat," Winston says, sharper than he means to.

Jenry sits on the only empty chair in the room, the one Winston cleared a few minutes before, readying the room like it was the set of a play. Jenry places his bag on the floor, his feet still clad in slides, though the temperature outside hovers around forty-five degrees.

"That's for you." Winston points at the cream-colored book on the table between them. Jenry picks it up, fingering the soft cover.

"It's a baby book," Jenry says flatly.

"It's *your* baby book."

Jenry flips through the stiff pages, like he's holding an ancient relic. "How did you get this?"

"You asked for something, when you were here last. This is what I have."

"Who gave it to you?"

Winston doesn't answer. Jenry stops on a picture of his six-month-old self dressed like a pumpkin. "Thank you," he finally says, his face creased in a smile. He looks at a few pages, then closes the book. "Is that why you asked me here?"

Winston sits back, hands folded on his lap. "That's not enough?"

"You could have mailed it."

"I thought we should check in, see how your semester is going."

"It's fine." Jenry crosses his feet at the ankles.

"Music Theory has been known to baffle even the most ardent composers."

"I dropped it. A few weeks ago."

Winston eyes widen. "I'm surprised your advisor allowed that."

"He didn't allow anything," Jenry says. "I made the decision myself."

"I see." Winston presses his fingertips together. "There are very few things in life that are autonomous decisions. People think they want to be an artist because it will guarantee freedom, the right to create as they see fit. But in truth, the life of an artist is often by committee, just like the rest of us."

"I also stopped playing with the orchestra." Jenry's dark eyes stare straight at his grandfather. "In case you wanted to know."

Winston gazes back at the boy. "Ah," he says with a laugh. "Okay, I understand."

Jenry looks confused. "I don't get what's funny."

"Quitting's not funny," Winston says sharply. "It's not funny at all." He shuffles through the papers on his desk. "What's funny is how you come in here with all that bravado, as if by some small chance you can deceive me into thinking you're not afraid, as if you're the first student who has struggled with college-level courses, with family problems and money problems and problems being young, gifted, and Black on a campus filled with privilege going all the way back to the *Mayflower*." Winston balances his elbows on the edge of his desk. "You can't bring me something I haven't heard of. Go ahead. Try."

Jenry leans forward. "Okay, try this. Two women have a baby with the one woman's brother and then he dies and they break up and the mother lies about the other one ever existing. You're telling me that's not original?"

Winston laughs again, this time more naturally. "Well, the specifics are a bit outrageous, I'll give you that."

"Oh, and the grandfather lied, too." Jenry reaches into his bag, pulling out a small photograph. He tosses it onto the desk like a bill he refuses to pay.

Winston doesn't move. He shifts his eyes slightly, enough to see that it is a picture of himself with Jenry on his lap, no more than a year old, sitting in the same chair he's sitting in now. He picks it up, fingers the rounded edge. It was taken seventeen years ago, but Winston looked essentially the same—his hair a bit thicker, more silver than white—but it seems inconceivable that the baby on his lap is the same person who sits before him now. He recalls how he'd kissed the top of Jenry's head right before the picture was taken, remembers the clean smell of his hair like swallowing sunlight.

"You act like you never knew me, but you did." Jenry's voice rises. "You spent time with me, right here, you held me in your lap, and then you let me go. Just like she did."

Winston gestures to the baby book. "Hand me that." When Jenry does, Winston flips through the pages, stopping when he finds the *Grandparents* section. He spreads the book open and hands it back to Jenry. "Do you see what it says under *Paternal Grandfather*? Do you see my name, right there in black and white?"

Jenry looks down, glancing over the page.

"I was there," Winston says, "when you were born. Just because you don't remember doesn't mean it didn't happen."

"And what about after? Why didn't you do anything to see me?"

"You have no idea what I've done. Who do you think paid for your piano lessons, for your music camp and all those symposiums?"

"I'm not talking about money." Jenry sits back in his seat. "You know that saying 'it takes a village'? Well, what happened to my village? As soon as my mom made this decision, it's like everyone else just fell in line. Like she was the only one who mattered."

"It's difficult to separate a son from his mother," Winston says, and as the words come out of his mouth he realizes just how true they are, thinking of Jasper and Faye and the bond they had, something he couldn't touch. "And you had your other grandparents. The ones who raised you."

"They lied, too. Everyone lied." Jenry shrugs, his eyes grazing the floor. "And for what? Who did it help?"

Winston is quiet for a while, wondering how much to reveal. "I believe it helped you, actually. We all believed that."

"You don't know them," Jenry says. "You don't know what they believed."

Winston folds his hands on the desk. "Fair enough," he says. It's true; he doesn't know them, not in any real way. "But you must know we wanted to help. To make things less complicated. No one set out to deceive you."

"Sure. If you call having your past erased just to learn how to play the piano *help*." Jenry isn't quite smiling, but there is a brightness to his eyes, as if he is enjoying having Winston's full attention. "But look at the rest of you. Juliet quit playing and she barely even talks to you, my mother doesn't have a life outside of work and me, and my grandparents . . ." He shakes his head, "There's like a wall around each of them, like they're these separate gardens right next to each other, but they can't see over the wall."

Winston takes off his glasses, cleaning them with a cloth napkin from his chest pocket. "Perhaps you're too young to realize it," he says, "but what you're learning is what we all learn eventually. Relationships are complicated. People. Families. Husbands and wives. Parents and children. When you're a child, you can't see how much work it involves, just keeping everyone connected."

Jenry plays with the frayed edge of the baby book, the nervousness back. He keeps his eyes down as he speaks. "What happened between you and Juliet?"

Winston recleans the glasses. "Nothing happened."

"So why don't you see her anymore? She lives a few miles from here, and you haven't seen her since summer."

"She told you that?"

Jenry doesn't answer. With his glasses back on, Winston feels more comfortable, more capable of handling the curveballs Jenry might throw. "I saw her on Tuesday night actually."

"This past Tuesday?" Jenry asks. "The night she came to my dorm?"

Winston sits up. He feels his face flush with heat.

"But it still doesn't make sense," Jenry continues, ignoring him. "The way you talk about each other. Something must have happened."

"We don't—" Winston stops himself. He glances around the room, as if there is something to look at, something he could find on the wall that would help him tell the truth. He wonders if he should open up to the boy, if he owes him that at least. "We don't trust each other," he admits.

Jenry sits motionless, his shoulders slack. "Why not?"

Winston realizes he needs something to hold, so he picks up his coffee, long cold, and takes a sip. "Juliet was always independent, even as a child. She wouldn't ask for help, wouldn't offer information unless you explicitly asked. She was . . . reserved, you might call it. But in college she stepped back even more. She was right here—her freshman dorm was Hope College, and then the Quad for sophomore and junior years." He points out the window, to the brick buildings that dominate his view. "I could see the dorms from my window, she was that close. But she hardly came by, barely called. She didn't bother to tell me when she started dating women, or when she first fell in love, can you imagine?" He turns to look at Jenry, but when his expression doesn't change, Winston shrugs. "And then a few months after graduation I got a postcard from Denmark, telling me she was staying to work on an album. Years go by, with hardly more than a letter here and there. No phone calls, no visits. Her brother had to tell me that she was back in the States, she didn't even come to see me. Her own father." His voice breaks on the word and he clears his throat. "And when they started living together, when your mother got pregnant, Juliet expected me to just go along with it, like it was no big deal."

"Was it a big deal?" Jenry shifts in his seat, playing with the tail of his shirt.

"Of course it was. To bring a child into the world. *My son's child.*" Winston stands up, as if he needs to leave. "It's not right, to do that to a parent. No matter what the state of your relationship is." He walks toward the window and stands with his back to Jenry, pretending to fix the blinds. Now he is the one with nervous energy.

"But you forgive her, don't you? That's the parent's job, to forgive their kids when they mess up."

"I don't know," Winston says, still not looking at him. "Is that my job?"

He adjusts the blinds, exposing the room to the bright morning light. A wide beam of sunlight falls across Jenry's lap.

"She's your daughter."

Winston chews the side of his lip. "Yes," he says, "she is."

He stares at the artwork on his wall—a Romare Bearden collage filled with jazz musicians, a Richard Yarde watercolor of Josephine Baker, and perhaps his most cherished item, though only a print from a museum gift shop: Jacob Lawrence's Panel no. 3 from *The Migration Series*, an image of African American migrants leaving the south on foot to travel north, seemingly guided by a flock of birds flying overhead—along with more personal items, including a black-and-white portrait of his parents standing in front of their brownstone in Harlem, their fingers entwined. All, he realized, were part of the lineage that brought him here; all, in some way, were ancestors.

"Doesn't that mean something to you?" Jenry asks, his voice bringing Winston back to the room, to the present.

"It means a great deal," Winston says, without turning around. "No one can disappoint you more than your own flesh and blood."

A silence holds the room captive. After a minute, Jenry dares to speak.

"Maybe I was lucky, then," Jenry says. "To not have a father."

Winston cracks the window. A stream of cool air slips into the room. "Maybe," he says, still not looking at his grandson.

"She told me you were heartbroken when she quit playing the piano."

"Heartbroken?" Winston turns to face him. "That's an interesting word."

"Is it true?"

Winston pauses thoughtfully. "Yes, I suppose it was." He props the window open with an iron railroad spike, one of the few mementos he'd kept from their summers in the Berkshires, from the long walks he and Faye used to take through the countryside, their land the only place he could be outside and not feel like a moving target. "But Juliet was an adult, she had the right to make her own decision. You don't."

Outside, a church bell rings. Jenry stands up, placing his bag on the seat. "I'm not a child." He slips the baby book into the main compartment, packed between textbooks. Then he closes the outside flap and fastens the leather strap.

"Then don't act like one. A lot of people sacrificed in order for you to be here. Don't throw that away out of spite."

"It's not spite," Jenry says. "I just want the time back. All those hours I gave to music, and for what?"

"This," Winston says sharply, his index finger aimed directly at the floor. "For you to be right here."

Jenry slings his bag over his shoulder. "I'm not sure it was worth it." He checks his phone. "Sorry, I've got an eight-thirty section."

"Do you know *The Emperor Jones*?" Winston calls out after him. "It was a very successful play in the 1920s, then an opera and a film. It made Paul Robeson's career before he was blacklisted. The first film to feature an African American in the starring role."

Jenry turns back. "I never saw it, if that's what you mean."

Winston continues, "The movie wasn't great, a white man's fantasy of watching the savage destroy himself, but Robeson was tremendous. The scene in the forest alone was worth the price of admission." Winston walks across the room to stand beside him. "The emperor goes into hiding and encounters these figures from his past, all the people who wronged him, all his mistakes and regrets made manifest, and he has to destroy them one by one, lest he be destroyed."

"How does it end?"

"He gets killed by a silver bullet, the only way the rebels believed he could be killed. But here is the great irony: it was the same way he planned to kill himself if he was captured."

"I'm not sure I get your point," Jenry says, squinting as he looks up.

Winston stares down at the boy, their eyes locked on each other.

"I think you do," he says, before clapping Jenry on the shoulder. "Thanks for coming by. These talks of ours, I've enjoyed them." He means what he's saying but can tell by the look on his face that Jenry doesn't believe him. "You're always welcome here."

Winston opens the door, waiting as Jenry steps into the hallway. He wants to say more, but he knows he can't rush the boy; whatever their relationship is going to be, it has to be on his terms. Winston might have set up the board, but he can't play both sides.

"Did Juliet give it to you? My baby book."

Winston knows he should lie, but he feels bad for the boy, searching so hard for the truth. As if such a thing even exists. "No," he says.

Jenry nods. "So it was my mother." He blinks against the sunlight now soaking the hallway and walks away.

It wasn't true, of course, but Winston doesn't correct him. Let Victor make his own confessions.

· 5 ·

Malcolm Sterling's office is in a three-story brick building on the eastern edge of the campus. Winston's known Sterling since the late eighties, when he was a newly hired assistant professor with a reputation for dramatics, a virtuoso who graduated from high school at fifteen, spoke several languages fluently, and played six instruments—but really, he came to Winston's attention when Juliet studied with him, the only freshman to earn a position in his coveted jazz ensemble.

Winston doesn't bother with an appointment. As long as he's known Sterling, his colleague has enacted the role of eccentric professor: he wore ill-fitting clothes, an expensive but moth-eaten overcoat, and was always in need of a haircut. He smelled like smoke—not from cigarettes, but from cooking meat over an open fire, preferably deer he hunted himself—and was always looking for something he just misplaced. He refused to hold office hours, began his classes at least ten minutes late, and never seemed to know what day of the week it was. Several of the college's presidents—there have been five since Winston began teaching here—have tried to get rid of him, but he is consistently the best-reviewed professor in the Music

Department, and his former students make up 10 percent of the endowment, through donations that were often more than his annual salary. What choice was there but allow him to stay?

Winston cannot hear the music until he is standing at the office door, waiting to be let in. He knocks again, louder this time, aware of the music's vibration against the closed door, almost more than the sound. He instinctively tries the doorknob, surprised to find it unlocked. The room is completely dark, except for the lights from the stereo system, which blink in rows of red, orange, and yellow, flashing brightly as the volume increases.

When the saxophone screeches, he watches the entire block of color light up, pulsing as if the receiver is straining to hold the music inside. It is too loud for Winston's liking, yet the melody is familiar. A strange jazz-like swing that reminds him of the dance halls of his youth, places whose music spilled from opened windows as he walked down Amsterdam Avenue, returning home from night classes at City College. At sixteen, he felt too young to go in alone, and the boys he knew who frequented those clubs were delinquents in one way or another: card sharks, hustlers, bookies; he feared the unapologetic smiles that lit their faces when he saw them on the street corner in the morning, certain they had yet to go to sleep. He knew better than to allow himself such pleasures, the slippery slope of temptation being, as his mother used to tell him, a one-way road to hell. Winston was her shining star; he had to be different, better, the best.

In the dark of Sterling's office, Winston waits for his eyes to adjust. When they do, he crosses the room in three long strides and plays with knobs until he finds the volume, turning it down to a rumble. As he looks for a light switch, a voice breaks the darkness.

"Who's there?" Sterling questions the dark. Winston can't place where his voice is coming from. He walks back to the entrance.

"It's Winston. I knocked but . . . I guess you couldn't hear me."

"Ah," Sterling says, his tone shifting. "Hang on, let me find the light."

Winston sees a figure rise from the shadows behind a file cabinet.

He watches an arm sweep across the wall, and a bright light illuminates the room. Both men squint.

"Winston." Sterling clears his throat. "What an odd surprise." He yawns fully, like a cat, his eyes pinched shut.

"I'm sorry I woke you," Winston says, unable to fathom how Sterling could sleep through such sound.

"What time is it?"

"About four thirty," Winston says, "In the afternoon."

Sterling nods, his disheveled hair flopping down to cover his eyes. "Well, yes, that sounds about right." He arranges the collar on his turtleneck sweater, a thick wool that makes him appear bigger than he actually is, which is quite an accomplishment.

"What can I get you to drink?" Sterling asks, his boyish face still crushed with sleep. "I've got a few fingers of that Glenlivet you brought for my birthday."

"No, no, I'm fine. It's too early for that."

"Is it?" Sterling scratches his shadow of a beard. "I'd imagine it's cocktail hour somewhere." He plugs an electric teapot into a socket by the window and goes in search of more supplies. From the closet he calls out, "What brings you by, my friend? I wasn't expecting to see you until the All Saints party."

"I'm here about a student actually. Jenry Castillo. He's a scholarship—"

"Of course, I know Jenry. He's in my music theory seminar."

Winston moves a stack of old newspapers to sit on the edge of a piano bench serving as a bookshelf. The piano is nowhere to be seen. "He said he dropped it."

"Well, yes, he tried. But so do half the students each semester. I don't sign off on the drop slips until Thanksgiving break. Just in case they have a change of heart." Sterling steps from the closet, holding two chipped mugs and a jar of instant coffee.

"Is he any good?" Winston asks.

"At music theory?"

"No, no, as a performer. Have you heard him play?"

"I'm on the scholarship committee, as you know, so I've seen hours of his video. He wouldn't be here if he wasn't exceptional."

"But you haven't seen him live?"

Sterling shakes his head. "He withdrew from the orchestra. Nothing I can do about that. The real test is the Winter Concert at the end of the semester. That's when we see what they've really got."

The light on the teapot clicks off and Sterling pours the boiled water into the mugs. He spoons coffee crystals into each one, stirring until the foam at the top disappears. "Sorry, I don't have cream," he says with sincerity.

"I'll drink it black," Winston says.

Sterling tips the bottle of scotch into each mug. The men toast, each holding their small mugs with a bent finger.

"Why the interest in this one?" Sterling asks. "Is he one of yours?"

Winston knows what he meant—is he one of your students—but he thinks of a different type of ownership when he answers, "Yes, he's one of mine." He sips his coffee, the scotch clearing his sinuses. "He's a good kid. Smart. But I wonder about his commitment. It might not be the right time."

"It never is," Sterling says. "You know that as well as anyone. Look at Juliet."

Winston scans the bookshelves, similar to the ones covering his office walls, but these are filled with record albums; from this distance, he can't make out any of the titles.

"She could be on stage in the best concert halls in the world," Sterling looks over his cup, adding with a grin, "or at least the best jazz clubs, if talent was all it took."

The men share a routine pause: they've had this conversation before.

"And Jenry?" Winston asks. "Does he have what she did?"

Sterling pushes the hair from his eyes again. "It's a fool's game, to compare musicians. Even when they're in the same band. All you know is how they make you feel."

"I just want to know if it's worth it," Winston says, wrapping both hands around his mug to warm them, "for him to work like she did. To sacrifice."

"Worth it to whom—the audience? The school? Them?" Sterling laughs. "What is any of it really worth?" He walks to the window, covered by thick blackout curtains, and pulls them open with a flourish. "What, my friend, is a sunset worth? Or a glass of scotch?" He raises his drink. "Or making love to a beautiful woman?" He smiles, leaning back against the window. "How do you put a value on the elements—the essence—of life? Either it is all meaningless, or it is all essential. You decide."

Winston finishes his drink. "Thanks, professor, for keeping the lecture brief."

Sterling smiles warmly. "Perhaps you want to join one of my seminars?"

Winston laughs at the suggestion, feeling the effects of the scotch—a looseness opening in his shoulders, as a warm current swims from the bottom of his stomach into his chest and throat. He feels the inside of his mouth tingle, aware of wanting more.

Sterling takes Winston's mug, filling it with scotch and just a touch of hot water this time—no coffee. He makes himself the same.

"The thing with Jenry is complicated," Sterling admits. "Like most students, he's under a lot of pressure . . . But it's more than that; he needs distinctions to keep the scholarship, that isn't a choice. And extracurriculars like orchestra or the ensemble take up a lot of time. Plus his core requirements for the concentration and his work-study—"

"Christ, how does he have time to practice?" Winston imagines Jenry working long shifts in the cafeteria, like he once did to get through school, his fingers pruned from hours in the hot soapy water. Perhaps he should have pushed them to take more money, but Victor insisted the work was good for him, the scholarship an incentive to keep him focused; they agreed they didn't want him to get soft.

Sterling sits down on the edge of his table, knocking a pile of papers to the ground. He glances down, then continues on like it didn't happen. "These kids, they work so hard just to get here. Sometimes that ends up being enough. Not everybody makes it."

Winston shakes his head. "No, not this one."

Sterling's expression changes, as if he just remembered a crucial fact. "You mentioned before, when we talked on the committee last spring, about some special circumstances. Do you care to elaborate?"

Winston considers the question. Should he tell him about Jenry's trust, the one that financed his musical education since the first grade? The one Winston set up for the boy, telling no one the truth about the origins of the money, and letting Victor—who withdrew funds monthly from the trust's executor, one of Winston's former students, now running an investment firm in Miami—believe it was an inheritance from Jasper's estate?

"It's a delicate situation," Winston says. "That's all I can say right now."

Sterling nods. He places his empty mug on the table and stands up. "And all I can say is this: the last delicate situation I was involved in lost me my wife and child. I hope the stakes aren't as high for you, my friend." Sterling claps Winston on the shoulder, squeezing him affectionately.

Winston rubs his hands together, blowing into them as if it were cold in the room, when in fact, he suddenly feels quite warm.

"Do you mind doing me a favor and losing that drop slip? I'd hate for him to fall behind in credits during his first semester." His voice is light and easy, but he knows what he's asking Sterling to do, knows it's a breach of the ethics code in their faculty guidelines.

"I already told you," Sterling says, "I won't sign it until Thanksgiving. That gives him several more weeks to figure it out. Plenty of time."

Winston stands, looks down into Sterling's eyes, understanding that he holds something powerful over his younger colleague, beyond his size or stature at the university, beyond his emeritus status or position on various committees: his audacity. That is Winston's greatest strength.

"I mean lose it completely," Winston clarifies. "So he can't drop the course."

Sterling's eyes shift, as he understands what Winston is asking.

"I don't mean it like that," Winston says quickly. "Just give him an Incomplete. I'll make sure he does the work. I just don't want him to have the opportunity to fail."

"That's what college is," Sterling says. "What life is."

"Not for him," Winston says.

They stand together sipping their drinks.

"Which are you more afraid of," Sterling asks, "for him to fail or to quit?"

Winston finishes his drink, placing the mug onto a stack of music sheets. "Isn't it the same thing?"

Sterling shakes his head. "Juliet quit, but she never failed. I'm guessing that's the fate you want to avoid?"

Winston doesn't respond. He thanks his friend for the drink and heads back into the cold, contemplating the answer. For him, quitting will always be the bigger sin. Failure is someone else's measure, but to quit is to fail yourself; a message he passed down to his children, making Juliet's decision much more difficult to bear. She had wanted to punish him, by throwing away the thing her mother had given her, but he didn't understand why. Talent was something he touched but never owned; ambition, drive, yes, but not that other magic, the kind you don't have to work for. What Juliet had in abundance.

He walks across the campus in the fading October light, a feeling of calm permeating his body. He never wanted to be an artist; he wanted to endure; to exist; to be seen. Not a small task in a country that had enslaved his great-grandfather. But now he wants more. Not for himself, but for the next generation. His daughter, his grandson, they have the best of him and Faye, of all the ancestors, if only they will claim it. If only they refuse to quit.

He passes Sayles Hall, its red granite exterior appearing almost black in the coming night. It has always been his favorite building on campus; one of the oldest and most striking on the Main Green, and the site of Juliet's many college performances—and soon enough, Jenry's. A seed of excitement sparks inside him. Winston has never been a gambling man, but he would wager all his possessions to reach this final goal: to have his family back together. What other choice does he have? If he fails now, to keep Jenry close, to bring Juliet closer, it won't matter anyway. There won't be anything left to lose.

· 6 ·

Winston spends Halloween night as he always does—hiding in his study with the porch lights off. In the morning, he drives through streets littered with candy wrappers and ribbons of toilet paper, jack-o'-lanterns rotted from weeks in the sun. The sky is thick with storm clouds, but no rain has fallen in weeks. The digital clock outside the Citizens bank reads 5:07 a.m., then flashes the temperature: 39 degrees. It's the first of November, and winter has finally arrived.

The pool feels colder than usual, so he shortens his routine, spends extra time standing in the hot water as he washes the chlorine from his body. Today the lifeguards offer him leftover Halloween candy along with the donuts, and he gives in, taking a bite-sized Snickers along with an old-fashioned, his wife's favorite, feeling a gnawing hunger in the pit of his stomach, though he knows neither treat will satisfy it. He wears his hat and gloves while he drives to his office, his scarf wrapped tightly around his neck, coffee balanced between his knees. The heater in his car seems to be blowing cold air, so he turns it off.

The History Department parking lot is more crowded than usual, but nothing else seems different or strange. He unlocks the building's front door, turning on the foyer light as he does every morning; checks his mailbox, checks the thermostat, and walks slowly up two and a half flights of stairs, each one creaking under his weight. His coffee is still too hot to drink. He finishes the last bite of donut in the hallway, which falls like a stone into his empty stomach. It's a relief to know he won't eat again for several hours.

He unlocks the deadbolt to his office door, turns the antique knob with a gloved hand. The lamp beside his desk is turned on, and sitting in his chair, arms folded across her chest, is his daughter. His first thought is *How wonderful,* but as he steps into the room, seeing the pile of papers on his desk, the opened file box sitting before her like a present, he feels the anger in the air; sees her face, stiff with fury, her eyes glassy, like black olives. He closes the door behind him, moving with measured steps, acting as if this isn't an unusual sight, as if he's expecting to see her this morning, with secrets he's held for more than a decade strewn across the desk, the bomb finally exploded.

"Hello." He places the newspaper on a stack of books, unfolding it neatly.

"That's your opening line?" Her tone is biting; he knows this won't end well.

"Do you have a better one?"

"How about, Why are you here? What's that box on my desk? What are all those pictures?"

He steps deeper into the room, closer to her, though his instincts are telling him to retreat, perhaps even to run.

"But no, you wouldn't ask those questions, would you?" Juliet sits upright in his chair. "Not when you already know the answers."

"I can see that you're upset—"

"So you're not blind," Juliet says. "Sick, but not blind."

He doesn't follow.

She gestures to the desk. "To do all this. You'd have to be sick. Or crazy."

He places his briefcase on the empty chair beside his desk, the one normally occupied by students. His movements are calm, careful. He needs his exterior demeanor to deflect from the growing sense of panic he feels inside.

"I'm not the one trespassing, dear." It's petty, but he can't think of anything better to say. His heart is racing, but his mind has gone blank.

"I used my key," she says, holding up a bulging key ring.

"So that makes it okay?"

"Are we really talking about what's okay, Pop?" Her voice rises. "Because from where I sit, you haven't done anything okay since Jenry was born."

"Don't be so dramatic." He takes off his overcoat and hangs it on the hook on the back of the door. He removes his gloves.

Juliet stands up suddenly, her hands slapping the desk. "You knew where he was. This whole time. You had an address and pictures. You have his fucking artwork. His report cards." She shuffles through the piles, spreading out stacks of paper. "You knew where he was, and instead of helping me find him, you collected this box of mementos like some stalker—"

"It wasn't the whole time."

"You have pictures of his birth," she shouts. "Pictures I took myself. Things you could have only gotten from his baby book."

"I didn't plan to keep it from you. I was trying to help."

"Help? How did this help me?"

He starts to talk faster, rushing to get the story out before she can say anything else. "I received a letter, when you were still living with me, from Marisa. She wanted to reach out to you. Who knows why. But you were just getting back on your feet. You seemed okay, and I thought it was better for you to go to London and get some of your life back, instead of heading down to Miami to get your heart broken again."

"So you went instead? So *you* could break my heart?" When he doesn't respond she lowers her eyes. He wants to reach for her, to cradle her head against his chest, to comfort her, but he doesn't dare. "You had no right," she says softly, shaking her head almost imperceptibly. "It wasn't your decision to make."

He walks to the corner radiator to turn up the heat. The knob is cold against his skin. "I don't know what I was expecting, I'm still not sure why I went." He places his hand along the cast iron columns, waiting for the heat to come. "But when I found her father, he had all this stuff, things she had given him, and he ended up giving them to me. The baby book, and all these pictures—"

"There are letters here," she interrupts. "Report cards. Programs from his concerts, things I didn't even know about. How could you collect all this and keep it from me?"

"I wanted to know that he was okay, to make sure he was taken care of—"

"*You* wanted to know?" She spits the question out, the words bitter on her tongue. "And you didn't think I wanted that same thing? To know something, anything, about the child I'd raised for more than two years?"

"Yes, of course. I was doing it for you. On behalf of you. And Jasper."

"Don't—" She points at him, her finger shaking with intensity. "Don't you dare bring him into this."

"How can I not? This is his son we're talking about. I had to make sure he was going to be okay, that he had opportunities to make something of his life." As the radiator fills with heat, Winston finally removes his hand. "Who else can carry on Jasper's legacy? This boy is the only remnant of my son I have left."

"*Your* son?" Juliet says, her tone almost mocking. "So that's what this is all about?"

Winston doesn't respond. Instead, his eyes travel to the row of bookshelves that line the room's longest wall, where a framed poster from Jasper's final show leans against the spines of his enormous set of *Encyclopedia Britannica*s. The thirty-two-volume set, bound in burgundy leather with gold trim, was a gift from his wife, celebrating his tenure.

Juliet's eyes follow his across the room, taking in all the same sights—an array of simple and sentimental objects that she, too, must recognize as being not just a part of her father's life, but a part of him, of how he defines himself—or better yet, lets himself be defined.

"Are you kidding me?" she says, her voice surprisingly restrained. "You had your son for thirty-three years. You got to raise him and watch him grow up. You saw him every single day. You watched from the audience as he turned from a skinny little boy into this amazing artist." Her voice is strained as she continues to speak; her face turns a deep shade of red as the veins in her neck bulge. "You got to see him perform all over the world, didn't you? You have memories and videos and dozens of photo albums from his childhood. Photos *you* got to take." Her voice shakes as she drops into a whisper. "You have his piano sitting right outside this door. You have his gravestone, right next to Mom's, and you can visit them every day if you want to." She takes a deep breath, shaking her head as she exhales. "Don't tell me you don't have remnants of your son. The one you named and raised and buried. It wasn't long enough, I know that, but you had his whole damn life."

Juliet sits back down, falling into the chair. She folds her arms, tucking her hands into her armpits, just like she's done since she was a child. Winston suppresses an odd sense of pride at the deftness of her argument and the calculated nature of her debating style, even when he finds himself on the opposing team. Even when she—his last living child—is skillfully articulating his shortcomings.

"Juliet, look." Winston takes off his glasses. "I know I can't make up for this. I can't make it right—"

"Let me get that on tape—that's the first true thing you've said in years."

"Just remember that we've all suffered, we've all lost things that were precious to us." He gives her a pleading look. "But Jenry was with his mother. His real mother." It occurs to Winston that perhaps he shouldn't say it like that, but why ignore such an obvious truth. It makes a difference. He feels certain it does. "Marisa was able to raise him when you couldn't."

"No, not *couldn't*." Juliet sits up straight. "Wasn't allowed to."

"Does it really matter? One good parent is enough. It's more than most people get."

"Well it wasn't enough for me."

Winston lifts his eyes in wonder, surprised by the venom in Juliet's voice and the look of anguish on her face. He allows the sting to dissipate before he replies. "I did the best I could. I hope you believe that."

"You were always a strict father, harsh, distant." She looks away, her dark eyes avoiding his. "But I don't remember you being mean. Not like now."

"You think it's mean to state the obvious?" Winston snaps back, hoping to get her to turn around, to draw her back into the argument. Any string of words, he thinks, no matter how harsh, will keep them in conversation, and at least has the potential to draw them together. But as soon as the question is out, he wants to take it back. Wishes he could be the father she remembers him being, or better yet, the one she wants him to be.

"What happened to our family?" Juliet asks, suddenly turning to look him in the eyes. "What changed?" Her mouth falls open, the jaw loose like a puppet's.

She looks to him like she is about to cry, something he will be unable to bear, and he pinches his eyes closed, refuses to see it. He stands for a moment in the darkness of the unseeing, feels the still air surrounding his body; pictures Juliet's eyes upon him, her judgment seeping into his core. He hears the wind outside, sweeping skeletal branches against his windowpanes, and hears the high-pitched hiss of the steam escaping the radiator. He opens his eyes. How thin the divide between man and the elements, he thinks, his eyes adjusting to the light—how transparent all lines of division really are.

Winston rests one hand on the desk, his fingers spread out on a stack of unopened mail. He remembers thinking retirement would mean a decrease in correspondence, but there's always someone who needs him. He knows how fortunate this makes him, to be in this elite category of the respected expert, and despite his age and race, to have risen to the top in such a demanding field, but in moments like this it feels irrelevant; he can't pretend to want any other form of acknowledgment than the admiration, appreciation, and love that only a daughter can give. It is Juliet's respect he longs for, and her forgiveness.

"I don't know," he finally answers, his voice trembling in a way he hadn't anticipated. He clears his throat, expecting to go on, but Juliet interrupts him.

"Was it because Jasper and I were both gay? Was that just too much disappointment for you?" Her voice is calm, but her eyes bore into him.

"What?" Winston asks, struggling to get the word out.

"This son you like to talk about, the one you're trying to resurrect through Jenry—why didn't you want him when he was still alive?"

"What are you saying?" Winston's eyes narrow as he tries to follow.

"You know exactly what I'm saying. You would go months without talking to him. You refused to meet his boyfriends—"

"He never brought anyone home, never introduced me—"

"And why would he, if this is what he would get? You were ashamed of him, admit it. And the worst part is that he knew it. Why do you think he never told you when he got sick? Do you think that was an oversight? A mistake? He died trying to protect you—"

"I was never ashamed of my son. Don't you dare say that to me."

"Or what?" Juliet laughs bitterly. "I already lost my brother and my son. What else can you take from me?" She is up now, walking around the desk. He wants to take a step back, to distance himself from her fury, but he can't show any signs of weakness now.

"We're done here," she says matter-of-factly. He stares at the key ring she cradles in her hands, watching as she works to remove a single key from the ring. He recognizes it, of course, the largest one, with the university's seal stamped on the bow. She lays the key on the corner of the desk, snapping it against the wood. "I don't want to see you anymore."

"You're upset. I understand that. But don't say something you don't mean."

"Oh, I mean it."

"You can't choose to step out of a family. It doesn't work that way." He looks down at her, suddenly overcome with anger. "You think I haven't been disappointed by you? Quitting the piano like it was a hobby, some game you used to play?" He throws his gloves onto the table. "Christ, if you only knew"—his voice is quieter now—"if you could see how your mother looked at you. How proud she was, just to hear you play. She stayed *alive* those last months just to hear you." Tears are welling in his eyes, and he suddenly doesn't care if she sees them. "But when you quit, I didn't walk away from you."

"You didn't?" Juliet scoffs. "You've spent my life walking away."

Winston reaches for the desk again, this time to steady himself. He takes a deep breath before speaking. "I took care of you the best I could. Worked to put a roof over your head. I wasn't perfect, but I was here. I've been here your whole goddamn life."

Juliet gathers her things and walks to the door. Her manner sub-dued, but still measured, resolute.

"My wife and I are about to have a baby, a child that I will legally adopt, and when we do, I don't want you to have anything to do with us. Don't write, don't call. You are relieved of the burden of caring for me or my family. Consider yourself free."

She leaves the door open as she walks out, leaving him to ponder the meaning of the word *free*, a state he isn't sure he's ever known. He closes the door a few minutes later, only after he's certain she won't return.

Alone in the office, warmed now and smelling faintly of her per-fume, he finds himself unable to sit in his desk chair, the one she had so skillfully commanded for the last ten minutes, before abandoning it as she had abandoned him. Instead, he sits against the edge of the desk, not bothering to remove the key Juliet had placed there. Certain he won't touch it for days or weeks, if ever.

He hears his heart thumping, loud like the beating of a drum, and thinks of Emperor Jones; wonders about his own silver bullet, the one thing that could destroy him. In the opera, they changed the final scene, and instead of being killed by the rebels, the emperor kills himself. But Winston preferred the original ending, where his death made him a martyr, allowing the audience to mourn him. His sacrifice turned him into a hero.

He picks up his coffee, lukewarm now, and drinks it quickly, numb to the burnt taste it leaves in his mouth. He feels his heartbeat slowly return to its normal rhythm. Waits for the lump in his throat to clear, for his hands to steady. He needs to act quickly, to fix the mess he's made, but he feels paralyzed, his limbs heavy with regret. The familiar hiss of the radiator fills the room as the heat clicks on, working to maintain its temperature. Warmth surrounds him like a presence, and he sits there, unmoving, for a very long time.

· 7 ·

Lying on its side, the piano looks like an odd-sized bed, its hard edges softened by the quilted moving blankets placed on all sides to protect it. One of the movers—there are four in all—kneels beside it, holding the tape dispenser like a gun. He covers the blankets in layers of packing tape, like a trainer wrapping a sprained ankle during halftime; around and around he goes, as the noise rips through the otherwise quiet air of the History Department, the sound of something being torn apart.

Winston watches the movers work. He stares at the covered piano and wonders why he's given it so much power over the years. Why did he believe so much life could be held inside a simple wooden box? One that doesn't hold their spirits any more than their coffins do, empty except for the dusty remnants of bone. It's irrational, he realizes, to give an instrument so much meaning. But grief isn't a rational thing. Played by his wife and then his children, it seemed to hold some significant part of their beings, more so than the pictures or clothing or stories he also kept, as if they had each left their mark on it, and in doing so, left an integral part of their selves behind. For years he felt certain of this, felt the weight of their ghosts. But something has changed now. Their fingerprints have been wiped from the keys, the burdens of the past lifted. A sense of clarity settles in him. Perhaps he could thank Juliet for this grace, her rejection serving to free him from the imprisonment of his own beliefs.

Earl, the maintenance man, arrives in a postman-blue coverall embroidered with the university's seal on a small patch above his heart. He greets Winston warmly, and together they walk to the fire escape, where he dismantles the alarm before unlocking the door, propping it open with his square body. The rush of cold air shocks both men, who blink their eyes against the drafts of wind. At the other end of the hallway, the movers take their time hoisting the piano onto the dolly; once loaded and secure, they roll it slowly through the halls. It moves like something from another time, a ship set adrift. It picks up speed as it nears the fire escape, propelled by the slope of the antique floors. Without hesitation, the movers jump on top of it, slowing it down with the weight of their bodies.

Winston looks back to where the old Steinway had stood. A wide rectangle of dust darkens the floor, its four corners marked by the small indentations the piano's feet have left in the wood. Earl sweeps away the dusty spot before Winston can stop him, then mops the floor with an oil soap. After, he smooths over the damp wood with a cotton rag; in a few minutes, he's removed all traces of the piano ever being there. The scent of lemon oil reminds Winston of his childhood, of cleaning the banisters in their old brownstone under his grandmother's watchful eye, polishing until his arm ached and the hardwood gleamed. It was his first experience of hard work, and with it came an unexpected reward: the simple pleasure of a task well done.

Outside, winter has arrived in full, and the cold December air smells like snow. He can see the men huddled together on the fire escape, threading pulleys through the wrought iron grates, tightening the harnesses, and eventually attaching a giant hook to the canvas straps that belt the quilts in place. The arm of the crane extends over the edge of the roof, elbow bent and ready; it looks like a child's toy from his sidewalk view, and when it first lifts the piano into the air, he imagines the whole thing crashing to the earth. But the ropes hold, and soon the crane brings the piano safely to the ground.

The last time Winston moved the Steinway—when he'd brought it from the cabin—he was in mourning, Jasper only one month in the ground. Today, he is in a different kind of mourning. He's done as Juliet asked—no calls, no letters, no questions—but Noelle surprised him with a phone call after the baby was born, telling him that everything went fine, and they were already taking him home. *Him*, she'd said: another boy. Winston asked if they'd named him yet, and she hesitated. "Yes," she answered, "we named him Jonah."

Winston found himself smiling. "A biblical name," he said. "That's good."

"It's after my father," Noelle said. "His middle name is Lucas, after Jasper."

"Yes, well," Winston had to clear his throat, "that's a nice tribute."

He'd sent flowers to the hospital, with no card, and arranged for meals to be delivered to their home for the first three weeks. That's what he remembers most about the newborn stage: how hard it was for Faye to find time to cook. He'd done his best, making her soft-boiled eggs and oatmeal for the first three days after Jasper was born, but each time she'd eventually push the bowls back to him, requesting lasagna and egg rolls instead, French vanilla ice cream beside a wedge of apple pie as thick as the Bible. He didn't make that mistake when Juliet came along four years later, ordering takeout from Faye's favorite restaurants for at least a month. Now, for Juliet and Noelle—members of the current food-obsessed culture of the middle class—he ordered from the campus caterers, known to be farm-to-table enthusiasts even before he'd heard the term on NPR.

The movers are on the sidewalk now, securing the dolly with blocks so the piano won't roll away before they get it into the truck. The History Department is perched on a hill, which makes the move especially tough, in addition to the narrow hallways of a building built circa 1854 with no elevator. Two more men have joined the team, and Winston watches as they guide the blanketed mass onto the dolly. They work together to push it up the steep incline of the street, and then onto the steel ramp protruding from the back of the truck. The ramp bows slightly under their weight, but soon they get the piano up and over the metal lip. The wheels screech in revolt, causing Winston to wince. Inside the truck, the movers strap the piano to the walls with bungee cords as thick as a man's wrist, a web of nylon holding it safely in place.

The driver appears, clipboard in hand. "Ready to sign?"

Winston places his signature on the line at the bottom.

"You mind writing down the address?" the driver asks.

"Of course," Winston says. He fills in Juliet's address and hands the clipboard back.

"COD?" he asks, his pen hovering above the paper.

"No, I'll pay now. It's a surprise." Winston hands him his credit card, which the driver tucks under the paper, rubbing over the numbers to make an imprint of the card. He turns it over to write down the security code.

"Quite a present," he says, nodding to the piano as he hands the card back to Winston. "I moved a lot of these uprights, and this is the best I've seen."

Winston pockets the card. "Thank you." The breeze kicks up, making his eyes tear.

"Just in time," the driver says, looking up at the sky. "Snow's about to fall."

He tears off the yellow copy and hands it to Winston, who folds it in thirds and tucks it into his coat pocket. The driver climbs into the truck and turns the engine. The smell of exhaust fills the air. Winston walks to the back of the truck, feeling the heat of the exhaust against his legs. The other men huddle on a low bench across from the piano, looking at their phones. He glances at the misshapen form, certain for the first time that he's doing the right thing. Juliet is, after all, the piano's rightful owner.

After the funeral, Juliet told Winston about her final night with Jasper at the cabin, how she sat for hours at the piano and played song after song from their childhood; how they tried to call him, but he wasn't home. Winston never told her that he was home that night, had sat by the phone and watched it ring. He convinced himself it was nothing important, and in doing so missed the last chance to speak to his son. The guilt feels like a wool scarf knotted around his neck, one he will wear for the rest of his life.

He asked Juliet—all those years ago, as they stood beside Jasper's yet unmarked grave, the earth packed hard from hundreds of mourners who had come to pay respects to their hometown star—if she wanted the piano for herself, and she said no. As if by refusing it, she could somehow push his death away, leave it confined to the cabin like the music she played that night, the notes trapped inside the walls. But Winston couldn't leave the piano behind. Like a fallen comrade, he wanted to bring the body home. So that's what he did, moving it from the cabin to the landing outside his office, where he'd been able to look at it almost every day, believing that through sheer proximity, he could keep some part of the past alive.

"Good morning, Dr. Patterson," says a voice from the pack of students exiting the building behind him.

"Good morning," Winston replies. He smiles noncommittally to the group, who button their coats against the falling snow.

"Supposed to get a few inches," he hears someone say. "Maybe they'll cancel class." The rest of the group laughs as they crossed the slippery street.

It is an odd sensation, to be known on campus as an almost mythic figure, as recognizable to students as the bronze statue of the bear or the bell tower, and yet to feel he knows no one at all. Perhaps it is time to leave; perhaps the piano is only the first of his many possessions that will depart from his office in the coming months. He has given his life to this institution, and they have taken it; does he need to give them his death as well?

He doesn't think of himself as morbid, but death consumes his mind now. Not just his own, but that of his colleagues—like his old friend

Bernie Bruce, the graduate school's first Black dean, and Winston's first ally on campus—as well as childhood friends and distant relatives, and of course the three he is still trying to get over: his wife and two sons. Or maybe not get over, but get through.

The truck beeps as the driver backs up, sending Winston onto the sidewalk. His dress shoes slip on the dusting of snow, but he catches himself, holds the lamppost for balance. The metal is so cold it burns his hand. He feels a deep sense of relief as he watches the truck pull away. Perhaps he has conquered the past, and his desire to part with the piano illustrates just that. But it is also a strategic move, and likely not his final one. Having just lost his queen, the endgame has now begun. The board is almost empty, and the king is no longer protected; to avoid checkmate, he will have to launch a skillful attack, using the few pieces he has left.

The snow is falling harder, and he blinks to clear his vision, glad to remove his glasses. The air is clean and cold in his lungs, and he takes several full breaths. His eyes follow the truck until it disappears around a corner, leaving dark, wet tracks in the freshly fallen snow.

BOOK VI

The Other Grandfather

May 1997

• 1 •

The sun had set over an hour ago, yet the den was still too hot. Victor cranked open the windows and turned on the ceiling fan, but Inés wouldn't leave the comfort of the bedroom, the only room in their small house that had air conditioning. He turned on the game—Yankees versus the Tigers—and sat in his new rocking chair, a birthday gift from his wife. The vinyl stuck to his skin, making him hotter, but he refused to get up. Not even June and already the Miami heat was suffocating.

If Victor had his way, he would live in New York. He liked the look of the city when they went to commercial break during the game, liked seeing the skyline, the signs for the subway, and the skyscrapers with their walls of glass; he liked seeing the bridges and the ferries that passed below, and whenever he saw the Statue of Liberty, he tried to imagine how it would feel to be inside, to walk along her crown. And then there was sports, especially baseball—the Yankees, of course, not the Mets—and he liked their nighttime cop shows like *NYPD Blue,* which Inés refused to watch with him, saying it was too vulgar, even though she liked that one actor, Jimmy Smits, who was Puerto Rican, not Cuban, but was so

314 ·   RACHEL M. HARPER

good it didn't matter. He liked the *Godfather* movies and all the other immigrant stories that took place in New York, never Miami, mostly it seemed because the people who made it to New York, even when they arrived with nothing, had at least fulfilled a long-held dream, while the ones who landed in Miami were just fleeing some other nightmare.

Like many Cubans who emigrated after the revolution, Victor's parents never wanted to come to Miami, but they thought it was better than staying in Havana and watching their freedoms slowly vanish. Lazaro and Ana were not political people, but they had managed to draw the attention of their neighbors; for complaining about the food rations and how their boys, Victor and his older brother, Emilio, were pressured at school to join the *pioneros* and fight for the cause; for throwing away the red initiation scarf Victor came home wearing one day, which he had borrowed from a friend because he thought it made him look handsome, like a bullfighter in Spain, and reminded him of the stories his abuela used to tell him about her childhood in Catalonia. They didn't realize their neighbors were part of CDR, a civilian spying network that Castro created to weed out counter-revolutionaries, but that wasn't who his parents were; Lazaro was happy Batista was gone and wanted what Castro promised, better health care and schools for their two boys, but in the kitchen after dinner, Victor heard him say to his wife, "When it becomes mandatory, it's no longer a revolution."

Lazaro was arrested a few times, but he always came home the next day, telling them he was okay, the soldiers only wanted to scare him, that he wasn't hurt, but soon the men on the docks wouldn't talk to him, wouldn't buy any of his catch, and one day they said his fishing license was expired and he had no other means of employment. Ana's parents owned a small tobacco farm on the outskirts of Havana and they helped for a while, but Lazaro was proud and didn't want to prove them right, that their daughter had made a mistake in marrying a *pescador moreno* instead of one of the educated *españoles* they picked out for her, so he refused their offer to leave Havana and move in with them, to work the land and leave the uncertainties of the sea behind.

Lazaro eventually found work with his younger brother, Rodrigo, at a sugar mill, and though the wages were low and the labor was difficult, he enjoyed the camaraderie between the men, like when they were boys on the baseball fields, and soon everyone got comfortable, thinking life would carry on that way for some time. And it did, until one day late in the harvest season when a bomb went off at the mill, starting a fire that destroyed all the stores of sugar cane and caused the roof to collapse. Several of the men were hurt, including Rodrigo, whose right arm, his pitching arm, was burned so badly it had to be amputated. Lazaro was arrested under suspicion of working with the dissidents and this time he didn't come back the next day. Months later, Lazaro still wasn't home.

At bedtime, Ana smiled at her boys, saying it would be okay, but while they slept she talked with families from their church, parents who sent their children to America to keep them safe. The program didn't have an official name, but it was funded by the U.S. government and the Miami Catholic Diocese, a covert humanitarian effort that allowed the boys to be taken care of until the family could be reunited. Padre Miguel assured her that they would be safe, that the host families were other Cuban exiles, and he promised to organize passage for Ana soon after; he would also use his position at the church to attempt to get Lazaro released. But Ana had to promise that she wouldn't tell anyone about it: not her parents or her sister, not the neighbors. Alone in her bed every night, Ana struggled to make the right decision.

Then Emilio got expelled after fighting other boys at school, ones who said his father was a traitor to the cause and deserved to die in jail; Ana contacted Padre Miguel that night, asking him to make the arrangements. Emilio was fourteen, three years older than Victor, and already toughened by the first two years of Castro's regime; he would be responsible for his little brother. While they lay in their bedroom at night, Emilio repeated the plan, trying to help Victor understand: It was just for a few months, until their parents could join them, and they mustn't talk about it with anyone; yes, they could still speak Spanish; of course, they would stay together, no matter what. They would play baseball every day and watch American television. Victor wanted to know one last thing: why would President Kennedy care about protecting *cubanos* more than El Comandante?

They left within a week and didn't say goodbye to their grandparents. They carried one bag each, with two outfits and four pairs of underwear. Victor brought a family photo album and a book about shipwrecks. Ana cut a lock of his hair and tied a ribbon around it, tucking it into the Bible she kept on her night table. She cried so hard when Padre Miguel came to pick them up, he worried she would cause a scene at the airport and asked her to stay home. Victor hugged his mother goodbye in the kitchen, holding on tight to the avocados she had given him for the trip, making sure he wouldn't drop them. The only things Victor remembered from the plane were the salted peanuts and bottles of Coca Cola poured over ice. Emilio slept beside him, his shirt damp with sweat. Victor looked out the window as the plane descended, awed by the view of Miami, and was instantly afraid. When they stepped onto American soil, he was holding his brother's hand.

It took nine months for Padre Miguel and the church to get Lazaro out of jail, and several more to get their papers to leave the country; during that time Victor and Emilio lived in three Cuban foster homes, all families who spoke English to the boys, trying to get them accustomed to life in America. They fed them two meals a day, mostly rice and beans, and gave them bedrolls to sleep on, laid out across the living room floor. Every night Emilio reminded Victor to say his prayers, to be grateful for what they had, even though all Victor could think of was what he'd left behind: the clean smell of his bed, eating *tostones* on the walk to school every morning, playing baseball in the streets with the older boys, the smell of garlic on his mother's hands as she washed his hair in the sink. On Victor's twelfth birthday, Emilio bought him a new baseball glove with money he made washing dishes at a local diner; Victor was so happy he started to cry. "*Aye, chiquito, no lloras*," Emilio said, kissing the top of his head. "Today is a happy day." Victor dried his tears on his shirt and made a wish that next year on his birthday they would all be together.

And even though he got his wish, and the family was reunited the following year, it was never the same; they had lost their home, their country, and Victor knew he had lost something else, not just his childhood but a sense of wholeness, of belonging. He knew he could never go back to Cuba, so he would have to find that feeling here, in America; not necessarily in Miami, but in the homes where he lived, and in the people. As far as Victor was concerned, he'd been homeless since they fled Cuba in the last hours of 1961, even though he'd lived in many houses since then, even though he owned the one he and his wife currently lived in, the mortgage soon to be paid off. But a piece of paper didn't make a house a home. People do, and he'd been missing most of his people, *sus abuelos y tíos, primos y amigos*, for longer than he could remember.

The game was tied 2–2 in the fifth inning, with the Yankees at bat. His beer was already too warm, but he finished it anyway. He called to his wife for another, but she couldn't hear him over the AC. Begrudgingly he shuffled into the garage to get a new can from the fridge. His khaki shorts hung loose on his waist, and he tightened his belt, retucking his shirt. Victor always paid attention to his appearance. He fixed his necklace, rearranging the cross that hung from a thin gold chain, and tucked it under his t-shirt, against the damp skin of his hairless chest. He combed his hair back with his fingers, smoothing out the waves. The pomade left a coconut smell on his hands.

He caught his reflection in the hallway mirror and smiled, still happy with how he looked. Customers always asked if he was working during a school break, complimenting his boyish face. He was the only forty-seven-year-old man he knew without a single gray hair and who had to shave only once a week. "It's the Spanish blood," his mother used to say, rubbing his cheeks like they would bring her good luck.

As he passed the couch, he saw the blinking light on their answering machine. He still didn't know why they had the stupid thing, since his in-laws were the only people who called, and he was happy enough to miss them. He pressed play and waited for the tape to rewind. There was a pause after the beep, and then a familiar voice.

"Hi, Papi, Mami, it's me, Mari. I just wanted to let know you that I had the baby. I'm in the hospital right now. And we're both okay, we're fine." She cleared her throat. "Oh, and it's a boy. Seven pounds, six ounces. Twenty-one inches. We named him Jenry. Jenry Sebastian Castillo. *Felicitaciones, abuelos.* You're grandparents now. *Adios.*"

Victor leaned over the answering machine, his finger hovering over the delete button. He thought of his wife, wondering if she could handle the news, if she could hear Marisa's voice without falling onto her knees like one of the old ladies from church. It had been months since they'd talked to their daughter, and Victor didn't see how this helped anything. But Inés insisted she needed more time, and he decided it was easier to go along with her, to keep the peace, instead of bringing the conflict into his house. He played the message again, trying hard to listen to everything she said. On the memo pad he wrote the details: "Boy. 7 pounds, 6 ounces. 21 inches. Jenri?" He underlined the word *boy* two times.

He lifted his drink, closed his eyes, and made a silent prayer for Marisa and the baby. It was hard to believe he was an abuelo now. He crossed himself and kissed the cross on his necklace. When he opened his eyes they felt wet, so he wiped them with his fingers. He wasn't ashamed of the tears. Lots of things made him cry—like when the Yankees won the World Series, or when his niece Danitza, Emilio's youngest daughter, got into a car accident, and even some commercials on TV, that one where the father dances with his daughter at her wedding. But this time, it wasn't a simple emotion like joy or sadness, it was a complex grief—part shame, part regret.

He played the message one more time, just to hear his daughter's voice. The last time she called was on Christmas, when she told them she was pregnant. Inés was so upset after, she couldn't eat any of the food she'd cooked for the holiday: not the *pernil* and *yuca con mojo*, not the rice and black beans, not the flan and *buñuelos*. She refused to go to

Midnight Mass and didn't open the door for the neighbors when they stopped by to wish them *feliz Navidad*. She said she couldn't face them, now that her dreams of being a grandmother were destroyed; now that her only daughter had shamed her. Victor tried not to think about it. He had hoped Inés would come around, but she still refused to mention their daughter's name, waving him off when he tried to bring her up, sometimes walking out of the room. He tore the note off the memo pad and folded it into a small square, which he put in his wallet. Then he erased the message. He sat down in front of the game and drank his beer.

Two days later, as he and Inés were walking to their car after eating lunch at Emilio's, his brother's newest restaurant, full from his order of *masitas* and *arroz con mojo*, and relaxed from the frozen daiquiri he drank to wash it all down, Victor felt ready to tell her. They were holding hands, something they still did in public, absentmindedly reaching for each other as they fell into step. It had started in high school, the first time he walked her home from school, and it hadn't stopped. A sign, he always told himself, he made the right choice in marrying her, despite the arguing and the miscarriages, the fact that she had given him only one child.

Many people were out and the streets were crowded, though this part of Little Havana wasn't as popular with tourists as Calle Ocho. Still, they had to be careful of children eating ice cream cones and old ladies with big purses walking very small dogs. Victor liked this neighborhood, whose colors and sounds reminded him of Old Havana—the blue and green and yellow buildings, the cars honking and radios blaring, the ever-present beat of salsa music in the background, and the smell of roasted pork and garlic fried in oil—but he didn't visit very often. Not since Marisa had moved away, and he no longer had a reason to come to the old neighborhood, hoping to give her a taste of the life he left behind in Cuba, a world she would never know.

They had parked several blocks away on purpose, to get some exercise, but the air was damp with humidity and Victor started to sweat. The curls Inés had pressed into her hair were beginning to expand in the heat, and he wondered if she would blame him if it all turned to frizz. Maybe he should wait until they were home? Before he could decide, she tripped on the uneven sidewalk, one of the painted bricks having come loose, and Victor caught her, his free hand coming down around her waist to hold her firmly.

"*Cuidaté, amor*," he said, squeezing her softly. She was no longer the skinny girl he had fallen in love with, but she was still beautiful, and when she smiled at him like she was doing now, he felt proud to walk by her side.

"My hero," she teased, leaning forward to kiss him. "*Dime la verdad*, you really like the tie?" She was asking about the early Father's Day present she'd picked up because there had been a sale. His wife was not one to miss a bargain, even if it was for something they didn't need. Maybe especially then.

"Yes, of course."

"I thought it would look nice with your blue suit."

"The one I never wear?"

She shrugged. "I thought it would give you a reason to wear it. It's very handsome on you."

He smiled. "Okay, *querida*." He squeezed her hand. The sun was warm on his face and he could feel beads of sweat breaking out on his forehead. He wiped it with his free hand, slicking it back into his hair. There was traffic in the distance, slowed down like in a parade, and he stared at the cars as they made their way. With his eyes squinting at the light as it bounced off the rooftops, he spoke again. "She had the baby. It's a boy."

He felt her hand tense. "Mari? She had the baby?"

"*Sí.*"

"*Cuando?*"

"Friday night."

"You spoke to her?"

He shrugged. "She left a message."

They came to a corner, but the cross street was empty so they didn't stop.

"A boy," she said. "What you always wanted."

He knew that would be part of the problem, that their daughter had done something she couldn't do: carry a son to term.

"This isn't what I wanted," he said.

She made a sound with her tongue. "What parent would want this for a child? It's not natural." He could see her shaking her head, but he kept his focus on the palm trees in the distance, and beyond that, the thin line of ocean.

"And what happened to us, is that natural? To lose all those babies?"

"It's God's plan," she said. "Not for us to question."

He wanted to keep walking, to the beach, the sand, but they had reached their car. He unlocked her door first, opening it to let the heat escape.

"*Como lo nombró ella?*" his wife asked.

"She said 'Jenri,' I think. I couldn't hear that well."

"What kind of a name is that? How do you spell it?"

"With a *J*, maybe." He shrugged. "You should call, ask her."

She took a tissue from her purse and blotted her face. "I can't stand this heat," she said. "I told you we should park closer." She pulled her hand away and eased into the car.

They drove with the windows down, waiting for the air conditioning to kick in. "Are you going to tell anyone?" he asked.

"What, that Marisa had a baby in a test tube? Like an experiment?"

"It wasn't in a test tube."

"No husband, no father. Oh, *pobrecito*, that poor baby. I can't imagine the life he will live." The wind blew hair across her face, blinding her.

"That baby is our grandson."

Inés shook her head, staring out the window at a group of children playing ball in the street. "Not like this," she said.

Victor gripped the steering wheel with both hands. "*Ay*, Inés. You're talking about our daughter. Mari. Our own flesh and blood." He wondered how bad it could be. A baby with no father—wasn't that like Jesus?

"I won't accept it." She stared out the window, still shaking her head.

"You don't have a choice." His voice got louder. "You either accept this baby or we lose our daughter." He felt the anger in his body come to the surface, leaving goose bumps on his skin.

She rolled up her window, though the inside of the car was still hot. With a plastic brush taken from her purse, she began to fix her hair. He watched as she slowly put it back into place.

"We already lost her," she said.

He heard the sound of her purse snapping shut, as final as a door closing.

LATER THAT SUMMER, when the baby's birth announcement arrived, Inés stood in the kitchen as she read it over several times. They didn't talk about it. Victor kept his eyes on the sports page, reading the denials from several Major League baseball players that they had ever used steroids. After dinner, when she took the birth announcement out with the newspaper, he pulled it from the recycling bin, realizing for the first time that he was spelling Jenry's name wrong in his mind. He kept the card, printed on expensive, cream-colored stock, the lettering pressed into the surface like an old-fashioned seal. It felt heavy in his hands, important. Victor liked how the paper felt between his fingers, smooth like a cat's ear. Once he had memorized it, he found an old magazine about car repair, something he knew she would never open, and tucked the card inside. He placed the magazine in the top drawer of his workbench, under a coil of extension cords, and slid the drawer closed.

Months passed before he looked at it again, but he liked knowing it was there. At Christmas, when Marisa sent a holiday card that Inés refused to open, he snuck into the garage while she was watching a *telenovela* and took out the birth announcement, drawing a strange comfort from seeing his grandson's name, the simple proof of his existence. On

Jenry's first birthday, Victor waited for something from Marisa, a photograph he hoped, or at least a letter with stories about how he was walking now or his favorite food, but nothing arrived. He cursed his wife for doing this to them, but he also thought about what he had done—or rather, what he *hadn't* done. He wanted to make things better, but he was certain it was too late for that. Some mistakes were too complicated to fix.

After Jenry's second birthday passed without any correspondence, Victor knew he had to accept what had happened. If he wanted to stay married, he had to give up on the hope he might meet his grandson or ever see his daughter again.

· 2 ·

Victor placed the ladder against the garage door and climbed up to hang the string of pumpkin lights from the roof. He used the same nails he'd put up two decades before to hang the Christmas lights Inés requested every year, claiming it made her feel more American. A funny statement, he'd always thought, since she was the one born here and he was the exile who gained full citizenship after marrying her.

He hung a paper goblin on a piece of fishing wire; it spun in the soft breeze, twisting around like a dancer. Every few minutes the spotlight on the roof went off, and he waved his arms in the dark until the motion detector turned the lights back on. It was late and he was tired. He had one more thing to hang—the TRICK-OR-TREAT sign above the front door—and then he could join Inés in bed, just in time for *The Tonight Show*.

He heard a car behind him, and then saw the headlights flash as the car parked in front of their house. He didn't recognize the small Toyota. He went back to his work. Then, a voice called to him, "*Hola*, Papi," and he had to grab on to the ladder to keep himself from falling.

He turned to see Marisa standing beside the Toyota, which was still running, the lights on. He felt the weight of the hammer in his hand.

"What are you doing here?" He was in shock, and he didn't know what else to say.

"I wanted to see you." Marisa shielded her eyes against the spotlight. "I wanted you to meet your grandson."

Victor climbed down the ladder. He looked behind her but couldn't see into the dark car.

"He's asleep," Marisa said. "Do you want to see him?"

Victor nodded and she opened the back door. Victor walked up slowly. He wanted to hug her, to touch her even in passing, but didn't. Instead, he peeked inside to see the baby, his long legs almost touching the floor. He had a full head of dark curly hair, skin browned from the sun. Not a baby anymore.

"He's big," Victor said. "How old is he now?"

"Two and a half," she said. "He eats like he's five."

"You were still nursing at that age. You didn't want anything else."

"Well, I didn't nurse him that long. I had to go back to work when he was three months old."

Victor shrugged. "Different times," he said.

He looked at his daughter, standing in the driveway where she had stood thousands of times; they'd bought the smallest house on the block just to get into the school district. Even then they were thinking about Marisa, what was best for her future, how to care for her. He could hardly believe she was almost thirty, let alone a mother. She looked so pretty standing under the spotlight, her eyes dark and focused, but he saw something else underneath, a worn-down resolve.

"*Ven aquí*, Mari," he motioned. "Give your old man a hug."

He held her as long as he could, pulling away just as the tears were welling in his eyes. She tucked her hair behind her ears and fixed her dress; she seemed nervous. Her eyes kept cutting to the house, and then back to him.

"Your mother's probably asleep by now."

Marisa nodded. "I thought she might be."

"I could wake her up, if you want to say hi."

Marisa shook her head. "I don't want to bother her."

"She would want to see you."

She glanced toward the car. "And what about him?"

Victor exhaled. "Mari . . . you know how she is. This has been very hard for her." He tucked his hands into his pockets. "For us."

"I know, Papi."

He shook his head. "I don't know what else to say."

She peeked into the car window to check on the sleeping boy. Victor couldn't believe she had a son, and yet here they were.

"Come inside and have some coffee."

"No, I don't want to wake him up. He hasn't been sleeping well."

"*Está él enfermo?*" Victor asked.

"No, he's fine." She pushed her hair out of her face. "It's been a long trip."

"And what about you?" He reached out to touch her shoulder. "You look tired, *hija*, like you drove straight through."

She nodded. "I am tired." She rubbed her eyes with the palms of her hands.

"So you should rest. Come inside." He waved for her to follow him, but she didn't. Instead, she began to cry. He went and wrapped his arms around her. Her head was heavy on his shoulder.

"Hey, it's okay."

"It's not okay," she said, moaning between breaths. "Nothing is okay."

"What happened?" He lifted her head to look in her eyes. "What's wrong?"

"I quit my job, I left my apartment, I left everything behind." She wiped her face on his shirt. "We broke up. Juliet, she left me. I know you're probably happy to hear it all blew up in my face."

He didn't know what to say. Happiness was not what he felt. He didn't have a name for this feeling, for this whole experience.

"I don't have anything, except my son. I need your help." She was crying again, harder this time. This was his daughter, and she needed him.

"*Claro.*" He squeezed her hand. "What do you need? Money?"

She was looking into the car. Jenry stretched in his sleep, exhaling softly.

"I need a place to stay. This isn't good for him, to be living in the car like some vagabond."

"Living in your car?" He couldn't hide the horror in his voice. "*Cuanto tiempo?*"

She shrugged. "We've been with friends, in different cities. I don't know."

"*Mira*, we'll go inside and tell your mother that you're here, that you need to stay for a while, okay? It will be fine."

Marisa shook her head. "She hates me."

"She's your mother. She doesn't hate you." Victor felt his heart ping in his chest. He didn't want to believe that was possible. "We could never hate you."

"You returned the Christmas card, the picture of my son. Like he was a stranger." Her voice was getting louder, sharp like glass.

"Give us time, *cariño*, we don't know him."

"You don't want to know him." She was shouting now, and he worried that the neighbors would hear. "You can't accept the fact that I'm gay. And that my son doesn't have a father. You can't stand who I've become. Who I am."

Victor held her shoulders, turning her to face him. He felt her strength underneath his hands, and he expected her to pull away, to explode any moment like a racehorse at the starting gate.

"*Mira*, this all happened very fast. We just don't understand." He glanced back to the house, looking for movement, a sign that Inés was still awake. "This wasn't how we raised you. You had boyfriends in high school, you went to the prom with Junior Vasquez, you wore dresses. Look at you, you're a beautiful woman, you could have any man, a good man, and yet you choose to do this strange thing—and for what? What did it get you?"

"It got me my son." Marisa's voice was calm now, matter-of-fact. "And I wouldn't trade him for anything." She pushed past her father and opened the driver's door.

"Yes, of course, I didn't mean that." He stumbled after her, stopped by the open door. He wanted to pull it off its hinges and fling it into his neighbor's yard. He wanted to break something, anything.

"This was a mistake. I'm sorry I came." She was sitting down now, gripping the steering wheel with both hands. He knew he needed to do something to make her stay.

"Don't leave like this. Where will you go?" Victor leaned into the car and turned off the engine, grabbing the keys. The metal was warm in his hands. "I'll get your things." He walked to the trunk, unlocking it before she could utter a reply.

He carried all four bags by himself, stacking them on the driveway. She was still in the car, her head bowed, but he didn't think she prayed anymore.

"You said you needed my help. This is me helping." He reached for her arm. His voice sounded harsher than he'd meant it, but he couldn't take it back. Instead, he softened the grip on her arm, squeezing her gently. "Please, *hija*."

"You can't make me into something I'm not." They stared at each other. He saw how tired her eyes looked, sad in a way he had never seen them before. "I'm never going to marry a man."

Victor touched her face, tucking a loose hair behind her ear. If he pushed too hard, he might not get another chance.

"So don't marry a man. Don't marry anyone! Just come inside, *mija*. You need to rest."

"I don't know how long—"

"Don't worry about that. *Créeme.* We just need time together. Like before."

She held up her hand. "I'm not in high school anymore, Papi."

"*Claro que sí*, I'm just saying . . . we've missed you. We want to help."

"What about Mami?"

He shrugged. "Give her time. *Ella es muy cubana*, stubborn and proud, but you know she loves you. Give her a chance to show that. To make up for what she missed before." He saw Marisa's expression soften as he talked, so he kept going. "But inside the house, you respect our rules. That's fair, don't you think?" He waited for her to nod. "And your past, for now it needs to stay in the past. All of it. The other girl, how you had him, everything." Victor believed what he was saying, which made it easier to say. He gestured toward Jenry. "Think about him. He doesn't need to be confused by all that. You have to do what's best for your son. This here, with us, is what's best."

He offered his hand and helped her out of the car. After retrieving her purse and sweater, she climbed into the backseat and unbuckled the latch on Jenry's car seat, pulling the boy gently onto her shoulder. He twisted his head, still asleep, and nuzzled his face into her neck. Victor picked up his blanket, which had fallen onto the seat, and tucked it around him, making sure not to cover his face. Marisa stood still, waiting for Victor to finish. He patted the boy's back, feeling the warmth of his body through the blanket.

"*Muy guapo*," Victor whispered, smiling at his daughter. She smiled back, to acknowledge the compliment, but there was no joy in the look she gave him.

"And he's dark," he added, "*como mi papá.*"

"Like his father, too," she said, giving him a look. "He's not just Cuban, Papi, he's Black. I won't let you pretend about that."

"*Sí, sí, es mulatto.*" He rubbed her shoulder. "Don't worry, *hija*. We are the same, him and me—*afrocubano.*" He was smiling as he touched the baby's curly hair, saying *afro* and then *cubano* as he touched his own.

She rolled her eyes and they laughed at his silly joke. But there was truth to it. Unlike his wife's family, he was proud to have the blood of slaves in his veins. It proved they were stronger, since they had survived the impossible.

They walked up the driveway together, Victor with his hand on his daughter's back. When they got to the front door, he leaned down to kiss Jenry on the head; he felt the softness of his hair against the prickly stubble of his own face. Closing his eyes, he breathed in the scent of him, recognizing something familiar in this sleeping boy, his flesh and blood. His grandson.

· 3 ·

Victor had no idea how long they would stay, but six months later, when they were still there, he was happy about it. Marisa told him she had a storage unit back in Providence, where she'd left all of her furniture and most of her clothes. She paid the bill for months, refusing to get rid of it, just in case she decided to go back. Victor thought it was a waste of money, but he knew she had to let it go on her own. One day, he asked why the bill stopped coming and she told him she'd donated it all to charity. He wanted to know why, what changed, but he was afraid to ask.

Inés took longer to adjust. She was cautious around the boy, hovering over him as he clamored around the house like a puppy, touching everything that wasn't fastened down. Jenry loved to be in the kitchen, to stand on the stool beside her while she cooked. He asked her questions and she answered them, talking to him as she would a much older child. He didn't always understand her, but it didn't seem to bother either one of them. He would eat anything she handed him—peppers, jicama, guava—and she soon adjusted her meals to his tastes, making the black beans without garlic that he preferred, rice with stewed tomatoes, and *plátanos maduros* instead of the green ones she liked.

Inés and Marisa barely spoke, but when they did it was always about the baby. As he got older, he carried messages between them, something they all preferred. He seemed to like being the messenger, having three grown-ups to run between. Even at the dinner table, when they were only a few feet from each other, they would direct all their questions at Jenry, and he would relay them back, translated into his toddler-speak for comic effect. He liked making them laugh and they liked being entertained. Unlike most young children, he didn't care about toys; he liked grown-up things: books, magazines, and newspapers. At the end of the day Jenry's fingertips were black with newsprint.

His favorite thing to do was look at photo albums. He'd sit between Inés and Victor on the couch, the album spread over his lap like a blanket, and point to each person in the photo, asking who they were and what they were doing. Inés told stories about her mother in her vegetable garden, her father who worked at a bank, and her brother who built houses. Victor showed him pictures of his boyhood in Cuba—the white sand beaches he ran races on, the lizards as big as his hand, the mangos he peeled with his teeth and ate straight off the seed. When they first moved in, Jenry had his own photo album, one of the few things Marisa had brought with her. There were pictures of Juliet inside, and when he pulled them out, talking about Juju, they would force themselves to nod and tell him yes, that's Juju, and when he asked where she was, they would say, *She's home, at her house.* "Wanna go home," he would say, "Wanna see her." They would shake their heads and say, "No, she has her own home now, and you have yours."

Victor saw how it bothered Inés, so he began to intentionally misplace the album, hiding it first in the linen closet, and then with the cookbooks in the liquor cabinet, later in his garage with his car repair manuals. Jenry always found them. Finally, without telling anyone, Victor packed up the photo album and all the loose pictures Marisa had of their old life in Providence, including Jenry's baby book, and put them into a file box he found in the closet. He brought it to work with him, not sure what he should do with it, and ended up storing it in the safe along with his boss's gold cufflinks and a baseball autographed by Minnie Minoso. Jenry continued to ask about the album and Victor continued to help him look for it, tearing up the house while Inés and Marisa looked on with curiosity, until Victor eventually told him it was lost. The lie made Victor feel a guilt he'd never felt before, but he was convinced it was the right thing to do, that soon the boy would forget about her, and life would be easier for all of them. At night after work, he distracted himself in the yard, pruning fruit trees until his muscles ached, his blistered hands finding no relief until they were wrapped around a cold bottle of beer.

A few weeks after Jenry's third birthday, when Victor was working late preparing the store for a Father's Day Sale, he had an unexpected visitor. Nothing could prepare him for the sight of Winston Patterson in person. To say that the man was intimidating was to say that Babe Ruth had a decent batting record. He was skyscraper tall, like he'd just walked off the basketball court, with a permanent scowl on his angular face. His skin was a medium brown, like half the men in Victor's family, tanned from hours of laboring in the sun, and then several more spent drinking beer on the docks as they weighed their catch for the day. He reminded Victor of his father, with the same deep-set eyes, the same air of authority. Maybe that was what had him on edge at first, as Victor stood on a milk crate and barely met his eyes, defending his daughter for decisions he himself was still questioning.

Victor eventually invited him inside for a beer, though Winston looked like he drank vodka martinis at hotel bars, or maybe a scotch on the rocks before dinner. The store was cold from the AC, and Victor could see appreciation in the man's eyes as they stepped inside. He was sweating like a boxer, so Victor offered him a towel, which he used to clean his face. The sweat beaded up again a few minutes later, and he wiped it again. Victor grabbed a six-pack of beer they hid in the stocking shelves and they sat in the footwear section to continue their talk.

"So what do you want?" Victor asked.

Juliet's father sat across from him, angled slightly so their knees didn't touch.

"I want to see the boy."

"No." Victor cut the air with his hand. "He doesn't even know who you are."

"And whose fault is that?" Winston cracked open the can and sipped at the top.

"All I know is that it's not his fault." Victor gestured to an empty chair. "If he saw you now, he would only be confused. Is that what you want?"

"I want to see how he's doing, to know that he's okay."

"I told you, he's doing fine. He's a happy little boy, never complains, never talks back." Victor shrugged. "He's a little spoiled actually. He's the first boy in the family. On both sides. Everybody wants a piece of him."

Winston's eyes narrowed. "It's a shame this acceptance didn't happen earlier, when he was first born." Winston leaned back in the small chair, which creaked under his weight. In more than two decades at this store, Victor had never made any of the seats do that. He wondered what it felt like to be that large, to look down on everyone you met. "That must be tough on your daughter, to see you change right before her eyes."

"Why would that be hard? Everybody's fine now." Victor sipped his beer. He knew it wasn't that simple, but he felt better saying it that way, as if by putting it into words, it would somehow make it true.

"And why is that—because my son is dead and my daughter is a thousand miles away, so you can pretend they never existed?"

Victor dropped his head, staring at the beer in his hands.

"I'm sorry about your son. That is a real tragedy. Everybody knows that part of the story and they feel really bad. They understand why Marisa has to do this on her own."

Winston shifted in his seat. "You think that's why Marisa's on her own?"

"The details of my daughter's personal life are not anyone's business."

Victor opened another beer, though he had hated the taste of the last one. He needed to do something with his hands.

"She made it my business when she devastated my daughter."

"Your daughter broke up with her," Victor said. "Marisa is the one with the broken heart."

He said it as a matter of fact, the words spoken simply to make a point, but as they echoed in his ears he began to feel sadness for his little girl.

Winston sat up in his chair. "Juliet cried every day for that boy, for months. Don't talk to me about broken hearts."

Victor swallowed, the fizz from the beer catching in his throat. "So maybe they're even."

Winston finished his beer. Victor held another out to him.

"No, I should be getting back to the hotel." He crushed the can in his hand and pitched it into a nearby trash can.

"How long are you in town?" Victor asked him.

"Just for the night. But Miami's a short flight, I can come back. Next time, I'll come for longer."

Victor squirmed in his seat. "Look, it isn't good for you to drop in unannounced. Who does that help?"

"I told you," Winston said, "I want to know how my grandson is doing."

Victor stood up. "Hang on, let me get something." He disappeared into the office, returning a few moments later with a file box. He opened the lid. "Why don't you take this—his baby book, a photo album, photographs of him and your daughter." Victor flipped through the stack. "Look, there are even a few of you." Victor shuffled through the pictures, handing several to Winston. "These belong to your daughter I'm guessing. But I'll give it to you, you can have all of it."

"A box? With some pictures?" Winston stood up, towering over Victor. "You think you can buy me off with that?"

"I'll send more," Victor offered. "I have much more at home. Pictures of his birthday party and the beach, the park, things your daughter hasn't seen him do. He's learning how to swim—"

"He's three years old—"

"I know, he's a natural. And what else . . ." Victor tapped his finger against his mouth. "Oh, I know, the piano, he sits at that little thing and just bangs out songs. You swear he knows what he's doing. The look on his face, it's like nothing you've ever seen."

Winston looked at him strangely, his head tilted to the side like he was straining to hear the words. "The piano?"

"Yes. He really seems to like it."

"But it's a toy, the one you have him playing. You don't have a real one, do you?"

"Well, yes, it's a toy. But it sounds pretty good."

"No, no, he must have a real piano," Winston said. "I'll buy it, if you can't afford to."

"We don't have a lot of space."

"Well, make space," Winston's voice bellowed. "If you want me and my daughter out of his life, then you have to replace us with something. This is what I want. I want him to play the piano." He looked hard at Victor. "I know you don't understand, but it was a big part of our lives. My wife and I, we raised our kids to appreciate music."

Victor nodded. "I understand your daughter plays."

Winston stared at him. "It would mean a lot to us if Jenry played, too."

"And the rest?" Victor asked, pointing at the file box.

Winston pondered this before answering. "I'll take it, but I want other things as well—report cards and drawings and school pictures. Christ, I want letters to Santa Claus, if you have them." His hands were gesturing wildly, and Victor imagined this was what he was like in the classroom, his voice booming as he made his point clear. "I want to hear about all the milestones, not just his birthday, but throughout the year. I want to know him, if not in person, then at least on paper." He lowered his voice now, stepped in closer. Victor could smell the beer on his breath. "And I want him to have music. Can you do that?"

"Yes," Victor said. "In exchange for what I've asked for, yes."

They shook hands and soon after Winston left, the file box tucked under his arm. Victor drank another beer in the empty room, letting the cold seep into his bones before heading back into the humid evening. He slept well that night. This agreement would benefit both of them, and he hoped it would offset some of the guilt he'd been carrying. When he saw Marisa in the morning, he was able to smile at her fully, unburdened for a moment by the terrible weight of her past.

· 4 ·

With the five-hundred-dollar check Winston sent him, Victor bought a used upright, which they moved into the dining room after giving the buffet table to Inés's sister. Jenry's first piano teacher was a retired librarian who lived two doors down, but later he moved on to classes at the local Y, and then private lessons with the music teacher at his elementary school. They never pushed him, but soon he practiced for several hours a day without being asked and could read music before he learned how to read books. His teachers each said he had something special; all the family had to do was allow it to blossom.

From the beginning, Victor was the one who took him to his lessons. It was an excuse to spend time with the boy by himself, the two of them free to bond on their own terms, away from the tension that continued to exist between his wife and daughter. Afterward, they would explore different parts of the city, just like Victor had done with Marisa when she was little, and like Emilio had done with him. At first people in the neighborhood thought Jenry was his son, that he and Inés had adopted the boy, but Victor was quick to correct them: this was his *nieto*, he would say, learning to ignore their looks of surprise and keep walking, squeezing Jenry's small hand in his as they crossed the street on their way to the park, or to feed pelicans on the beach. When Jenry got tired, Victor would lift him by his arms to swing him around in circles, both of them dizzy by the end, and when they fell to the ground Jenry would say "Again, again," as they both erupted with laughter. Looking skyward, his arms held tight around the boy, Victor felt his chest expand, releasing a tension he didn't know he carried; his preoccupation with the past began slowly slipping away, as his body grew more rooted to the present, and to his grandson's future. He knew he was in the right place and had made the right decision.

As the years passed, that feeling only grew stronger. Despite their obvious differences—at six, Jenry would sit for hours at the piano, while Victor, in his fifties with two bad knees, couldn't sit still—they spent much of their free time together. Victor tried to get him interested in athletics, along with the piano, but Jenry disliked games with balls, and avoided team sports like soccer and basketball, preferring miniature golf and chess to activities that made him sweat or could injure his hands. They did other things together, like working in the yard and collecting vintage hubcaps, and when he wasn't too busy with schoolwork or watching his abuela in the kitchen, Jenry helped Victor at work, unpacking boxes of new baseball gloves, the rich smell of the leather bringing him back to his own adolescence, those early days living in strangers' houses, when he slept with his new glove from Emilio tucked under his pillow, freshly oiled and holding an old tennis ball as he tried to make a deep pocket; playing catch by himself to mold the glove to his wide fingers, to break it in.

Baseball was their final holdout, a sport Victor so revered that Jenry didn't complain when his grandfather signed him up for Little League each spring, agreeing to stand in the outfield with the other kids who had no fixed position, looking for four-leaf clovers while he should have been racing to catch pop flies. After playing for years without much improvement, and with a batting average of .075 and no putouts to his credit, Victor accepted that his grandson wasn't going to be the next Derek

Jeter; by the time Jenry started high school, Victor put all his energies into supporting his passion for music, taking him to local festivals like Jazz in the Gardens and buying season tickets to the Miami Symphony Orchestra, even though he fell asleep during many of the concerts. And of course, he continued to bring him to his weekly piano lessons. His new teacher was a prodigy himself, the son of Marisa's colleague, who had graduated from Juilliard. As agreed, Winston funded all his musical training. Even when they no longer needed his help, after Victor had bought the sporting goods store from Mr. Caplan with money he inherited from his parents, Winston continued to send it, most likely out of his own need. Victor didn't want to take it, yet he imagined how the other man felt, how it allowed him to believe he was making a difference in his grandson's life. Victor couldn't deny him that simple gift, not after taking so much.

By sixteen, Jenry was performing with a group of top youth musicians, traveling around the state for recitals. Beyond talent, it was his drive that impressed Victor the most, his willingness to practice the piano for hours, in search of just the right note. He was old enough to go without a chaperone, but Victor preferred to accompany the boy, just to spend a few hours alone with him in the car. He had grown up so quickly, and Victor knew he didn't have much time left. Every fall, while Victor prayed the Yankees would make it to the playoffs, Jenry prepared for the Youth Music festival in Key West, a three-day event to commemorate Franz Liszt's birth. Jenry had been attending since he was seven and playing in it since he was ten; this year, though only a junior in high school, he chaired the committee to choose the honored guest, writing a song for the orchestra to perform on the final night in front of the entire town. Everyone assumed he would be the honored guest himself one day, after getting a scholarship to the best music school in the country; it was an expected path, the one they all planned for.

After two standing ovations and three toasts at the reception, Victor and Jenry walked to their hotel room under a hazy sky, the almost-full moon covered by a string of stratus clouds. Victor thought he heard waves crashing against the shore but wasn't sure; on a small island like this, they were never far from the ocean.

"I can't believe what those people were saying about you," Victor said. "I'm so proud, *hijo*."

"It's just words," Jenry said. "Famous people like to talk."

Victor scratched a mosquito bite on his wrist. "You don't like to talk."

"I'm not famous—"

"Not yet," Victor interrupted, clapping him on the back. They both laughed, and Victor kept his arm around Jenry as they walked. The air was cool now, and Victor felt grateful to be outside on such a beautiful night, to be healthy and alive, and to be with his grandson.

A cat darted across the street in front of them, a streak of tan and white. Victor heard a yowl in the distance but there were no lights on this part of the street, and he couldn't see more than ten yards ahead. It reminded him of his childhood in Havana, walking home after baseball games that lasted deep into the night, the simple pleasure of exhaustion, of triumph. It felt strange to be an old man, to forget what he ate for breakfast, yet be able to remember so clearly the joys he felt as a boy, so many decades before.

"It's never too early to think about the future. College is just two years away, a blink of the eye."

Jenry nodded. "I think about college all the time." He kicked his feet over the loose pebbles on the road. A thin layer of sand covered the asphalt in this part of town, as if the wind had purposely blown it onto the streets, wanting to expand the beaches, to one day turn it all back into dunes. "Everyone says Juilliard is the best. But New York is a huge city. I don't want to get swallowed up."

"There's Boston, too. That Berklee College of Music is very good."

Jenry stopped to look at him. "What do you know about Berklee?"

They were eye level, the same height for three months now, but Victor assumed he would soon tower over him, as Winston had done all those years ago.

"I read about it on the computer," Victor said. "I want what's best for my only grandson." It was true, but he'd only known to look it up after talking with the college recruiter Winston had put him in touch with, the older man saying that if Jenry chose a school in New England, he would pay for whatever the scholarship didn't cover.

"Maybe a music school isn't best," Jenry said. "Maybe I need a regular school, where I can do regular things."

"What kind of regular things?" Victor's eyes narrowed. "If you want to play video games and be on Facebook all day, you can stay home and do that for free."

"I don't even like video games. And you know Mami won't let me on social media."

"Because she's a smart woman. And she knows you're better than that."

Jenry kicked at the pebbles again. "Sometimes I don't want to be better. I just want to be normal."

Victor glanced over to see Jenry staring into the dark in front of them. He had said things like this before, when classmates teased him for leaving school early to perform for the mayor, or being interviewed by the *Herald*, but this seemed different.

"Of course you want to fit in, that's natural. And at these schools, you will."

"But it's more than that. I don't want to go to a fancy music school, just to be with a bunch of other kids like me. I want to go . . . where Mami went."

Victor tried to hide his surprise. If he didn't know better, he would think Winston had planted the idea in Jenry's mind himself.

"I want to go to Brown," Jenry continued.

"*Sí*, I know where she went," Victor said softly. "I helped pay for it."

This wasn't their plan, but he imagined it was what Winston wanted all along, not just a prestigious music school, but the Ivy League, his own university. His support had always come with conditions, and Victor now saw it for what it was, a chance for Winston to turn the tables and bring his grandson back home.

Jenry turned to him. "So, what do you think?"

Victor shrugged, careful to stay calm. "It's a good school. An expensive school."

"I can get a scholarship. Or, at least I can try."

"Money . . . isn't the only problem." Now Victor was the one peering into the dark. There was a break in the houses up ahead, and he imagined he could see the lights of Havana in the distance, just over a hundred miles away.

"What is the problem?" Jenry asked, his voice clean and innocent like salt.

"A lot is tied up there. For your mother. A lot of old wounds." There was more to say, of course, but Victor knew it wasn't his story to tell.

Jenry nodded. "I know," he said. "She met my father there. And lived in Providence when I was born." Victor looked away as Jenry recited the story they had repeatedly told him about his life. "That's also why I want to go, to find out more about him."

Victor saw a look in his eyes he wasn't used to seeing. A hunger, or maybe desperation, and it made his stomach tighten. "I understand," he said, turning to the path ahead. "What boy doesn't long to know his father?"

He thought of himself at eight or nine, sitting for hours next to his own father on their old fishing boat, his clothes damp and smelling of the sea, his bare feet browned in the sun, as he waited for something to happen—the fish to start biting or the winds to shift—anything to let him know they were right to come out this far, and would have good luck on the water. Lazaro always left the harbor before sunrise, and Victor's job was to balance the coffee pot between his knees, making sure not to spill when they cut sideways into a wave, even when he couldn't see it coming. His other job was to be quiet, to not complain, to not ask any questions. When Victor stared at his father, his muscled forearms white with salt residue and scarred from run-ins with marlins and barracuda much longer than he was tall, he knew he would never know what his father was thinking, or how he felt. As he watched him cut the engine, letting the boat float along with the current, their voices low so they didn't startle the fish, Victor understood that this couldn't be changed, it was who his father was, but he also knew that he could be a different type of man one day, a different type of father.

"I know how hard it's been for you, to know only his name and not the person he was. But I've tried to be a father to you—"

"Of course you have, Abuelo, and you've done a great job. A great job." Jenry repeated. "I'm just saying . . . it's different for me. I don't fit in with everyone else. I don't really look like any of you, and I don't do the same things, like worship the Yankees or listen to Celia Cruz all day long." Victor laughed but Jenry was serious, talking quickly to get it all off his chest. "I love Cuban food, you know I do—Abuela is a great cook—but I also love American food, like bacon and pizza and fried chicken. And I like jazz and hip-hop and R&B, not just salsa, okay? I mean, sometimes I just want to listen to Prince."

Victor nodded, unsure of what to say. Of course there were differences, but they had tried not to see them, or at least not to emphasize them. Yes, he was darker than the rest of the family, with curly hair if it grew too long, something Inés rarely allowed to happen, but when Victor looked at pieces of him—his eyes, the dimples when he smiled, his square chin—he saw his daughter, the girl she used to be, and even a bit of himself. But he knew there was more, an entire family line Jenry wasn't familiar with. It was an experience Victor couldn't relate to, and therefore couldn't begin to comprehend.

"I have this whole other side to my life," Jenry said, "and I just want to see what it's like. I want to see where I came from."

Victor patted his shoulder. "You don't have to convince me," he said. "It's your life. You can decide." It was the right thing to say, and also, Victor hoped, the right thing to do. He wanted Jenry to make his own decision, to choose his fate. It was a burden Victor had carried too long.

"Will you help me, with Mami? She's always said she wanted me to go to a different college, because the double legacy would be too much."

He kissed the side of Jenry's head, smelling his hair cream, a faint spicy vanilla, but also the salt of the nearby ocean. "Of course I'll help you." What other choice did he have?

Jenry smiled, wrapping an arm around his grandfather. Victor knew the risk of sending him back to that world, but he also knew the risk of keeping it from him. He never expected to carry the secret this long anyway, and a part of him didn't want to hold it anymore.

· 5 ·

As promised, Victor did his part to help; after talking with the guidance counselor, Jenry's piano teacher, and the admissions officer, Marisa was convinced that Brown was a better choice than a strictly focused music program and would allow him more opportunities to get a well-rounded education. Jenry applied Early Decision and got in, having received a special scholarship from the Music Department, the first of its type ever given. Nine months later, and less than two years after the conversation in Key West, Jenry left Miami for Providence, just as his mother had done more than twenty-five years before.

An hour after the plane took off, Victor drove Marisa to her doctor's office. She'd found a pearl-sized lump a few weeks earlier and had waited to schedule her appointment; she didn't want anything to interrupt Jenry's final days at home. After her initial examination, the doctor sent her to get a biopsy, a word that scared Victor, but Marisa claimed was routine. She used connections at the hospital's lab to get seen the same day, which Victor knew meant she was worried; he insisted on bringing her to the follow-up appointment the next evening to get the results. They both agreed not to tell Inés.

The waiting room was almost empty. Two women sat together looking at the same magazine. At first Victor thought they were mother and daughter, but when he looked again, they seemed too close in age, so he guessed they must be sisters. The room was cold, and Victor offered Marisa his sweatshirt. She shook her head, saying she was fine. When she showed him pictures from a tabloid magazine, he pretended to be interested, but he didn't know who any of the celebrities were.

Marisa finished the magazine, tossing it onto the table. "I'm going outside."

"Do you think that's a good idea?" Victor lowered his voice. "To smoke, right before your appointment? The doctor will be able to smell it."

He saw the look on her face as she debated whether to deny it. She shrugged. "It will calm me down."

"Take a walk," Victor said. "Try meditating."

"Are you serious, Papi?" She rolled her eyes. "I'll be right back. Don't worry."

He watched her slip out the door. The scent of her perfume lingered in the air after she was gone.

Victor glanced again at the two women, who were now holding hands. One rested her head on the other's shoulder. *Oh*, Victor realized, *not sisters*. He looked away. The world was like this now, people doing in public what they used to be ashamed to do behind closed doors. What had changed? These two seemed decent—fully clothed, modest haircuts, no weird piercings—but the men he saw in South Beach, the ones necking on the street corner and always laughing, they were expecting too much. They said they wanted equality, but it seemed to Victor that what they really wanted was attention; and then when it came, they had the nerve to complain.

He wondered if Marisa had ever marched in a parade, if she'd held hands with a woman in public, if she flaunted her body to strangers. He'd thought about asking years ago, but then realized he didn't want to know. She had followed his rules all these years—no conversations about the past, no unexpected phone calls with the woman, no letters, almost as if it hadn't happened at all—and he was grateful for her discretion. Inés thought it meant she was cured, just a college phase that extended longer than it should have, like sleeping on futons and burning sticks of incense, but Victor knew better. This was a business transaction: he had helped her, and now she was helping him. Nothing had changed as far as who she was on any fundamental level; she'd only changed how she lived. A sacrifice she was willing to make for her son.

If she had a private life, she didn't show it. During the years she'd lived with them, she never brought anyone home, never said she'd met someone, never had that look—the dazed delight—of someone falling in love. At first, he encouraged her to go out, with friends or on dates, just to have fun, and he set her up with guys he knew, ballplayers and single men from church, but she accused him of being a hypocrite, and worse, of trying to make himself feel better, so he eventually stopped. He didn't want to argue with her, not when he realized she was right. He *did* want to feel better, and he wanted the same for her—was that so wrong? It bothered him to see her this way, living her life like a spinster when she wasn't even middle-aged. And it wasn't fair, he knew that, what he had asked her to do, but there was no other choice. They had made an agreement, and it was working, the boy was happy, and they were all together in one house. They were a family again. Maybe that was enough for now. Maybe he should let God handle the rest.

He felt a vibration in his pocket. The cell phone was from Inés, hardly a gift, more like a fancy leash. This younger generation and their gadgets, they had no idea how they'd fulfilled a housewife's dream—to always know exactly where her husband was. He saw Jenry's name on the screen and his eyes lit up. He flipped open the phone.

"*Hijo?*"

"*Sí*, Abuelo. It's me."

"Of course it's you. Who else calls me?" Victor laughed, but Jenry was silent on the other end.

"I don't want to talk," Jenry said. "I just want you to know that I know."

"You know what?" Victor's voice stayed calm, but his heart immediately began to race. He shifted in his seat.

"About my father. About her. What happened when I was born." He cleared his throat. "Before I was born."

Victor searched the room for a clock. How long had Marisa been gone?

"I think we should talk about this. Your mother—"

"I just spoke to her. And I'm done talking for now. I want you guys to leave me alone." He paused. "Just let me sort this out."

"Jenry, wait. *Escúchame.* I'm so sorry—"

"I don't want to hear it," Jenry said. "You had years to make this right, and none of you did."

"We were just trying to protect you."

"From the truth?"

"It wasn't my truth to tell." Victor's voice had gotten loud, and when he glanced up the women were looking at him. He dropped his head down, shielding his eyes with his hand like it was suddenly too bright in the room.

"Whatever, Grandpa," Jenry finally said.

The word sounded wrong to Victor's ear, foreign and cold.

"*Hijo*, please."

"I'm hanging up now. Don't call me back. And tell her not to call either. I need time to think."

"Jenry, wait. *Por favor ... perdóname.* Don't punish me."

The front door to the doctor's office opened and Marisa stepped inside. Victor could see that she had been crying.

"*Hijo*?" Victor spoke into the phone. The line was dead.

Marisa sat down two seats over from him, waving a magazine in front of her face to dry her eyes. She put on sunglasses and reapplied her lipstick. Victor put the phone back in his pocket.

They waited like that until the nurse called her name.

· 6 ·

Marisa's condo felt warm, so the first thing Victor did was take off his sweatshirt. She had stopped running the AC at night; she was always cold. He'd brought extra blankets from home, draped them on her like sweaters, but that didn't keep her from shivering. They said this type of chemo would be better—fewer side effects, faster results—but they had nothing to compare it to. Eight rounds over eight weeks, plus radiation, and the cancer should be gone. Sixty percent were cancer-free after a year. "Good odds," the doctor had said. "I'm sure your daughter will be one of the lucky ones."

He knew Marisa wouldn't eat, but Victor brought food anyway—plain rice, yogurt, frozen chunks of mango—that was all she could keep down. She'd lost ten pounds already, though to his eyes it was closer to twenty. He wondered where the weight had come from, if her muscles were deteriorating from the inside. He begged her to move home, so they could take care of her. But this was her home, she kept reminding him, for several years now, and even if she was sick, she wanted her own space. Victor visited most evenings, walking the half mile from their house to bring the food Inés cooked for her.

Marisa was lying on the couch, made into a bed these last few weeks, so it was easier for her to get to the bathroom. The TV was on in the background.

"Just leave the food on the table." Marisa pointed to the kitchen.

Her hair was tied back, like she used to wear it as a little girl. But she didn't look younger. This past month she'd aged several years at least.

"You gotta eat, *mija*. You know the garlic is good for you." He unpacked the cooler her mother had sent with him. "Rice and beans, yucca with *mojo* sauce, your abuela's famous *ropa vieja*, you know that's my favorite. And of course"—he held up a small cake pan, hoping to entice her—"flan so thick you could eat it with your fingers."

"I just ate," she said. "Sorry, Papi."

He saw an eight-ounce yogurt container on the coffee table, and beside it, a child's juice box. Nothing that would count as a meal.

"Oh, and there's ice cream," he said, grinning like a kid. "I found a new flavor, to help with the nausea." He pulled out a small paper bag, cold against his hand. "Who knew they put ginger in ice cream? But the lady said it was the only thing that kept her going during her pregnancy. Money-back guarantee, she said." He held it up to her, a spoon in his other hand.

"Right," Marisa said. "Because pregnancy and cancer are exactly the same thing." She turned over, shifting the pile of blankets she was hiding beneath.

Victor walked into the kitchen. He made himself a plate, hoping the smell would make her change her mind, and left the ice cream on the counter to soften.

They watched a game show together, both annoyed by the second round, and then a reality show that followed several two-person teams—mother-son, father-daughter, newlyweds, sisters—as they raced across several continents.

"We should do that, you and I. We're much better than those other father-daughter pairs." He laughed at the screen. "Look at them, they can't even run."

"I can't even *walk* ten feet to the bathroom."

"Not now, *tonta*. Next year, when you feel like yourself again."

"Next year. Yes. I'm sure I'll feel like traipsing around the world." Her tone was sharp, but he pretended not to notice it.

Victor shrugged. "You never know what miracles will happen." He held the ice cream out to her. "Here, try some." She took the bite, a drop falling onto her chin. He caught it with the tip of the spoon, like he did when she was a baby spitting out her rice cereal. She wiped her mouth while he smiled.

"Good, no?"

She nodded. He fed her another bite, alternating with his own until they had finished the pint. When he set it on the table, he felt a sense of accomplishment. And relief.

Before, he'd thought that cancer was a foreign invader, a mass of cells that came from nowhere to destroy the body, but he'd learned that it was your own tissue turning against you. One part grew too big and your body tried to attack it. Now that this had happened to his daughter, he wondered about the parts she had tried to deny, and if those were the ones that had turned against her. And since she had done it at his request, didn't that make some of it his fault? Or even all of it?

He brought the dishes to the kitchen and cleaned up, putting leftovers in the fridge next to dishes from days before. He didn't have the heart to tell Inés that Marisa barely ate anything she made. Let her think she was helping in some way, which he knew was her attempt to try to fix what they had broken. At home Victor hated to clean, but here it felt easy; in five minutes he could make the place look new again, and it would stay that way until he came back. This was a space he could control. He loaded the small dishwasher and sprayed down the counter, wiping it with a paper towel until the tiles gleamed. He liked the smell of the window cleaner in the air, and later, the smell of liquid soap on his fingers after wringing out the sponge. There were a few lingering kernels of rice, which he picked up by pressing them into his fingertips. He brushed his fingers over the sink and watched the kernels fall into the garbage disposal.

Marisa appeared to be sleeping. He stood above her, taking in her face, the parts he didn't normally get to stare at—the still-black hair he wondered if she dyed, the wide-set eyes, the smooth, pale skin just like his mother's. He looked for himself in her face. And then Jenry—what did he have from her? The eyes perhaps, though his were darker, like a coffee bean. What was this mystery they called genetics? How strange to share blood and DNA and yet see nothing on the surface, while other mixtures produced almost identical copies, the dominant traits passing down through all the children. If he had had another child, a boy perhaps, maybe he would see himself in that blend—but maybe not. It was all a gamble, the whole of life, and he had no idea where to place his bet.

She stirred and the blankets slipped down, exposing her needle-marked arm, veins blown from repeated IVs. He tucked her arm against her body and pulled the blankets back up, tight over her shoulders. He felt her bones, hard and small under his hands, and found himself wanting to cry. It wasn't fair to feel his daughter's frame like this, under such fragile flesh, nor was it easy to see that sometimes there were only inches between life and death. To hug her now was to feel the bones in her back, the skeleton of a fish. He had just buried his mother the year before, and his father two years before that—was it really God's plan to also put his daughter into the ground? It's not right for a parent to have to bury a child. He thought of Winston Patterson, his wife and son long gone, and he couldn't imagine what that loss did to a person; he didn't want to know.

Victor leaned down to kiss Marisa's head and saw she was awake. He rubbed her cheek. "Close your eyes, *hija*. Go back to sleep."

She shook her head. "I wasn't sleeping," she said, but he could tell by her eyes that she had been. She patted the couch and he sat down. "Do something for me, Papi."

"Anything," he said, smiling at her.

"Remember that boat we went on, when I was a little girl? How we went way out off the coast, beyond the islands—"

"The fishing boat, with Emilio?" He smoothed the hair from her face.

"No, before that. Just you and me. We went snorkeling, out by that coral reef off Key West."

"With the sunken ship?"

"Yes, exactly." She gave him a weak smile. "Do you remember how scared I was? To swim over that huge black hull?"

He nodded as the memories came back: her hair wet and sticking to her face; the sunflowers on her bathing suit, bright yellow like the fish that swam throughout the coral.

"And the current was so strong," she added, "we got separated from the group."

"I remember the boat had to come back around to pick us up." He patted her hand. "You were such a good swimmer, no one could keep up."

"You could," she said, turning her eyes away. She stared at the wall, as if she were seeing the waves again, feeling the resistance of water. "I want to go back there—"

"Of course, when you're feeling better—"

"No, I mean later, when I'm gone. I want you to bring my ashes there, spread them at sea."

Victor looked away. "It's not good to talk like this."

"When will we talk about it? When I'm already dead?"

He stood up—not to leave her, but to do something with his body.

"You can't run away from this, Papi."

He had his hand over his mouth, biting his fingers to keep from crying. "I don't know what to do," he said.

"It's okay." She held out her hand and he took it, returning to the edge of the couch. He was careful not to put any weight on her.

"I'm so sorry that you have to go through this. It's not fair, none of it."

"But I don't *have* to," she said. "I'm choosing to. The alternative is waiting for me at the bottom of the sea." She squeezed his hand. "We always have a choice."

He shook his head, tears falling from his eyes. "I'm sorry, *hija*. I did what I thought was right. I thought it was best for you."

She looked him straight in the eyes. She had always done that, even as a child. She wasn't afraid to look at things.

"I know you did," she said, and he knew she meant it. "You wanted to protect me."

They were suddenly talking about Jenry.

"I was thinking about the boy and your mother. What would be easier for everyone."

Marisa nodded, her eyes glassy.

"And now I think, I know, it was wrong," he said. "I was wrong."

"Yes. You were." Her voice was even, calm, as if she were agreeing that he was born in 1950, and not that he had been wrong to convince her to lie to her son, lie to everyone, about where he came from. And she didn't even know the worst part, Victor thought, how he had communicated for years with the same family that he denied, and taken money from them to finance Jenry's education.

"I don't know if you can ever forgive me, or if it's even fair to ask. I just hope that one day you'll understand where I was com—"

"Maybe I don't need to understand," she interrupted. "I don't think that's what forgiveness is about." She pointed to the coffee table. "Can you pass me that?" He handed her a cup of lukewarm tea. She drank it slowly, pausing between swallows. "There is so much I don't understand," she said, her voice soft but steady. "I will never understand what it was like to be you, Papi, and to have my daughter show up out of the blue, with a baby and a broken heart, asking for help." She drank more of the tea. "I will never understand what it's like to believe that a gay relationship is not as important as a straight one, or to worry that God won't accept a part of yourself, your child, just for choosing another path. I'm not you, I haven't lived your life. But I also know that you haven't lived mine. And there is so much about me that you don't understand."

She paused, letting her words hold the space between them. Victor wanted to say something in response, to explain or justify what he'd done, to apologize even, to try to make it right, but he somehow sensed that words would not be enough, so he stayed quiet. It was her time to talk. And his time to listen.

"Maybe one day that will change, but until then I will focus on what I do understand, and what I know." She finished the tea, holding the cup between her small hands. "I know that you love me, and you love my son. And I know that if I die, whenever I die, I don't want to carry any of this with me. I don't want to die angry. So I know what I have to do: I have to forgive you." She reached for his hand. "I forgive you, Papi, for doing what you thought was right to help us. Even though it was wrong, I forgive you. Who better than I to understand the mistake of doing the wrong thing for the right reason?"

She handed him the cup and closed her eyes. Victor thought about his own mistakes, wondering if she was paying the price for his crimes.

"Promise me," she said, "that you'll take me back to that water."

He held the cup in his hands, feeling as if he could crush it. "And if you don't die?"

"Then we will go together. We'll swim through the coral and count the schools of fish, and when the current takes me too far from the rest of the group, you will bring me back."

"Yes," he said. "I promise."

She was smiling now, and he sat with her until she fell asleep.

· 7 ·

Marisa finished the first course of chemo by Thanksgiving. She lost fifteen pounds and most of her hair. The doctor said it had gone well, just before telling her she would likely need a second course in the new year. He wanted to schedule radiation right away, but Marisa told him she had an important business trip in December, and it would have to wait.

Victor thought the trip was a terrible idea. He told her for weeks that she shouldn't fly on an airplane with all those germs, shouldn't travel to the Northeast during the winter, with snow and ice and temperatures just below freezing, but she wouldn't listen. It was Jenry's first college performance, and she wasn't going to miss it. She had the same response each time he mentioned it: *Not while I'm still alive.*

Her flight was in the afternoon, but Victor drove her to the airport in the morning and parked in the short-term lot, walking her into the terminal. He carried all of her bags. They checked her in and got an early lunch at the airport lounge—fish tacos for him, a bowl of bean soup for her, which she didn't finish. She claimed to feel better, her appetite was back and the headaches were mild, her nausea almost gone, but he knew it was an exaggeration at best, at worst a bald-faced lie. She was fed up with Jenry ignoring her calls, and was determined to see her son perform at the concert. Victor worried something deeper was driving her, that she knew something about her future she hadn't told him yet.

"You can still change your mind," Victor said, wiping hot sauce from his mouth. "Wait for him to come home at Christmas. That's only a few weeks away."

"And what makes you think he'll even come home?" She was cleaning the table with her napkin, trying to remove the watermarks from her pot of tea.

Victor didn't know how to respond. "He's a good boy," was all he could think to say.

Marisa leaned forward in her seat. "I wanted to thank you, Papi, for everything you've done to help me. Now, and in the past few months. Always, really."

"You're my daughter. It's my job." He squeezed her hand as it lay on the table. She smiled but didn't seem happy.

"I know you don't understand," Marisa said, "why I have to take this trip. It may seem foolish—"

"Reckless, is what the doctor said—"

"But it's not just about the performance. Or going back to campus." She stirred her soup with the plastic spoon but didn't take a bite. He always watched her eat, counted her bites at each meal, to calculate just how much food she was missing. He didn't do anything with the information, but it made him feel better to know it. "I need to see my son, face-to-face. There are things I've never told him. Things he deserves to know."

Victor put up his hands, as if to stop her from saying any more. "You have to do what you think is right. I just don't want you to get sick."

"Sicker than I already am?"

Victor finished his lemonade, ignoring her question. He shook his head. "I don't know how you ever survived those winters."

"You get used to it," she said, pulling her hat down to cover the back of her neck, adjusting her wig. She had started wearing one a few weeks earlier. He tried to imagine her hairless and more frail than she already was, but he couldn't. It was impossible for him to picture her any other way than what she had always been—healthy, hopeful, and strong. But it was a lie. He could see in her face how she pretended, her skin sallow, dull like wallpaper.

"And I have to see her," Marisa added, "I have to see Juliet."

Victor shifted in his seat. He couldn't remember the last time she'd said the woman's name. This was a moment he hadn't anticipated. "Do you think that's a good idea?"

"I think it's necessary," Marisa said. "It's been a long time coming."

"Just remember," Victor said, tapping the table, "you don't owe her anything."

"I don't?" Marisa rolled her eyes, something she'd done more often of late. "Oh, Papi, if only it were that easy . . ." She took a small sip of water. "You and Mami want to make it so simple, to cut her out like she wasn't important. But Juliet was there, at the beginning. I loved her. She helped me do everything. She was there when you weren't."

"I've apologized for that—"

"And I've forgiven you. But what about her? Where's her apology?" Marisa pointed her spoon at him, which shook in her hand.

"You need to calm down, *hija*. You're in a fragile state."

Marisa lowered her voice. "I'm not fragile, I'm sick. And I might not be alive next year. Which is exactly why I need to go now. My son has another family, people who've wanted to love him, and I prevented that from happening. I did that. Because I couldn't stand up to you and Mami. Because I couldn't accept the truth."

"We couldn't accept it." Victor forced himself to look directly into her eyes. "We couldn't accept who you were." His voice cracked and he coughed to cover it up. He watched as her eyes filled with tears.

"I let your shortcomings, your failures, become my own." She pushed her bowl away, spilling soup onto the table. "But you know what? I'm not going to allow my son to do what I did. I'm not going to let him give up something he doesn't have to, just because I don't want to face my own mistakes. I'm just not going to do that anymore."

He patted her hand, forced himself to smile.

"Let's get you to the gate."

He walked with her to security, where he placed her bags on the conveyer belt. He wondered how much radiation the x-ray machines poured into the luggage, and how it compared to the poison that was coursing through his daughter's veins. The guard asked for his ticket, and when Victor explained that he wasn't flying, the guard told them to say their goodbyes. Victor kissed his daughter on both cheeks, holding her by the shoulders.

"Have a good trip." He felt her bony frame beneath the coat. "*Ten cuidado.*"

She nodded. "I'll call you when I land."

"Only if you remember," he said. She smiled, and he knew that she would. "I love you, *mija*," he said, his voice filled with emotion.

"It's just a few days," she said, squeezing his hand. "It's not like you're sending me off to college again." She laughed, and he saw a glimpse of her younger self, the girl who was open to surprise and happiness, when she hadn't quite figured out who she was yet, and no one held it against her. He could see that she had struggled to fit herself into someone else's image—his, his wife's, the world's—and that it hadn't been good for her.

"Just tell the truth," Victor said suddenly, "about everything. Whatever you need to clear your conscience. You deserve some peace."

"Now you get it, Papi." She flashed a quick smile as she fixed her hat.

"I am proud of you, *mija*. So very proud." He rubbed her shoulders with both hands and leaned in to hug her again.

"What if he never comes home again?" Her voice was trembling in his ear. "What if he has a new home? Up there, with them."

He squeezed her softly. "A boy's home is always with his mother," he whispered.

Victor stood back as she walked through security, lifting her arms so the machine could scan her body. The guard waved her on and she picked up her things on the other side, glancing back to him. He waved, but she didn't see him.

Other passengers kept moving around her, and soon she was caught in a mass of movement, and Victor could no longer find her in the crowd. His daughter disappeared right before his eyes.

BOOK VII

The Other Son

December 2015

· 1 ·

When Jonah Lucas Patterson is born neither of his mothers is in the delivery room. Instead, they are home, lying together on their own bed, fitted with freshly laundered four-hundred-thread-count sheets that ride up every time their weight shifts. Tonight, they are making love and making amends and making a baby.

The call from the adoption agency comes in just after six the following morning, and by seven thirty they are sitting with the social worker in the hospital's bright lobby, signing paperwork as thick as a manuscript. When the birth mother, a teenager from Central Falls with straight As and dreams of becoming a veterinarian, requests to see them in the recovery room, she asks them to post a yearly picture on the agency website if it's not too much trouble, and to tell the baby that she tried to do her best by him, that giving him up was her way of giving him a better life. After, hearts aching and hands ink-stained, Jonah's new mothers stand outside the nursery's thick window, looking for their son. A nurse wheels him over in the pram, where he's swaddled in a soft cotton blanket, a blue knit cap tight on his head, with hair oily black like a baby seal. Noelle is flooded with tears, which fall on the stuffed elephant she's brought for their son. After checking their wristbands, the nurse lets them in, holding Juliet's hand as she escorts her to the rocking chair. Juliet is the first to hold him. She feels nervous, her arms trembling, and Noelle places her hand on Juliet's elbow to steady her.

The weight of her son is both heavy and light; he feels substantial, like he alone is holding her in the seat, yet also weightless, like he could float out of her arms if she doesn't hold him tight. His skin is papery smooth and a shade of brown so light it's almost translucent, showing the veins beneath like a miniature map.

"Don't worry," Juliet says, "his color will come in later."

Noelle nods and strokes his hand, and he immediately relaxes his fist; as his fingers unfurl, she slips her pinky into his grasp and he reflexively squeezes. Together they watch as the skin over his knuckles turns a rosy tan, awed by his strength.

"Look at his fingernails," Juliet says, "how tiny they are."

"Christ, are all babies this strong?" Noelle asks. The nurse nods as she opens a bottle of pre-mixed formula and screws a clear nipple onto the top. She gives the bottle to Noelle, who looks to Juliet.

"You do it," Juliet says, letting Noelle take her place in the rocking chair. Juliet props her arm up with a pillow.

"I haven't done this since eighth grade," Noelle says, laughing, "and even then, the baby wasn't this tiny. My God, he looks like a little bird."

"He looks perfect," Juliet says, rubbing his head with the back of her hand. She notices a few curly hairs at the nape of his neck, peeking out from beneath the cap, and her eyes fill with tears. He is alive; he is hers.

His eyes open briefly, but as soon as Noelle brushes the nipple over his lips, he begins to suck, and his eyes close again. The nurse places a blanket over them and leaves the room. Juliet's face aches from smiling.

"I can't believe he's finally here." Noelle hasn't taken her eyes off of him. Juliet kisses her on the forehead.

"We're a family now," she whispers into Noelle's ear.

———

THEY TAKE HIM home two days later, with a free diaper bag from the hospital and a starter can of powdered formula. They are nervous, sleep-deprived, and giddy like children playing dress-up. Noelle takes the day shift, Juliet, the night. Time slows to almost a standstill, each minute feels like an hour, each day a week. One night Jonah seems restless, twisting in his sleep as Juliet holds him against her chest, hoping to calm him with the steady sound of her heartbeat. It works for a while, but soon he wakes again, now with a whimpering cry. She checks the clock; almost time for his 4 a.m. feeding. After sucking down a few ounces of formula, he refuses to go back to sleep, so she takes him downstairs.

She dims the lights in the dining room and turns up the heat. The floors creak under her footsteps. She pulls on her shearling slippers and heads to the kitchen to reheat her tea. The baby's hand has fallen out of the blanket and she re-tucks it, protecting him from the heat of her mug. He looks up at her, blinks slowly, and opens his mouth to let out another cry. Rocking doesn't work, so she burps him again, patting his tiny back with her opened hand. He lets out a small burp and resumes his cry, sounding more like a motorized toy, one whose batteries are dying, than an infant.

She walks to the window to show him the snow outside, but all she sees is her own reflection—wild-haired, sleepy, too old to get in the ring with a newborn. The sight makes her laugh, which distracts the baby from his cries. He looks at her and she stares back, noting the gray-brown of his eyes, how they look milky, like a paint color that hasn't been fully mixed. She kisses his forehead, breathing in the scent of him: baby powder, A&D ointment, just-washed laundry. The smell brings her back to the only other baby she held like this, the first time she had felt this type of love. She's relieved to feel it again, closing her eyes to capture the moment like a photograph.

Soon he twists in her arms and yawns, a whimper escaping his lips. This is a different cry, like a kitten meowing, cute and strange simultaneously, and she finds herself looking at him so closely she can count the grooves in the roof of his mouth. She tries to imagine what he will look like with teeth and more hair, tries to hear his voice. The sound of the cry is stronger now, so she takes him back to the dining room to try the bouncy chair. It is the only thing on the table, a long mahogany oval that sits ten comfortably, and when she buckles him in and turns on the switch, all she can think is that he looks like some sort of twenty-first-century prince on his throne. She hears the chair vibrating, an annoying sound, so she presses another button, this one marked with a musical note, and the tinny sound of "The Itsy Bitsy Spider" rushes from the underside of the chair. The baby seems more surprised than comforted, but the end result is a weakening of his cry, so she leaves it on.

She bumps into the piano as she steps back, startled once again by its presence in the room. It has been sitting against the wall for the last few days, since after returning from the hospital she found piano movers on the porch, asking where she wanted it set up. She had them bring it into the dining room, moving a buffet table to make it fit against the wall. Part of her wanted to send it back, but Noelle gave her a look that said *Be reasonable*. The driver gave her a business card for a piano tuner, but she said she wouldn't need it. She wasn't planning on playing.

"Keep it anyway," he'd said, smiling at the baby still bundled into his car seat. "Maybe he'll play one day."

Juliet doesn't want to think about that now. She sits backward on the piano bench and looks at the baby. Her elbow brushes across the keys, making a terrible sound. It startles both her and the baby, who throws his arms out stiffly, fists unfurled. She is surprised to see his eyes are still closed. After a few seconds, he starts to whine again. Juliet plays a C sharp, and he quiets down immediately. Intrigued, Juliet turns to face the piano. She plays a few chords and then looks over her shoulder to see him sleeping peacefully. She stops and counts, waiting for him to cry. At fourteen seconds, he begins to squirm, and by eighteen he's officially whimpering. She plays another chord progression and once again he settles down. *Well,* she thinks, *this is one way to get me back on the bench.*

She plays a few of her old favorites, everything from Jelly Roll Morton to Beethoven, and before she realizes it thirty minutes have passed and the baby is asleep. The stairs creak but she ignores the sound, focused solely on her fingering, and suddenly Noelle is beside her, sleepy-eyed and wrapped in a fleece bathrobe. She places her hands on Juliet's shoulders.

"Waking up to that sound, it's like going back in time."

"He made me do it," she whispers. "It's the only thing that calmed him down."

"It's lovely." Noelle kisses her head and shuffles into the kitchen, coming back with a cup of warm coconut milk. She sits at the bench, watching the baby while Juliet plays.

"Well, isn't this a Norman Rockwell moment?"

"Sure, if he had painted lesbian families and their adopted children."

"You know what I mean."

Juliet smiles at her wife as the sound of the piano fills the small space.

"It's almost suffocating, this type of love," Noelle says. "I can't believe people do it more than once."

"People are brave."

"Or stupid."

"Or both."

After a moment Noelle asks, "Was it like this last time?"

Juliet is surprised by the question, and takes her time answering. She wants to make a joke, to diminish the memories she has of those first few years, as if by making them seem less important she can protect Noelle from thinking the experience is redundant, that it means less the second time around.

"If you're asking, did I play the piano to get him to sleep, then yes."

Noelle shakes her head. "Did you feel this same way about him?"

Juliet looks at Noelle as she answers. "Yes. I think so."

Noelle nods. "No wonder it's been so hard to get over."

Juliet stops playing. "The hardest part is knowing that I could have protected myself, and it would all be different."

Noelle places her empty glass on the table. "Different, yes. But not necessarily better."

"Who's to say what's better?" Juliet looks at her. "I should have acted better. Been a grown-up. Claimed my son."

Noelle reties her bathrobe, cinching the waist tight. "So now what?"

Juliet starts playing again. "You sound upset," she says.

Noelle fixes the baby's blanket, leaves her hand resting on his feet. "It's just, when I hear you say *my son*, you should be talking about Jonah, you should be talking about *our son*—but you're not, and it breaks my heart."

"You knew about Jenry, when we first met. I told you about him."

"You told me the story, yes, and that's what I thought it was. A story from the past, not a person. Not someone who would show up in our lives and—"

"And what?" Juliet walks to Noelle's side. "Take me away from you? You're my wife. Jonah is our son. This is our family."

"But where does Jenry fit? How can he be your son and not a part of our family? I just don't understand how this is supposed to work."

"We'll figure it out, okay? Trust me." Juliet offers her hand to Noelle, who doesn't take it.

"I want to believe you," Noelle chooses her words carefully, "but you've said that before. Right after drinking a bottle of wine and disowning your father."

Juliet exhales, letting the words sink in. Even though they are all true, it is still difficult to hear. "I've got thirty-seven days sober today. It's a start."

Noelle softens, reaching for her. Their hands make a long shadow that stretches over the sleeping baby, his eyes twitching as he dreams. "Maybe I don't say it enough, but I'm proud of you. I know it's not easy."

"It's our only shot of keeping this family together," Juliet says, finishing the thought. "I know that. I realize what's at stake."

Noelle nods, smiling down at Jonah. "What about having Jenry over, to meet the baby?"

"I was thinking I'd wait until after the Winter Concert. I don't want to add any stress before his big day." Juliet pulls Noelle closer to her, their fingers entwined. "If that's okay."

Noelle squeezes her reply, then says, "You're still going then?"

"Of course. I said I would. I've been helping him prepare, just coaching him a little."

Noelle rests her head on Juliet's chest. "You think your dad will show?"

Juliet makes a face. "I'm not sure he's invited."

"Winston Patterson goes anywhere he wants, welcome or not."

Juliet gives her a half smile. "I'm hoping he won't want to go."

"You can't avoid him forever."

"Actually, I can. And let's face it, his forever isn't going to last too long."

"That's a horrible thing to say."

Juliet looks down at the baby. "What he did was pretty horrible."

Noelle exhales. "I know." She squeezes Juliet around the waist. The blanket slips off the baby's foot and they both reach to fix it. "But what good comes from you being awful back? Hurting him doesn't make you feel better, and it doesn't bring those years back." She brushes the hair from Juliet's face to see her eyes.

"If you can't do it for yourself, do it for him." Noelle nods toward the baby. "My father is dead, so Jonah only has . . ." Her voice trails off. Then she adds, "Don't leave him with no one."

Juliet is quiet, thinking about what Noelle has said, until she finally nods in agreement. "You're right about Jenry. He should meet his brother."

"He should meet all of us," Noelle says. "His whole family."

Juliet rests her head against Noelle's cheek as they stand together, staring at their son.

· 2 ·

At the urging of her sponsor, Juliet finally takes a thirty-day chip at her home meeting. It's long overdue, and she has the new baby as an excuse, but the truth is she's been avoiding it; the last thing she wants is to stand in front of her peers and speak for three minutes about her slip. Her voice is gravelly and a few times she almost cries.

"I should have taken this two weeks ago, on the day my son was born, but I was embarrassed. To have only thirty days, after more than five years in the program. That wasn't something I wanted to celebrate. But I guess that's just my ego talking." She stops to take a deep breath. "A month before, on the first of November, I only had a few hours. That day was my bottom. I felt like a failure, knowing I was no longer one of you. That I had to start over. I had to walk in here, look you in the eyes, and tell you I wasn't sober." She fingers the plastic chip in a room of familiar faces. They aren't quite friends, most don't even know her last name, but she feels a bond with them, a peculiar type of affection.

"The worst part was when I got out of the shower that morning. When I had to get dressed and do my hair, when I had to look at myself in the mirror." All the other heads nod in agreement. "I had to look at my wife, who no longer trusts me. And now my new baby, who I could lose if I get this wrong, if I screw up again." Juliet feels her face get warm, her voice starts to crack, but she forces herself to go on. "I already lost one son to my drinking—maybe not directly, but it was certainly a factor— and I can't afford to lose anything else now." Her boots feel hard against the soles of her feet, and she wants to sit down, to be done confessing. She wonders how these stories can ever help someone else. But then she re- members what kept her at those first meetings, how hearing other people tell their truth helped her find her own.

"I was sober for five years, but I was a dry drunk. I stuffed things into boxes and thought if I put them away, they wouldn't affect me. I hadn't really worked through anything." She makes eye contact with a silver-haired woman in the back of the room. "My sponsor keeps telling me: it's not just about being sober, it's about emotional sobriety—not just putting the past away but coming face-to-face with the pain of it, that's how you can release it. I don't know how I'm doing with that, but at least I'm trying. I hope it's enough." The person timing her share gestures that she should wrap it up. She holds up the plastic chip, *30 days* written in thin gold letters, and watches it dangle from the small chain around her finger. "I'm grateful for my slip, since it brought me back into the rooms and forced me to face my shit. And I'm grateful to be here, forty-five days sober. Thanks for letting me share." The room claps as she sits down.

At the break, she fills up her coffee and gets a second donut, not worried about spoiling her dinner. Sugar seems to help—with what, she's not sure. Some people say you end up trading addictions, from booze to sugar to exercise, until you are finally addicted to something with less dangerous side effects. She wonders if it's a cop-out, but today is grateful for the crutch.

She feels a hand on her arm and turns around, expecting to see an- other familiar, sober face, someone wanting a hug, a handshake, or a phone number—someone desperate for hope. Instead, she finds Marisa's unfamiliar face. She looks at least ten years older than she is, her skin wrinkled, with pale, gaunt cheeks. Her hair is thinner and shorter than Juliet remembers it, less radiant. It's also a different color, almost burgundy. She looks like a middle-aged woman, something Juliet herself must also look like, but seeing it in someone else—someone she knew as a teenager, and still thought of as a young person with her whole life ahead of her—is unsettling.

"What are you doing here?"

"I'm sorry. I should have called. But I worried you'd refuse to talk to me." Marisa is nervous, and it helps dissolve Juliet's shock, before it can turn into anger. "Jenry mentioned the restaurant a while ago, and when I went by, they told me you were at a meeting." She shrugs, adding, "Santiago sent me here. You know how Cubans are, can't keep our mouths shut."

"Yeah, I know." Juliet can picture him talking to her, wanting to help.

"Congratulations on your chip. That's really great." Marisa smiles warmly. "I've been going to Al-Anon for years. I think it helps."

"Thanks." Juliet doesn't know what else to say, but she keeps talking. Anything to cover the silence, which feels too intimate for her to bear. "I had five years and then I lost it. It doesn't make any sense"—her voice turns serious—"how easy it is to throw away something that means so much."

"Yes," Marisa says, stepping aside to let someone pass between them. "And how we can spend the next fifteen years regretting it." She offers a weak smile.

Juliet, surprised at the implication, looks around the room, feeling exposed, but no one is paying them any attention. "What are you doing in Providence?"

"I'm here to see Jenry, in the Winter Concert. But also," Marisa lowers her voice, "I wanted to see you. There are some things we have to talk about."

Juliet glances at her empty seat, wanting to put some distance between them, but her boots feel bolted to the floor.

"What you said before, about your sobriety, it was very moving." Marisa touches her arm with her gloved hand. "I mean it—I'm really happy for you."

"And I'm really ... surprised to see you," Juliet admits, "after all this time." She barely recognizes her own voice, which sounds cold and uncaring, when she only meant to suggest nonchalance. "Is everything okay?" She feels nervous now, imagining what had really made her come all this way. "Did someone die?"

"No, no, nothing like that." Marisa bites the edge of her lip, peeling off the faded lipstick. "I was hoping we could talk outside. Just for a few minutes." She tightens her scarf around her neck, adjusting her hair. Juliet thinks she sees her hairline shift. *Is she wearing a wig?* "And then I'll leave you alone."

Juliet's stomach relaxes a bit. She glances at the clock, then nods toward the door. "We can talk in the sanctuary."

She grabs her coat and they leave the meeting hall together, walking down a cobblestone path. The sanctuary is cold and empty, lit only by the colored rays of late afternoon sunlight that stream in through the stained-glass windows, a scene depicting angels riding on horseback. Soon the sun will set, leaving the room filled with shadows. Juliet watches Marisa lean against the back of a pew to catch her breath. She stares at her old, unrecognizable friend and still can't quite believe she's here, after all these years.

"First, I want you to know how sorry I am. I made a big mistake by keeping Jenry from you for so long. It wasn't fair, to him or you, and I wish I could change how it happened. I really do."

"You could have reached out any time—"

"I did my best." Marisa shakes her head, leaning against the pew for support. "Listen, I can't pretend I wasn't angry. I was devastated, I had just lost you, and I wanted to protect my son."

"He didn't need protection from me."

"You say that now, but you were drinking a lot and you were unstable—"

"My brother had just died—"

"I know. I don't say any of this to blame you, or to rub it in your face. But back then ... Christ, Juliet, I was out of my mind with grief. I wanted to hurt you—I did, I can admit it now—because I wanted you to know how it felt to be rejected. To be abandoned." Marisa's voice softens and Juliet can see that her eyes are filled with tears. "It was selfish, I know, but I was a single mother, and I had this kid to raise, and you had refused to adopt him. I wanted to punish you." Juliet starts to interrupt, but Marisa puts up her hand, asking for the space to finish. "I don't know how much time I have here, but I don't want to leave without telling you this. I have only a few regrets in my life and that's one of them. How I ended things between us." She waits until Juliet looks her in the eye to continue. "I'm sorry. I hope you can forgive me."

Juliet has been waiting a long time for that apology, but now that it has arrived, it doesn't feel like she thought it would. It doesn't make her feel better or vindicated, it doesn't help her understand why it happened. It only makes her heart ache—for what she took from Marisa, and for what Marisa gave up to protect her son.

"I've been angry a long time," Juliet begins, "and I planned to stay that way. It felt better than being sad. And I blamed it all on you. I know it wasn't fair, but that's what happened. It was the only thing I could do back then. To make sense of it all."

Marisa nods. "We do what have to do to cope, to get through the day."

"But I know it wasn't easy for you either. I can hear that now. Even though it's hard, I'm trying to understand you." She knows she needs to say more, but pride makes it difficult. Then she thinks of all the times she was the one who needed forgiveness, and the words arrive. "You did what you had to do, to take care of your son. I get that. I didn't leave you many options." She takes a deep breath, tries to picture the person she was back then—selfish and driven, a little reckless, but also fundamentally decent, no better or worse than anyone else, just human, flawed—and she thinks of what she's done to get to that understanding, all the work she's had to put in to forgive herself; how she's shown up for others and made sacrifices, how she's had to be honest, how she's been forced to grow. And if she can have that much compassion for herself and for other alcoholics, if she can give them a second chance, can't she do the same for Marisa? "I'm sorry I wasn't there for you. I was so focused on my music, my dreams, that I didn't realize you had your own. And that I was destroying them."

Marisa wipes the tears from her eyes. Juliet stares at her drawn face, wonders what has happened to her. Could her life have been that hard?

"The only thing you destroyed was an illusion," Marisa says, her voice without pity. "You didn't love me. A person can't lose what they never had."

"I did love you," Juliet says, "just not in the right way."

A church bell rings in the distance. Tiny pieces of dust float like snow in the air above them.

"The other reason I'm here," Marisa begins, her voice tentative, "is to let go of something we both decided a long time ago. A secret we agreed to keep, that no longer feels . . . appropriate. Or fair. Given what Jenry has been through."

"Marisa—" Juliet interrupts, certain she knows where this is going.

"I know you're going to be upset, but just hear me out. I've been thinking a lot about this, I've done some real soul-searching," Marisa says, "and I think we have to tell Jenry the truth, that Jasper is not his biological father. That we used an anonymous donor."

Juliet's first thought is *No*, and she shakes her head instinctively. A barrage of questions runs through her mind, but the only one she asks is "Why now?"

"Why not now?" Marisa already sounds defensive. "Everything else has finally come out. He deserves to know the entire truth, Juliet, and to hear it from us. I'm just not comfortable keeping the secret any longer. I did that before, and it blew up in my face. I'm sorry, but I don't want any lies between me and my son. Not anymore."

Juliet hears the words she chose—*me and my son*—ringing in her ears. Does she even have a vote in this? She tucks her hands into the deep pockets of her down jacket. "I just don't see how it helps him. Not right now. We're just starting to build something. He thinks he's a part of my family, why take that away?"

"He *is* a part of your family, regardless of his DNA."

"You don't get it. He thinks he's one of us—me, my father, Jasper—that he's part of a long line of talented people, and it makes him special. If you take that away, what does he have? The file number to a donor he may never meet?"

"He's eighteen, he can contact the donor if he wants."

"And will that really help him fit into our family? Being Jasper's son gives him something, makes him feel like he belongs. That's what he needs."

"He needs the truth." Marisa's voice is filled with desperation. "If he finds out we lied about this, before we can explain it to him, he may never trust us again."

"But this isn't about us," Juliet says, her voice rising, "it's about Jenry. About giving him a family. A real family, not a biological spreadsheet." She is thinking of Jonah and Noelle, too, of how the bond between them feels as strong as the blood she shares with her family, maybe stronger. "We can't do this just to make ourselves feel better, we have to do what's best for Jenry. Even if it makes us uncomfortable."

Marisa shakes her head. "What aren't you telling me? Is this about Jasper? Or your father?" Her eyes knit together. "Who are you protecting?"

"Jenry," Juliet spits out. "I'm trying to protect Jenry. Why aren't you?"

Marisa's head jerks back in shock, her face colored with anger. But then, before it has a chance to settle, her expression shifts, until her eyes grow wide with a different thought. She shakes her head, replacing her glare with a wry smile. "Oh, Juliet," she says, her voice almost tender, "you always did know how to astonish me. I wish I had more energy, just for the fun of going a few more rounds." Marisa moves to sit down on the bench. Juliet watches as she takes a protracted breath.

"You've always been a good mother. Even when you wouldn't claim him. The two of you had this connection. I had to work for mine." She coughs into a folded handkerchief, then tucks it back into her purse. "After we left, I had to figure out a way to replace you. To mimic that bond.

So I gave him the piano. It was as simple as that." Marisa stares at her gloved hands, resting on her lap. "Blood didn't connect you. It was your gift he needed. That is how I tried to protect my son."

Juliet sits down next to her. The wooden bench feels cold against her legs. "Is that why you got my father involved?"

"Your father?" Marisa looks up, blinking several times. Up close, her skin looks dry and pale.

"I found it all," Juliet says, "the photographs and letters, the report cards, the updates on how Jenry was doing. I saw everything you sent him."

"What are you talking about?" Marisa's eyes are drawn together, framed by a look of genuine surprise. "I sent your father a letter, *one* letter, many years ago. That first winter after we left. He never wrote back."

"He has things he could only get from you." Juliet starts listing with her fingers. "Photos I took during his birth, pages from his baby book—"

"I don't even have the baby book." Marisa's voice rises. "My father lost it years ago . . ." Her voice peters out as a look of realization blooms on her face. "Well, I'll be damned," she says, her voice falling to a whisper now. "I always assumed he'd destroyed it."

Her father, Juliet thinks, *not her*. She realizes it was Victor who sent her father all those things, not Marisa; it was his betrayal, not hers.

"Well, isn't that cute. Our fathers were pen pals." Marisa's voice drips with sarcasm. "I'm sorry but," she says, shaking her head, "this whole thing is crazy."

Juliet doesn't say anything, as her mind tries to figure it all out. What had she missed that day in her father's office? Had she been so focused on collecting evidence of Marisa's guilt that she overlooked other clues?

"I wonder how they managed to pull it off." Marisa looks over at her. "Two old men, two strangers, doing something we couldn't do. Communicate."

Juliet sits up, as something occurs to her. "You wrote to my father—why?"

"You know why," Marisa says, meeting her stare. "I was looking for you."

Juliet, feeling suddenly warm, unzips her jacket. She notices Marisa's eyes flicker across her body, stopping at the old belt buckle she's worn since college.

"Still wearing that?"

Juliet nods. "Still waiting for it to bring me luck."

Marisa laughs. "We never change, do we?"

After a thoughtful beat, Juliet says, "Sometimes we do."

Marisa leans her head back, gazing at the ceiling. "I think we should tell him together," she says. "Maybe he'll take it better coming from us both." Her voice is calm, almost soothing, but the meaning behind her words lands like a rock on Juliet's chest. She feels her lungs constrict, as if the pressure were real, and has to force herself to take a deep breath before responding.

"I think that would be a mistake." She tries to stay composed, to reason with Marisa. They need to become allies, a position she could not have imagined suggesting an hour ago, but which now seems like her only hope. "I know you think the truth will somehow help him understand, but I think that's naive. We need to look at the big picture." She exhales with a heavy breath.

Marisa remains very still. "I just don't want him to find out by accident and have another reason to shut me out."

"He won't find out," Juliet says. "That secret died with my brother."

"I thought you might have told your wife."

Juliet looks away, ashamed to admit that she still keeps things from people who love her. "How do you know I'm married?"

"You mentioned it in your share."

Juliet nods. "I always forget what I say up there. It's easier that way."

"I get it. It must be hard for her to understand," Marisa offers, her smile kind.

"I just wanted Jasper to have a place here, to be alive in her eyes."

Juliet pauses. "It breaks my heart that she never got to meet him. To her, I'm all alone."

But after saying the word out loud, she can't help but think how untrue it is. She's not alone; she has a father, and Winston has a daughter—one so loyal that she is still willing to protect him, despite what he's done to hurt her. She hasn't admitted it yet, but shielding Winston from the truth is the main reason she's fighting to keep the secret. Believing Jasper had a child gave him so much hope after his son died, just to know that some part of him lived on. She knew then she could never tell him the truth. Despite all the years and the distance that has grown between them, that fact hasn't changed.

"It's not just for Jenry," Juliet finally admits. "If my father ever finds out he isn't Jasper's biological son . . ." Her face shows a look of anguish. "It would destroy him."

"Okay, so we ask Jenry not to tell him," Marisa suggests.

"What are you saying? We tell Jenry the truth just to make him lie? That doesn't make any sense."

"We have to tell him something," Marisa says firmly. "I can't keep lying to my son."

Before they can agree, the door swings open and the janitor enters, pushing a large trash can. Juliet stands up, startled by his presence. Behind him, the sky shows signs of twilight.

Marisa bows her head and makes the sign of the cross as she leaves the pew, so quickly that Juliet almost misses it.

"Are you sure you're feeling okay?" Juliet asks, as she holds the door open for Marisa. Without the sun, the temperature seems to have dropped ten degrees. "This weather must be a shock to your system."

Marisa puts on a brave smile. "I'll be fine," she says, buttoning the collar on her coat against the brisk evening air. "Just have to make it through the concert."

Juliet stares at her, certain there is more she's not saying.

"We've talked enough for one day, haven't we?" Marisa jokes, brushing off Juliet's concern as she heads up the darkening path. A few steps later, she slips on the cobblestone and Juliet catches her by the elbow.

"Careful, you can't always see the ice." Juliet steadies her as they climb the stairs to the meeting hall.

"I forgot about the dangers of winter." Marisa's cheeks are red from the cold and for a second she looks like her old self again. Juliet holds the door open to let her pass through.

"It's amazing how quickly it all disappears."

"And how quickly it all comes rushing back."

As they step into the warmth of the hall, Juliet is aware of a new sensation spreading through her limbs. She thinks of the anger she's carried all these years, imagines it like a grenade in her pocket, threatening to explode at any moment. She always thought she'd unleash it if given the chance, pull out the pin and toss it into Marisa's lap, watch her get blown apart—but here she is, standing inches away, and all Juliet wants to do is bring her to the fireplace, give her a steady hand to lean on. She pictures the grenade, but instead of a dark, hard casing, it's pale like an egg, the shell so thin it cracks under the weight of her breath. Inside, instead of gunpowder, she imagines a small bird, whose wet limbs expand into feathered wings, the filament bright and clean like a dove, and all she can do is stand there and watch it fly away.

· 3 ·

The Winter Concert begins at eight o'clock, though Jenry isn't scheduled to go on until well after nine. It is standing room only in the auditorium at Sayles Hall, and its two hundred seats are taken within ten minutes of opening the doors. Not everyone is a classical music fan, but there are fancy appetizers and wine, and even the most diligent students need a break from studying for exams. Marisa takes a seat near the front, on the side closest to the exit. Juliet sees her walk in and purposely waits near the back, below the room's enormous organ, to watch her. When Marisa scans the crowd, they make eye contact and Juliet nods, thinking it will end there, but Marisa waves her to the front, where she has saved her a seat. She is wearing makeup tonight, and looks better than she did the day before, more rested. The room is warm from all the bodies, but Marisa never takes off her coat.

Winston arrives late and stands in the rear, leaning against one of the tall entrance doors, his reflection filling the large, square windowpane. To Juliet, it looks like he is standing beside his identical twin, a terrifying thought—her father in duplicate. When she was a child, he used to say the only thing wrong with her was that she wasn't twins, but she doesn't remember ever feeling the same about him.

The stage is small compared to the size of the room, a rectangular platform elevated several feet above the floor to guarantee a good view. The piano, a shiny black concert grand, waits patiently in the center of the stage, massive and sturdy like a ship in the harbor, docked but eager for the sea. Before Jenry goes on, the announcer—who sits below the stage in a folding chair, holding an old-fashioned microphone—mispronounces Jenry's last name and incorrectly states that he is a sophomore. The audience claps loudly, and Jenry bows his head slightly as he walks down the aisle to the stage. He wears gray slacks, a striped tie, and a dress shirt that fits him perfectly, and stands with his shoulders back, head up, as Juliet instructed.

Juliet feels her own stomach drop, as if she were the one performing. Beside her, Marisa's knee bounces with nerves. When Jenry sits down at the piano, he adjusts the bench and straightens his tie, then pulls the microphone close to his mouth.

"It's Castillo, actually," he says with the Spanish pronunciation, "Jenry Castillo." His voice sounds confident and clear. "And I'm a first-year," he adds with a smirk, as pockets of laughter spread through the room to break the silence.

He pushes the microphone back and adjusts the sheet music. Juliet takes a deep breath as he readies his hands over the keyboard. The first notes, deep and loud, erupt from the piano like a thunderstorm, and soon the room is wet with sound. It is a song Juliet knows well, Liszt's Piano Sonata in B Minor, but he plays it faster than she has ever heard it played, his fingers seeming to blend into each other as he pounds out the notes, almost merging into the keys themselves, as they race from one end of the keyboard to the other. The sonata is one giant movement, almost thirty minutes long if played in its entirety, but he has excerpted several key parts, cutting and blending the most dramatic measures, as he moves deftly from a brilliant tone to broader sounds and back again. He plays with the confidence of a composer, as familiar with the changing character of the music as if he had written the piece himself.

Several minutes into the performance, when no one is expecting it, he pulls back and slows down the tempo so much it sounds like he is playing a different song—exactly the effect Liszt seemed to be going for, as he moved from allegro to andante to scherzo, before the climactic finale, a technique of thematic transformation the composer was known for. The acoustics in the room are surprisingly good and the notes ring clear. Juliet is impressed by the depths of contours he's been able to re-create in his rendition, knitting together the musical equivalent of gently rolling hills and steep alpine peaks in order to make a cohesive, uninter-rupted landscape—not one composed of similar parts, but of distinct, often discordant elements, which nonetheless come together in a harmo-nious flow. The effect is extraordinary.

Jenry looks as comfortable as Juliet has ever seen him, more natu-ral than she remembers feeling at her first Winter Concert, an event she wouldn't even remember if her father hadn't taken photographs and put them in an album. The look on Marisa's face is pure amazement, the same expression Juliet remembers her father having when he watched her play; partly pride, but more than that—it was awe, at what this person who came from you could do, something you can hardly comprehend. Jenry has kept the sonata's final climax, which after a loud flourish seems to turn in on itself, dissolving into a dramatic silence that ushers in the finale, the last three chords played so delicately they seem to evaporate. When he plays the final note, holding the pedal to stretch the sound, it amplifies beauti-fully, capturing the understated eloquence of the entire performance.

There is a long silence afterward, and then the room bursts into ap-plause. Juliet turns to watch her father, who is the first to begin clapping, and will likely be the last to stop. His wide smile makes something ache inside her. Before she knows it, she is out of her seat with the rest of the room, giving him a standing ovation, clapping so hard her hands burn. Jenry takes a single, deep bow before walking down the aisle to sit beside the other performers, his forehead damp with sweat. Marisa reaches out, without looking at her, and squeezes Juliet's forearm.

By ten, the concert is over. A reception is set up in the foyer, where audience members mill about waiting for the performers. Photos are snapped for the *Brown Daily Herald* and *The Providence Journal*, as Professor Sterling poses proudly with his star students, Jenry standing tall in the middle of the pack. Juliet stands off to the side, sipping on a club soda while she watches the spectacle with faint recollection. His friend Lexi is there, wearing a fancy dress, and she grabs his tie to pull him away from the crowd, wanting to be the first to talk to him. She hugs him tightly and can't stop herself from gushing over his performance. He nods and smiles as he shakes hands with the other students that surround them. It is his moment, and Juliet is happy to witness it.

WINSTON HEADS TO the bar, a safe place to avoid his daughter, but is instead intercepted by Marisa, who approaches him with a confidence that seems both familiar and familial. He recognizes her right away, not by how she looks, but how she speaks to him.

"Dr. Patterson," she says, "I can't believe it's been fifteen years. Time certainly has been kind to you."

"How are you feeling?" he asks, skipping the formalities. He looks at her with concern, his eyes saying the rest.

"Better than I look," she says with a laugh, stepping around him to order a white wine from the bartender.

"Should you be drinking?"

"Tonight, absolutely."

They stand together awkwardly, surrounded by others with the good fortune to be caught in easy conversation. Finally, Winston says, "It was a stellar performance. Your boy's got chops."

"Thanks in part to you." Marisa raises her glass to him. "I wanted to tell you face-to-face. What your support this fall has meant."

Winston dismisses the implication. "I won't take credit for his efforts."

"Of course not." Marisa sips her wine, the alcohol instantly going to her head. "We've all worked hard to get him here."

"Parenting is the toughest job there is," Winston says. "High risk, no job security, and most of us are dreadfully underqualified."

"And it's even harder when you're doing it alone, wouldn't you agree?"

He locks eyes with her, examining her face for some ulterior motive, but she seems genuine enough. "Yes," he answers, "especially then."

"Tell me, does it ever get easier?"

He stirs his drink, waiting for the ice to melt. "Not really. They just move further away. Literally and figuratively."

"I'd imagine it's different when you're a grandparent. They seem to move closer with time. At least that's how it was for my parents."

"I certainly hope that's true," Winston says. He thinks of saying more, how different he feels with Jenry than he did with his own children, how he finds himself wanting to hover over the boy, like it's his last shot. But he doesn't want to say too much. "Jenry is quite special to me, I hope you know that. I've got my eye on him."

Marisa takes a step back. "Jenry's special to all of us. It sounds cliché to say about my own son, but I mean it. He's been a real blessing to me. In ways I didn't understand before, ways I couldn't see until all this happened." He sees her expression and knows she's not talking about the concert or the Ivy League school, she's talking about this right here, the family, all of them together. "I needed to come here, to see for myself. Jenry's in good hands. He's going to be just fine."

Winston sips his drink, wanting to agree with her, but wondering if things are ever that simple.

"I know it's not my place," she continues, touching his arm as if that will help her get through to him, "but maybe your eye should be on Juliet. She's the one who needs you the most right now." Before Winston can react, she picks up her glass and walks away.

AFTER COMPLETING HIS obligatory social rounds, Jenry makes his way to the dessert table, where he eagerly pops brownie bites into his mouth. Seeing he's finally alone, Marisa approaches him. Juliet watches from across the room, partly concealed behind a banner promoting the upcoming Chorus Concert. She sees Marisa smile at her son, sees Jenry pull back when he notices her, unable to mask his surprise.

"I didn't know you were coming," he says, talking through their brief hug.

"You know I would never miss it," she says, telling him how much she enjoyed the performance. "Is that a new song? I didn't recognize it."

"A new arrangement," he clarifies. "I've been working on it for a while."

Juliet spots her father talking with Professor Sterling at the bar. The two men share a smile over raised glasses, then peer into the crowd, no doubt looking for Jenry. She feels a moment of panic at the thought of them seeing her, bewildered by the bizarre coincidence of this night, of so many important people from every phase of her life coming together, reuniting on this old, familiar campus. She wishes she had a better place to hide, feeling too vulnerable to face her past—but she knows she must.

"Juliet was supposed to come," she hears Jenry say. "Have you seen her?" She notices a barely detectable smirk on his face. He seems to be rubbing it in, trying to make her uncomfortable, but Marisa doesn't fall for it. Instead, she smiles brightly. "Actually, yes. We sat together."

Before Marisa can say more, Juliet reveals herself, moving to cover the space between them. "It was a marvelous performance," she says to Jenry with conviction.

"You came." His face lights up, and a moment later, she's hugging him. "Liszt was a bold choice." She beams. "I'm thoroughly impressed." She catches Marisa's eye as she pulls away.

Jenry shrugs. "I figured I should wake these people up."

"Well, it worked," Marisa says. "They seemed to clap forever after you finished."

"They clapped for everyone." He spoons extra sugar into his coffee.

Professor Sterling moves into their loose circle, patting Jenry's shoulder. "If you want to be a star, you have to learn how to accept compliments. Anyone courageous enough to choose Liszt for their first concert, and reckless enough to edit a half-hour sonata down to eight and a half minutes without their professor's approval, surely possesses the necessary discernment to admit when he's pulled it off."

Jenry's face reddens with embarrassment, but then Sterling breaks into a grin. "And to think, you tried to drop Music Theory. Good thing I never signed that slip."

"I've been wondering about that." Jenry sips his coffee, wincing at the taste. "How did you know I'd change my mind?"

"First-years always change their minds," Sterling quips, taking a swallow of his drink.

"Sweetheart," Marisa cuts in, slipping her hand through Jenry's arm, "can we borrow you for a few minutes?"

Sterling eyes Marisa over his glass. "And who might this be?"

"My mother," Jenry says. "She surprised me with a visit."

"Of course, I should have known." He shakes Marisa's hand with gusto. "How lovely to meet you."

Jenry gestures toward Juliet. "And this is . . ." He pauses, not sure how to define her.

"Juliet," Sterling exclaims, "as I live and breathe, how is this possible? Two of my brightest stars, together in the same sky." He kisses her three times in a row, alternating cheeks.

"The heavens must be shining on you," Marisa says under her breath, as she sips her wine.

Sterling holds Juliet's hands. "I was just chatting with your father about you. We must bring him over." But when he looks around, the old man is nowhere to be found.

Jenry turns to Juliet. "You never said you studied with Professor Sterling."

Sterling throws an arm around her. "She did more than that. Juliet got me through the Cold War." He drops his voice to a whisper. "I'm talking about the administration, not the Russians. The president didn't want to give me tenure until he heard her play. At this very concert, wasn't it, dear?"

"You're exaggerating, Sterling. As usual." Juliet feels her face flush. "I had nothing to do with it."

"What is it with this crowd? I've never known musicians with such humility. It can't be good for the future of our profession."

"Speaking of the future—" Marisa tries again to interrupt.

"Oh no, dear," Sterling cuts her off, taking her arm, "we mustn't talk about anything as dreadful as the future right now. Here, let me fill up that glass before the bartender leaves." Sterling escorts Marisa to the bar. "We'll be right back," he calls over his shoulder, "if she doesn't steal my heart and run away with me."

"I'm glad you didn't drop the class," Juliet says, moving closer to Jenry so she can speak at a normal volume, despite the crowded room.

"I didn't want to lose my scholarship." Jenry exhales. "As long as I did okay tonight, I should be fine."

"I wouldn't worry about it. Sterling may be odd, but he's no fool."

Jenry's voice turns flat. "Your father was here, but he didn't come over." He looks disappointed, even hurt. "I take it he wasn't impressed."

"I'm sure he stayed away because of me. He knew I didn't want to see him." She glances around the room, surprised she can't find his head above the crowd. "If it makes you feel any better, he clapped for like three minutes."

He looks into his cup as he drinks the last of his coffee. "It's weird, to be here with both of you."

Juliet nods. "It's weird for us, too. But in a good way." And then, feeling inexplicably bold, she adds, "We've been apart too long, don't you think?"

LATER, WHEN MUCH of the reception has cleared except for parents and friends, Juliet notices Lexi standing by the coat check with a group of students, clearly waiting for Jenry. Lexi smiles at her. "You must be so proud."

"Yes. I am," Juliet says, and then, looking at Marisa, adds, "We are."

"Well, thanks for coming." Jenry's eyes shift between his mother and Juliet once again.

"I'm sure you want to run off with your friends, but we wanted to talk to you first," Marisa says. "It won't take long."

"About what?"

"It's not a big deal," Juliet interjects. "It can wait." She shoots a pleading look at Marisa, who carries on undeterred.

"Can we go somewhere else? Someplace private?"

"Maybe this can happen tomorrow," Juliet suggests, hoping for more time to convince Marisa. "When do you leave?"

"In the morning." Marisa knots her scarf. "It can't wait."

Jenry recognizes the gravity of his mother's tone. "Give me a second then." He goes to the coat check to talk with Lexi and the others. While waiting, Marisa and Juliet grab paper cups and fill them with hot water for tea, just for something to do. When Jenry comes back he pours himself another coffee and grabs a plate of desserts, seeming to know he will need fortification.

"This way," he says. "We can talk in the dressing room."

They cut through the dark, vacant auditorium, passing by the stage. The grand piano, with its singular, smooth architecture—its remarkably silent presence—is the only thing that remains. Juliet stops to glance at the empty seats, enjoying the view for a brief second. She thinks she hears someone call her name and peers out into the dark, as black as the night sky. No one is there, just the distant sound of the caterers cleaning up in the foyer. She laughs to herself, slightly embarrassed, and rushes to catch up with them, her footsteps echoing across the stage.

· 4 ·

When they get to the dressing room, Jenry closes the door behind them. Marisa speaks first.

"I came here to bring you home," she says, her voice calm, matter-of-fact. "You need to know that upfront, so you can understand where I'm coming from."

Juliet looks as surprised as Jenry. "That's not what we talked about."

"Just hear me out." Marisa sits down on the couch, her coat still buttoned.

The room has a tall ceiling, making it feel larger than it is, and a small oriental rug covering the dark wood floors. Jenry pulls out a chair for Juliet, who sits in it backward, across from the only mirror in the room. She tries not to look at her reflection. Jenry stands by the shuttered window, arms crossed over his chest.

"I think we can agree this has been a difficult fall for all of us. And I came up here to try to fix it, to admit that I think you coming here was a mistake."

"Are you kidding me right now?" Jenry shakes his head.

"Maybe we should do this later," Juliet offers. "Let him have tonight."

"The timing isn't great, I'm sorry about that. But this needs to be said." Marisa adjusts her coat. "It was something we didn't prepare you for, and now it's blown up in our faces. I blame myself, because I could have told you the truth a long time ago, and maybe prevented all this upset. Or at least some of it." She balances her tea in her lap, sipping from it occasionally. "I knew I had to see you in person, because you wouldn't take my calls, but also because I felt you slipping away from me, becoming this person who didn't want to know me."

"I never said that," Jenry says.

She holds up her hand. "I'm just trying to tell you what I felt. I was afraid I was losing you, and I thought I could convince you to come home and we could go back to our old life. It would be just you and me again, and Abuelo *y* Abuela, and we would have our family back. You would be safe. That's all I've ever wanted." She stops to take a deep breath, looking at the floor. They wait for her to continue.

"But then I got here, and I saw you, and you have another life up here—classes and teachers and friends. And you have the piano, your music, which is so beautiful, I don't even understand how you can make something so beautiful." She lifts her head to look at Jenry. "And then I see something else: you have Juliet and your grandfather, you have this whole other side, and they want to know you. They want to love you. Because that is what they have always wanted. They are your family, too, do you understand?"

Jenry leans against the radiator, his face a swirl of unreadable emotions.

"You don't remember them, but they were there, at the very beginning, and they remember you." Marisa's hands are trembling. "And I realize that you have something here, something I can't give you. But I understand something else, too. You have to want it, if it's going to work. You have to choose it."

"I don't get what you're saying," Jenry says. "I already chose to come here."

"To this university, yes, but not this family. You didn't know what you were choosing by coming here. Now you do."

Juliet is afraid to move, to shift in her seat even, in case her movement alters the outcome of this moment. This is all she's ever wanted, for Marisa to acknowledge her role, to have another chance with Jenry, but now that it seems possible, she's worried that he won't choose it, won't choose her.

"But before you say anything, we have to tell you something—"

"Marisa, don't—"

"Don't what?" Jenry asks, looking at Juliet.

"Don't put all this pressure on him to choose," she says, trying to cover.

"I'm not asking him to choose between us." Marisa looks at her. "I just think he should have all the facts."

"Why does it have to be like this?" Jenry asks, obviously irritated. "You guys arguing and cutting each other off, trying to convince me to believe each of you, despite the fact that neither of your stories makes much sense." He throws up his arms in frustration. "Is this what it's like to have two parents? Because it's a pain in the ass."

"Watch your language, please."

"Oh, Mami, come on. Why do you have to say that whenever I get upset? Calm down, be quiet, don't get mad. It's like you're afraid to let me express myself, to even have feelings if they don't line up with yours." Jenry looks down at his hands. He picks food from his fingernail and flicks it onto the floor.

"That's not what I'm afraid of."

"So what then, that I'm going to choose someone else over you?"

"Do you think it's easy doing this alone, having all the pressure of another human being's life on your shoulders?"

"But you chose that, didn't you? You left Juliet."

"It's not that simple," Juliet says, surprised to hear herself defending Marisa. "I broke up with her. I didn't make it easy for her to stay."

"Well, we know she didn't make it easy for you either." Jenry starts counting on his fingers. "Taking me out of the state, never letting me see you, telling me about my father when she should have been telling me about you."

Marisa leans forward. "How could I know you would have wanted that?" She raises her voice, frustration starting to show. "I was alone, making decisions the best way I knew how. I was trying to protect you."

"But you're not alone now, are you? And I'm not a little kid anymore," he says. "I don't want you making all the decisions."

Marisa takes a sip of her tea. "Good, because that's what I'm getting at. I want us to decide together what the next step should be." She turns to Juliet. "All of us."

"Well, I can tell you right now, I don't want to go home," Jenry says. "Not that you care what I want."

"Of course, I care. But there are other factors to consider."

"Like what? If this is about money, I still have the scholarship."

"This isn't about the scholarship." Marisa pauses. "It's about being ready—"

"You don't get to decide when I'm ready."

"You're right." Marisa clears her throat. "But you weren't ready when you came up here, to meet this side of your family—"

"I didn't *know* about this side of my family," he interjects.

"What your mom is trying to do," Juliet speaks calmly, attempting to be a bridge between them, "is figure out what you can handle, so you don't get in over your head. That's all."

"Maybe college is too much right now. You've been acting irresponsibly. Dropping classes and threatening to quit. That's not the boy I raised."

"The practice schedule for orchestra was crazy, three nights a week, and I hated the music they played," Jenry admits. "That's why I quit. But other than that, I'm good. I'll take an incomplete in Music Theory and finish it next semester. By the summer I won't even be behind."

"I think we should discuss other options." Marisa picks lint off her coat.

"What other options?" Juliet has a sinking feeling in her stomach.

"He could always withdraw. Take a leave of absence until he's clear on what he wants." She turns to Jenry. "You can always come back to school later."

"You think it's going to be easier when he's older? In a few years he might not have the skills he's got right now." Juliet speaks quickly, the words tumbling from her mouth. "Do you know how many people can play the song he played tonight, the way he played it? Not many. And most of them would take a year to do it that well. He had just a few months." Juliet feels angry, and she spits the words from her mouth. "Music won't just wait around for you. It's not like a rifle you can pick up and shoot whenever you want. It's a gift that you have to take care of."

Marisa sits back on the couch, disappearing into the plush cushions. "Music was your dream, that doesn't mean it has to be his." Her expression is firm as she turns to Juliet. "It has to be his decision."

"Music *is* my dream," Jenry says. "I never said it wasn't."

"But that doesn't mean you have to pursue it here, at this school, more than a thousand miles away from home."

Jenry looks at her. "I think it does."

Marisa raises her voice. "You can't *think* at a school like this, you have to *know*." She points at the door, indicating the stage and the campus outside, the privileged throngs who filled the auditorium less than an hour ago. "To compete with those kids, you have to be completely dedicated. You can't have another semester like this one." Her tone is harsh, but she's speaking the truth.

"You act like this was a waste. Like I failed out." He looks at Juliet for help.

"I think he's done well," Juliet offers, "considering the circumstances." She glances at Marisa, who holds her gaze before turning to Jenry.

"If you want to stay, and you're serious, fine. I will support that. But if it gets hard and you want to quit, and you think that's the way to punish me, it won't work." Marisa takes a breath, steadying her voice. She unbuttons her coat to reveal her small body inside, bundled in layers of bulky wool that still manage to make her look vulnerable. Juliet knows it is her turn to step in, to be the ally that Marisa has finally admitted she needs.

"You're not going to lose him," Juliet says, speaking directly to her fear. "You raised a good boy. Now we have to let him become a man."

She watches Marisa lean back into the couch, not relaxing, but letting it support her. Juliet hands her a napkin, which she uses to dry her eyes.

"I don't want to punish you." Jenry leans his head back against the door. "I just want things to be easier. Now that I know the truth, can't the fighting end?" He lifts his head, looking between the two of them. "Is that possible?"

"I suppose anything is possible," Marisa says, tucking the napkin into her pocket. "The fact that we are here together is proof of that."

A radiator bangs in the distance, and they can hear water rushing through the pipes overhead.

"So we're good now," Jenry stands up. "That's all you wanted to say?"

Juliet stares intently at Marisa, willing her to end the conversation. It's clear that Jenry can't handle anything else, and Juliet wants to respect that, even if it means there will always be a secret between them.

Marisa gets up, her body straining to make it appear effortless. "You want to be a man," she says, "then you need to act like it." She holds him at arm's length, looking into his eyes for emphasis. "Return phone calls when you get them. Complete the classes you sign up for. Be responsible." He nods and reaches out to hug her, folding her head into his chest. Juliet looks on, relief flooding her body.

"Something's different," he says to Marisa. "Did you change perfume?" She smiles at him instead of answering. "Wait a minute, did you quit smoking?"

Marisa nods. "I did, in fact."

His face lights up. "Good for you, Mami." He squeezes her shoulders. "I'm proud of you."

She tucks her arm through his. "Come, walk me to my rental car. I'll tell you the whole story."

They walk through the doorway arm in arm, Juliet watching from behind. It's strange for her to see them together after all these years, to notice the places where they are alike, as well as the differences. He looks a little bit like her, she has to admit, but he also looks like himself, and possibly the donor. And even though they aren't related by blood, there is something about him that reminds her of Jasper. The confidence, maybe, the bright, curious eyes. But regardless of who he looks like, and even with no blood shared between then, she'd recognized him back in September, felt something familiar in his manner; she knew him instantly, as if no time had passed. That alone speaks to the power of their connection.

In the foyer, Jenry waits for Juliet to catch up. As they leave the building, Jenry stands in the middle, as he's always been. When he was learning to walk, they would each hold one of his hands, supporting his whole body with their combined effort, and as he began to run, they would hold him back to keep him from going too fast, to keep him from falling. Now, as he is about to fly, she wonders what their job should be, if they are supposed to hold him or let him go, if pushing him is necessary to propel him forward, to give him the proper acceleration, or if that is the very thing that threatens his ascent.

It is something all parents must consider, and to think of it now allows Juliet to realize an important truth: she is here to fulfill that role for him, along with Marisa, whether or not anyone else understands it. She knows who she is to him.

They walk down the steps together, facing the Main Green and all its ghosts, but for Juliet, it no longer feels haunted; the lamplights glow along the path, welcoming and familiar. Marisa turns to Juliet, and the two women share a look, not a goodbye really, but an understanding— they will always be connected, and won't ever have to say goodbye again.

"Where are you parked?" Jenry asks Juliet. "Maybe we can all walk together."

"No, you two go ahead." She lifts her collar against the wind. "I'll be okay."

Juliet takes a shortcut across the grass, while Marisa and Jenry head toward Simmons Quad, recently renamed for the first female and first African American president in the university's history. It's a part of campus she doesn't know well, yet it still feels familiar.

"Is it hard for you to be back here?" Jenry asks.

"Not really," Marisa says. "It was actually harder to stay away."

"That's the problem with college," he offers, trying to relate. "You make all these connections, and then in four years it's gone."

Marisa looks around, surprised by how much she still recognizes. "But it's not gone. It's all still here." She wants to say more, awed by the potency of her surroundings. "And you're here now. That's all the proof I need." She squeezes his hand. "Nothing real is ever gone."

· 5 ·

On Christmas Eve, after a ten-inch snowfall, Juliet finds herself standing with Jenry in the middle of the street. Mounds of densely packed snow have been plowed onto the sidewalk and there is nowhere else to stand.

"I'll admit," he says, "when you said you'd pick me up, I expected a car."

Juliet laughs, climbing a small embankment. "That is what I meant, before the storm. But I was too lazy to shovel out the car. Besides, it's safer than driving. Half the streets in my neighborhood aren't even plowed yet."

It's almost five and the sun has already dropped below the hill, making the sky dark with blue. The air smells clean and cold.

"I can help you," Jenry says, falling in step beside her. "After we eat."

Juliet looks doubtful. "I bet you've never even held a shovel."

He smiles. "True. But if you can do it, it can't be that hard to pick up," he teases. "Certainly easier than playing the Fifth Symphony without the sheet music—which I can also do."

She laughs at his confidence. "Exams are over, so now you're invincible?"

"*Relieved* is a better word." He blows into his hands and keeps walking.

A few minutes later, they stop at a crosswalk, waiting for a city bus to pass. The exhaust warms the air as it pulls away, a cloud of gray pooling at their feet.

"You think you did okay?"

He shrugs. "I think I passed. Which is good enough for now."

Juliet crosses to the corner and he follows behind. "I bet you used to get straight As, right?" When he nods, she says, "Say goodbye to high school."

He mimes saying goodbye, waving at a passing car. Juliet laughs when the passenger waves back. "Curse of the small town," he says. "Everybody thinks they know you." He kicks at a pile of plowed snow, which explodes against his foot.

"And they might." Juliet's breath streams from her mouth like smoke. "You're a double legacy, your grandfather taught here for forty years, and your concert was just covered by three newspapers—not exactly anonymous."

The snow crunches beneath their feet. "I've been debating whether to tell you something," Juliet says, breaking the silence.

"Oh boy." He drops his head dramatically. "There can't possibly be more."

She shoves him playfully, causing him to lose his balance and fall into a snowbank. When he climbs out his jeans are covered with powder. She helps him clean off, swatting at his legs with her mittens. They start walking again, and Juliet wonders if she should let it go.

A few minutes later he asks if she's still debating, and she points to the next street, a one-way that goes straight down to the river. "We used to live on that street, when you were born. We can swing by the house if you want to see it."

He takes his time before answering, "Okay."

They turn at the stop sign and walk along a row of parked cars, all snowed in. Halfway down the block, Juliet stops in front of a three-story brick house with a shiny black door. The lights are on in the first-floor apartment, and they can see a small Christmas tree in the corner of the living room, burdened with too many lights. A thick red candle burns in the window.

"That's it," Juliet says. "We had the whole first floor."

Jenry looks the house up and down. "Seems like a nice place," he says.

She nods. "It was. I hated to leave."

They look at the house until a woman walks into the living room carrying a tray of drinks and they both glance away.

"I don't remember it," he says. "I'm sorry."

"There's nothing to be sorry about," Juliet says. "You were too young to remember." She turns away, continuing down the hill. Jenry follows, glancing back a few times at the house. She pretends not to notice.

"I wish I recognized it," Jenry says several minutes later, when they are cutting across the river. "This whole thing would be easier if I just remembered something about you, anything."

Juliet stops at the corner, scraping snow from the bottom of her boots.

"I don't," she says. "I think you were spared." She thinks of her own mother, how it might have been easier if she hadn't known what she was missing.

"What I wanted to tell you before is that a lot of this is my fault." She looks down as she speaks. "Why I didn't get to see you again, after your mother left."

They reach the sidewalk and stop on a corner of bare concrete. Everything around them is cleared of snow, as if something has blown it all away. "I didn't have any legal rights because I didn't adopt you when I had the chance." He is playing with the zipper on his jacket, zipping it up and down. She wants to stop there, but she knows there is more to say. "Your mother wanted me to, but I said no." His eyes open wider, but he still looks straight ahead. "I was afraid, really, of being responsible to you and to your mother, for the rest of my life. I was young and I was selfish." She grabs his arm so he will look at her. "And I'm sorry. I could have saved us both a lot of time."

Jenry shakes his head. "You don't need to apologize."

"I just want you to know that I have regrets. That I would do it differently if I had another chance."

He looks down at her, eventually shrugging. "That's nice, but it doesn't really change anything." His eyes are glassy, tearing from the cold. The streetlamp lights up one side of his face, making his skin glow yellow, then red. The other side is dark, and his features blur into a person she doesn't recognize.

"I know," Juliet says, trying to mask the resentment she feels surrounding that simple truth—that nothing she can do will ever change the past. "Believe me, I know."

She feels embarrassed, longing for something he obviously doesn't need, and it makes her want to give up, just leave it all behind. She walks ahead, hoping to put distance between them, but when she looks back, he is still there, trudging through the snow just a few steps behind her. They continue like this for many blocks, cutting through the still, snow-blanketed edges of downtown until they finally reach her street. She sees the Christmas lights on her next-door neighbor's house twinkle in the distance and suddenly has a strong desire to be inside her own home, to be able to rest. At the corner, Jenry catches up with her.

"There's something you don't know," he says, his voice loud and oddly desperate, cracking like an adolescent. "I wouldn't want you to change anything. It is what it is. And it's okay." He touches her shoulder, tries to comfort her. "All we can do is pick up the pieces and move on. That's all I want to do."

Juliet nods, knowing there's nothing else for her to say. A block later, she stops in front of a sage green house with white trim. "Here we are." She opens the wooden gate and climbs the stairs to the porch, knocking her boots on each step to clear off the snow. Jenry peeks through the front windows, taking in the Christmas tree and the fancy dinner table set for the holiday.

"Pretty nice spread you got here."

"It's all Noelle. She's the one with the vision." Juliet unlocks the door, but before she can turn the handle, Jenry grabs her hand.

"You know, I do think you get another chance." His eyes blink quickly. "Not to be my mother, but to be . . . something else entirely. And I want that. I want you to be that for me." He stares at her for a few seconds before starting to laugh. "It sounds dumb when I say it out loud."

"No, it doesn't. It sounds honest." She squeezes his hand. "I like the way it sounds."

She opens the door, and they step into the house together.

· 6 ·

After dinner and two rounds of hearts—a card game Jenry has never played before, which Juliet considers a travesty—they sit in the living room to eat dessert. Jonah is sleeping in his bouncy seat, on the floor near the fire. Noelle serves three types of Christmas cookies, plus a sweet potato pie Juliet made the night before. Jenry tells her he's never eaten a pie so good, a compliment she rewards by serving him another slice. They drink eggnog as thick as pancake batter from small teacups, which Jenry places gingerly on the table between sips.

"Let me fill that up," Noelle says, even though his glass isn't empty.

Juliet cuts her eyes at Noelle, worried that he will feel smothered, but he seems quite content—happy even. Maybe this experiment will work after all.

Noelle puts down her cup with dramatic flourish. "So, we have a Christmas Eve tradition—"

"We do?" Juliet interrupts.

"Which is to open one present tonight and the rest on Christmas. But since you're not going to be here tomorrow, you get all your presents right now."

He blushes. "But I don't have anything for you."

Noelle waves him off. "Presents keep college kids alive."

Jenry opens the gifts with a look of mild embarrassment. A wool scarf, two button-downs, a Gap gift certificate, and a DVD box set of *The Wire.*

"I told her a Netflix subscription would make more sense, but she insisted."

"It's a special edition," Juliet groans. "Promise you'll watch it over the break, or else we really can't keep hanging out."

Jenry laughs.

"She's not kidding," Noelle says. "I got Season One on our third date."

"Actually." Juliet pops a cookie into her mouth. "It was your birthday."

"See what I mean?" Noelle jokes. "It's like some sort of initiation."

Jonah cries out from his chair, twisting in his sleep. They all turn to look at him. He continues to squawk, so Noelle goes to him, unbuckling the straps.

"Can I hold him?" Jenry asks.

"Of course you can."

Jenry puts down his cup, wiping his hands on his jeans. He sits upright on the couch, a pillow propped under his arm, and waits for Noelle to place the baby in his lap. Jonah continues to squirm in Jenry's arms, eyes still shut.

"Hey, little man," Jenry says, looking intently at the baby's face.

"Put your finger out," Juliet suggests, and when Jenry reaches out, the baby wraps his tiny hand around the extended finger. Jenry's eyes grow wide, sparkling with surprise. "Damn, he's strong."

"Say hello to your brother," Noelle says, talking to the baby, but without missing a beat, Jenry says, "Hello, Jonah."

He brings his face closer to the baby's face, and then, as if sensing a shift in the room, Jonah opens his eyes. "Hi," Jenry says again, "I'm Jenry," and the baby looks at him for a long time before he wriggles and lets out a soft cry.

"He's probably hungry." Juliet looks at her watch to check the time.

"Do you mind feeding him?" Noelle offers Jenry a bottle, which he tips gently into the baby's mouth. As Jonah begins to suck, his body stills.

They are all surprised by a knock on the front door a few minutes later. Juliet looks at Noelle, who shrugs. "Maybe some carolers," she says, as Juliet gets up to peek through the eyehole.

"Jesus Christ." Juliet stands back from the door, like she's just seen a ghost.

"On Christmas Eve?" Noelle smiles. "That's ironic."

"It's my father." A look of astonishment colors Juliet's face.

"Now that *is* a Christmas miracle."

Noelle puts down her cup and straightens her sweater, gesturing for Juliet to let him in. Juliet takes a slow, extended breath before opening the door. A wave of cold air greets her first, and then, her father's familiar face.

"Merry Christmas," Winston says, stamping his boots on the doormat. "I hope I'm not interrupting." His eyes scan the room as he waits to be invited in.

"No, of course not," Noelle says. "Please, come inside." She glares at Juliet, who steps back to let him pass; he leaves a trail of snow on the floor behind him.

"Thank you." He takes off his hat as he enters the house, ducking under the doorframe from habit. His face is flush with cold.

Noelle leans forward to kiss him on the cheek. "It's nice to see you, Winston. It's been a long time."

"Too long," he agrees. He steps into the living room, standing beside the Christmas tree. "Beautiful tree," he says, reaching to straighten an angel tangled in a string of lights. "I'm glad to see you're using your mother's ornaments."

"I always use them," Juliet says. "You're just usually not here to see it."

Winston doesn't respond. He holds the hat in his hands, a charcoal-gray fedora, which he spins around nimbly, like a dealer with a deck of cards.

"Well, he's here now," Noelle says brightly, trying to lighten the mood. "Winston, what can I get you to drink?"

"I just came to meet the Christmas miracle." He looks around for the baby, his glance eventually landing on Jenry, bottle and baby in hand. His eyes widen in surprise. "I thought you'd be long gone by now. Flown south like the geese."

"Tomorrow," Jenry says. "Flights are always cheaper on Christmas Day."

Winston nods. "And how's everything with the baby? Looks like he's growing well." His eyes dart between Noelle and his daughter.

"He's already ten pounds," Noelle says. "Eats round the clock."

Winston laughs, a smile spreading across his face. He looks so happy and kind, so handsome, that it makes something inside Juliet turn, and it cramps in her chest. She faces her father, done with the pleasantries.

"Why are you here?" she demands.

"Juliet." Noelle says her name once, soft like an exhale, as she reaches for the cuff of her sleeve. Juliet pulls her arm free and steps closer to her father.

"I thought your pride prevented you from going anywhere you weren't welcome." Juliet says it like a statement, not a question.

"I was hoping you'd changed your mind. The Christmas spirit and all that." He stares at the fireplace, his eyes trailing from one stocking to the next.

"That's optimistic of you." Juliet tucks her hands into her pockets. Behind her, the front door is still cracked, and though she feels cold, she doesn't move to close it. She wants to make it easy for him to leave.

Winston picks up a shopping bag filled with wrapped presents. "I brought a few things."

"For who?" Juliet questions.

Winston shrugs. "Everyone." He clears his throat, correcting himself. "Well, I didn't know Jenry would be here. But I already gave him his present."

"Let's not worry about presents just yet," Noelle says, taking the fedora from his hands. "Come in, take your coat off. We have plenty of food."

"He's not staying," Juliet says. "You can't stay, right?"

Winston unbuttons his coat. "Actually, I'd love to."

Something about him seems different. He has a slight smile when he speaks, and his normally booming voice seems hushed, as if trying to fit within the confines of their small home. Even his body seems smaller, more amenable. As he stands in the living room, he appears unremarkable in every way, and for the first time in years Juliet doesn't feel intimidated by him, worried that she will say or do the wrong thing. Her anger has allowed her to feel more confident in his presence, perhaps the only benefit of continuing to hold on to it.

Noelle takes his coat, raising her eyebrows in Jenry's direction. "Come on, Jenry. Let's get that baby more milk." He shifts the baby in his arms, holding him carefully as he follows her into the kitchen. Suddenly Juliet is alone with her father. Winston gestures toward the front door.

"Aren't you going to close that? It's thirty degrees outside."

"Since when does the cold bother you?"

"I was thinking of the baby."

"Yes, of course you were." She closes the door. "You do tend to think about the children, don't you?"

Winston steps toward the fire to warm his hands. "Your mother had that gift. Of insulting someone, but masking it in a compliment. I didn't realize things like that were hereditary."

Juliet laughs. "Oh yes you did. That's why it bothers you."

She watches her father stare into the fire. "It doesn't bother me," he finally says. "It's a comfort, actually. To see her in you." He glances into the dining room, spotting the piano. "I see you got my present."

"I thought it was an apology."

"I should have given it to you a long time ago. Despite your refusal. I should have known better." He turns to face her. "I'm sorry."

Juliet feels her pulse quicken. The sound of her father apologizing is such a rare occurrence it makes her physically uncomfortable, like being injured or sick.

"Can I get you something to drink?" she offers. "We have eggnog or spiced apple cider." Then she adds with a smirk, "Sorry, no scotch."

"Eggnog sounds perfect."

She uses the ladle to fill a small cup and hands it to him. He nods his thanks. As he looks around the room, his eyes stop to linger on the poster from *Don Quixote* that used to hang in Jasper's loft, an image of her brother suspended in flight. He was still looking over her, setting an example for Juliet to follow; not just how to defy gravity, but how to expand the definition of success, of survival. It was what they were raised to do.

"I suppose this could go on for days," he says, "but I suggest we cut it short and just get to the bottom line." He sips his drink while she continues to look at him, biting the inside of her cheek to keep her mouth shut. Let him try to fix this.

He clears his throat before speaking again. "I didn't tell you about finding Jenry because I wanted to help. You were having a hard time, first your brother's death, and then Marisa leaving—it was too much for you to handle. And when you started to get back to yourself, to your music, I thought that was a good thing. I thought it would help you." He seems nervous, and walks to the fireplace. "Then her letter came, out of the blue, and I didn't know what I was supposed to do. All I wanted was to protect you, Juliet. Not from him, but from her, his mother—from what she wanted you to be. But mostly from yourself. You were too young, and you had so many plans. I thought it would take you off track, if you opened all that up again. I thought you were better off focusing on something you could control."

"You had no right to make that determination."

"You're right. I didn't." He places the cup on the mantel, looking into the fire as he speaks. "I convinced myself that I was protecting you, when really I was protecting myself. I thought I could hold him at bay, could know him only from a distance, and protect myself from any risk of losing again." He straightens the stockings that hang from the mantel, running his fingers over the embroidered names, tracing each letter. "We made an agreement, me and her parents, and in exchange for supporting his education, they sent me regular updates—as long as I kept you out of it. That was one of the conditions." He stops and takes a breath. "But now, seeing how it's all gone, I'm sorry I went along with it. I was wrong."

Juliet feels lightheaded. In more than forty years, her father has never apologized to her for anything—and now twice in one conversation.

He clears his throat again. "But the larger thing, the thing I didn't want to admit to myself, was that I didn't want it to be true, this thing you were telling me, this thing you believed—"

"What *thing*?" The question bursts from her mouth before she can stop it. She is suddenly terrified of the answer.

"That you were, in fact, his mother." Winston turns his head to look her in the eyes. "That he was your son. I couldn't accept it. In fact, I ignored it. And in doing so, I slowly made it untrue."

Juliet shifts her feet, hot from their proximity to the fire. "But you kept in touch with Victor, so you clearly thought of Jenry as your grandson—"

"He is my grandson," Winston says forcefully. "That has never been in question." He reaches for his cup, swirling the remaining eggnog before tipping it into his mouth.

Juliet looks at him, realization blooming on her face. "You mean because you thought Jasper was his father?"

"Because I knew Jasper was his father. And I wanted to know his son, in some small way, so I could keep my son alive. It may sound selfish, but it's the truth."

Juliet feels a mixture of anger, excitement, and fear rushing under the surface of her skin. "And how did you know, Pop? Because you felt it? Because you saw something in him that reminded you of your son? Or was it because I told you?"

He looks away before answering. "All of those things, I presume."

"But when it was me doing the same, telling you what I felt," she says, her voice beginning to rise, "when I told you he was my son, it meant nothing?"

"You told me no such thing," Winston barks. "You never once said that *you* were having a baby, and you never used the word *son*. After you lost him, maybe, but not in the beginning. Not when you were raising him."

"Would it have made a difference? If I had adopted him, made it legal?"

Winston puts down his cup. "I honestly don't know."

Juliet steps closer to him, feeling the warmth of the fire on her face. "And if Jasper wasn't his father, what would you think then?" She feels powerful in that moment, like a hunter standing above her prey—arrow pulled back, bow taut, string vibrating with the pent-up tension of knowing she has the power to determine another being's fate. She can crush his whole world right now, just by telling him the simple truth—that Jenry isn't Jasper's son.

"I can't possibly answer that," Winston says. "I can't go back and disbelieve something I already know to be true."

She points her finger at him, something she's never done before, realizing that she is no longer afraid of her father—if anything, she is afraid *for* him. "You know because I told you. And you believed me. But here's what I don't understand—why believe that and not the other? If it's all just my word."

She watches him stare at her, his focus shifting from her eyes to the tip of her finger. She can see that he is struggling now, that he wants to understand what she is really saying, beyond the implications and word-play, and it makes her feel sorry for him. And then, in an astonishing moment of clarity, she understands that something has shifted: she is stronger than her father. Now she must protect him.

She lowers her voice, dropping her finger as well. "Don't worry, you don't have to answer. Just know that I feel the same way. I, too, can't go back and disbelieve something I already know to be true." Her voice drops to just above a whisper. "Jenry is my son. Mine. That is why you are his grandfather."

After saying it, she realizes it is the most honest statement she can make, that really nothing else needs to be said. This whole thing is about belief—not fact, not proof—and in that way it puts her and her father on the same side. She believes Jenry is her son, and her father believes he is Jasper's son—it doesn't matter that neither is correct in any technical sense. The belief is what matters, and what they do with it—the life they live as a result of it.

"It might not help you understand, but I'm talking about the past," Winston says, "the way I felt back then. Not now."

Juliet kneels down next to the log rack, searching for dry wood. She's tired, and doesn't want to hear any more excuses, but she is curious about one thing.

"What changed?" She glances up at him.

"Meeting him, just having him here. I see things differently now." Winston shrugs, lowering his voice. "I don't know if I can put it into words."

Juliet adds a log to the fire, pushing it into the embers with a pair of steel tongs. She holds it there, waiting for the fire to catch, until her arms begin to ache.

"When I saw him sitting on that piano bench," Winston begins, "in front of all those people, the look on his face—it reminded me of you."

Juliet stands up. Her eyes are so dry they burn. Yet when she blinks, they fill with tears. "Now was that so hard?" She looks at her father, her voice filled with emotion. "All these years, that's all I've wanted to hear— that you could see our connection, see me somehow in him."

Before Winston can respond, they hear another voice.

"My mom said the same thing."

They look over to see Jenry standing in the doorway.

"It was the first thing she said in the dressing room," he continues. "*You looked just like Juliet.*" The expression of pride on Jenry's face is one

Juliet hasn't seen before. She smiles at him as the tears fall from her eyes. A feeling of relief floods her body.

Winston stands motionless, afraid to break the spell; as if with one wrong word or gesture, the connection he worked so hard to establish will disappear. After all he's done to bring Jenry and Juliet back together, to heal the wounds he caused and the ones he fell victim to, a part of him worries it won't be enough; their bonds so tenuous that even the slightest wind, a door swinging open, will cause them to collapse.

"Maybe genes don't account for everything," Noelle says, walking into the room with the baby asleep in her arms. "Because I swear this one looks just like you, Winston." She lifts the baby to show him.

"All babies look like old men," he says dismissively.

"No, I think she's got a point," Jenry peers over her shoulder. "He definitely looks like you, Gramps."

"*Gramps?*" Juliet laughs, wiping the tears from her face. "How do you like the sound of that, Pop?" Her tone is playful, and Winston, seeing it as an offering, an olive branch, follows her lead.

"I prefer *Granddad*," he says with a shrug, "but I'll defer to my grandson."

"What do you think, Juliet?" Noelle hands her the baby, who squirms in her arms but stays asleep. Juliet looks down at her son, scanning his face for any signs of resemblance, of recognition.

She smooths the tiny hairs of his eyebrows, traces the curls at the top of his head, kisses his broad forehead. His face, so new and unexamined just a few weeks ago, is already familiar; his small, brown body already known and accepted as one of their own.

"I agree," she says, lifting her eyes to meet her father's gaze, to give him this small gift. "He looks like you, Gramps."

But what she keeps for herself is also true: that the baby reminds her of Jenry. Not just in features, but in experience; how she looks at him; how he makes her feel. She believes all of this, knows it to be true, but doesn't have to say it out loud.

· 7 ·

The scene in the dining room is a classic holiday affair—cluttered table with starched white tablecloth, poinsettia centerpiece, turkey drying out on a sterling silver platter—though the family that brings it to life, crowding around the piano, carols ringing out, is modern in every way that matters. If a picture were taken, it would be difficult to determine allegiances, who went with whom, a possible indication of things to come.

Winston has a bias against any Christmas song that isn't Nat King Cole, but he tries to be a good sport about it, making up lyrics to "The Twelve Days of Christmas" when he can't remember the words. He is given the job of turning the sheet music whenever Juliet nods in his direction, and he takes the position seriously, springing into action whenever needed.

At first Jenry and Juliet take turns at the piano, but once they've exhausted their holiday repertoire, they move on to more interesting songs, and are soon sitting side by side on the bench. It has been more than two months since the first time they played together in the practice room, and she is surprised by how much has changed in his playing since then. His confidence, his presence.

Sitting next to him, she is aware of the proximity of his body—the scent of his cologne, the sound of him exhaling as he makes a mistake, the tightening of his leg muscles as he pumps the damper pedal, connecting their notes—but she doesn't think about what it means. In fact, she thinks of nothing at all as she plays. She hears the music filling her, feels the vibration through her fingertips and up into her chest, but that is all. She isn't aware of thinking or breathing—simply of being. It is a gift she allows herself to unwrap slowly.

Once they begin to improvise, Winston is no longer needed; he sits at the table while Noelle makes him a plate of food. He won't normally eat a meal so late in the evening, but tonight he can't say no, smiling and lifting his plate to everything Noelle offers. Later, when he is done eating, pushed back from the table with his arms folded over his vest, she offers him the baby, and he accepts that, too. He holds Jonah's body in the crook of his arm, memorizing his tiny features—the silky dark hair, the wrinkled fingers, his long eyelashes—and finds himself transported through time, back in that hospital with his young wife, innocent of all the heartache that lay ahead.

While the baby sleeps, lulled by the music, Winston's eyes fill with tears, as if all his feelings have floated to the top of his body and are now about to spill onto the table for the whole world to see. He doesn't care. Through glassy eyes he looks at his daughter, watches her effortlessly play song after song on that old piano, her movements mirrored by the boy at her side as if he has spent his whole life watching her play. What a miracle, it seems to Winston in this moment, how people can both know and not know each other, and how thin the line between what is remembered and what is forgotten, like the line between harmony and discord, redemption and betrayal.

Juliet looks up from the piano to find her father staring at her. She sees the tears in his eyes as he looks down at her son, and she feels something inside herself open, as if she can hear even the faintest whisper on the other side of the world. He still has it—the power she has given him—not because he is her father; not because they share the same blood and the same last name; not because he raised her by himself for more than half her life; and not even because he supported her study of music from the time she could walk—he has that power, that privilege, because she loves him. Love is what makes someone powerful, not anger, not fear.

And through it all, Jenry continues to play; his eyes gaze ahead as he seems to stare through the case and all the way inside the piano, where hammers strike strings and turn vibrations into song.

"Don't worry," he says to Juliet, "I'm still here." As if he can read her mind and knows her greatest fear: that it will all dissolve like a dream.

But it isn't a dream. It is simply a moment, a holiday like so many others, the only difference tonight being a matter of proportion; the living have finally outnumbered the dead.

Later, when they close the lid over the keys, the house becomes unusually quiet. Juliet feels her body ache from playing, her fingers numb. She sees her father standing over the record player, delicately placing the needle's tip onto the vinyl. It is one of the quintessential images from her childhood: her father standing apart from the rest of them, an album balanced between his steady hands.

She hears the scratch and hiss of the music taking shape, the familiar comfort of notes filling the air. She can probably guess the song he will play, but she doesn't want to be certain of anything. *Let him surprise me,* she thinks as she steps into the living room to join her family, *let all of them surprise me.*

Acknowledgments

And now, the fun part.

The publication of this novel is a result of the hard work and dedication of many people whom I respect and admire. I first want to thank my agent, Anjali Singh, for her early enthusiasm and ongoing support, and my editor, Dan Smetanka, for his unflinching editorial eye and fierce love of these characters. My gratitude goes to the whole team at Counterpoint, for their extraordinary commitment to this novel. Many thanks to Robin Billardello, for the gorgeous cover, and to Laura Berry and Wah-Ming Chang for their interior design magic. Thank you to Megan Fishmann, Rachel Fershleiser, Selihah White, and Katie Boland—you are rock stars. For their steady work and swift responses, my thanks to Dan López and Yukiko Tominaga.

I began writing this novel years ago, and the story has been influenced by several formative relationships. I want to thank my parents, for filling our house with books and taking me to the library every week when I was a child. Special thanks to my two older brothers, both voracious readers, for seeing my gifts early and encouraging me to shine. This book would not exist without the partnerships I had in my twenties and thirties; I am grateful for the lessons they taught me.

I was fortunate to have a residency at MacDowell during the revision process, which provided sanctuary, sustenance, and stimulation. I am thankful for the time and for the friendships I made there. Thank you to the librarians and staff at all the Brown University libraries, especially the Rock, where I worked as a student, and the John Hay, which offered much inspiration. I am also, and always, thankful to my colleagues at Spalding University's School of Writing, along with the students and alums, who heard excerpts of this work over the years and whose warm responses kept me going during many dark nights. Shout-out to the MFA students and faculty at Otis College of Art and Design; I will never forget the work we did.

For their advice, assistance, inspiration, wisdom, and support, I wish to thank my many friends and family in Providence, New York, Los Angeles, Atlanta, Oakland, Seattle, Philadelphia, Washington, D.C., Minnesota, Arizona, Massachusetts, and Mexico. I appreciate the interest you've all shown in my writing over the years, but also the many conversations, trips, and meals we've shared when I desperately needed a break from this fictional world.

And, finally, my deepest offering of thanks is to my wife, Rebecca. Without her patience and devotion, without her encouragement and love, without her vision and confidence, this novel would still be a manuscript. She is my first and best reader, my greatest champion and fearless defender. She was the first person to fall in love with this book, and the last person to fall in love with me; every day she gives me a reason to smile, to care, to dream. This book, and every story I tell, is for her.

© Sam Zalutsky

RACHEL M. HARPER is the author of the novels *Brass Ankle Blues* and *This Side of Providence*, which was short-listed for the Ernest J. Gaines Award for Literary Excellence. Her work has been nominated for a Pushcart Prize and has been widely published and anthologized. Harper has received fellowships from Yaddo and MacDowell, and is on the faculty at Spalding University's School of Writing. She lives in Los Angeles. Find out more at rachelmharper.com.